OLIVER PÖTZSCH

The Council of Twelve

A Hangman's Daughter Tale

Translated by
LISA REINHARDT

MARINER BOOKS
HOUGHTON MIFFLIN HARCOURT
BOSTON NEW YORK

First Mariner Books edition 2018

hmhco.com

The Council of Twelve: A Hangman's Daughter Tale was first published in 2017 by
Ullstein Buchverlag GmbH as *Die Henkerstochter und der Rat der Zwölf.*
Translated from German by Lisa Reinhardt. First published in English by
AmazonCrossing and Mariner Books in 2018.

Library of Congress Cataloging-in-Publication Data
Names: Pötzsch, Oliver, author. | Reinhardt, Lisa, translator.
Title: The council of twelve / Oliver Pötzsch ; translated by Lisa Reinhardt.
Other titles: Henkerstochter und der Rat der Zwölf. English
Description: Boston : Mariner Books, 2018. | Series: Hangman's daughter tales |
Includes bibliographical references and index.
Identifiers: LCCN 2017053540 | ISBN 9781328508317 (paperback)
Subjects: LCSH: Fathers and daughters—Fiction. | Executions and
executioners—Fiction. | Germany—History—17th century—Fiction. |
Murder—Investigation—Fiction. | BISAC: FICTION / Mystery & Detective /
Historical. | FICTION / Historical. | FICTION / Mystery & Detective / General. |
LCGFT: Historial fiction | Thrillers (fiction)
Classification: LCC PT2676.0895 H4813 2018 | DDC 833/.92—dc23
LC record available at https://lccn.loc.gov/2017053540

Printed in the United States of America
DOC 10 9 8 7 6 5 4 3 2 1

Maps on pages vi–viii copyright © Peter Palm, Berlin / Germany

For Elijana, Quirin,

Vincent, Leon, Camira,

and all others yet to come.

Welcome to the Kuisl clan!

In memory of Lee Chadeayne

◆

"A foreigner is only a foreigner in a foreign land."

—Karl Valentin

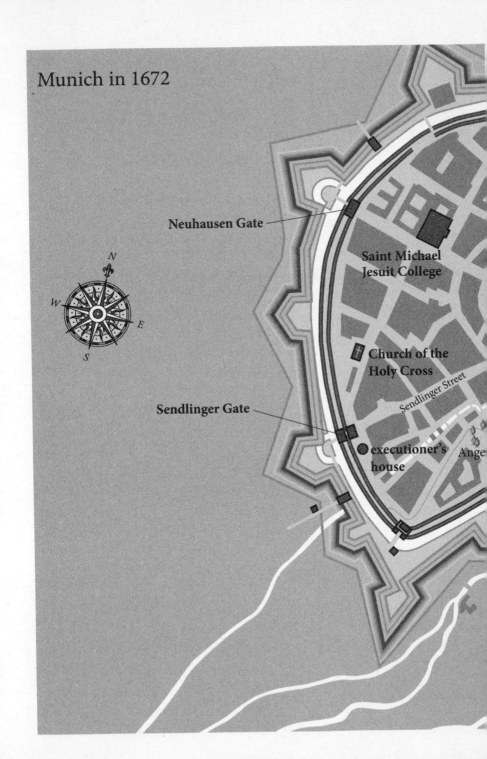

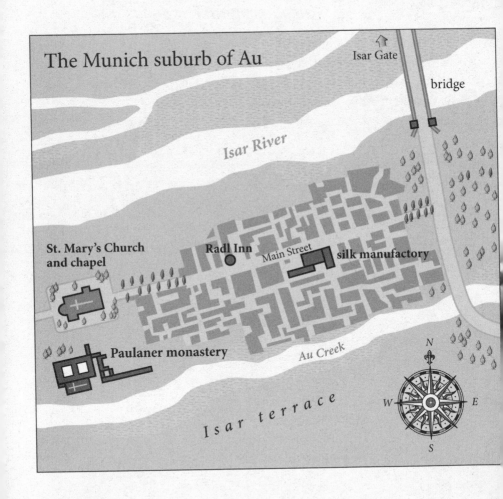

The Munich suburb of Au

Isar Gate

bridge

Isar River

St. Mary's Church
and chapel

Radl Inn

Main Street

silk manufactory

Paulaner monastery

Au Creek

Isar terrace

N
W   E
S

DRAMATIS PERSONAE

THE KUISL FAMILY

JAKOB KUISL, Schongau executioner
MAGDALENA FRONWIESER (NÉE KUISL), Jakob's elder daughter
BARBARA KUISL, Jakob's younger daughter
SIMON FRONWIESER, Schongau medicus
PETER, PAUL, AND SOPHIA, children of Magdalena and Simon
GEORG KUISL, Jakob's son
BARTHOLOMÄUS KUISL, Jakob's brother

THE COUNCIL OF TWELVE

MICHAEL DEIBLER, Munich executioner
JOHANN MICHAEL WIDMANN, Nuremberg executioner
MASTER HANS, Weilheim executioner
PHILIPP TEUBER, Regensburg executioner
CONRAD NÄHER, Kaufbeuren executioner
KASPAR HÖRMANN, Passau executioner
JÖRG DEFNER, Nördlingen executioner
MATTHÄUS FUX, Memmingen executioner
MICHAEL ROSNER, Ingolstadt executioner
LUDWIG HAMBERGER, Ansbach executioner
BARTHOLOMÄUS KUISL, Bamberg executioner
JAKOB KUISL, Schongau executioner

MUNICH CHARACTERS

ELECTOR FERDINAND MARIA, ruler of Bavaria
ELECTRESS HENRIETTE ADELAIDE, his wife

PRINCE MAX EMANUEL, their son

JOHANN KASPAR VON KERLL, electoral court conductor

DOCTOR MALACHIAS GEIGER, physician

DANIEL PFUNDNER, Munich city treasurer

JOSEF LOIBL, captain of the guard

LUKAS VAN UFFELE, manufactory director

MOTHER JOSEFFA, brothelkeeper

WALBURGA DEIBLER, wife of the Munich executioner

VALENTIN, city musician

GUSTL, Au clerk

LORENTZ, city dogcatcher

ANNI, ELFI, EVA, AGNES, AND CARLOTTA, weavers at the silk
    manufactory

SCHORSCH, SEPPI, AND MOSER, members of the Anger Wolves

LUKI, leader of the Au Dogs

PROLOGUE

THE SMELL OF DEATH WAS as rotten as decaying fish, and
it roused Johanna Malminger from the sweetest dreams.

Only a moment ago she'd been dancing with a strapping
young lad, twirling so fast her brow was sweaty. They had
danced very close, her hips pressing against his loins, his hand
stroking her back and bottom demandingly, their lips almost
touching. But when she tried to kiss the handsome stranger, he
was suddenly wearing a mask.

And when she tore off his mask, she was looking at a grinning
skull with black, stinking eels creeping from its eye sockets.

The stench had woken Johanna. The stench and the cold.

She shook herself, but the foul smell and the cold didn't go
away. She had a terrible headache, and her tongue was dry and
sticky, but for some reason she seemed unable to move it. Her
eyes were still closed, sticky with sweat and dirt. When she managed to open them, Johanna found that she wasn't lying next to
her sister on the flea-ridden mattress at the Au hostel, nor underneath the dance floor put up for the Jakobi Fair over on Anger
Square. No, she was lying in some kind of cold, damp hole.

Bright rays of sunshine streamed in through a square opening in the opposite wall. Johanna squinted—it was broad daylight outside.

Broad daylight?

Panic shot through Johanna. She had overslept! Now old Trude would throw her out for certain, and she had only started at the sewing workshop two weeks ago. The old hag had given Johanna her final warning the last time she was late. What would become of her and her sister Liesl then? Liesl was only ten. They would have to live on the street and beg, like so many other girls who had come to Munich in the hope of a better life. Johanna and Liesl's parents had died of the Plague in their small village near Straubing, and marauding soldiers had slit open their older brothers like cattle. That was during the last attack of the Swedes, before the long unholy war finally came to an end. Johanna had hoped to find work as a maidservant or nurse, but she soon realized that young women like her were a dime a dozen in Munich. They were dross; dirty strays who were pelted with rotten fruit and vegetables by the arrogant citizens of Munich—if they were paid any attention at all.

All Johanna had was her body.

Back in Straubing the lads had told her how pretty she was, and here in Au, too, outside the gates of the big city, she had noticed the looks. Johanna had resisted at first, but the young journeymen had lured her like a cat with sausages and bacon. In the end, she'd even begun to like it. She was already nineteen and life was short and dirty, why shouldn't she be allowed a bit of fun? And at least that way she and Liesl got a decent meal from time to time and a bed that was better than the dirty straw mattress at the hostel, where they had to sleep together with all the other lost girls from the country.

But then something had happened that never ought to have happened, and Johanna had decided to change her life. Miraculously, she had found employment at the Haidhausen sewing workshop, and Johanna knew it was her last chance. And now she had danced, boozed, and overslept. That accursed Jakobi Fair! Some fellow had probably taken her home with him. Not a baker's apprentice, judging by the stench, nor a dapper musician, but a fisherman. Why was it so cold in this stinking shack? She really needed to get going, if it wasn't already too late.

Johanna tried to sit up but found to her astonishment that she couldn't. Again she tried to move her tongue but something was stuck in her mouth and making her gag. She realized the strange taste in her mouth came from a rag — from a rag and something else, something metallic-tasting, like a coin.

She was bound and gagged.

Slowly it dawned on Johanna that the merry dancing at the fair had landed her in a mess much worse than merely losing her job. Tossing back and forth, she frantically tried to remember what had happened the night before. She had danced with a young man, blond, blue eyes, and a smile as sweet as cherries in June. She couldn't remember his name or his profession — the beer had flowed freely. Johanna remembered Liesl tugging at her skirt, but she had shaken off her little sister like a bur and danced even more vigorously. It was the first Jakobi Fair since the end of the Great War, the biggest fair in town. People had caroused like there was no tomorrow. The blond fellow had kept refilling her jug. Hadn't the beer tasted a little odd at the end, too bitter? But the harder Johanna tried to sort last night's events in her head, the more muddled they became.

She started at a sudden noise — a scraping sound followed by a slap. Her eyes had somewhat adjusted to the light, so she looked over to the window where the noise had come from.

She caught her breath. The window had become smaller.

Was it possible? She squinted, and now she saw where the scraping and slapping were coming from: the opening in the opposite wall wasn't a window, but a square hole at hip height that grew smaller by the minute. Johanna saw a trowel deposit a portion of wet mortar in the opening, then a hand placed a brick on top.

Slap and scrape, slap and scrape . . .

Someone was walling her in.

Johanna wanted to scream, but the gag pressing against the roof of her mouth made her want to vomit. Again she thought she tasted metal. Or was it blood?

If I vomit, I suffocate . . . Who is going to look after Liesl?

Johanna forced herself to stay calm. With a pounding heart she tried to listen for any other sounds from outside. Where was she? She could hear the steady rushing of water, so she guessed she was close to the Isar River. Could she be on one of the fishing islands near the great bridge? Or somewhere by the lower raft landing? But why was it so terribly cold? It was the middle of summer. Now she could hear voices shouting and laughing. There were people out there, not far from her. Again she tried to scream but only managed a rattle in her throat.

The river rushed by, people walked past not far from her, and Johanna even thought she could make out the music of drums and fiddles coming from Anger Square. The fair cheerfully went on, while her window to the outside world was getting smaller and smaller.

Not much longer and it would shut completely. Probably forever.

Slap and scrape, slap and scrape, slap and scrape . . .

Tears welled up in Johanna's eyes as she tugged at her fetters in vain. What kind of devil had done this to her? Why did she have to dance with the handsome stranger?

A painting from the church in her village came to her mind, one that used to frighten her to death as a child: a young man asking a woman to dance. A goat's foot protrudes from his right trouser leg, and his tongue is long and black like a snake's.

The third deadly sin.

Lust . . .

Johanna whimpered softly and prepared herself for the inevitable. Was God punishing her for her sins? Surely he must know about her most terrible crime. Evidently, all her prayers in the Haidhausen church hadn't been enough to appease the almighty.

Slap and scrape, slap and scrape . . .

The bricks kept filling the opening mercilessly. Soon the hole was down to the size of a man's head, then a child's head, then a fist. One last ray of light fell into Johanna's prison and caressed her face. Desperately she strained toward it.

My God, I'm so sorry, so very sorry! Please, dear God, show mercy!

But God wasn't merciful.

The final brick slid into place with a crunching sound, and all that remained were silence, cold, and darkness.

Johanna was alone.

I

IT'S NOT THAT IT'S HIS own fault. It's just that he makes it too easy for the other children."

"And what exactly do you mean by that?" Magdalena glowered at the old Schongau headmaster, Hans Weininger, who was kneading the brim of his hat with embarrassment. Then her eyes went down to her son Peter. Snot and blood ran from the nine-year-old's nose and dropped on his only white linen shirt, leaving greenish-red streaks. Peter sniffed and stared straight ahead, clearly struggling to hold back tears.

"Are you trying to say my son *asks* to be beaten up?" Magdalena continued. "Is that what you're trying to say?"

They were standing outside the Schongau Latin School in Münzgasse Lane, a gloomy building whose chimney was so crooked that Magdalena feared it might fall down any moment and kill all three of them. The town slaughterhouse was situated on the first floor, and the sweetish smell of blood and meat was in the air. A dry breeze blew through the lanes and drove solitary snowflakes into Magdalena's face. It was bitterly cold, but Magdalena seethed with rage.

"This is the third time this month already!" she shouted.

"Why can't you give those good-for-nothings a healthy beating with the switch so they know what it feels like?"

"Er, I never actually see them do it," the headmaster said quietly and kept his eyes fixed on his hat, as if he was studying a tiny louse. "So I don't know who they are."

Of course you know, Magdalena thought. *It's probably the Berchtholdt children or the Semer brats, or some other imps with fathers on the city council.*

"Perhaps your son should hold back a little with his Latin exercises," Hans Weininger suggested. He was a scrawny, angular man who liked to sing cantatas most of the day and hide behind the lectern the rest of the time. Magdalena had known him since childhood. Having studied theology and even law for a little while in Ingolstadt, Weininger was far better qualified than the boozy headmaster of the German school by the cemetery, where the poorer children merely learned the Lord's Prayer and some basic math with the abacus. That's where Peter's younger brother, Paul, went, when he wasn't skipping school and playing down by the Lech River.

"The boys just don't like to be corrected by their classmate all the time," Weininger said. "Especially when . . . um . . ."

He faltered, but Magdalena knew very well what he was trying to say.

"Especially when this know-it-all is a hangman's brat," she added bitterly. "I haven't forgotten what family I'm from, thank you very much."

Magdalena had almost gotten used to the fact that, in Schongau, she would always be the dishonorable hangman's daughter. Even though her husband, Simon, had been made town physician nearly two years ago, the citizens still steered clear of her. What pained her most was that the stigma of her lineage had also transferred to her children.

It also made her angry.

"My son has more between his ears than all those darned patrician boys together." Magdalena raged at the headmaster. "One day he's going to be a respected physician, and it'll be no thanks to your pathetic tutelage."

Weininger winced, and Magdalena sensed she'd gone too far.

"If you believe your son is too good for me and Schongau, why don't you send him to another school," he said sardonically. "How about the Jesuit college in Munich? I hear you're planning a trip to the big city anyway." He smiled. "Why don't you knock on the door and introduce your dear son. Let's see what the padres think of him."

Magdalena swallowed hard. Weininger had touched a sore spot. "You know very well that's impossible," she replied curtly. "Not with his grandfather. And now I bid you a good day, Herr *Headmaster.*"

She left Hans Weininger where he was, took Peter by the hand, and stomped down Münzgasse Lane until they were out of sight. She was seething with rage, and not only because she'd once again had to experience firsthand what it meant to be the daughter of the town's executioner. This city was one big rumor mill! Evidently, all of Schongau already knew that the Kuisls were going to travel to Munich.

One month ago, Jakob Kuisl received a very important invitation: he had been elected to the so-called Council of Twelve, the supreme body of the Bavarian executioners' guild. Next week, over Candlemas, Bavaria's most influential hangmen would meet in Munich, and Jakob Kuisl had been asked to introduce his family. Magdalena hadn't been sure at first whether she should even go. Little Sophia, her youngest, had only just turned one, and it was ice cold now, some of the rivers frozen. But she knew she couldn't turn down her father's invitation—it had been more like an order anyway.

And who knows, it might be his final journey, Magdalena thought. Involuntarily, she tightened her grip on Peter's small hand.

Her father was old — nearly sixty. He was still a feared hangman, his last execution only a few weeks back — a thieving vagabond whose remains now swayed in the breeze on the Schongau gallows. But even though Kuisl was as strong as an ox and as clever as a fox, his movements had become slower lately, more erratic. The weight of decades gone by were in his eyes, the burden of the Great War and all the humiliation he'd had to experience as an executioner since then. Magdalena suspected the invitation to Munich was also partly a redress for their years of living in contempt. She and the rest of the family would have to accompany their father, whether they wanted to or not.

To take her mind off these gloomy thoughts, Magdalena stopped and dabbed the blood and snot from Peter's face with a handkerchief. A thin stream of blood was still running from his nose, reminding her of the injustice her son had suffered. He was even paler than usual, the skin around his right eye was slowly turning black, and one leg of his expensive trousers was torn and would have to be mended.

"Why don't you fight back?" Magdalena bitterly asked her skinny eldest child, who was visibly shivering under his threadbare shirt. "This would never have happened to your brother. Paul is a whole year younger than you but even the ten-year-olds run away from him. Why can't you defend yourself?" She was sorry the moment the words were out, but it was too late. Peter turned away from her, his thin body stiffening.

"There were five of them," he said quietly. "Not even Paul could have held them off."

"Who was it? Tell me! That mangy Berchtholdt? Fat little Seiler? I'll give them a good talking-to. I'll go to their parents and—"

Peter shook his head and Magdalena stopped abruptly.

"You'll only make it worse," he whispered. "They're just dumb. They only have their fists." He attempted a smile. "When they hit me, I simply close my eyes and think of something beautiful. Of the painting in Altenstadt Church, for example, or a poem by Ovid."

Magdalena sighed. When she and Simon decided to send their elder son to the Schongau Latin School, they had known that it wouldn't be easy for Peter. Previously he had attended school at nearby Oberammergau, but that hadn't lasted long. As the son of the town physician, Peter had the right to attend the local Latin school, and apart from that, he was intelligent, sensitive, and talented. His drawings and anatomical sketches showed great promise.

But he was also the grandson of the Schongau hangman.

"What do you think about paying your father a visit?" Magdalena asked with a wink. She knew Peter loved nothing better than to be with his father at his treatment room. He probably learned more in an hour there than in a week with doddery old Weininger. But sometimes the never-ending stream of questions from his eldest child became too much for Simon, and twice already the boy had ruined valuable anatomical sketches by adding his own drawings — much to his father's dismay.

Peter nodded enthusiastically and wiped the remaining snot from his face. Hand in hand they hurried up the icy lane to the Hof Gate Quarter near the old castle, where Simon's office was part of their family home.

When Magdalena saw the freshly whitewashed half-timbered building with the lean-to stables and the garden out back, she was once again filled with secret pride. Not long ago, she, Simon, and their children still lived down in the stinking Tanners' Quarter in her father's house. Now they not only lived in town, but in the prestigious Hof Gate Quarter, where the wealthy citizens and patricians had their houses.

The same patricians whose children beat up my son, she thought, and her happiness vanished like snow in the sun. *Just like the Berchtholdts used to beat up me and my brother, Georg. Will it never end?*

She opened the front door and saw immediately that Simon was going to have a long day. More than half a dozen men and women were seated on the bench in the dark hallway, with their dripping noses, wheezing coughs, and feverish eyes. It smelled of sweat, smoke, and burned herbs. The end of January was high season for colds and flu. People sometimes knocked on the door in the middle of the night, asking for a little thyme or hogweed to soothe their cough. A fever was also going around at the moment and had already claimed two children and several elderly people.

Magdalena greeted the patients with a nod and walked past the door to the family's living room with the tiled stove. The treatment room—also heated—was on the left, and a well-worn staircase led up to their bedrooms.

From the corner of her eye, she noticed two elderly women on the bench, whispering and pointing at Peter. She guessed they were gossiping viciously about the dirty hangman's brat with his ripped trousers.

But they still seek out his father the medicus, those backstabbing snakes.

Without giving the women a second glance, Magdalena stepped into the treatment room with her son. In her anger over the whispering old biddies she completely forgot to knock.

She recoiled at the sight of the man in the center of a room that was cluttered with cupboards and trunks.

His trousers down around his ankles, alderman and cloth merchant Josef Seiler was bent over the table. A massive red boil gleamed on his buttock, shining like a star in the night. Simon stood beside him with his scalpel raised, ready to make his cut.

Magdalena struggled to suppress a laugh. Portly old Seiler was puffing like an old boar, and clearly he hadn't noticed that someone had entered the room. Magdalena thought it was highly likely that Josef Seiler's boy had been among those who beat up her son, and now the father was standing here, pants down and bare-arsed, as if waiting for a good hiding.

Simon looked with surprise at his wife, who stood with one hand pressed to her mouth.

"Um, please excuse me for one moment," he said to Seiler.

He put down the scalpel and walked to the door. "Are you crazy?" Simon hissed at Magdalena. "How many times do I have to tell you not to disturb—"

"It's about your son," Magdalena cut him off softly and gestured at Peter. "You may have noticed he's bleeding."

Simon glanced at Peter, who was studying the red boil on Seiler's backside with interest. Irritated, the medicus shrugged. "What's a brawl among boys? I can't see anything serious about it. Nothing that can't wait, anyway."

"Your son is *bleeding,*" Magdalena replied a little louder. "How about *Herr Doktor* takes a proper look? Or is Seiler's arse more important to you than your firstborn's nose?"

"Are we done yet?" Josef Seiler asked from behind. He was still bent over the table and evidently hadn't overheard their quiet conversation. "I didn't feel anything."

"Er, I'm just looking for a salve to ease your pain," Simon said. "I'll be back in just a moment." He pushed Magdalena and Peter out into the hallway, where the waiting patients stared at them as if they'd grown horns.

"Can't you see that I'm busy?" Simon whispered.

"Is it too much to ask you to take a quick look at your son?"

Simon sighed, then leaned down to Peter and briefly studied his nose. "It's not broken, that's the main thing. Stick some shepherd's purse up his nostrils, that'll stop the bleeding." He straightened up and looked around. "Where's Sophia?" His eyes darkened. "Don't tell me you left her with her grandfather again?"

Magdalena shrugged. "What did you want me to do? Old

Weininger sent two boys to fetch me. It's freezing outside. I couldn't take her in a hurry."

"Then let's pray your father doesn't do anything stupid. You know what he's like as a nurse — especially when Paul is with him. Who knows what that boy could do to Sophia." Simon raised a finger. "Remember the sled ride down Peitinger Castle hill last week?"

Magdalena rolled her eyes. Simon's constant fretting about their daughter's safety got on her nerves sometimes. She guessed her husband worried so much because they had once before lost a little girl after only a few months. That had been five years ago; it had taken a long time for Magdalena to fall pregnant again. And Sophia was the apple of her father's eye.

She looked at the patients, old men and women the lot of them, clearly looking forward to a continuation of the marital row.

"Perhaps you didn't take Sophia because you didn't want people talking about her," Simon said in a strained voice. "Because you're embarrassed."

"That's . . . that's utter nonsense." Magdalena flared up. "Are you serious?" She no longer cared if people heard her. The two women started to whisper again.

"Go to hell, the lot of you," she hissed. She turned to the cracked door of the treatment room and called out: "I bid you a good day, Herr Alderman! Give my regards to your bully of a son. Next time I see him, I'll pull down his trousers just like my husband did with yours."

She grabbed Peter's hand and turned around, leaving Simon gaping after her.

Magdalena regretted her harsh words even as she hurried past the surprised patients. She could practically feel the people's eyes on her back. Why did she always have to be so hot-tempered? She had inherited her father's temper and it got her into trouble almost as frequently as it did him. But she couldn't take back her tantrum now. Chances were Simon had lost a wealthy patient because of her—and just when the patricians were beginning to accept him as town physician. Each month they struggled to pay the rent. She could have slapped herself. On the other hand—how dare Simon suggest she didn't want to be seen with their daughter? With the child she loved more than anything?

The cold air outside helped to clear Magdalena's head. When she looked around, the town she knew so well suddenly seemed awfully small and cramped. Once upon a time Schongau had been a flourishing place, with large numbers of merchants and travelers passing through all the time, but since the end of the Great War more than twenty years ago, the town had become small and sleepy. The old castle had fallen to ruin, plaster and paint were crumbling off the formerly picture-perfect houses along the market square. Magdalena noticed only now that her own house, which she'd admired proudly not long ago, was also in dire need of a fresh coat of paint. The houses in the Bavarian capital of Munich would certainly be much grander.

Just like the minds of the people of Munich—unlike the boarded-up Schongau numbskulls, Magdalena thought.

The parish church bells chimed the third hour of the afternoon and reminded her that she had indeed left Sophia alone with her father and Paul for too long.

"You heard what your father said," Magdalena said to Peter and stroked his head. "Let's go see your grandfather and Sophia." She gave a thin smile. "Grandpa knows more about bloody noses than your smart-arse father, anyhow."

"Faster, Grandpa, faster!"

Puffing like an old horse, Jakob Kuisl pulled his grandson Paul across the frozen pond behind the executioner's house. Sharp skates made from deer bones were strapped to the boy's feet, ploughing through the thin layer of snow atop the ice. Kuisl was pulling on a thin hemp rope tied around Paul's waist. From time to time the ice creaked and groaned beneath their feet, but Kuisl knew it would hold despite his considerable weight. He used to skate across the ice every winter as a child, and now, at the end of January, the temperatures were so low that small icicles adorned his impressive beard. What worried him, however, was the fact that Paul was dragging a small bundle of fur along behind him that swerved merrily from left to right.

Inside the bundle, tightly wrapped, lay Kuisl's youngest grandchild, Sophia.

She seemed to enjoy the ride across the ice, because she giggled and cooed happily. But something told Jakob Kuisl that Sophia's mother would never have agreed to Paul's idea.

Panting, he stopped, and Paul immediately complained: "Keep going, Grandpa! Don't stop!"

At eight years old, Paul was already taller and stronger than his older brother, and he had clearly inherited his grandfather's build. Kuisl sometimes wished Paul was a little less boisterous and rowdy, but he could also see already that Paul would one day make a worthy successor. Executions were his everything. Paul had already watched two beheadings close up, and just two weeks ago he'd helped his grandfather prepare the ropes for a hanging.

Kuisl wiped the cold sweat from his forehead. "Your grandfather is an old warhorse, not a young colt," he grumbled, then gave his grandson a conspiratorial wink. "You need to give your horse a break. And then I'll tell you about all the people we're going to meet in Munich next week."

Paul's eyes brightened. "Lots of hangmen, right? Are they stronger than you?"

"Bah! You know very well no one is stronger than your grandfather." Kuisl smiled grimly and picked up Sophia, who had started to cry in her bundle of furs. It seemed she wanted to be dragged across the ice again. The hangman gave her a wet rag to

suck on and placed her gently beside the snowman he and Paul
had built earlier. Then he turned back to his grandson.

"The most famous and best hangmen from all over Bavaria
meet in Munich next week," he began in his deep voice. "From
Regensburg, Passau, even all the way from Nuremberg. And
your old grandfather from Schongau as well. It's a great honor,
you know."

Kuisl was indeed very proud to be elected onto the Council of
Twelve—although he made sure not to show it. He'd been considered a good executioner for a long time, perhaps even one of
the best in Bavaria, plus he was an excellent healer. But his quick
temper, his sharp wits, and his stubbornness were almost equally
famous. And some of his colleagues thought him too lenient.
There were certain forces on the council that had always managed to keep him out of the innermost circle. Only once, more
than ten years ago, Kuisl had received an invitation to a meeting
in Nuremberg, but he had never made it onto the Council of
Twelve before.

"For a long time, the elector of Bavaria forbade the hangmen
to meet," Kuisl explained, sitting down in the snow beside Paul.
"Because we're dishonorable. But all guilds must meet up from
time to time to discuss things, even us executioners."

"I want to be a good hangman too, one day," Paul said solemnly. "Like you and great-uncle Bartholomäus. And Georg."
He gave Kuisl a pleading look. "Georg is coming to Munich too,
isn't he?"

Kuisl nodded gloomily. "Yes, your uncle will be there. And
your great-uncle."

The fact that his younger brother was already on the Council
of Twelve had bothered him for a long time. He and Bartholomäus had never been the best of friends, not even as children. Jakob's brother had moved to Bamberg and become the
city's executioner many years ago. Kuisl's son, Georg, was com-

pleting his journeyman years there and was likely to remain in Bamberg. Jakob Kuisl had never fully recovered from this blow. At least he would see the boy in Munich—a reunion he'd been looking forward to for months, even though he'd never admit to it.

"I bet Georg won't mind teaching me how to behead," Paul said cheerfully. "Maybe we can practice on turnips or dead goats. Goats have the toughest neckbones—you said so yourself."

"Um, we'll see," Kuisl replied. "You know, we hangmen have a lot to talk about in Munich. There are new laws and we haven't met up in a long time—"

"I'm really quite good at beheading already," Paul interrupted. "Watch!" He picked up an icy stick and, with one clean stroke, separated the snowman's head from its round body. The head rolled down to the pond and came to rest with a crooked grin. But Paul wasn't done. He kept thrashing the snowman with his stick until it was nothing but slush and lumps of ice.

Kuisl winced involuntarily. Sometimes his grandson's blood-lust scared him a little. He had always viewed the executioner's task as a necessary evil, never as something fun. On the contrary—the older he became, the more often he felt disgust at his job.

But someone has to do it, he thought. *And I'd rather it was me than some unscrupulous monster . . .*

Thoughtfully, he watched Paul, who was dancing atop the mound of snow, singing some nursery rhyme. The snowman's nose—a rotten turnip—lay trampled on the ground.

"There you are! I've been looking everywhere for you three."

Jakob Kuisl looked up and saw Magdalena walking toward them at a brisk pace from the executioner's house.

The hangman got to his feet and brushed the snow off his coat. "I came outside with Sophia and Paul. The stove isn't drawing properly and smoked the house out. The fresh air is good for the children."

He shot Paul a warning glance. They had agreed to keep silent about dragging little Sophia across the ice. He could only hope his grandson remembered, or else he'd be in trouble.

"I hope you wrapped Sophia up properly," Magdalena said threateningly.

Kuisl pointed at the fur bundle beside the mound of snow. Magdalena was the only person in the world who could speak to him thus. Magdalena and his beloved wife, Anna-Maria, when she was still alive.

Magdalena bent down to pick up Sophia, who had started to whimper softly. She lifted her daughter lovingly and held her to her chest. Suddenly she wrinkled her nose. "You didn't . . ."

She pulled the rag from Sophia's mouth and sniffed it. "Schnapps," she stated with disgust. "How many times do I have to tell you I don't want you to give her liquor?"

Kuisl shrugged. "That's what my parents used to do. It's only a few drops. I can't see any harm in it."

"And I'm telling you for the last time that I don't want a drunk baby," Magdalena replied. "I've got plenty of other things to worry about with Sophia and Peter — who is at your house, by the way, where I've given him some shepherd's purse. A bunch of his classmates bloodied his nose."

She sighed and shook her head, then pointed at the executioner's house, which lay not far from the pond. "Let's go in. Sophia has been outside long enough, and I must feed her."

They followed the muddy track through the snow to Jakob Kuisl's home. Since Magdalena and her family had moved up to town, eighteen-year-old Barbara had lived here in the Tanners' Quarter with their father. She cooked for him, did the washing, and looked after the chickens and the dairy cow in the stable next to the house, as well as the small vegetable garden. On the outside, the house looked increasingly decrepit. Several shingles were missing from the roof and the paint was flaking off all over. But inside, Barbara kept a tidy house.

Peter was sitting on a bench next to the stove and, as he did so often, he leafed through a book from Jakob Kuisl's small library. His nosebleed had stopped, but he still looked very pale. He only looked up briefly when Paul grabbed the bowl with the now cold porridge and finished off the remains of their shared breakfast with great appetite. Magdalena sat down at the table and started unwrapping her daughter.

Sophia had bright blue eyes and raven hair, and her almost always smiling face smelled of milk and honey. She gurgled happily and kicked her little legs. If you didn't look too closely, you couldn't see anything amiss. But Jakob Kuisl had seen her flaw too many times to blank it out any longer.

His granddaughter's right foot was twisted to the inside and slightly thickened, the toes strangely grown together.

Sophia had a clubfoot.

She was almost fourteen months old now, and other children started to walk at this age. But Sophia would probably never walk very well. Jakob and Simon both tried their best to stretch the tendons every day amidst heart-wrenching wails, but they knew the foot would never be straight. And worse, it hadn't taken long for Sophia's handicap to become public knowledge. To most people a clubfoot was much more than a small flaw, especially when the child's grandfather was a living, breathing hangman.

To many Schongauers, Sophia bore the mark of the devil.

Since time immemorial the devil was depicted with horns and a goat's foot. He was a great actor, able to turn himself into handsome youths and beautiful women—but no matter how hard he tried, his limp always gave him away.

For her entire life, Sophia would limp like the devil.

When Magdalena had finished feeding the child, she turned back to her father, who had been sitting at the table in silence.

"Where is Barbara? I haven't seen her all morning. She could have looked after Sophia."

Kuisl tightened his lips; he had been waiting for this question. Magdalena guessed the meaning of his silence.

"You had another fight, didn't you?" she asked.

"She said she didn't want to go to Munich. Told me I couldn't make her. My own daughter!" Kuisl spat into the reeds on the floor. He pulled out his pipe and began filling it. "She's a pigheaded, quarrelsome thing," he growled. "And that's because she doesn't have a husband to teach her some manners."

"She's only as pigheaded and quarrelsome as her father," Magdalena replied with a sigh.

Kuisl fell silent again. His quarrels with Barbara had been an almost daily occurrence lately. He would have liked nothing better than to marry his younger daughter to the Schongau gravedigger, or perhaps the knacker, who had already given her two bouquets of dried cornflowers. But Barbara remained stubborn and did as she pleased. She had the reputation of being a wanton girl who liked to mess about with lads from neighboring villages or with traveling journeymen. She danced passionately and frequently and didn't seem to care what people thought. Kuisl had tried to speak with her about it many times.

Well, if he was honest, he usually did more shouting than talking.

But nothing he said or did changed Barbara's behavior. Particularly in recent weeks she had become increasingly irritable and withdrawn—something was up. But Kuisl had never been very good when it came to women's emotions, not back when his beloved wife was still alive, nor with his daughters. And Kuisl's order to accompany him to Munich hadn't helped improve Barbara's mood.

That and the message that had gone with it.

Perhaps I should have broken the news a little more gently, he thought.

"When was the last time you saw her?" Magdalena wanted to know, drawing Kuisl back to the present.

The hangman moved his head from side to side. "Hmm. Earlier this morning. She was crying, the silly goose, when all I said was . . ." He faltered.

"What?" Magdalena pressed on.

"Well, that she must come to Munich with me because I'm finding her a husband."

Magdalena stared at him, aghast. "You said *what?*"

Kuisl shrugged. "For God's sake, a guild meeting is the perfect opportunity for an engagement. Lots of hangmen do it. You'll see, Barbara will be swamped with suitors. She's a good match with her looks, especially now that I'm on the council. It's for the best."

"And you wonder why she's run away? You . . . you . . ." Magdalena pinched her lips and inhaled deeply. "Where did she go?"

"She ran off toward Katzenweiher Pond. But—" Kuisl broke off. He'd just remembered the last thing Barbara had shouted at him.

You can't just sell me off like a piece of meat! I'd sooner die . . .

"Katzenweiher Pond!" Magdalena breathed. "Where they found the body of a girl only a few weeks ago."

"What are you talking about?" Kuisl tried to laugh, but it came out more like a croak. Suddenly, he felt weak and helpless. "You don't seriously believe my Barbara would . . . well, you know . . ." His voice faltered and he slammed his fist into the table. "Goddamnit! If she does that to me then . . . then . . ."

But Magdalena had already turned away. She handed Sophia to Peter, and the girl immediately started to cry again.

"Look after your sister. I'll be back soon. And as for you, Father, pray to God that Barbara hasn't done anything stupid."

Magdalena walked out of the house and hurried toward Katzenweiher Pond.

The hangman muttered a curse and followed his elder daughter across the icy fields.

• • •

Up in town, Simon closed the door behind the last patient and took a deep breath. He'd had to ask several people to come back tomorrow, and others he'd sent home with a cheap cough syrup made from an ivy decoction and honey. He needed some peace and quiet, which was a rare commodity this time of the year. Why did everyone always fall ill at once? It was like a conspiracy of all the noses and throats in Schongau.

Simon had had to use all his powers of persuasion to appease Josef Seiler. Finally the corpulent patrician had let him cut open the boil, though not without a barrage of curses on womankind in general and the doctor's wife in particular. At least Seiler had paid three thalers for his efforts — that was more than a doctor usually earned in a whole day.

Simon still couldn't believe how Magdalena had behaved. Didn't she see that her loose tongue could cost them their income? The rent they had to pay to the city was huge, and there were still plenty of wealthy citizens who hadn't accepted him as the town doctor, not least because of his wife, the hangman's daughter, whom many avoided. But he also knew he had used the wrong tone. What devil had possessed him to say Magdalena didn't want to be seen with Sophia? He decided to apologize to his wife as soon as he saw her.

Exhausted, Simon trudged back to the treatment room to clean up. Bloody rags and the scalpel he'd used to cut open the boil were still lying on the table, next to dirty urine vials, more knives, and some blood-caked pincers. He fetched a jug of hot water from the stove and poured it over the scalpel, knives, and pincers in a bowl. Then he started to clean his instruments thoroughly — a ritual he had begun about a year ago.

Simon had only told Magdalena and a handful of close friends about his obsession for cleaning. Martha Stechlin, the old midwife who gave him a hand from time to time, thought that washing surgical instruments was utter nonsense, and Simon guessed that many other Schongau citizens shared her view. Dirt and filth were as much part of the human body as blood and saliva. The old bathhouse owner over at Altenstadt even prescribed mouse droppings for gas and cemetery soil for back pain. For burns and amputations, respected doctors used egg yolks and moldy bread. So what harm could come from a little dirt on surgical instruments?

But Simon had found in recent years that wounds tended to heal better if treated with clean tools. He even went as far as washing his hands before examining a patient—although he did so secretly, because he was afraid of gaining a reputation as a charlatan and a quack. But somehow he knew he was doing the right thing, even if he couldn't prove it.

Perhaps one day it will be possible. Maybe when Peter becomes a doctor . . .

He winced at the thought of Peter. He had forgotten all about his son's bloody nose. Well, some shepherd's purse and a few kind words from his mother would have to do this time. It hadn't been anything serious, after all, unlike Sophia, who would need the help of her family for a long time to come. Nevertheless, Simon decided to pay his boys a little more attention, Peter especially, who had a hard time with his classmates. The trip to Munich would do everyone good.

But before they left for Munich, Simon had to finish the job for which he had closed his doctor's office early once again. It was the perfect opportunity, with Magdalena and the boys down at his father-in-law's. Finally he'd found a quiet moment to finish the last few lines.

Simon placed the clean vials back on the shelf and went over to the living room. The last light of the afternoon fell through the crown glass panes, and Simon lit a pine chip so he could see better. On the shelf next to the family shrine lay a folder full of loose pages. Many of them were smudged or had lines crossed out and written over. On the first page, written in thick letters, was the work's Latin title. Simon nodded contentedly. At least the title stood, and he liked it, too, especially the ending, *De Rebus Sanitariis et Sanitate Adnotationes Auctore Doctore Simon Fronwieser.*

For almost two years Simon had been working on his treatise on cleanliness and well-being. He had put down his observations over about fifty pages, and all that was missing was a poignant conclusion.

That, and the recommendation of a famous doctor, because who would read a book written by a completely unknown physician from the middle of nowhere?

When his father-in-law had first asked Simon to travel to Munich with him, he hadn't been overly enthusiastic. It wasn't that he'd miss out on work, as the trip to Munich would be at Candlemas, the feast on which servants received their annual pay and no one worked — which was also the reason Jakob Kuisl had been granted permission to leave by the city clerk. It was just that Simon could think of better things to do than sit in some drinking hole with a bunch of dirty hangmen and watch them down beer and swear. But then he'd had an idea.

The recommendation of a famous doctor . . .

He knew of such a doctor in Munich. If Simon could only convince him he was right, nothing stood in the way of his treatise being published. His work would get printed, with his very own name on the front page. The scholarly world would be scrambling to get their hands on a copy, even the erudite *doctores* in faraway Rome and Avignon. Not to mention his former professors at the University of Ingolstadt, which he'd had to leave when he ran out of money. Ha! He'd show them all . . .

Loud knocking tore Simon from his daydreams, just when he was about to start writing.

He tried to ignore it. Maybe the unwelcome visitor would go away again. Frowning, Simon tossed words back and forth in his mind, but the knocking grew louder and louder. Eventually he gave up. Annoyed, he put down his quill pen and walked to the door.

"All right, for God's sake," he called out. "I'm coming!"

When he opened the door and saw the patient, he knew right away that every second counted.

Magdalena ran as if the devil were after her.

She saw her father following her to the pond from the corner of her eye. If she wasn't so worried about Barbara, she would have cursed and sworn at her father. The old man truly was as sensitive as a rock! He had probably told Barbara in just a few blunt words that she was to meet her future husband in Munich, whether she wanted to or not. Couldn't he see how that would make Barbara feel? Especially when she had been more withdrawn than usual lately. Magdalena had tried speaking with her several times, but she was always met with a wall of silence. Magdalena had a hunch what her sister's behavior might be about, and it was high time she got to the bottom of it.

If it isn't too late already, she thought.

She headed east across the frozen fields and through a small wood until she reached a large pond not far from the old castle. It was much larger than the pond by the executioner's house, and the snow-covered surface was broken by several brownish clusters of reeds, the dry leaves whispering in the breeze. Magdalena had hated this gloomy place even as a child. The Schongauers believed the small black lake was cursed, and no one liked to come here. It was called Katzenweiher—the cat pond—because it was often used to drown unwanted litters of kittens.

And many women had suffered the same fate here.

A chill ran down Magdalena's spine as she looked out onto the frozen pond. While male felons were usually hanged, women—convicted child murderesses in particular—were drowned. The hangman would hold the bound and gagged woman underwater with a wooden pitchfork, and sometimes she was put inside a sack as well. It was a slow, cruel death because the victims kept rising to the surface.

In Schongau, Jakob Kuisl had ensured years ago that these brutal killings were abolished, but from time to time young women sought out this unfortunate place to take their own lives. Only a few weeks ago they had found the body of sixteen-year-old Anna Wiesmüller here. The girl had been a local farmer's maid and had fallen pregnant. She had confided only in her sister. The girl had drowned herself in her despair, and the father was never found.

Breathing heavily, Magdalena paused and ran her eyes along the opposite shore. In the fading light of the afternoon sun, Magdalena made out a person sitting on the small rotten pier that had jutted out into the water since time immemorial.

It was Barbara.

Magdalena breathed a sigh of relief and made the sign of the cross. Her worst fears hadn't come true. Then again, had she really believed her sister would take her own life? And perhaps Magdalena's hunch was wrong, too—her sister could be incredibly hard to read.

Only Georg, Barbara's twin brother, seemed to understand her without words. But he'd been living in Bamberg with their uncle for almost six years now.

Meanwhile, Jakob Kuisl had reached Katzenweiher Pond too. He circled the small lake from the other direction so that he and Magdalena reached the pier at almost the same time. But Magdalena had already heard her father's thundering voice from right across the lake.

"By Jesus Christ and all the saints, do you have any idea how worried we've been?" he ranted, his face bright red from the exertion. "Goddamnit! You have no business being up here by yourself, do you know that?"

"So now I'm not allowed to go outside anymore?" Barbara

snapped back. Her eyes were red from crying. She looked pale and she shivered underneath her thin woolen coat. Magdalena noticed once more how beautiful her younger sister was, with her raven curls and full eyebrows. The two sisters looked much alike, though Barbara looked a tad wilder and perhaps a little wicked, which was why the lads in town sometimes called her the devil's wench.

"Or have I done something wrong *again*?" Barbara continued, looking at her father. "Have I not swept the house properly, or fed the chickens, or milked the cow well enough? Is that it? Go on, tell me!"

"Father was just worried, that's all," Magdalena tried to soothe her sister and placed her own coat around Barbara's shoulders. She understood Barbara's frustration well. Their grumpy old father wasn't an easy man to live with, as she knew from years of experience. It was high time for Barbara to find a husband before she did something stupid.

"How dare you talk to me like that," Kuisl snarled at his younger daughter. "You won't be doing so for much longer. As soon as—"

"I'm not going to marry one of your stupid hangmen," Barbara said. "Forget it!"

"What would be so bad about it?" Kuisl shrugged. "They're a decent lot, no cutthroats, knackers, or gravediggers. The Nuremberg hangman, Widmann, earns so much that he owns several townhouses. And then there's also a bunch of dashing apprentices." He attempted an encouraging wink, but failed. "They're strapping, handsome young lads. Ha! Not skinny rakes like my dear son-in-law."

"All right, you've gone too far," Magdalena interjected. "Simon is a doctor after all, and—"

She broke off when she saw the flicker in Barbara's eyes. Why couldn't she shut her mouth? How many times had Barbara lamented how lucky Magdalena was—a husband who had been appointed town physician and three children—while she, the younger sister, had to keep their father's house and put up with his tantrums.

"I think you should leave us alone for a while," Magdalena said to their father. "As you can see, Barbara is fine, and now we need some sister time."

Jakob Kuisl ran his fingers through his icy beard, then he nodded. "If you must. But don't start thinking she can get out of the Munich trip. We're finding her a husband, and that's the end of it."

Barbara was about to make a retort, but Magdalena squeezed her hand. "All right, Father," she said. "Now go."

"It's only for the best, Barbara, believe me," Kuisl said quietly without looking at his daughter. "Only for the best. You'll thank me one day." He turned around and trudged back toward the River Lech.

Magdalena waited a little while, then she stroked Barbara's hair. "Maybe going to Munich isn't the worst idea," she started softly. "Why not take a look at those fellows? And if you don't like any of them, at least you'll have seen Munich. I heard there's a real theater—not just one in a tavern, but in its own house of stone. And they say that since the elector's Italian wife lives in town, everyone who's anyone comes to Munich. It's full of music, dances, gardens, and—"

"You don't understand!" Barbara burst out. "I can't!" Crying, she collapsed, her whole body racked by sobs.

Magdalena took her sister's face between her hands and gave her a determined look. "Barbara, talk to me. What's the matter? You've been acting strange for weeks. Talk to me now."

Barbara's sobs turned into hysterical laughter. She pushed Magdalena away. "You don't see it, do you?" she shouted. "You're a midwife, you've given birth several times yourself, but you don't see it. And why should you? I'm just the baby sister who cleans up after Father. Why the hell didn't I get rid of it like Father's trash? Why? Now it's too late."

Magdalena knew then that her hunch was right.

It's true. I should have noticed much sooner. Why couldn't we talk about it?

"Dear God," she breathed. "You're . . . you're pregnant."

Barbara had cried herself out of tears, but the silence that followed said more than a thousand words. For a long time, the only sound was the wind in the willows along the shore.

"Whose is it?" Magdalena asked eventually.

Barbara sniveled. "Remember the traveling jugglers that passed through Schongau early in the winter? The good-looking blond one who was throwing the balls so cleverly at the parish fair?" She laughed desperately. "I always fall for the same clowns."

"But you didn't have to—" Magdalena began.

"I told him I didn't want to," Barbara cut her off. "In the hay barn, I kept telling him no. It was nice at first, but then . . . then he wouldn't stop. I tried to fight him off, but he pinned me down, held my mouth shut, and took me like . . . like a dog. I couldn't do anything. He laughed when he left and said I'd wanted it too. It was the first time, since . . . since . . ." She broke off, racked by dry sobs. After a while, she continued.

"I only realized well after the jugglers had left. I . . . I was numb. I cried for days, secretly, in bed, in the woods, so none of you would notice. The shame . . ." Barbara wiped the tears from her eyes. "Then I wanted to get rid of it. But it was the middle of winter, no herbs anywhere. And to whom could I have gone for a brew of savin or some dried hellebore? Old Stechlin, who's constantly on my back about my supposed wantonness? Or maybe Father?" She gave another desperate laugh. "He'd never have believed that I hadn't done it willingly. No one would have."

"You could have come to me," Magdalena said softly. "I would have helped you."

Magdalena used to work for Martha Stechlin, the Schongau midwife, and people still sought her out when they needed herbs or advice regarding female issues.

Only my sister didn't come to me for help . . .

"Believe me, I . . . I wanted to," Barbara replied haltingly. "I don't know how many times I stood outside your door, but something always happened. Simon would be there and look at me strangely, or the boys wanted to play, or Sophia would cry . . . I kept putting it off, kept hoping it would go away by itself, but now it's too late, I fear." Barbara hung her head. "I haven't bled for three months."

Magdalena groaned. *Too late,* she thought. *Much too late.*

An abortion induced by herbs and plants like savin, hellebore, or mugwort was only safe in the first few weeks. If women were caught during that time, they could expect fines, the stocks, or banishment. But the longer they waited, the more dangerous the consumption of such remedies became—not only because they could die of the poison, but they might also be sentenced to death. And the midwife or wise woman who had given the plants could also be hanged or drowned in the sack. Many desperate young women killed their newborns shortly after birth, smothered and buried them, hoping no one had noticed the pregnancy. Others stuck needles in their lower abdomen, and often the mother died along with the child. Jakob Kuisl once told Magdalena that more women were convicted as child murderesses than as witches.

But Magdalena also knew that Barbara would never be capable of killing a child. Especially not now that little Sophia reminded her aunt every day how dainty and fragile such a little person was.

"It is what it is," Magdalena said after a while. Her expression hardened. "The child's in your belly now, and, God willing, you'll give birth in half a year's time." She hesitated just for a moment, then nodded decidedly. "At least we're traveling to Munich next week. We're going to find you a husband."

Barbara stared at her, dumbfounded. "But . . . but . . . how? I'm pregnant . . ."

"You're only in the third month. If you marry now, no one's going to care where the child came from. Not if you get married in Munich. Father can't find out yet, nor Simon. It's going to stay our secret." Magdalena took Barbara's hands in hers and squeezed them tightly. "I promise to make sure you won't get an ogre for a husband. I give you my word as your big sister."

"Damn you, I'm not going to marry any of those accursed hangmen!" Barbara yelled. "How many times do I have to tell you? No way! Father, you, and even old Stechlin always try to tell me what I should and shouldn't do. Why can't you just leave me alone?"

"So you're just going back to doing nothing, like you've done for the last few weeks?" Magdalena continued mercilessly. "Are you going to wait until the child is born? A dishonorable hangman's daughter with a bastard? They'll chase you out of town like a mangy dog, like they do with all unwed mothers. And that's not all. Have you considered the consequences for our family? For Father, especially?"

"What kind of a family is this, anyway?" Barbara hissed. "A family of dishonorables, hated like the Plague."

"But it's *your* family," Magdalena replied quietly. "You only have the one."

Suddenly they heard a faint crying. Magdalena turned around and saw Peter trudging through the snow toward them, carrying Sophia.

"I swear I haven't done anything!" he exclaimed. "But she just won't stop crying. I even tried to read something to her."

"Silly!" Magdalena smiled despite herself. "When a little thing like that one cries, it's either hungry or needs a fresh diaper. I fed her not long ago." She took Sophia from her son and wrinkled her nose. "So I'm pretty sure it's the latter."

Gently, she laid Sophia on the pier and unwrapped the furs Peter had put her in. As expected, the cloth around the little bottom was wet and soiled. Magdalena didn't have a spare diaper with her, however.

"Take this." Barbara had stopped crying and was holding out a cloth. "My handkerchief. We can wash it later."

Magdalena gratefully accepted the cloth and wrapped it around Sophia, who was much happier already and tried to grab her mother's hand.

"She's so beautiful," Barbara whispered from behind Magdalena. The grief had left her voice. Barbara and her niece had shared a special connection since the day Sophia was born, when Barbara had helped Martha Stechlin, the midwife, deliver her.

"Even though she'll probably never dance at her wedding," Magdalena remarked bitterly. "Not with her foot."

"Then she just won't marry, like her aunt," Barbara said with a thin smile. "They call me the devil's wench, too." She gave a dry laugh and wiped her tears away. "Barbara and Sophia, the two devil's wenches. How does that sound? Let the men go to hell!"

Barbara leaned down to Sophia and stroked her soft cheek. "Don't ever let a man near you," she whispered. "They bring nothing but tears and misery."

Outside the doctor's door stood two men and a young woman. A cold breeze drove snowflakes into the hallway as Simon scrutinized the group.

The older of the two men wore a bearskin coat and a hat made from squirrel pelts, while the younger man wore red and yellow woolen garments. Between them, they held the woman, who was clearly very weak and struggled to stand. Her face was ghostly pale, her eyes closed, and sweat ran down her face despite the icy wind. Like the men, she was dressed in costly garments. Behind them in the twilight, Simon made out a carriage with two white horses.

"We were told the town physician lives here," the older man said gravely. He spoke with a strange accent, and Simon guessed he came from south of the Alps. The man cast a searching glance down the hallway, as if hoping to find someone else.

"Um, that's me," Simon replied. "How can I be of help?"

The old man, a good head taller than him, frowned and looked Simon up and down. Simon's height had caused him grief since childhood, and he occasionally tried to make up for it by wearing high-heeled boots and fancy hats.

"You're very young to be a *dottore* —" the older one started, but the young man cut him off.

"My wife needs your help." He spoke with the same accent. "She gave birth to a healthy son a few days ago." He motioned at the carriage. "The wet nurse is looking after him. We were in Munich on business and thought we'd be back in Verona for the birth . . ." He shook his head with a sigh. "But the child came in Landsberg, much sooner than expected."

"Why didn't you stay in Landsberg?" Simon asked.

"We had already wasted enough time," the old man grumbled. "We have lots of work to do in Verona. I told my daughter-in-law not to come. But she didn't listen, as always, and wanted to see the Munich court. And now this!" He tapped Simon's narrow chest. "Can you help us? Yes or no? She has a fever. Give us some medicine so we can leave this dismal place as soon as possible."

If it is what I fear, then no medicine is going to help her, Simon thought glumly as he studied the semiconscious woman. But he didn't say anything. The old man didn't look as though he would enter into lengthy discussions with a country doctor. Simon guessed the father and son were wealthy foreign merchants, perhaps even lesser noblemen. Simon was in for a world of trouble or even a court case if the woman died in his care. On the other hand, he felt incredibly sorry for her. He tried to imagine what he would feel like if it was Magdalena standing in front of him, or Barbara. It could happen to any woman.

Any woman that gave birth, anyway.

"Bring her inside," Simon said eventually. "I'll see what I can do."

The two men carried the woman to the treatment room, where a small, hard bed stood in one corner. The old man glanced disparagingly at the crooked shelves with surgical instruments, scratched vials, and ancient jars of medicine that had been passed down to Simon by his father, the Schongau bathhouse owner.

"Perhaps we should have continued on to Füssen," he growled.

Simon was about to give a harsh reply but changed his mind. He leaned over the woman and checked her pulse and reflexes.

"Who helped with the birth?" he asked and carefully unbuttoned the young mother's coat.

"A . . . a midwife from Landsberg," the young man replied hesitantly as he watched Simon.

"*Maledetto!* What are you doing to my daughter-in-law?" the old man flared up when Simon lifted the woman's skirt. "Are you a medicus or a rascal?"

"If I'm going to find out what's wrong with her, I have to examine her," Simon explained.

The man hesitated, then nodded reluctantly. "As long as you don't use your knives down there," he grumbled.

Simon pushed a thin, holey screen between the patient and the two men, then he began to examine the woman's abdomen from the outside. In the medical world, there was a strict distinction between learned physicians and the more hands-on barber-surgeons. Only the latter were permitted to conduct surgery, while the learned doctors—the group Simon now belonged to as well—merely examined the body on the outside. But once Simon had removed the bloody rags tied around the woman's pelvis, he suspected that not even surgery could help her. A putrid smell spread through the room. Simon heard the old man exhale in disgust behind the screen. He washed his hands and walked to the two men.

"How long did she stay in bed following the birth?" Simon asked.

The young man shrugged. Simon could tell he had a bad conscience. Fear for his young wife had dug deep grooves in his otherwise youthful face. "About a week," he said quietly. "My father felt that—"

"We have good doctors in Verona," the father interrupted. "Should we have left her in that old Landsberg hag's stinking hole for longer? We can't afford to stay away from home this long. I need my son in the office."

"This woman should have stayed in bed at least three more weeks," Simon replied curtly. "Her abdomen became infected following the birth."

"Then give her something," the old man snarled at him. "Are you a doctor or a whining quack?"

Instead of replying, Simon disappeared behind the screen again and carefully cleaned the young woman's abdomen with warm water. Even though he had washed his hands first, he had a feeling it was already too late for her. He had seen too many women like her, dying of a strange fever soon after giving birth. His colleagues believed that some yet undiscovered substances began to fester inside a woman's body after birthing. Simon, however, was convinced those substances came from the outside; he'd included this theory in his treatise. Unfortunately, he couldn't prove anything at this stage, he could only presume.

Simon fashioned a bandage from clean cloths and inserted dried yarrow, arnica, and comfrey to alleviate the infection. Then he dressed the woman, who had started to moan softly.

"You must change the bandage daily," he told the anxious husband. "I'm going to give you more herbs. I would advise you to remain in Schongau for a while—I can recommend an inn . . ."

"We don't have the time." The old man shook his head. "And I want my daughter-in-law in good hands. Our physician in Verona swears by cupping, and I'm sure that'll fix her. Also, the Rottenbuch abbot can offer us better accommodation than this foul-smelling town."

"She must not lose any more blood," Simon warned them. "I truly believe—"

But the old man cut him off by putting a few coins in his hand. "That should be enough. And now farewell, Herr *Medicus*."

The man had practically spat the last word. Now he put on his hat and coat while the young man helped his wife to her feet. Simon helped to carry the woman out to the carriage, where he caught a brief glimpse of the rotund wet nurse holding a screaming little bundle. The driver cracked his whip, and soon the carriage disappeared in the dusk.

Godspeed, Simon thought.

But he didn't have much hope for the woman. He guessed she would die before they made it to Verona. This fever so many women contracted after giving birth was brief and merciless.

Deeply saddened, Simon returned to his treatment room. The coins the old man had given him jingled in his pocket—a whole week's wage—but it didn't make him feel any better. Simon took a closer look at the coins. They were five silver thalers, the same kind the Schongau cloth merchant Josef Seiler had given him earlier that day. These, however, were brand new, displaying the Wittelsbach lozenges and the year 1672 on the front, and a Madonna on a half-moon on the back. Evidently, the Verona merchants had received the coins not long ago in Munich. They were shiny, as if they were fresh out of the mint. Simon let them slide through his fingers and was about to put them away when he noticed something.

Could it be?

He studied each coin individually. Then, to confirm his suspicion, he fetched the scales he usually used for his medicines. He placed the fat cloth merchant's three coins in one pan and three of the Verona merchant's coins in the other.

The scales instantly tilted to the side with Seiler's coins.

Simon frowned. His suspicion had been correct, the coins of the Veronese men were not only newer, but also lighter. He guessed they were made with some kind of cheaper metal, like copper or tin. The only question was: had the merchants known, or had they been betrayed?

Once more Simon studied the beautifully shiny silver coins. There was nothing he could do about it now, anyway. The carriage would have left Schongau by now and was on its way to Rottenbuch. Simon absentmindedly let the thalers slide into his purse. He shrugged. Money was nothing more than pressed metal.

Not even ducats and doubloons of the finest gold could help the young woman now.

When Magdalena and Simon finally lay in their bed that night, they didn't speak for a long time. Each listened to the breathing of the other, knowing their spouse couldn't get to sleep either. Next to their bed, in a crib made by her grandfather, Sophia slept peacefully. Magdalena reached out and stroked her daughter's little hand.

So small and fragile, she thought. *And so beautiful. I pray to God that we may keep her.*

As if the Lord had tried to make up for his mistake with Sophia's foot, he had blessed her with all sorts of positive traits. Sophia was the happiest child imaginable, full of laughter; she was attentive, her curious blue eyes studying everything; and her lips had recently formed a few first words. Magdalena thought she could already tell that her daughter would one day be as beautiful as her aunt.

And just as shunned, she thought with a pang.

So far they hadn't spoken about their argument that afternoon, but Magdalena had told her husband about Kuisl's plans to find a husband for Barbara in Munich. She hadn't told him that her sister was pregnant, however. She didn't think it was a good idea to tell Simon, not yet. Simon liked to talk, and it was just too risky. Her father couldn't find out under any circumstances. Not even Magdalena could tell how the Schongau hangman would react if he found out that his younger daughter was pregnant with an illegitimate child. This was something for the sisters to deal with themselves.

Magdalena was about to say something to her husband when he also started to speak.

"Listen," he said. "I'm sorry for what I said about you and Sophia this afternoon. It was stupid of me and I know it's not true. I think I've just taken on too much lately."

Magdalena squeezed his hand. "It's all right. You are working too much, it's true. The neighbors said a carriage was here until after dark."

"They were travelers on their way back to Verona," he replied quietly. "The woman was very ill. I don't think I was able to help her."

Haltingly, Simon told his wife of the young mother and her father-in-law, whose haste and greed were probably the death of her.

"It's that accursed fever that befalls women after birthing," he finished, shaking his head. "I just wish there was a cure."

"Maybe there can't be a cure for every ailment in the world," Magdalena responded. "Have you ever thought about that? Perhaps we simply have to put up with some diseases."

"Like Sophia's foot? Is that what you're trying to say?" Simon tossed and turned in bed. "I will never stop looking for reasons. I haven't become a medicus only to cut open boils on fat patricians' backsides. If only my treatise could be published . . ."

Magdalena groaned. "*That* again. I think we have more important things to worry about. Barbara needs to marry. And I'm praying to God there's going to be at least one half-decent fellow among those hangmen in Munich." She shuddered. "I only hope they're not like the Schongau gravedigger. Or the knacker— you can smell him ten paces against the wind."

"At least you've convinced your sister to come to Munich," Simon replied. "I'm surprised she even agreed to that much. I would have thought Barbara would refuse no matter what."

"I . . . I just sweet-talked her." Magdalena hoped her husband wouldn't notice her shaking voice. "I think my descriptions of the new theater and the many palaces and gardens helped. Munich is supposed to be one of the most beautiful cities of the German Empire since Elector Ferdinand Maria employs so many foreigners at court. Apparently, they've built a stunning new cathedral, new fortifications, and a magnificent residence. And . . . hey, what is it?"

Simon was laughing. "Well, I'm just trying to imagine a dozen executioners of your father's caliber sitting at one table. That's probably the exact opposite of Munich court life." His hand wandered over to Magdalena. "I've never understood how a clump of a man like that could make such a beautiful daughter."

"Why not," Magdalena teased, "when a weed like you can do it?"

When they were lying in each other's arms a while later, a smile crossed Sophia's face. She gurgled and laughed in her sleep.

It seemed she was having a lovely dream.

2

On the Loisach River, 2 February,
Anno Domini 1672

ʙARBARA STOOD AT THE FRONT of the raft with her eyes
closed, taking in the noises and smells around her. The steady
rushing of the river, the groaning and cracking of the ice on the
water, the calls of the helmsmen from neighboring rafts . . . The
faintest hint of spring lay in the air, barely detectable, but Barbara sensed it wasn't far away, a few more weeks, perhaps. A
slight thaw had set in recently, and even though there was still
snow on the fields and frost at night, the longer days promised
warmer and merrier days ahead.

When Barbara opened her eyes again, the feeling of safety and
comfort vanished. In front of her was the raging river, carrying
the raft at a scary speed past villages and narrow towpaths, where
a handful of peasants trudged through snow still knee-deep in
places. But most of all, Barbara saw the many raftsmen with
their felt hats, blue jackets, and pike poles, which they used to
push off other rafts or navigate around a dangerous rapid. All of
them were young, strong men and all of them were gaping at
her. Just then one of them whispered something to his colleague,
laughed, then they winked at her suggestively and touched their
hats in greeting. Barbara turned away.

Will it never end? she thought. *Are we nothing but fair game to men?*

They had left Schongau early the previous morning. Until the last moment Barbara hadn't been sure whether she should go. But did she really have a choice? Her older sister was right after all; if she bore a child out of wedlock in Schongau, her life would be over. And her disgrace would affect the whole family. Her father would likely be expelled from the Council of Twelve as well.

What if she kept her pregnancy secret and left the baby outside someone's house when it was born? At a monastery, perhaps?

The thought made Barbara feel sick. It didn't matter who the father was—the child was her flesh and blood. For years—decades—to come she would be haunted by the question of whether her child was still alive or not, whether it was well or dying of starvation at that very moment, freezing somewhere in the streets, wondering to the last who its mother had been. No, she couldn't do it. She should have gotten rid of it when it was just a tiny speck, but now it was too late.

So Barbara had decided to follow her sister's advice and travel to Munich with her family. What did she have to lose? As soon as Schongau had disappeared behind a bend in the road she had breathed easier.

Anywhere is better than that narrow-minded hole . . .

Her father had heard that the first rafts of the year were operating on the Loisach River, and so they had decided to travel via Rottenbuch and Oberammergau to the Loisach valley. A wagon driver had taken them as far as Baiersoien. After a night at a drafty, flea-infested inn, a master raftsman had agreed to take them to Munich for a few hellers.

Barbara looked to the back, where, between several marketeers from Partenkirchen, a haggard old scissor-sharpener with his huge pack, and two journeymen dyers sitting on their bales of cloth, the Kuisl family sat on a number of barrels. Peter and Paul visibly enjoyed the ride on the raft, unlike their father, who continually tried to stop his sons from playing catch among the many crates, bales, and barrels. Magdalena was feeding little Sophia, and their father sat smoking his pipe, staring into space. Barbara knew Jakob Kuisl hated to death knowing there was water beneath his feet, but he would never dream of showing fear in front of his family.

"Watch out! Ice!"

The helmsman next to Barbara yanked the front rudder around hard, and she lost her balance. She managed to hold on to the man's broad back at the last moment and saw the large floes of ice drifting past the raft. She could hear some of the other passengers screaming in the back; an old farmer's wife prayed to Saint Nicholas, the patron saint of raftsmen. The raft turned dangerously to the right and the helmsmen at the front and rear fought hard against the current, cursing viciously. The big man next to Barbara toiled and groaned; the huge muscles on his arms flexed as he pulled the oar through the water again and again. Finally, they were back on course.

The helmsman wiped the sweat from his face with a grim laugh. Only now did Barbara realize the man was Alois Seethaler, the master raftsman from Garmisch who had agreed to take them aboard that morning. He was a bearded, sinister-looking fellow who carried a heavy purse full of jingling coins around his belly. He had charged considerably for his courage to attempt the trip to Munich this early in the year.

"That was a close call!" he boasted and winked at Barbara. "But you were a big help, girl. Feel free to hang on to me anytime. Pretty little thing, you are." With a loud laugh, he slapped her on the bottom, and Barbara winced.

"Leave it," she said between clenched teeth.

"Don't be like that," the raftsman grumbled. "I gave your family a good price, the least you can do is show a little gratitude."

"I don't remember being part of the deal," Barbara replied.

Alois Seethaler grinned. "Who knows. Soon we'll be at Wolf-ratshausen and more travelers are going to want to come aboard. Perhaps the price will go up then, and you won't be so squeamish anymore. How do you like that?"

Seethaler's hand suddenly went down her backside and right between her legs. She froze. In the past, she would have slapped the man for doing what he did, no matter how big and strong he was, but now she simply felt sick — like so often in the last few weeks. The raftsman took her silence for consent, and his fingers made their way under her coat, under her skirt, in between her thighs, when he suddenly stopped and yelped.

"Is there a problem here?" a booming voice asked from be-hind Barbara.

She turned around and saw her father. He was more than a head taller than the big master raftsman and his bulky boot stood on Seethaler's foot, pinning him to the spot.

"I said, is there a problem here?" Kuisl repeated menacingly. His arm came down on the raftsman's shoulder like a felled tree trunk.

Alois Seethaler winced and then slowly shook his head, and Jakob Kuisl lifted his boot off Seethaler's foot. But his arm re-mained firmly planted on the raftsman's shoulder. Moments like these reminded Barbara that her father was still as strong as an ox, despite his ripe age. His height alone intimidated most people — especially if they knew that the giant was the notorious Schon-gau hangman. Clearly, Alois Seethaler had no idea that he'd just flirted with the daughter of an executioner.

"No . . . problem . . . ," he wheezed.

"Then I thank you kindly for the pleasant journey, Herr Mas-ter Rafter," Kuisl said and patted the man's shoulder, then he carefully picked some bits of fluff off his coat. "When do you think we'll reach Munich, hmm?"

"Seven ... maybe eight hours," the other man stammered. "Once we reach the Isar River, we can go faster."

"That's great, because I'd really like to taste some Munich beer tonight, one of those smooth dark ones, brewed by the monks who renounce all flesh. Can you be one of those monks until tonight?" Kuisl gave the raftsman a glowering look. The latter nodded but didn't say another word.

"I'm so pleased we have an understanding. Are you coming, Barbara?"

The hangman turned around and made his way to the back of the raft. Barbara followed him unwillingly. Kuisl stopped abruptly.

"Do you understand now why I want you to have a husband?" he asked angrily. "I can't always keep an eye on you. Men are like beasts. They smell fresh blood like stalking wolves."

"I know that," Barbara replied quietly.

Better than you think, she added in her thoughts.

Jakob Kuisl sighed. The anger vanished from his face and he gave his younger daughter a loving look. "By the way, I'm glad you decided to come without a fight in the end. And ... and ..." He wrestled with himself. "I'm sorry about the way I sprung the news on you the other day. God knows I'm a rough bugger — your mother always said so."

"You really are." Barbara smiled. It didn't happen often that her father apologized to her.

Jakob Kuisl took a deep breath. "Then do me a favor and just take a look at the three lads I chose for you. Then you can still decide on someone else."

"*Three* lads?" The smile was wiped from Barbara's face. She stared at her father with astonishment. "What in God's name ... ?"

"Well, I wrote a few letters, just to see who's coming. And I may have mentioned my beautiful daughter." Kuisl shrugged.

"In my opinion, there are three possible candidates for you. Of course, I don't know if they're ugly, but at least all three are a good match."

Barbara gaped in amazement. That was so much more brazen than she had feared. "And what exactly did you tell them about me?" she asked eventually. "Big breasts, black hair, even teeth? What assets do I have that I don't even know about? Wide hips, good paces, like a horse?"

Kuisl's eyes darkened again and he clenched his fists. "You're going to take a look at those men, whether you want to or not. Damn it! I've turned a blind eye for far too long. If your dear mother knew . . ."

Barbara left her father midsentence and disappeared between a few crates, her face red with anger. She needed to be alone—a difficult thing on a raft twenty paces long and seven paces wide. Everywhere she turned, passengers who had witnessed the argument between her and her father were staring at her curiously. Magdalena was also looking at her with concern, but she had her hands full with Sophia. And what could her sister do, anyhow? Magdalena had assured her they would get through this together, but they were just hollow words.

No one could help her, not even Magdalena.

Crying softly, Barbara slid down between the crates and closed her eyes.

The steady rushing of the water helped her calm down a little. After a while, she wiped her tears away and stared defiantly at the icy green waves. Life would go on. She had already endured much in her life; she would find a way through this, too.

She was a Kuisl, damn it!

They finally neared Munich in late afternoon. The woods had become sparser in the last few hours and they had seen more and more onion-shaped domes of small village churches jutting into the blue sky. After they passed an old castle near the Isar River, the first walls of the city fortifications came into sight.

Simon was standing at the front of the raft with his two boys, gazing at the impressive skyline. Trenches, walls, and massive fortifications separated the snow-covered fields outside the city from the magnificent houses, churches, and towers on the other side. The previous elector, Maximilian, had commissioned the imposing fortifications during the Great War, but they hadn't yet been completed when the Swedes attacked. Nevertheless, these walls told each passing traveler that they were looking at one of the most advanced and magnificent capital cities of the German Empire.

Simon could make out two particularly high onion domes in the city center, which he guessed belonged to the Frauenkirche, the well-known Munich church. The wide, sullen Isar River ran through fallow hop fields, meadows, and patches of forest not far from the city. The raft passed by gravelly, sparsely vegetated islands and eventually glided under a long bridge. Simon had heard that this bridge had been the start of Munich. Apparently, a powerful duke had it built so he could demand a bridge toll from the salt merchants from Reichenhall. In time, a monastery and a few shacks had turned into a mighty city, known far beyond the boundaries of the German Empire.

Pleased, Simon stroked his red coat and the fashionable breeches he'd put on especially for this journey. He knew one had to dress better in Munich than in Schongau, the stinking provincial backwater whose narrow-mindedness Simon increasingly resented. He had always felt more at home in larger cities than in his hometown. Simon fervently hoped the meeting of the executioners would take place somewhere central, so he could stroll through the streets of the city and visit the churches, the theater, and the electoral residence, called simply the Residenz.

Once they had passed the bridge, the river became very busy. Wooden landings and piers protruded from the left bank for several hundred feet. Countless rafts and barges were tied to posts and bollards; poorly dressed laborers carried bales, barrels, and crates up the bank, which probably earned them a kreuzer or two. Simon could barely hear a word with all the shouting that went on in this place.

"The raft landing," Kuisl grumbled happily. "We're almost there."

"So where is this meeting taking place?" Simon asked. "At a tavern in town, or near the market square? Perhaps we could visit the Frauenkirche on the way. I heard it was . . . hey, wait!"

Ignoring Simon's questions, Jakob Kuisl had jumped off the raft and climbed up narrow steps to a wide, busy lane. The hangman made his way past tired-looking peasants with packs and crates on their backs, caterwauling market women, and drunken raftsmen who came staggering out of a tavern near the raft landing. Even though Candlemas was supposed to be a time of peace and rest, the streets of Munich were buzzing.

"They're already drinking away their annual pay," Magdalena guessed while she struggled to catch up with her father. "For Christ's sake, can't you slow down?"

"Where is he headed to, anyway?" Barbara asked. She hadn't spoken in hours and Simon was pleased she wasn't looking quite so surly anymore. "To the next tavern for a beer, while we twiddle our thumbs in the cold? I wouldn't put it past him."

"Hmm. I thought he was headed for the house where the hangmen are meeting," Simon replied. "But I wonder why he isn't going toward the city gate."

Simon was right: instead of turning toward the massive city gate, Kuisl walked on to the busy Isar Bridge with its high bridge tower. Carriages and oxcarts drove through the tower's gatehouse toward the city. It reeked of sweating animals, beer mash, and fresh horse dung.

"For crying out loud, Father, you owe us an explanation!" Magdalena demanded when she finally caught up with Kuisl. "Where are you leading us? I'm not taking another step until you tell us."

The hangman stopped and pointed to the far bank, where Magdalena could make out a number of poor-looking huts. They seemed crooked and scattered randomly, as if a drunken giant had accidentally dropped them. Several mills stood out from among the shacks, their ice-crusted wheels driven by a creek. A dark cloud of soot and smoke hung over the entire settlement along the swampy bank.

"That's where we're going," Kuisl said. "To Au."

"Oh my God, it looks awful," Magdalena breathed. "What is it? A village for beggars and cutthroats?"

"That's pretty much it." Kuisl grinned. "Did you really think a dozen dishonorable executioners would meet at the Munich Residenz over wine and some pheasant? Au is a good place for hangmen. There's always something to do."

"Great," Simon sighed as he abandoned his plans of evening strolls through the city. He cast a depressed glance down at his best coat and breeches. "I might as well hang a sign around my neck that reads 'please rob me.'"

"Nonsense, you'll like it there," Kuisl said affably as they walked across the bridge. "I've been here before. Folks might be a little rough around the edges at Au, but they're cut from decent cloth."

Almost on cue, two ragged-looking figures staggered toward them, holding on to each other and bawling some Bavarian folk song Simon couldn't understand. Like the raftsmen down at the landing, these two clearly didn't want to spend Candlemas sober.

Soon the Kuisls had reached the first huts of Au. There was neither wall nor gate, just a wide road covered with icy mud that ran parallel to the Isar River. Every now and then, the rows of shacks along the road were broken by larger buildings with narrow stairways on the outside that led to balconies and doors of all shapes and sizes. Old men and women with weather-beaten faces leaned from the windows, eyeing the strangers curiously. Narrow, winding alleyways led off the sides into a maze of wooden houses, backyards, mills, and hostels. There was only a handful of stone houses, the largest of which was a three-storied building that lay a little off to the side.

It was getting dark by now, but Simon could make out at least a half dozen taverns right away. Every single one seemed to be packed, the carousers audible from the street; at one tavern, an out-of-tune fiddle played a lively melody. The next moment, the door of the tavern was yanked open and a drunken man stumbled toward the family. He just made it to the next corner before vomiting noisily.

Barbara wrinkled her nose and glared at her father. Then she turned to Magdalena. "So, is this the beautiful Munich you promised? The theater, the countless gardens . . ."

"Grandpa, why is everyone drunk here?" Peter asked.

"Well, they're celebrating a year of hard work," Kuisl explained with a shrug. "Servants and journeymen get a few days off after Candlemas. Then it's back to work for another year. A little booze-up never hurt anyone."

"If they keep drinking like that, their money for the year will be gone by morning," Magdalena muttered. "I for one don't want to spend another day in this—"

She broke off when someone screamed in one of the alleyways. It sounded different than the usual shouts of drunken men —anxious and terrified. Jakob Kuisl hesitated briefly, then he turned into the narrow lane. Simon and the rest of the family followed him. Soon they saw a group of people gathered along the creek that ran through Au. A mill stood on their right, and something was lying on one of the waterwheel's paddles. In the dim light, it took Simon a moment to figure out what it was.

It was a body.

Some of the people were straining to turn the wheel against the current, but it kept slipping from their fingers and the body was carried higher and higher. Soon it would be thrown down on the other side.

Jakob Kuisl cracked his knuckles, then he pushed the people aside like blades of grass until he stood by the waterwheel.

"Out the way!" he growled.

Oohs and *aahs* came from the crowd as the hangman grabbed one of the icy paddles and pulled on it. At first, nothing happened, but Kuisl grunted and groaned and finally the wheel began to turn against the current.

"Who is that?" a bullnecked fellow near Simon whispered. "I wonder if he's from Giesing. A beer driver, perhaps?"

"I don't care where he's from, all I know is I don't want to start a brawl with him," another man replied. "With his shoulders, he could carry a dozen kegs of beers up Au Hill at once."

The people watched and whispered while Kuisl kept pulling on the wheel. Finally, a few men came to his aid and together they dragged the lifeless body off the paddle and placed it gently on the ground.

Simon winced when he saw that the body belonged to a girl of about sixteen or seventeen. She was dead, without a doubt. Her glassy eyes stared blankly into the night sky, icicles hung in her strawberry-blonde hair like glittering jewelry. The cold water had preserved the body well, so it was hard to tell how long she'd been in the creek. Simon couldn't see any obvious injuries, either.

"Hey, that's enough now, folks, show's over. Beat it!"

A haggard man carrying a lantern in one hand and a cudgel in the other appeared from one of the alleyways. He swung his stick threateningly. "Beat it, I said!" he repeated. "Or do I have to make you? I'll lock up anyone who keeps staring."

Grumbling, the crowd dispersed until only a handful of curious onlookers remained. Finally the tall, skinny man reached Jakob Kuisl. His nose was red from the cold and probably a dram of brandy, too. A drop of snot hung from its end. The man sniffed and glared at Kuisl out of small, nasty eyes.

"That goes for you, too, big fellow," he said pompously. "This is a case for the officials, and I'm the Au clerk, goddamnit. Or do you have something to do with her death, hmm?" He pointed his cudgel at the girl's body. "You didn't want to pay and threw her in the water once you were done with her, is that it? Spit it out!"

"We only just arrived," Simon said now. "My family can testify to that." He pointed at Magdalena, Barbara, and the children, who had remained in the background.

The haggard man moved his head from side to side. "Hmm. Strangers." He sniffed again, pulling a big lump of snot back up his nose. Then he gestured with his cudgel toward the main road. "We've already got enough hungry mouths at Au, so get out of here, you dirty country rabble!"

"This poor girl was probably also country *rabble*," Kuisl said, ignoring the man's order.

"Huh?" The skinny man rubbed his nose. "What makes you think that, big one?"

"Well, there were several dozen people from Au here before. Every one of them saw the girl, but no one called out her name. And I'm guessing everyone knows everyone in Au, right?"

"Er, that's right," the clerk admitted. "But still—"

"Also, tying a sack of stones around someone and throwing them in the water is a pretty elaborate murder. If I was the murderer, I would have knocked her over the head and chucked her in the creek. The cold does the rest."

"Sack? Stones?" The clerk looked confused. "What are you talking about?"

Kuisl leaned over the body and turned it onto its back. Now everyone could see the small sack of stones tied around the girl's waist.

"I could feel it when I lifted her off the paddle," Kuisl explained. "She was damned heavy. I bet it's at least thirty pounds

—that would drag you down like a lead weight. If the water-wheel hadn't picked her up, she would have stayed at the bottom of the creek until summer."

The clerk scratched his nose, then a grin spread across his blotchy face. "Ha! Case solved, then," he announced triumphantly. "The wench drowned herself. Happens all the time. Young things like her get knocked up by some clown from out of town, they can't see another way, so they jump in the water and Munich's down another pretty girl."

Kuisl frowned. "Hmm. Possible . . ."

"What do you mean, possible, it's—"

"Possible, but unlikely. Or would you jump in the river if you had a purse full of coins?"

Now Simon was confused, too. "How in God's name do you know if she's carrying a purse?" he asked his father-in-law. "I mean, you haven't even examined her."

Kuisl grinned. "If you hadn't been so busy shouting at one another, you would have heard the jingling when I lifted her down." He leaned over the body again. "I think we'll find it just here under the skirt . . ."

"Hands off!" the clerk hissed. "If she really carries money on her, it's my job to determine—"

"And line your own pockets with it, no doubt," Magdalena added and stepped forward. "No way. The money belongs to the poor girl's family. It's your job to find them."

"How . . . how dare you talk back to me!" the skinny man exclaimed. "I am an official. You just wait!" He raised his cudgel and started toward Magdalena and Barbara, but Jakob Kuisl got to him first. He grabbed the club like a matchstick and lifted the clerk in the air with it.

"Let me go!" the man shouted. "I'm going to lock up the lot of you! I . . . I . . ."

"Let him go, Jakob. The fool has embarrassed himself enough."

Simon turned to the voice that had come from one of the alleyways and saw a short, broad-shouldered man whose arms seemed much too long for his stocky body. He had a square face with alert, friendly eyes. The man was about Jakob Kuisl's age and wore a thick, wide coat made from blood-red wool. Now he approached the small group with long steps.

"Bloody hell, it's Michael Deibler!" Kuisl exclaimed happily. He dropped the whining clerk like a rotten apple. "How did you know we were here?"

The man called Deibler grinned, exposing a row of black teeth. "Well, a bunch of Au folks just told me about the giant who isn't from around here who's helping fish a body from the stream. I put two and two together—I knew you were coming today, after all." He laughed drily. "Clearly, it's true what they say about you, dear cousin: you attract dead bodies like flies."

"This . . . impertinent fellow stuck his nose in matters that are none of his concern!" the clerk complained, getting to his feet. "He refused to follow my order and—"

"Just shut up, Gustl," Deibler cut him off. "You should be grateful for any help from this impertinent fellow. The Schongau hangman has a reputation for solving murders."

"Ha . . . hangman?" The clerk took a step back. "Why didn't you say so sooner?" He eyed Kuisl fearfully and made the sign of the cross. Simon knew most people reacted that way when they found out his father-in-law's profession. Hangmen brought ill luck, especially if you looked them in the eyes or touched them.

"So how many bloody executioners are hanging around Au now, huh?" the clerk asked.

"Twelve, to be precise." Deibler shrugged. "Most of them have to leave again in a few days. Then it's only you and me again, Gustl." He grinned and pointed at Kuisl and the dead girl. "Now let the man do his job."

Without another word, Gustl stepped aside and Kuisl examined the girl's skirt. He soon found what he was looking for and produced a small purse. He opened it, and tipped out a number of silver coins. Simon leaned down to get a closer look.

The coins seemed familiar to him.

It must be a coincidence, he thought.

He looked again. They were indeed silver thalers. All of them were new and bore the lozenges and the year 1672.

They looked exactly the same as the coins Simon had received from the Veronese merchants the week before.

"My goodness! That's a lot of new money for someone who drowned herself." Kuisl jingled the coins. "If you ask me, something's fishy here. The girl couldn't have been that unhappy, not with a purse full of thalers. And if she was murdered—why didn't the murderer take the money?"

"Maybe he didn't notice the purse?" Magdalena guessed.

"The purse was right underneath the sack of stones," Kuisl replied. "Whoever did this would have noticed. Which takes me to my next question: if the girl didn't kill herself, then why the rocks?"

For a while no one said anything, then Deibler's dry laughter rang out again.

"Damn it, Kuisl!" he called out. "You've only been here for half an hour and already there's a mystery. You really do live up to your reputation." He brought his hand down on the hangman's shoulder. "Now let's go and have a beer to celebrate our reunion. Welcome to Munich, cousin!"

While Jakob Kuisl and Michael Deibler walked ahead, prattling, Magdalena and the rest of the family followed a few paces behind.

"Welcome to Munich, bah!" Barbara hissed and kicked at a frozen pile of horse dung. "This is the gateway to hell. The stinking Schongau Tanners' Quarter is paradise by comparison."

"It's only a short walk to the city," Magdalena said. "I'm sure we'll have plenty of time to visit the beautiful palaces, cathedrals, and the theater, too." She smiled encouragingly, though inwardly, she had to agree with her sister. This trip was turning out quite differently than what their father had promised them. Barbara had told her that Jakob Kuisl had already chosen three candidates for marriage, which would make it harder for Magdalena to help her sister find a suitable husband.

Also, Magdalena was annoyed because Michael Deibler hadn't even greeted her. Clearly, Deibler was the Munich hangman and knew her father from years ago. She understood the two of them had much to talk about, but did that mean common courtesy had to go out the window? Who did he think she was, a maidservant?

Next to her, Simon was deep in thought as well. Something seemed to be on his mind, but Magdalena was too exhausted from the long journey to ask. And her back was sore; she had been carrying Sophia in a sling around her belly, from where the infant observed all the goings-on attentively.

After a while, they reached a large tavern. Loud noise came from inside. Just then a jug shattered, men laughed and yelled. Then the door swung open and a man staggered into the street. He fell into the muddy snow and continued on hands and knees, leaving a thin trail of blood with his tracks. Evidently, he was bleeding heavily from the nose.

"Ah, the famous Au nightlife." Deibler grinned. "Looks like it's packed already. But there's always room for us at the executioners' table."

"Is this where we're staying?" Simon asked reluctantly and pointed at the sooty, cracked crown glass windows on the second floor.

Michael Deibler nodded. "The Radl Inn is the best tavern in Au, with stoves and glass windows, even a privy in the courtyard. I reserved two nice rooms especially for you."

"The best tavern in Au," Magdalena said flatly. "How kind of you." With a deep sigh, she followed the others into the dingy establishment.

They were immediately enveloped in a cloud of sweetish tobacco fumes. The dense smoke made Magdalena's eyes water. Smoking had been prohibited in Bavarian taverns several years ago, but clearly no one cared at Au. Several dozen patrons, most of them men, were puffing on their pipes and drinking beer from large mugs. Magdalena suspected most of them were servants and workmen who were drinking away a good chunk of their annual pay. The atmosphere was accordingly exuberant. People were singing, laughing, and dancing on a kind of stage, where several garishly made-up girls swayed their hips seductively.

Magdalena saw a man vomiting out of one of the back windows and then taking another swig of his beer. Every bench was tightly packed—except for one table in the far corner, where a handful of somber fellows sipped on their beers in silence. They seemed different from the other revelers.

"A few of our colleagues are already here," Deibler shouted at Jakob Kuisl over the noise. He pointed at the brooding fellows one by one. "Kaspar Hörmann from Passau, the Memmingen hangman Matthäus Fux, and even your old friend Philipp Teuber from Regensburg."

Jakob Kuisl looked around the room. "Has my brother arrived yet?"

Deibler shook his head. "I'm guessing he won't come until tomorrow. Just like Johann Widmann from Nuremberg, the popinjay. He likes to make people wait." Deibler rolled his eyes. "But he can afford to, since he's the richest and most powerful man of our guild."

"Now, now, Michael," Kuisl wagged his finger with mock severity. "You're the executioner of our electoral capital, so don't hide your light under a bushel."

Deibler waved dismissively. "Being the Munich hangman

isn't the same anymore since the whores are no longer part of my jurisdiction. The few tortures and executions a year aren't what they used to be—"

"I hate to interrupt your most important palaver," Magdalena cut the hangman off. "But the children are tired." She pointed at Peter and Paul, who were struggling to keep their eyes open. "If you would be so kind as to show us to our rooms . . ."

"Of course." Deibler nodded. He seemed to notice Magdalena for the first time. He gave the innkeeper an imperious wave. Visibly uncomfortable, the bald, potbellied man came over to them, trying to avoid the Munich hangman's gaze.

"Take the children to their room," Deibler ordered and gave the innkeeper a severe look. "I only hope you smoked out all the vermin, or I'll squash you like a louse."

The fat man kept his head down and made the sign of the cross. Magdalena knew how superstitious people were with one hangman—how would they feel with a dozen in the room? Deibler probably paid a lot of money so the hangmen could meet here at the Radl Inn.

"I'm going upstairs with the children," Barbara said to Magdalena. Barbara looked exhausted. When Magdalena looked closely, she could tell that her sister's body was indeed a little rounder, her breasts a little fuller. "If you like, I'll take Sophia," Barbara suggested. "I could do with the distraction."

Magdalena hesitated briefly, then she handed Barbara the small woolen bundle. Sophia happily reached out her little arms to her aunt, and Magdalena smiled. After all the excitement with the dead girl in the creek she wouldn't be able to sleep yet anyhow, and a mug of beer would help.

Once Barbara and the children had followed the innkeeper up a narrow, well-worn staircase, Magdalena and Simon sat down beside Deibler at a scratched table, sticky with beer. Jakob Kuisl was already deep in conversation with Philipp Teuber, the Regensburg executioner. Several years ago, the two of them had

had a few eventful days in Regensburg and had only just escaped with their lives. Magdalena smiled when she saw her father like this. Some weeks Kuisl didn't utter more than a handful of words, but when he was among his own kind, he seemed to flourish.

Next to Teuber sat a man whose nose was huge from drink and boasted a shiny red boil on top of that. A young lad, presumably his apprentice, had fallen asleep next to the man, his hair swimming in a puddle of beer. Opposite him sat a red-haired fellow who stared sullenly into his beer. Magdalena gathered from Deibler's words that the two older men were the Passau and Memmingen executioners.

"I must apologize if I was a little gruff earlier," Michael Deibler said to Magdalena. Only now did she notice the warm, friendly eyes in the grouchy-looking face. Deibler had taken off his woolen coat, and underneath he wore a clean white shirt with a lace collar and a vest of dyed fustian. The Munich executioner was no pauper. "It's no easy task to organize this guild meeting," he continued. "And then those dead girls . . ."

"Dead girls?" Simon looked at the hangman with confusion. "Are there more?"

Deibler slowly shook his head. "Well, that is the second girl this week. Of course, it could be a coincidence. But both cases are rather unusual."

"What happened to the other girl?" Magdalena asked. Thirstily, she reached for the mug of beer a maid had set down in front of her.

"Nasty story," Deibler said darkly. "They found the poor wretch by the raft landing, near Sendlinger Gate. Some log drivers pulled her out of the water."

"Did she drown?" Magdalena asked. "That doesn't sound very unusual."

"Er, no. She was impaled."

Simon and Magdalena froze for a moment, the noise of the

tavern suddenly seemed to come from far away. Magdalena pushed her beer aside, her thirst gone.

"*Impaled?*" Simon repeated. "You mean someone hammered a stake through her heart? That's terrible!"

"Indeed." Deibler nodded. "It used to be a common form of execution in my great-grandfather's time. They used to believe the angry soul of the deceased was nailed to the earth that way. Sometimes the stake would be inserted through the anus, and the condemned person would be sat upon it. It would make for a very slow—"

"Jesus Christ, spare us the details," Simon exclaimed, having grown visibly pale. "What do you know about the victim?"

"Well, she was one of those countless young girls who come to Munich in the hope of a better life. As far as I know, they don't even know her name." Deibler sighed and took a long sip of his beer. "I feel sorry for those girls from the country. They come to Munich to find work as maidservants, but often they find only misery. She probably fell victim to some drunk bastard."

"Who went on to impale her?" Magdalena frowned. "I don't know . . ."

"Hey, you! Are you B-Barbara Kuisl?" slurred the fellow with the bulbous nose—the Passau executioner Kaspar Hörmann, presumably. Until then he hadn't uttered a word, but now he seemed to have woken from his trance. His white shirt was speckled with gravy and beer stains, and his hat lay trampled on the ground.

Magdalena only gave him a brief glance. "No," she replied curtly. "Barbara is my younger sister. She's gone upstairs."

Kaspar Hörmann giggled. "I knew you were too old."

"How dare you—" Magdalena flared up, but Hörmann held up his hands apologetically. "I didn't . . . mean it like that," he mumbled. "I only meant, to . . . to marry." He pointed at the unconscious young man at his side. "My charming son, Lothar, heard about your sis-sister. Your father wrote us a letter."

Magdalena turned white. She looked over to Jakob Kuisl, who was still engaged in conversation with the Regensburg hangman. They had already amassed a row of empty mugs in front of them.

You can't be serious, Father, Magdalena thought.

"M . . . my Lothar is a strong lad," Hörmann said and pulled up his son by his hair. Lothar gawked like a calf, his teeth crooked and his nose already turning like his father's. He burped loudly once, then Hörmann let his son's head fall back on the tabletop. "He may drink a little much, but he'll make a good hangman one day. I'm sure your father and I will come to an agreement." Grinning, Hörmann raised his mug to Magdalena, who turned away in disgust.

"Barbara is going to scratch Father's eyes out once she sees who he has chosen for her," she whispered to Simon. "We can only hope the other candidates are better-looking." To her annoyance, she realized Simon was somewhere else in his thoughts.

"What's the matter with you?" she asked. "You were strange earlier, too, with the dead girl."

"It's about those coins your father found," Simon replied, making sure no one else could hear him. "I think I've seen coins just like those before — the ones the merchants from Verona paid me with a few days ago."

Magdalena listened intently as Simon told her about his suspicions. "So you think the coins all come from the same mint?" she asked eventually. "The same counterfeit money?"

"Not really counterfeit, just too light. And they're all brand-new. The dead girl's coins looked just as new, and I'm pretty sure they had the same embossing." Simon rubbed his nose. "But to be absolutely sure, I'd have to take another look at them and hold them in my hand."

"I'm sure that could be arranged — Michael Deibler confiscated them. I don't think he'll just keep them." Magdalena looked over to Deibler, who was talking to the red-haired executioner from Memmingen and laughing loudly. She smiled. "He doesn't seem like a bad fellow, for a hangman." She reached for her mug and raised it to Simon. "Let's just make the most of this trip, damn it. Maybe Barbara's other suitors won't be as bad as this one." She took a large gulp of beer and wiped the foam from her lips. "At least the beer is tasty in Munich."

A few hours later, two drunken figures made their way through the lanes of Au. They swayed a little and had to hold on to each other from time to time. Beggars, scoundrels, and cutthroats watched their progress from dark nooks and crannies. Usually drunks were easy prey for thieves, who were as numerous as stones in the Isar River here at Au. But no one touched these men.

That was probably because one of them was the Munich hangman, and the other one looked very big and dangerous.

Potential robbers crossed themselves and turned the other way. After all, they might one day depend upon the hangman's goodwill—or at least a quick hand at their execution.

The two men stopped at the Au creek, and the giant stuck his head into the water. Then he shook himself like a wet dog.

"Brrr! That's better," Jakob Kuisl grumbled. "I think the last beer was off."

"Damn it, I hope for your sake this won't turn out a waste of time," Michael Deibler growled. "I should never have agreed to come along. Do you have any idea how much I still have to prepare for tomorrow? And my Walburga must be worried sick."

"Your dear Walburga would be even more worried if she knew her husband had been lying under the table with all the other drunks at the Radl Inn not long ago," Kuisl replied with a grin. "You should be glad I got you out of there."

"You're probably right. Damn that godforsaken booze!" Deibler dipped his head into the ice-cold water, too. When he straightened up again, he gave a roaring laugh. "You turn up here and immediately stick your nose in someone else's business. So it's true what they say, even outside hangmen's circles: you and that scrawny medicus, you're a proper pair of sleuths."

"Well, my son-in-law's more like a puppy," Kuisl replied with a wink. "And now let's go. I want to get to bed before sunrise."

He walked ahead and Deibler followed, still swaying slightly. Kuisl had boozed with the other executioners for half the night, especially with Philipp Teuber from Regensburg, who was a good friend. Kuisl didn't drink as much as he used to a few years ago, since he promised his daughters, but an executioners' meeting was a special occasion, and the Munich beer tasted exceptionally good.

But a nagging thought had kept Jakob Kuisl from enjoying himself properly all evening, ever since he fished that dead girl from the water. He simply had to double check, if only to satisfy his curiosity. And curiosity had always been a better friend to the Schongau hangman than alcohol. Therefore, he'd asked Michael Deibler to take him to the house of the Au clerk.

In an alleyway near an old papermill stood a house that looked a little more solid than the shacks around it. Deibler had told Jakob Kuisl on the way that Au didn't have its own prison, so the clerk sometimes locked suspects in one of his rooms at home until the trial—sometimes even in his sitting room.

Kuisl hoped fervently the girl's body would still be there, too.

Michael Deibler knocked at the door with a grim expression. The short walk had sobered him up a little, but he still struggled to stand up.

"Gustl, open up, for heaven's sake!" he shouted, bracing himself against the wall. "It's me, the hangman!"

A moment later they could hear a thud from inside the house, as if someone had rolled out of bed.

"By the Holy Virgin," Gustl's squealing voice rang out. "I swear I haven't done anything, I—"

"Idiot!" Deibler cut him off. "Open the door, we're not going

to hang you. We just need to"—he swallowed back a hiccup—
"check something."

The door opened and the ashen-faced clerk stood in front of
them in his nightgown. "I can't sleep anyway with a dead body in
my house," Gustl said, shivering. "The priest wouldn't wake up
to take care of the wench. But first thing tomorrow . . . Hey!"

The two hangmen pushed past the clerk into the sitting room,
and Kuisl knocked his head on the low doorframe on the way.
He grumbled ill-humoredly. As if his head wasn't sore enough
already.

The body was lying on a table in the middle of the room,
poorly covered with a cloth. The sight sobered Kuisl instantly.
He hadn't noticed before how appallingly thin the girl in front of
him was, and how young. She couldn't have been older than sixteen or seventeen years, with pale skin, reddish-blonde hair, and
a remarkable number of freckles for wintertime. The hangman
was overcome with pity for this girl who only yesterday had the
same dreams and worries as so many other young women. Kuisl
imagined the body on the table was Barbara. But then he pushed
the thought aside and focused on his task. He leaned over the
girl . . .

And sniffed.

"Hey, what's he doing?" Gustl started up from behind. "This
is my house, he can't do that. That's disgusting!"

"This is the Au prison and my friend is helping to solve a
crime," Michael Deibler said, still struggling with his hiccups,
"so shut your mouth, Gustl." Thanks to the hiccups, Deibler appeared even grumpier than usual. His face was as pale as a ghost.
Frightened, Gustl stepped back and didn't say another word.

"So? Find anything?" Deibler asked after a while.

Kuisl deeply inhaled the smell of the dead body, which had
begun to stink a little despite the cold. The hangman had always
been able to rely on his nose, but the faintly sweet smell he had

noticed earlier that evening had vanished. Just like the dilated pupils. Down by the creek, the girl's pupils had appeared wider to him than those of other dead bodies. Or had he been mistaken? He leaned close to the open mouth. There was still a faint trace of the smell here. His nose wandered down to her hands, which had clenched into fists in her final struggle. Kuisl was about to turn away when he thought he saw something sparkle between the fingers of her left hand.

"She's holding something," he said with a frown. He turned to the clerk. "Do you have a pair of pliers? Rigor mortis has already set in, I can't get into her fist."

"Oh, God, don't tell me you want to—" Gustl started, but Kuisl cut him off.

"I think I can just . . ." He pushed against the hand until they heard a loud cracking. The clerk winced.

"Ha—here we are!" Triumphantly, the hangman pulled out a thin chain with a tiny medallion. He took a closer look.

"Hmm. A woman with a crown and aureole. The Virgin Mary, I guess. I wonder why it was in her hand."

"Perhaps it was meant to protect her?" Michael Deibler suggested.

"Well, whatever it means, at least I think I know what the poor thing died of," Kuisl replied. "But I'd have to cut her open to know for sure."

Gustl groaned, and Deibler didn't seem too enthusiastic either. "Damn it, Kuisl!" he hissed. "I could lose my job over this. If the Munich judge finds out—"

"Come on, you're just as curious as I am to find out what this murder is about," Kuisl replied, "so don't be like that. It wouldn't be the first time a hangman cut open a corpse."

"Yes, but not that of a *murder victim*. I've done it with gallows birds that no one claimed, out of curiosity, or if someone offers good money for a thief's heart. The Munich judge even gave me express permission. But this can get us both in serious trouble."

Kuisl shrugged. "Not if I stitch her up neatly afterward and put her dress back on. No one will notice a thing."

Deibler hesitated, then sighed. "All right, then, for truth's sake."

He handed Gustl, who had been listening to their conversation with wide eyes, two silver coins. "These are from the girl's purse," Deibler said. "You can keep them if you keep your mouth shut. You'll get another thaler in one week. But if you talk . . ." The Munich hangman looked at him darkly.

"I-I'll be as silent as the grave," Gustl stammered and quickly stashed the coins away.

"Then let's do it." Kuisl pulled the girl's dress up. He got out his knife, which he sharpened as frequently as his executioner's sword, and made the first insertion from the breastbone downward.

The hangman had cut open dozens of bodies in his life. Like Deibler, he was fascinated by the inside of humans, of which very little was known as yet. Kuisl believed he had more medical knowledge than most learned physicians from here to Schongau. He was the proud owner of a small Latin library at his house, hundreds of medicines, and countless surgical instruments, which he sometimes lent to his son-in-law.

But he's the physician and I'm just a dishonorable hangman, Kuisl thought.

Once he had cut through the thin layer of skin and fat at the top, followed by the connective tissue, he carefully pushed the innards aside. He briefly examined each organ, but he was mainly interested in one particular one, a plump, red sack. When he found the stomach just beneath the breastbone, he slit it open, and out came a blackish-red mass.

Floating in the mass were seeds and half-digested skins. A

sweet, familiar scent wafted through the room, confirming Kuisl's suspicion. He grinned triumphantly.

"Just as I thought," he said.

"By God, *what* did you think?" Deibler groaned, holding his nose shut. "Tell me! I already feel sick, anyway."

Gagging sounds from the next room indicated that Gustl hadn't been able to stand the sight and smell of the dead body any longer. Jakob Kuisl threw the cloth back over the corpse and turned to the Munich hangman.

"Her stomach is full of deadly nightshade," he explained. "The poor thing must have eaten a whole bowl full of the berries, as a compote, I'm guessing, maybe mixed with blueberries or blackberries. I smelled it earlier. Her pupils were still dilated down by the creek, so she hadn't been poisoned long before she was found." He pointed at the body under the sheet. "Her stomach held the proof."

"Hmm. So you think she poisoned herself, tied the sack of stones around her waist, and jumped into the creek?" Deibler asked.

Kuisl thought. He would have liked to smoke a pipe, but he already had a headache from all the smoke in the tavern. "Deadly nightshade is nasty stuff," he said contemplatively. "Three, four berries make you lusty, but any more and delirium sets in, until death. The wide pupils show that the girl was already out of her mind when she came to the creek. You don't tie a bag of stones around yourself in that state. And someone would have noticed something—poison victims scream and rave as if they're possessed."

"So what do you think?" Deibler jutted out his chin. "Go on. I can tell you've got a suspicion. It's written all over your face."

"I believe someone poisoned this girl. The berries must have been preserved or dried, because she couldn't have picked any fresh ones in winter. She probably devoured the berries with great appetite — I also saw traces of some kind of pastry in her stomach. The murderer waited for the poor thing to die and then carried her to the Au creek, tied a bag of rocks around her, and threw her in."

"Maybe that explains the medallion," Deibler said. "Maybe she hoped it would reverse the poisoning and reached for it as she lay dying."

"Not even the mother of God could have helped her with that amount of berries in her stomach. Either way . . ." Kuisl pointed at the body. "This was no suicide but cunning murder, Michael. And the murderer is somewhere out there." He stretched tiredly. "And now fetch me some needle and thread, so we can still get a few hours of sleep before the meeting."

As he stitched the corpse back together, Kuisl couldn't shake the feeling of having overlooked something. But he was too exhausted to think clearly.

And so this important detail slowly vanished from his consciousness again.

3

Two MEN CROSSED THE ISAR BRIDGE to Au late that
morning. One of the men had a limp, and the other was tall and
broad-shouldered and had no trouble making his way through
the crowd with his intimidating stature. He carried a sack on his
back and looked around. His bushy beard hadn't seen a barber in
a long time.

And his nose was just as big and crooked as his father's.

Magdalena spotted her brother and uncle from over a hundred paces away. Waving, she ran toward them.

"Georg, Georg!" she called out. "Over here!"

Now Georg recognized her, too. He raised his arm and walked
faster, and the older man struggled to keep up. Jakob Kuisl's
brother Bartholomäus had limped since childhood, but it hadn't
stopped him from becoming an excellent executioner. He had
been the hangman of Bamberg for many years now, and he also
had a seat on the Council of Twelve. Georg, his nephew and
journeyman, was supposed to take over from him one day. Jakob
Kuisl had never gotten over the fact that his own son had chosen
Uncle Bartholomäus, the more successful hangman, instead of
staying in Schongau with his father.

Meanwhile, Magdalena had reached Georg, and the siblings laughed happily as they embraced. They had last seen each other over two years ago, when Georg came to Schongau for a visit, and Magdalena could see that her brother had changed. He was almost nineteen now, a proper man and nearly as tall as his father, but more sinewy and almost sturdier. It was hard to believe he was Barbara's twin. Magdalena thought about how she used to sing lullabies to Georg and Barbara. It seemed like yesterday, but now she was looking at a man.

"I can hardly call you *little* brother now," she said and pinched Georg's biceps. "What's Uncle feeding you? Roast pork and sausages every day?"

"With dumplings on the side," Georg replied with a grin. He rubbed his belly with mock sadness. "But I haven't eaten a thing since breakfast. It's about time for a feed."

"The trip from Bamberg was worse than getting stretched on the rack," Uncle Bartholomäus grumbled when he reached them. He, too, had the Kuisl nose and broad body. Nearly all his hair had fallen out in recent years, so now he was almost bald. "I don't even know why I bothered coming," he groused. "I only hope there'll be some decent beer."

Magdalena smiled. The two brothers, Bartholomäus and Jakob, couldn't stand each other, but they were very much alike when it came to grumbling and growling. That seemed to be another Kuisl characteristic.

"The beer here is excellent, Uncle," she assured him as she massaged her temples with a grimace of pain. "That is, if there's any left. Some of the hangmen arrived yesterday and had a big night. Especially Father and Deibler."

"And you, too, by the looks of it," Georg said with a laugh.

"Well, I'll go and see if there's a keg left for us," Bartholomäus said. "I'm so thirsty, I could drink the Isar dry."

He limped ahead, and Georg looked at the narrow, foul-smelling lanes of Au. "What a nice neighborhood for the meeting." He grinned. "I should have known, actually. The Vienna hangman once said he'd like to know where that big city of Au was, because he was hanging so many men from there."

"Don't tell Barbara that one," Magdalena said. "She's upset enough about our accommodations as it is."

Georg beamed at the mention of his twin sister. The two of them used to be inseparable as children. Magdalena guessed that Georg was part of the reason Barbara had agreed to come to Munich in the end. She briefly considered telling her brother about Barbara's pregnancy, but the timing didn't seem right. Barbara might tell him herself soon — they always used to share their worries.

"Believe it or not, I sometimes dream about my dear sister," Georg said with a smile. "I still know exactly what she looks like, even though I haven't seen her in ages. How is she?"

Magdalena sighed. "Not too happy, thanks to Father's plans." She told Georg about their father's intentions and the three candidates from the executioners' guild. "I've already met one of them, the son of the Passau hangman," she said. "A drunkard and as ugly as sin."

"A good match, though," Georg objected. "Passau is a large town; lots of work for a hangman."

"Now you sound like Father." Magdalena shook her head, then she pointed at the Radl Inn. "She's upstairs with Sophia. I'm guessing the boys will be there too, waiting for you."

"Sophia?" Georg frowned, then he remembered. "Of course, you wrote about her. I can't believe you have another child now. How time flies."

Magdalena gave a thin smile. "Well, you should have come back to Schongau, little brother. Father isn't getting any younger."

"Who knows, maybe I will," Georg replied grimly. "Perhaps even sooner than I'd like."

"How do you mean?"

He waved dismissively. "You'll find out soon enough. Now let me say hello to everyone. We have much to talk about."

Together they crossed the icy road to the Radl Inn. Magdalena remained silent, racking her brain about Georg's last comment. What could he mean? Perhaps Barbara wasn't the only Kuisl in trouble.

The meeting of the executioners started punctually, when the bells struck noon, in a side room of the inn that was usually used for weddings. Magdalena assumed the innkeeper wasn't shouting today's meeting from the rooftops. Who wanted a dozen dishonorable hangmen in their tavern? She gradually came to realize that her father was right: this guild meeting couldn't take place in Munich; if anywhere, then here at Au, the home of scoundrels, unfortunates, and other stranded characters.

Magdalena leaned against the wall near the door, watching the hustle and bustle. Almost all twelve executioners had arrived by now, accompanied by many journeymen and several apprentices, bringing the total to around thirty men. Magdalena thought how different they all looked, yet they had one thing in common: they all were paid workers of death.

Many of the executioners present had become wealthy doing what they did. Several of them wore expensive garments, some even very brightly colored ones, making them look like exotic birds. Their faces were hard, their expressions reserved, and yet they seemed to come to life here among their own kind. Magdalena spotted her father deep in conversation with Uncle Bartholomäus; evidently they weren't arguing for a change. The other hangmen seemed to be in high spirits as well, which probably had something to do with the large keg of beer sitting on the table in the middle of the room, from which they helped themselves. Each man had his own pewter mug engraved with his name — an old tradition, but also a measure of precaution, protecting honorable citizens from accidentally drinking from the hangman's mug and turning dishonorable themselves. Many of the men puffed on long-stemmed pipes, and the room was thick with smoke.

In the far corner, Georg and Barbara looked like they were having a serious conversation. Magdalena wondered whether Georg already knew about his sister's pregnancy. They had also talked for a while that morning, but Peter and Paul had kept interrupting them. Paul especially adored his uncle, who had whittled swords and other wooden toys for him during his last visit to Schongau. Now Paul was racing around outside with a bunch of street children, while Peter was upstairs, reading and looking after the sleeping Sophia.

"A bunch of rough, boozing, smoking fellows like us must be an unpleasant sight for a lady. Forgive us, madam."

Magdalena started at the sound of the sonorous, pleasant voice coming from behind her. It was one of the men from the table last night, but he hadn't arrived until later. She thought she remembered his name was Conrad Näher, the Kaufbeuren executioner.

"Oh, I'm used to worse, with my father," she replied with a smile.

"I believe you," Näher said, grinning. "I've heard a few things about your father that would take getting used to."

Magdalena laughed. For a hangman, Näher was a very likeable person. He had soft facial features; his eyes were compassionate and friendly. He was around fifty years old and looked very tidy with his neatly combed graying hair and freshly starched lace collar. His speech was more like that of a nobleman than a rough executioner. After taking a sip of his beer, Näher pointed at Barbara, who was still talking to Georg.

"That must be your younger sister. Your similarity is just striking—and your beauty, too. Your husband is a lucky man." Conrad Näher's gaze traveled around the room. "Is he not attending our guild meeting?"

"Um, he'll join us later," Magdalena replied. "He had some business in town."

She bit her lip. Näher had reminded her of the fact that Simon still hadn't returned. Shortly after Georg and Uncle Bartholomäus had arrived, he had walked across the Isar Bridge into Munich to find this oh-so-famous physician he apparently needed to help get his treatise published. Magdalena had forgotten the doctor's name, and if she was honest, she didn't really care. Simon's constant palaver about his treatise was getting on her nerves.

Her husband had promised to be back at noon, and now he was almost an hour late. And all because of some scribbled bits of paper that had been driving the whole family insane for months. Magdalena knew Simon loved her more than anything, but he loved his work, too. And sometimes he became so engrossed in the world of medicine that he forgot everything else around him.

"Would you possibly be so kind as to introduce me to your sister?" Näher suddenly asked.

Magdalena started. "Er, for any particular reason?"

The Kaufbeuren executioner smiled. "Well, your father wrote me a letter. I'm sure you know its contents . . ."

Magdalena couldn't suppress a soft sigh. *Aha, candidate number two. Could have been worse, I guess . . .*

"Well, um . . . ," she stammered. "I don't think this is the best time. But if you insist —" Relieved, she broke off when the door opened and another executioner entered the room. All eyes turned to him and the room fell silent.

The man was tall and lean with long wavy hair and a carefully groomed moustache. His coat and the shirt underneath shone blood-red and were of the finest fabric. He held a bone-handled cane in his left hand, and his fingers were studded with rings. He looked around the room with an arrogant expression until he spotted Michael Deibler.

"Blimey, Deibler, what sort of a stinking hole is this?" he

snapped at the Munich hangman. His broad Franconian accent didn't go at all with his elegant appearance. "My carriage almost rolled into the ditch on the way here, the streets reek of shit and piss, and my four journeymen have to sleep in the stables. By crikey, is that the way to treat me?"

"Good to see you, too, Johann Widmann," Deibler replied with a grin, completely unfazed by the Franconian's grandiose entrance. He stood up slowly and gave the newcomer a nod. "We've been waiting for you."

"When I hosted the guild meeting in Nuremberg a few years ago, the wine flowed freely," Widmann continued his lament while looking about the room disparagingly. "We dined on duck and pâté at the Golden Eagle—"

"And you held long speeches until the small hours, yes, yes," Deibler interrupted. "I remember well. It was just after the war, and no one cared about a few hangmen because everyone was a murderer. Times have changed, Widmann. We're lucky we're even here at Au. How long do you think it took me to get the elector's permission for this meeting?" He pointed at an empty seat. "And now move your arse over here so we can start."

Johann Widmann's eyes scanned the men. "I only count eleven of us. One's missing."

"We're not waiting any longer," Deibler replied. "Or half of us will be drunk before we even start." He clapped his hands. "So, dear cousins, please take your seats."

Magdalena still hadn't gotten used to the fact that the executioners called each other cousins. But since families of executioners usually intermarried, most of them were related somehow.

And we might soon be related to the Memmingen or Kaufbeuren hangman, she thought sadly. *Or whomever Barbara ends up marrying . . .*

While the eleven executioners sat down at the table with their mugs, the journeymen and families took their seats on the chairs along the wall, like the front row at an execution. Georg sat down next to Magdalena, while Barbara sat stony-faced near the door. She looked like she would jump up and run out at any moment.

"What did you two talk about?" Magdalena whispered to Georg.

"She told me about her pregnancy," Georg whispered back. "Already this morning we had an argument." He frowned. "She still doesn't seem to understand that she must marry."

"Thank God Father has no idea," Magdalena hissed. "Let's pray it stays that way."

Georg nodded glumly. "Barbara is lucky she still has the chance to get away pretty much unscathed here in Munich. We'll have to tell the fiancé, of course. We can't keep it secret from him for long. But I think that'll just be a matter of money. And she's by no means a bad match."

"I know." Magdalena sighed. "I've met the second candidate now. It's Conrad Näher, the Kaufbeuren hangman."

"Hmm. Not bad," Georg said. "Näher is a decent man. His wife died not long ago, and he doesn't have any children, as far as I know. And Kaufbeuren isn't too far from Schongau—not as far as Passau, anyway, where that drunkard Hörmann lives."

"Or as far as Bamberg," Magdalena replied sadly. "Tell me, what did you mean when you said you might soon be back in Schongau?"

Georg was about to reply when Michael Deibler clapped his hands three times.

"I declare the meeting open!" he called out. "By the black cat and the thrice-knotted hangman's noose."

"By the black cat and the thrice-knotted hangman's noose," the other executioners murmured and brought down their fists on the tabletop so hard that the keg almost toppled. Magdalena guessed it was an old ritual like those of other guilds.

Deibler, the guild master, sat at the head of the table and lit a black candle with a piece of kindling. The other hangmen had black candles in front of them, too, and now they started to light them, each on the candle of his neighbor. The tense silence reminded Magdalena of the moment following the Holy Communion at church.

When all candles were lit, the Munich hangman picked up a thin stick, raised it above his head, and broke it in two. The silence was lifted. The executioners raised their mugs to one another and drank deeply while Deibler gave his opening speech.

"My dear cousins, I'm pleased we finally managed to reinstate the Council of Twelve after all these years," he began. "We have much to talk about. Most importantly, we need to discuss the issue of the learned physicians, who are increasingly pushing for a withdrawal of our license to heal in the German Empire."

"Damned quacks!" Passau hangman Kaspar Hörmann ranted. "The devil take the lot of them." His slurred speech told Magdalena how drunk he already was. Several hangmen muttered their agreement.

Perhaps it's just as well Simon isn't here, Magdalena thought.

"Quiet!" Deibler raised his hand. "Before we talk about physicians and the other points on our agenda, let me introduce a new member in our round. You know that only the best and most experienced executioners of Bavaria get a seat in this council, and it's my pleasure to announce that Bartholomäus Kuisl's brother, the Schongau hangman, Jakob Kuisl, will be sitting at the table with us from now on. The twelfth seat became vacant when the honorable Philip Hartmann of Augsburg became a burgher." Deibler pointed at Kuisl, who was sitting opposite him with folded arms. "Well, I think you all know Jakob. You voted him onto the council with a large majority."

"Although it was not unanimous," Johann Widmann remarked pointedly as he stroked his moustache.

Michael Deibler ignored the comment. "We all know Jakob Kuisl is an excellent executioner and healer—"

"Who's much too lenient," a red-haired, scar-faced man interrupted with a grin. Magdalena remembered he was Matthäus Fux, the Memmingen executioner. He had been there the night before. "If he continues like this, he'll ruin our reputation as blood guzzlers. The poor sinners will shake our hands and say 'thank you kindly!'"

The others roared with laughter, and Jakob Kuisl lowered his head in mock embarrassment. Michael Deibler now walked over to him, carrying a full pewter mug with Kuisl's name on it.

"Flesh of our flesh, blood of our blood," Deibler chanted. "Welcome to the Council of Twelve, dear cousin. Prepare to be christened." As was the custom, he emptied the mug's contents over Kuisl's head before handing it to him with a bow. The Schongau executioner shook himself off, and the other hangmen laughed and rapped their mugs on the table.

"As is customary, our cousin brought his family along," Deibler continued and pointed to the chairs along the wall. "His son Georg, the Bamberg journeyman, and his daughters Magdalena and Barbara. Jakob's younger daughter is a stunning beauty and unmarried." Smiling, Deibler turned to Barbara, who sat by the door as if frozen.

"Go on, girl, stand up so we can all see and admire you," he said. Barbara stayed seated, her lips pinched and her arms folded.

Magdalena saw her father turn red with anger. Just when Jakob Kuisl was about to speak, Barbara stood up and smoothed her dress. She trembled slightly and her eyes blazed, making her look like a mad fury.

A very attractive fury, Magdalena thought.

The executioners clearly shared her opinion, as they whistled and cast teasing glances at Jakob Kuisl.

"Are you sure the girl's yours?" a short, hunchbacked hangman remarked with a giggle. "She doesn't look anything like you. Where's the hooked nose?"

The others howled, and no one but Magdalena seemed to notice the solitary tear running down Barbara's cheek.

"This is worse than a horse market, goddamnit," Magdalena whispered to Georg. "Why isn't Father doing anything?"

"It's just men," Georg replied with a shrug. "Barbara can take it."

"I wouldn't be so sure," Magdalena said grimly.

Now drunk Kaspar Hörmann got to his feet and staggered toward Barbara. "You can all forget about it," he slurred and looked at the men. "Her father sent me a letter, it's a done deal." He bowed to Barbara with a grin, then pointed at his son, who was busy picking bits of meat from his teeth. "So why don't you kiss your future husband and—"

He slipped on some spilled beer and fell flat on his face. The other hangmen roared with laughter. Eventually, the Kaufbeuren hangman, Conrad Näher, stood up and addressed Jakob Kuisl in a gentle voice.

"Dear cousin," he began, "not only Hörmann, but I, too, received a letter from you about your daughter. I thank you kindly, but I don't think this is the right place to get to know such a lovely girl." He turned to Barbara with a smile. "Perhaps in the coming days the opportunity might arise for a stroll along the—"

"Do you really believe a pretty young thing like her would look twice at an old bag like you, Näher?" Johann Widmann cut him off. "Your bed is as cold as a midwinter night in the forest —no movement in there for a long time, as one hears. Or perhaps there never has been any movement, seeing as you're without offspring."

Again the others laughed, while Conrad Näher winced. Fists clenched and trembling with anger, he took a step toward the Nuremberg executioner, but Michael Deibler stepped in between.

"No brawl among cousins!" he ordered. "At least not while I'm around." He turned to Widmann. "As for you, pull yourself together, Johann. You may be the wealthiest of us, but that doesn't give you the right to insult others. If you've got something to say, say it plainly."

"Just a joke." Widmann held up his hands in apology. "But you're right, Deibler, I do have something to say." He smiled broadly and turned to the others. "Jakob Kuisl wrote to me, too. He knew my wife passed away giving birth to our fifth child last autumn. I didn't reply to the letter because I thought a hangman's wench from Schongau had no place in Nuremberg city life. But now . . ." He studied Barbara and licked his thin moustache. "Well, I must admit that her beauty makes up for a lot. And my sons need a new mother to cook, nurse, and change the little ones' diapers." He gave Kuisl a questioning look. "Can she nurse? Her breasts seem well developed to me."

"If you need someone to milk, find yourself a goat—that would fit much better into your family, Herr *Goat's Beard!*"

It was the first time Barbara had spoken. From one moment to the next, the room had become dead silent.

"How . . . how dare you . . ." Johann Widmann finally spat out. His face was red with anger. He shot up, and the men to his left and right restrained him, pushing him back down on his chair. "You dirty little hangman's wench!" he shouted. "I don't have to put up with this! Not from you!"

"Oh, you're a *hangman* too," Barbara replied coolly. "Remember? Every one of us in this room is dirty, dishonorable, and shunned, even the illustrious Nuremberg executioner, Johann Widmann. You don't shit gold, either."

Some of the men muttered angrily and rapped their mugs on the table, while others grinned stealthily.

"I must apologize for my daughter," Jakob Kuisl said eventually. He stood up and Magdalena saw that he was shaking with anger and embarrassment. He seemed gray and bitter and, all of a sudden, very, very old. "Sometimes she just . . . opens her mouth before she thinks."

"Then teach her some manners, Jakob, by God," Widmann snapped. "You can't tolerate—"

He broke off when the door opened almost without a sound. It was as if a gust of wind had blown it open.

A very cold gust of wind.

A man with white hair that was tied together at the back stepped in. He had broad shoulders, a beefy neck, a face as white as chalk, and he was dressed entirely in black. His eyes gleamed as red as those of a rat. A chill ran down Magdalena's back and she almost screamed out loud. She knew this man, but she would never have expected to see him here.

The twelfth member, she thought. *My God, did Father know?*

The eleven other executioners were silent. It was as if there was an invisible wall between them and the man.

"Welcome, Master Hans from Weilheim," Michael Deibler said frostily. He pointed at the last empty seat. "We started without you."

"Forgive me, beloved cousins." Master Hans twisted his face into a smile that didn't reach his red eyes. "Work kept me. An accursed offertory box thief from Pähl who wouldn't confess. Reckoned he was innocent." Hans rubbed his hands on his coat, and Magdalena thought she saw dried blood on it. "Well, never mind," he said softly. "They all confess in the end, don't they?"

Suddenly Master Hans turned and looked straight at Barbara. Her face was almost as white as his.

"Greetings, Barbara," Master Hans whispered and twisted his lips into another crooked smile. "How nice to see you again. The circumstances last time were, well . . . a little unfortunate."

Barbara sprang to her feet, her chair crashing to the ground. She ran to the door and disappeared. Only her receding steps could be heard for a while.

"Barbara, don't be silly!" Magdalena shouted. "Barbara!"

Without waiting for Georg, she ran after her sister, through the tavern, past the patrons and the maid carrying armfuls of mugs and shouting angrily after her, out into the icy street. But there was no sign of Barbara; she had probably turned in to one of Au's many alleyways. Magdalena pulled her coat tighter and set out to look for her sister with fear in her heart.

She was terrified by the nagging thought that she might never see Barbara again.

Master Hans had come back into their lives.

Not far away, on the other side of the river, Simon was in a different world.

He was wandering along a wide cobblestoned street that was lined on either side with half-timbered houses several stories high. Countless taverns lured the traveler with colorfully painted signs, and the street buzzed with carts and carriages. Their progress went haltingly, drivers swearing and cracking their whips. Street children were picking up frozen horse dung, getting dangerously close to the huge animals.

Simon closed his eyes and inhaled deeply. Munich streets were smelly, too, but unlike at Au, the smell here was . . . well, rather exquisite. He could smell stews with rare spices, spilled wine freezing into red ice on the street, fresh blood from the butcher's, expensive lamp oil in the houses, and fresh pine logs that were being carted to the many construction sites in the city. It was busy and loud, a babel of voices from which Simon could occasionally make out bits of Italian and even French.

On his right, Simon spotted a square where a small market was being held. Among other things, Simon could see small bundles of dried herbs for sale. He smiled. Surely he'd find his beloved coffee beans here. So far, merchants from Augsburg had always brought them to Schongau, but he had run out a while ago. Evidently, Munich had everything the heart desired. The electoral city was the most amazing place he had ever visited. Living here must be . . .

"Hey, watch out, you idiot!"

A carriage with a blue canopy was headed straight for him.

Simon only noticed now that he was walking on the road. He jumped aside at the last moment and got splattered with mud. The driver shook his fist at him angrily.

"I beg your pardon," Simon mumbled even though the man was long out of earshot. Despite the cold he felt rather flushed, which might also have something to do with the two glasses of wine he'd just enjoyed at one of the taverns. He had time to kill. Simon had gone into Munich that morning and asked a number of people on the street where the famous physician Malachias Geiger lived. Finally, someone had pointed him in the right direction. Now Simon went over and over in his mind the words that he was planning to introduce himself with.

Greetings, dear colleague. My name is Doctor Simon Fronwieser from Schongau, and I believe I have made some medical observations you might find interesting. If you allow me . . .

Simon shook his head. Maybe he should leave out the "dear colleague" at the beginning. To call himself a colleague of Doctor Malachias Geiger was perhaps a little presumptuous. The Geiger family was one of the most respected physician dynasties in the country—there was even gentry among them. The Geigers had cured kings and electors, they had studied in Paris and Padua, they had published countless papers that had become standards of medical literature. Malachias Geiger's treatise *Precautions Against the Plague* in particular was regarded as a medical milestone, and Simon must have read it a dozen times. It had also given him the idea of telling Geiger about his own treatise and asking him for help with its publication.

An idea that seemed absolutely crazy to him now that he was in Munich.

Nevertheless that morning he had asked his way to Geiger's house, which turned out to be an imposing half-timbered building on Sendlinger Street, one of Munich's main thoroughfares. But Geiger hadn't been in; a servant told Simon to come back later, and so he had sat down to wine, cheese, and bread in one of the many taverns and worked through his treatise again and again. By now he had crossed out and overwritten so much that he struggled to decipher his own writing.

For the second time that day, Simon ascended the stairs to the entrance of Geiger's house with his papers rolled up in his hand and knocked cautiously at the door. After a few moments, a young man with a pince-nez and a snow-white ruffled shirt opened it.

"What do you want?" the man asked impatiently. He was holding a glass half-filled with urine. "If you're a servant, please use the back door."

Simon swallowed hard. Did he look like a servant? He had specifically put on his new vest and clean hat. Who did this puppy think he was?

"I was here this morning about a meeting with Doctor Geiger," Simon replied a little too frostily. "I was asked to come back after lunch."

"What is it about?" the fellow asked rudely.

"I would like to tell the doctor in person. I'm a colleague."

The young man smiled disparagingly as his eyes went up and down Simon's now dusty, mud-stained clothes. "A colleague, I see," he jeered. "Then we're *colleagues,* too. I'm Geiger's assistant. And I can tell you right away that the master doesn't have time for you. An important examination of a lady from court." He held up the urine glass and gave it a little shake. "Slight opacification, probably stones that will need to be removed."

Simon waved his hand and sniffed. "Hmm. I think the pungent smell indicates a bladder infection. Perhaps you should—"

"I'm hardly going to discuss the urine of the venerable councilor's wife at the door," the assistant interrupted him. Uncertainty flickered in his eyes. "If you want to see the doctor, come back another day."

Simon wasn't going to give up that easily. "When exactly would it suit him?" he asked. "I've made important—"

"Another day. I bid you a good day." The assistant was so quick to close the door that Simon couldn't do anything. He raised his fist to pound on the door angrily, but thought better of it. Seething inwardly, he walked down the stairs. That arrogant whelp was several years younger than him and treated him like any old quack! He probably had wealthy, influential parents who got him the position as assistant, and now he washed urine glasses for his master and threw his weight around with misdiagnoses. Simon sighed. It had probably been a mistake to call himself a colleague. He had a feeling it would be much harder for him to get anywhere near Dr. Geiger from now on.

He wandered, deep in thought, along Sendlinger Street into the city center toward Old Peter, as the people of Munich called their parish church, St. Peter's. Why had he been so stupid? But then again, maybe his observations weren't good enough to bother the great physician with. Well, there was nothing more he could do today, anyhow. He really needed to get back to Au if he didn't want to ruin things for good with Magdalena.

His wife had been unusually withdrawn toward him lately. Perhaps it had something to do with Barbara's mood swings. Simon struggled to believe his young sister-in-law would really get married here in Munich.

He was about to head for the Isar Bridge when the sign of a shop on the right caught his eye.

BOOKSHOP JOHANNES WAGNER AND SON,
PURVEYOR TO THE ELECTORAL COURT

Entranced, Simon stopped. He had heard of shops that sold books but had never seen one. The few books he owned came from his father-in-law or itinerant merchants. The thought of a shop full of nothing but printed pages made his heart beat faster.

Simon cautiously pushed down the handle and the door opened with a soft creak. Immediately, he was enveloped by the smell of bone glue, leather, paper, and parchment, which he'd loved since childhood. Simon stopped reverently, as if he'd entered a church. The only source of light was one window covered with old cobwebs, so that most of the shop remained in the dark. Ceiling-high shelves were laden with books of every size, most of them bound in black or brown leather, though some huge tomes bore gold letters on the spine. There were scrolls of parchment, thin booklets, and piles of loose pages that were still waiting to be bound.

Will my works ever be for sale here? Simon wondered.

When he approached one of the shelves, he noticed the shop counter that had so far been hidden from view. Behind it stood a skinny, very pale elderly man with thinning hair who looked as though he only lived off books and dust. He wore a stained, threadbare coat but somehow carried it with great dignity.

"Looking for anything in particular?" the book dealer asked with a smile, putting down the large book he had just been reading. "A book of prayers, the Holy Bible, some inspirational martyr legends, perhaps?"

"Um, I was just looking," Simon replied hesitantly. "But since you ask — do you have any medical works?"

The old man nodded. "Of course. So long as they don't conflict with the teachings of our church. We are purveyors to the electoral court and the Jesuits at St. Michael, so we can't offer any heretic works." Carrying a flickering candle, he led Simon to a shelf full of books with Latin titles. Simon immediately recognized several works from his father-in-law's library and also saw a number of more recent publications that had the world of medicine talking. Johann Scultets's *Wunderarzneyisches Zeughaus* was one of them, and a new edition of Jakob Ruf's book of midwifery another. Next to it lay a thin booklet whose strange title aroused Simon's curiosity.

Observationum microscopicarum centuria.

Simon picked up the vellum-bound volume, opened it, and saw several drawings of creatures that looked like monstrous insects.

"An interesting read," the old book dealer said. "The author is a French doctor named Pierre Borel who claims to have made some exciting discoveries in the blood with the aid of magnifying lenses — although some of it seems a little too adventurous for me." He pointed at the creepy animals. "Or do you really believe something like that is crawling around inside us?" He laughed. "Well, each to their own. We only just printed it in our own press. Twenty copies. It's quite cheap, actually."

"How much is it?" Simon asked.

"Well, you seem to be just as crazy about books as I am, so I'll make you a good price." The old man winked at him. "Let's say, half a ducat?"

Simon thought. That was indeed cheaper than he had expected. Books had become more and more affordable in recent times, which probably had something to do with larger printing shops and the fact that paper was getting cheaper. Simon reached into his purse where, together with some smaller coins, he still had the silver thalers from the Veronese men. He knew they were too light and therefore forgeries, and he felt bad. But on the other hand, this bargain was just too tempting. He'd long been wanting a book about the new art of microscoping.

"I can give you five thalers as a down payment," Simon suggested. "A little more, perhaps. I'd have to get the rest from my, er . . . accommodation in Munich," he added hastily.

The book dealer sighed but didn't object. "Let's see how much you have in your purse, then."

Simon emptied the contents of his purse onto the counter. The old man put on his monocle and took a closer look at the coins. When his eyes reached the silver thalers, he paused. Then his expression hardened.

"Where did you get these from?" he asked sharply.

"Well, I'm a physician. A . . . a patient paid with these."

"A patient, you say." The bookseller eyed him suspiciously. "Wait here," he said with a strained smile. "I'll go and see if I can find a cheaper version of this book for you."

He disappeared between the shelves, and a moment later Simon heard a door creak at the back of the shop. Evidently, there was a second exit. Simon shifted his weight from one leg to the other.

Damn it, what have I done?

Cold sweat ran down his forehead, his heart raced. Why did he have to give those accursed coins to the old man? The man had noticed the false thalers instantly, as if he had seen others like them before. He was probably on his way to the city guards. Simon thought about the punishment coin counterfeiters in Bavaria might expect. A hand was chopped off, and if they were unlucky, the hangman would dip them in boiling oil or burn them at the stake.

Without hesitating any longer, Simon ran outside, leaving the silver thalers on the counter. At any moment he expected to hear shouting and the sound of men running after him, or armed guards leaping out of an alleyway and arresting him.

But all remained calm.

He ran down Sendlinger Street, past carriages and carts, whinnying horses and cursing drivers. He randomly chose narrow lanes and crossed squares, trying to use the sun for orientation, not slowing down until he finally saw the Isar Gate. When he stopped to catch his breath, he noticed that he was still clutching the book about microscoping. He had accidentally taken it in all the excitement.

Isn't that just great? he thought. *Now I'm not only wanted for coin counterfeiting but also theft. I might as well hand myself in to be broken on the wheel by Deibler now.*

With a wildly beating heart he walked through the gate, not

noticing the dark, hooded figure that had followed him through the lanes.

When Simon crossed the Isar Bridge, the man slowly followed—like a bad smell one couldn't shake.

"Barbara? Are you there? Come back, we can talk about everything!"

Magdalena was still running through the maze of Au alleyways in search of her sister. Georg and Jakob Kuisl had joined her. They had spread out as well as they could, with Magdalena first checking at Au Creek. She thought of the poor drowned girl and became terribly worried. But Barbara wasn't by the creek, or behind any of the mills along the creek, or on the slope of the Isar bank.

After some time, Magdalena came to a church and a small chapel that stood on a large grazing area at the back of Au. A handful of tethered horses searched for some of last year's grass underneath the crusted snow, while a few children held a snowball fight among the trees. Just then Georg came out of the chapel, shaking his head sadly.

"I thought she might have hidden in there," he said. "As a child she often used to go to churches or chapels when she was sad." He gave Magdalena a quizzical look. "Why did she run off like that when Master Hans spoke to her? Hans may be scary and rough, but no one asked her to marry him."

"Ask Father," Magdalena replied grimly. "I would love to know if he was aware that Hans was a member of the Council of Twelve."

Now Jakob Kuisl arrived at the frozen pasture, too. He was breathing heavily and his face was bright red—Magdalena couldn't tell whether it was from anger or exertion. And he reeked of beer from the hangmen's christening.

When Kuisl saw that his younger daughter was still missing, he cursed. "Jesus bloody Christ, that girl is a nail in my coffin.

First she makes me look like a fool in front of the entire council, and then she just runs away. Widmann is the richest hangman in the country, and he almost bit. And now this!"

"Did you know Master Hans was on the council?" Magdalena asked sharply. "Tell me, did you know?"

"No, damn it, I didn't know. I . . . I . . ." Kuisl's anger evaporated like water on a hot stone. Still breathing heavily, he sat down on a snow-covered pile of timber next to the church. Suddenly, he looked very tired.

"Believe me, if I had known, I would have given Deibler hell," he muttered. "I can understand why Barbara doesn't want to see Hans." The hangman rubbed his reddened eyes. "But now he's here, and life goes on. Like it always does."

"Can someone please tell me what you two are talking about?" Georg asked impatiently.

"Hans nearly tortured your sister," Magdalena said angrily. "At the order of the Schongau City Council, when Father was in Oberammergau two years ago. Barbara still has nightmares from those days. Master Hans had already shown her the instruments. We never told you because . . . because . . ." She broke off.

"Because you thought I'd do something stupid?" Georg asked. "I probably would have."

"Hans was merely doing his job," Jakob Kuisl said quietly, though his fists were clenched. His voice sounded husky. "They had given the order, and he was the executioner. We're only tools of the high and mighty."

"And so you torture the daughter of a colleague, because you're just a *tool*? This is your daughter we're talking about." Magdalena spat on the ground. "You disgust me, Father. All that killing and torturing, the bargaining with your sons and daughters, it's repulsive."

"You know we didn't choose our profession," Georg replied bitterly. He stepped next to his father, and Magdalena noticed again how similar they were.

"You just said you would do something stupid to Master Hans for your sister," she said. "And now you're saying torturing people is just part of your job. So, are you just a tool as well, Georg?"

"I was speaking as a brother, not an executioner." Georg sighed. "Even if we wanted to, we can't do things any differently. You know that, Magdalena. Our profession has been in our family for centuries. Being hangmen is what God has chosen for us."

"May God help me so my children won't have to say that one day," Magdalena replied coolly. "And now excuse me, I'm going to continue to look for my little sister."

She turned and walked off. Only now did she notice how cold it was. She'd been hot when she was running, but now she was shivering, and with the cold, her anger gradually cooled off, too. Georg was right, of course. But it was just so unfair! Her father had wanted to marry her to the Steingaden hangman years ago, and in hindsight, she considered herself incredibly lucky to have been allowed to marry Simon, the Schongau bathhouse surgeon. It appeared her sister wouldn't be so lucky. And now Barbara was somewhere out there, possibly doing something stupid.

Seeing Master Hans again had probably roused memories in Barbara, dark memories, buried deeply. Magdalena had a sense of the awful things that had happened to Barbara in Schongau, but she had never truly spoken with her sister about it.

First the pregnancy, and now Master Hans, Magdalena thought. *Everyone has a breaking point.*

Without paying much attention to where she was going, she had walked back to the Isar Bridge. Would her sister have crossed the bridge and gone into town?

Magdalena decided it was worth a try. Leaving Au behind, she walked onto the wooden bridge that was the only way into the city from the east. And it was accordingly busy. Carriages and carts drawn by massive steers rolled past Magdalena. A half dozen guards stopped every single vehicle and collected the bridge toll. Farther ahead, several wagons rumbled down the steep access road to the raft landing; from there the freight was shipped to Freising, Landshut, or all the way to the Danube and on to Vienna. A thought struck her.

The raft landing!

Why hadn't she thought of it sooner? If Barbara really wanted to run away, the raft landing was the perfect place. She only needed to hop aboard one of the countless rafts to leave Master Hans, her pigheaded father, and yes, her whole family behind forever. Magdalena gathered her skirt and ran down the access road to the piers and landings.

The raft landing was as busy as ever. Two rafts laden with oil and wine had just arrived, three others were taking off. Magdalena's eyes frantically searched the crowd of merchants, raftsmen, and travelers, but she couldn't see Barbara anywhere. Several barges were bobbing at the piers farther back. Had Barbara asked a fisherman or an itinerant merchant to take her with him? Magdalena ran north along the raft landing until boats and people became sparser. She walked past a row of wooden storage sheds and saw numerous tunnels and cellars that had been dug into the bank along the river, probably to store perishable goods. In such rock cellars, the temperatures remained freezing even in the middle of summer, especially if they were filled with ice. Magdalena watched a group of men store a few crates and barrels, but other than that, no one else was this far down the raft landing. The shouts of the raftsmen and the horns sounding a departure seemed far away now.

A hunched figure sat at the far end of the last pier.

Magdalena immediately recognized her sister.

"Barbara!" she called out. "Thank God, Barbara. I'm so glad to see you."

She ran along the icy, slippery walkway, almost fell, and finally wrapped her arms around her little sister. At first it seemed like Barbara was going to push her away. She stiffened, but then she laid her head against Magdalena's shoulder and cried bitterly. Her whole body quaked.

"Everything is going to be all right, darling," Magdalena said soothingly and held her tight. "Everything's going to be fine."

"Nothing's going to be fine," Barbara sobbed. "Absolutely nothing!"

"Hans can't hurt you," Magdalena said. "I'm going to speak with Deibler. We'll find somewhere else to stay and—"

"I don't give a damn about bloody Hans," Barbara burst out. "The devil take him!" Her body was racked by another crying fit. "Don't you understand?" she continued after a while. "When I saw Hans, everything came back to me. Everything those men . . ." She broke off. "I don't want to marry at all. No hangman, no knacker, no gravedigger, not even a fat merchant or blacksmith. They're all monsters."

"Not all of them," Magdalena objected. "Think of Simon or Georg."

Barbara gave a desperate laugh. "I can hardly marry either of them."

"But that Näher from Kaufbeuren doesn't seem so bad. Will you promise me to at least take a look at him?" She squeezed Barbara's hand. "But most importantly, you must promise me one thing: don't run away again without telling me. If it comes to that again, I want to know where you are."

Magdalena thought again about the dead girl in the creek. She had probably run away from home too, in the hope of finding her luck in the city.

"Promise me," she asked her sister again.

"I . . . I promise." Barbara nodded, and the two sisters hugged harder than ever. For a brief moment, Magdalena felt like she was holding the little girl she used to sing lullabies to.

We will always stick together, no matter what. Nothing can break our family. That's what makes us strong.

In that moment, a commotion broke out behind them. Magdalena let go of her sister and looked around. About twenty paces from them, the men that had been carrying crates and barrels into the icy cave moments ago were clearly very agitated about something. They were carrying something out of the cellar, a longish bundle that didn't seem particularly heavy, but the men were handling it as cautiously as if it were a sack of gunpowder. The shouting became louder, and some of the men made the sign of the cross.

"Let's go find out what's going on," Magdalena said.

They walked over to the group of men, who had set the bundle down on the ground near the last pier. Some of them were muttering prayers, all had taken off their hats.

"Evil is coming to the city," a broad-shouldered raftsman whispered. "First the impaled girl at the upper raft landing, and now *this*." Trembling, he pointed at the bundle. "I'm telling you, the dead are returning."

Peering through the men's shoulders, Magdalena finally saw what was lying on the ground. She winced, and Barbara gave a soft cry.

The dead are returning . . .

Shocked, Magdalena stared at the face of a mummy as tiny snowflakes fell into its black, empty eye sockets. The mummy's mouth was wide open, as if in a final, desperate scream that no one had heard.

Or in a curse, Magdalena thought.

"God help this city," one of the raftsmen said quietly. "Fetch the guards before this thing comes back to life."

4

Move along, people! Get out of the way!"

A half dozen guards were struggling to make their way through the crowd on the raft landing. From an alleyway above the river, Jakob Kuisl watched the people pushing and shoving each other to get a glimpse of the corpse. Around the strangely bent body, which still lay near the last pier, the people of Munich had left a wide space, as if they feared the ominous thing might suddenly come back to life.

"Goddamnit, if you don't make way this instant, I'll give you a taste of this." Raising his sword, the first of the guards—evidently the captain—started dealing blows left and right with the flat side of the blade. Grumbling, the crowd finally began to yield.

"So you're saying it's a mummy?" Jakob Kuisl asked his elder daughter, who was standing next to him. Magdalena shrugged.

"Well, at least it looks like the one you once told me about. A stiff puppet covered with leather. Don't the Egyptians use them to make this powder you sell to people for a lot of money?"

Kuisl snorted. "Ha! It's probably just dirt and ground-up mouse droppings. Believing is everything." He pointed to the corpse. "That's definitely a person. Or at least it used to be one."

Following the gruesome discovery, Magdalena had sent one of the many street children over to Au with the message for her father that she had found Barbara. The news of the mummy in the rock cellar had spread faster than wildfire, and Kuisl had already heard all about it by the time he reached the bridge. Michael Deibler and Georg had gone with him, and now Georg was holding the visibly shaken Barbara in his arms. Kuisl hadn't had a chance to speak with his younger daughter yet—he was just relieved to find her alive and well.

"Shall we go down and take a closer look at this mummy?" he asked, turning to Michael Deibler.

The Munich hangman grinned. "I thought you'd never ask. Let's go, you nosey old dog. I know the captain. Josef Loibl is almost as grumpy and uncommunicative as you, but he's not a bad fellow."

Kuisl and Deibler took a narrow flight of steps down to the raft landing while Georg stayed with the two women. Unlike the guards, the hangmen had no trouble making their way through the crowd. People were quick to make room when they saw who was approaching: an over-six-foot-tall bearded hulk together with the well-known Munich executioner.

Finally the two men reached the group of guards standing around the corpse and awaiting further orders. The captain, an old warhorse with a scarred, stubbled face and the only one of the guards to wear a cuirass, eyed the hangmen with suspicion.

"I'm afraid you're too late, Deibler," he said. "She's already dead, can't execute her anymore."

"But perhaps the one who did this," Jakob Kuisl retorted.

He looked down at the bundle in the snow. It was clearly the corpse of a young woman. Her facial features and the high cheekbones beneath the skin were well preserved, just like the formerly blonde hair, now brittle and dull like old straw. Her mouth stood open in a silent scream, exposing a row of healthy white teeth. Kuisl estimated the girl had been around eighteen years old—roughly the same age as Barbara. She wore a plain skirt with an apron, like those customary for maidservants. Her body was bent, as though the dying woman had curled up like a sick cat. Parts of her fingers, toes, and nose were missing, probably chewed off by rats, and her skin resembled tanned leather.

The executioners could make out remains of leather fetters around her wrists and ankles, and scraps of a gag sticking to her lips.

The captain stood beside the two hangmen, his head tilted back, trying to size up Kuisl. "And who do you think you are, big fellow, dishing out advice to me?" he snapped. "You're not from Munich, anyway. I'd remember your face."

"He's the Schongau executioner," Michael Deibler replied. "We're holding our guild meeting over at Au over Candlemas, remember?" He winked at the captain. "You didn't want us in the city."

"And that's how it should be. And now, hangman, pack your giant away and go back to—"

"Have you had a look at the bag yet?" Kuisl asked.

The captain gave him an irritated look. "What . . . ?"

"The bag." Kuisl pointed at the corpse. "On her apron. Maybe its contents will give us a clue."

Loibl turned red. "*Us?* Now listen here, you block—"

"Just let him," Deibler interrupted him with a sigh. "He'll do what he wants anyway. And he actually knows a thing or two about dead bodies. Besides"—he gave a thin smile—"none of you wants to touch the corpse. People are already whispering about the return of the dead and witchcraft, so you might as well let us dishonorable executioners do the job. We wouldn't want any upstanding citizens to get their hands dirty."

"Well, all right, then, go ahead." Reluctantly, Loibl stepped aside, but Kuisl noticed the glint of relief in his eyes.

The Schongau hangman leaned over the dead girl, whose stiff clothes and leathery skin were covered in a thin layer of ice. The bag hanging at her side was as dry as old timber, and when Kuisl tried to open it, it fell apart. Inside, he found a few rusty kreuzers, a small medallion, and some dried plants that crumbled between Kuisl's fingers and blew away with the next gust of wind.

"Ha, nothing but rubbish," the captain said. "I knew this wouldn't get us anywhere."

"Rubbish can tell a story, too," Kuisl replied, studying the items in his palm. He sniffed at the last plant crumbs sticking to his fingertips. Then he closed his eyes and took a deep breath.

"This girl came to Munich from somewhere around Altötting not long after the Great War," he started in a monotone, keeping his eyes closed. "She was unmarried, found employment as a simple maidservant, and fell ill in her final days. Someone tied and gagged her and walled her in alive in the rock cellar over there."

Everyone was silent with astonishment for a while, then the captain burst out laughing. "Bloody hell! Who are you? A wizard or just a good liar? No one can possibly know all that just by looking at the body."

"As I said, he's the Schongau executioner," Michael Deibler said with a grin. "Murder is his passion. He did something very similar with a dead girl in Au yesterday."

"Another dead girl at Au?" Loibl frowned, then shrugged. "People are dropping like flies over there. That's Gustl's problem, the clerk. None of my business." He turned back to Kuisl. "And now tell me, why do you think you know so much about this dead bit of meat, big fellow?"

Kuisl stood up and pointed at the dead body. "She's young and isn't wearing a ring, so she probably didn't have a husband. The rusty kreuzers were minted in 1647 and bear the Latin name of Elector Maximilian, the father of the current elector. So she's been dead for at least twenty years. Her clothes tell us that she was a plain maidservant, like so many young girls who come to Munich to find their luck."

"Twenty years. Hmm. You might be right." Deibler nodded. "Those rock cellars are as cold as the devil's arsehole, and drafty from countless little air holes. A dead body would dry like a stockfish."

"The cave the men found her in had been walled shut quite a while ago," Loibl added. "You can tell by the mortar and bricks. They just opened it today. Perhaps she was already dead when the fellow put her there. No one noticed the body, they closed the hole, and—"

"For crying out loud, she was bound and gagged," Kuisl interrupted. "Why would the murderer go to this trouble if she was already dead? Also, I can't see any external injuries. I'm telling you, the bastard walled her in when she was still alive."

Loibl spat on the ground. "And what if he did? This happened decades ago, so it doesn't concern us. Most likely the murderer is just as dead as his victim."

Meanwhile, the guards struggled to keep the crowd at bay. People were still shouting excitedly, and several strong lads pushed their way closer to the corpse.

"It's a ghost, I can see it clearly!" one of them yelled. "A living dead! Drive a stake through her heart, like the other one!"

"I'll drive a stake up your arse if you don't shut up!" Loibl shouted back. He took a threatening step toward the young men, and they retreated, grumbling. For a while, people remained relatively quiet.

Deibler grinned. "Perhaps finding out what happened to the poor girl wouldn't be so bad after all, Josef. Otherwise the taverns are going to be crawling with ghost-hunters by tomorrow, wielding their stakes and crosses."

"Damn it, Deibler, don't start with me." Loibl raised a warning finger. "But your friend has aroused my curiosity now." The captain turned back to Kuisl, ignoring the chaos on the raft landing around him. "The fact that she's from Altötting was a guess, though. Admit it. You couldn't have picked it up from her accent, now, could you?"

"No, but the necklace spoke to me." Kuisl held up the medallion from the bag, a cheap piece of tin on a rusty chain. "A Black Madonna like they worship in the Altötting area. I'm guessing that's where the girl got the necklace from, and she's too young for a long pilgrimage."

"Damn, now you only need to explain why you think she was ill," Deibler said, scrutinizing the corpse. "Then your trick is complete. Have you seen any injuries on her? Rotten teeth? Dried blood?"

"None of those things." Grinning, Kuisl shook his head. As always, he thoroughly enjoyed holding out on his audience. "It's the herbs she was carrying. If you buy herbs for cooking, you buy them at the market and put them in the basket with your other groceries. In a sack like this, you keep medicinal herbs." He frowned. "Although I can't say for certain what the herbs were. The smell was too faint. Ingredients for a cough syrup, perhaps? Linden flowers? Ivy?" He scratched his nose. "Goddamnit, I just can't figure it out."

"I'm just glad you don't know her name and that of her murderer," Captain Loibl replied with a laugh. "Or I'd have to arrest you for witchcraft." He gave the hangman a box in the side. "I like you, big fellow. Next time I find a strange corpse, I know who to ask for."

"Let's hope there won't be another one," Deibler grumbled. "Three murder victims a week are plenty for my taste. Although this one can't be connected to the other two—it's too old for that. Or . . . hey, what are you doing, Jakob?"

Michael Deibler watched in confusion as the Schongau hangman bent down low over the mummy. He reached into her mouth and pulled something out.

A tarnished black amulet.

"What in God's name is this?" Loibl asked, alarmed.

"Hmm. It's barely recognizable," Kuisl said, studying the pendant closely. "But I think it's another Virgin Mary. I can make out a woman with a halo, but it's very faded."

"And why was it in her mouth?" Deibler asked. "She was hardly going to eat it, was she? Especially since she was gagged."

"Put it away before anyone sees, damn it," the captain hissed. "Or people really will start believing in ghosts."

Kuisl put the tiny medallion in his pocket. He gave Deibler a meaningful glance but didn't say anything.

"Let's wrap up this show as fast as we can so people stop talking about witchcraft and living dead." Loibl looked around the groups of agitated people on the raft landing. Every other moment, someone glared at the hangmen and spat over his own shoulder.

The captain signaled to his guards. Reluctantly, and visibly afraid, they spread a blanket over the stiff body and wrapped it up.

"We'll take her to the cemetery at the Church of the Holy Cross," Loibl said. "There's a paupers' grave where she can finally rest in peace." Then he turned to Kuisl and Deibler. "I'd like to shake your hands to thank you, but I'm afraid I'd lose my job. Anyone who touches a hangman turns dishonorable themselves, as you know. So I'll just say God bless you." He nodded at Deibler. "And give my regards to Walburga. The cough medicine for my children really helped."

With that, Josef Loibl turned around and led his men up the raft landing. Deibler's eyes followed the captain for a long moment.

"A decent fellow, that Loibl," he said eventually. "Trusts me and my wife more than the quacks in the city. He treats us practically like honorable folks and always pays right away for his medicines." He paused, then continued slowly: "The amulet in the mummy's mouth . . ."

"The Virgin Mary with an aureole," Kuisl said, nodding. "Just like the one the dead girl at Au was holding."

"It has to be a coincidence. There's more than twenty years between the two murders," Deibler said as he considered the similarities. "I've heard that people used to bury their dead with a coin in the mouth to pay the ferryman to bring them to the realm of the dead. Perhaps that's what the medallion in the girl's mouth was for?"

"A murder victim who was walled in?" Jakob Kuisl rubbed his huge nose again. "Then it could only have been the murderer himself who put it in there. After all, she was gagged."

"For God's sake, Jakob." Deibler rolled his eyes. "Stop your guesswork and look after your family. They need you more than some ancient mummy." He gave his friend a pat on the back. "Speaking of family—I've got a feeling my Walburga wouldn't mind at all if the Kuisl family moved in with us for a few days."

Kuisl frowned. "What makes you say that?"

"Well, since I heard what Master Hans nearly did to your Barbara, I can understand why she doesn't want to sleep under the same roof as him. And admittedly, Au isn't the best neighborhood for your grandchildren."

"Nonsense." Kuisl waved dismissively. "That's not necessary. I'll speak with Barbara and—"

"Now don't be like that, you stubborn old dog." Deibler grinned. "Walburga and I don't have children, so we've got plenty of room in the executioner's house. You can stay at the Radl Inn if you want, but your family would be better off with us. Go on, shake on it, or I'll sulk." He held out his callused hand to Kuisl.

"Well . . . all right, then. Perhaps it is for the best." Kuisl grabbed Deibler's hand and smiled, although it was hard to tell under his thick beard. He felt deeply grateful. The rest of the world might shun them, but hangmen would always stick together. And Deibler was right: what did he care about a corpse that had been dead for more than twenty years? He was here as a member of the Council of Twelve, and that was all. Also, he had enough problems with Barbara.

"It's a pity you're already married, Michael," Kuisl said. "Or I'd gladly give you my Barbara."

"Thank you very much, but I love my Walburga dearly." Deibler laughed out loud. "And I think your daughter would have a word or two to say about that. As far as I can tell, you'll have a hell of a time getting that hothead hitched." He wrinkled his nose. "And now, dear cousin, it's time to dip your head into Au creek once more. You stink like an old barrel of beer after the hangman's christening."

When Simon finally reached the Radl Inn at Au, he realized that something was amiss. Inside, several hangmen he had already met the night before sat at a table, but neither his father-in-law, nor Georg, nor Magdalena was among them. He remembered the meeting had started at noon. Was it already over? Then he'd be in a world of trouble. The Passau hangman Kaspar Hörmann came wavering toward him, fiddling with his codpiece. Evidently, he was on his way to the privy.

"Um, pardon me," Simon began, still clutching the stolen book. "I'm looking for my father-in-law and my wife. Do you by any chance—"

He broke off when he noticed Hörmann's angry glare. "A lovely family you have," the Passau hangman slurred. "As soon as the Kuisls are on the council, everything turns higgledy-piggledy." He waved his finger in Simon's face. "And you can tell that fresh sister-in-law of yours that I wouldn't want her for anything, the little hussy. Who does she think she is? My son deserves better. Just wait till Widmann gets hold of her."

"I . . . I'm afraid I don't follow . . . ," Simon stammered. He increasingly got the impression he had missed more than just a boring guild meeting. "Is the meeting already over?" he asked.

"Over?" Hörmann laughed. "It hasn't even started properly. Thanks to you Kuisls, we have to wait. God knows when we can continue." The hangman burped loudly. "And now let me pass before I piss my pants." He stumbled past Simon through the door.

When Simon saw the grim looks of the other hangmen, he decided to continue his search outside. To his great relief, he spotted Paul out in the street. Dressed in dirty trousers and just a thin shirt, he was playing with a group of street children with a whip and a spinning top. Of all the family members, Paul — together with his grandfather — seemed to have the least problem with Au. He looked happy among the other filthy children. Simon tapped his son on the shoulder, and he turned around reluctantly.

"Where's everyone else?" Simon asked. "Your mother, Grandpa, your brother . . ."

"Peter's upstairs, looking after Sophia and reading some boring Latin stuff," Paul replied. "And the others are looking for Barbara. I think she ran away."

"Ran away?" Simon was shocked. What on earth had happened here while he was out? He was about to ask more when he noticed a man watching him on the other side of the street. He was wearing a black coat with a hood. Now he came toward him with long strides. Suddenly Simon felt hot despite the icy temperatures.

Oh my God, a city guard! he thought. *How could I forget? They followed me all the way from the bookshop. Now it's all over.*

He was about to turn around and run when the man called out to him.

"Hey, you! Are you Simon Fronwieser?"

Simon paused. They already knew his name? Then there was little point in running now. He could only hope for a mild sentence, because after all, he had only been given the coins. Or was it about the stolen book? With a deep sigh, he turned around.

"Yes, that's me," he said with bowed head.

The man pushed back his hood and revealed long, wavy hair and a well-groomed beard. On his coat Simon saw a silver cloak pin studded with tiny diamonds. Christ, if this was a plain city guard, Munich was truly wealthy. The man gave him a formal smile.

"I'm so glad I found you, Doctor Fronwieser," he said. "I'm an envoy from the electoral court."

Now Simon was completely confused. All right, the coins he'd tried to give the shopkeeper were counterfeit, but there were only five. Or were they trying to accuse him of minting them, large scale? Would they boil him in oil as the supposed head of a gang of counterfeiters?

"Listen, I . . . I think there must be a misunderstanding," he stammered. "I only had the thalers for a very short time; they came from a pair of Veronese merchants. And . . . and the book was an accident, I swear—"

"Thalers? Book?" The man looked puzzled. "I don't know what you're talking about. I am here as the personal envoy of the highly esteemed serene electress Henriette Adelaide. She heard about your abilities and your sharp mind and wishes to see you at an audience at noon tomorrow."

Simon's jaw dropped. He didn't know what to say. He heard the words over and over in his mind. Or was he dreaming?

She heard about your abilities and your sharp mind . . .

Could it really be possible that the Bavarian court had heard about his medical observations? He had discussed them with several colleagues from the wider region, he supposed. And once he had treated a traveling alderman from Munich who had seemed somewhat interested in his theories. But he never thought . . .

He swallowed hard before he finally thought of something to say. "I . . . I'll be there. Please tell Her Electoral Excellency how deeply grateful and—"

"That's settled, then." The envoy handed him a folded and

sealed document. "This is your permit, you must present it at the audience. Don't forget, when the bells ring at noon." Then he looked around the stinking narrow street with disgust. "And now you'll have to excuse me. I have several more errands to run, in *other* quarters." He hinted at a bow, pulled the hood over his carefully combed hair, and strutted off.

Simon remained in the middle of the street for a long time, standing as if frozen, the sealed document in his trembling hands. He was aware neither of the children playing around him nor of the noise from the tavern. Over and over he heard the sentence that would surely change his life forever.

The electress . . . heard about your abilities and your sharp mind . . .

He only woke when his son's snowball hit him right on the nose.

When Magdalena arrived back at Au with Barbara and the others, Simon ran toward her, visibly excited. He was bleeding slightly from the nose, but that didn't seem to bother him.

"It's . . . it's a miracle," he said, panting. "She . . . she's heard about me!"

"What are you on about?" Magdalena stopped and shook her head. "Are you delirious because someone punched you on the nose?"

"Er, no. That was Paul." Simon absentmindedly pulled a handkerchief from the pocket of his vest and dabbed at the blood. "Never mind my nose—I'm destined for greater things!"

"For God's sake, I think a greater thing fell on your head," Jakob Kuisl growled. "Now tell us what you're talking about before Deibler locks you in the madhouse."

"An envoy from the electress has just been here. Because of me." Breathlessly, Simon told them about the strange encounter and the audience at noon tomorrow. For a moment, everyone was silent with astonishment.

"*You* are supposed to meet the electress?" Magdalena gaped at him. "Are you sure it's not a misunderstanding? Maybe the messenger thought you were someone else."

Simon shook his head and held up the sealed document. "He explicitly mentioned *Doctor* Simon Fronwieser. And my sharp mind. I'm guessing the court is interested in my treatise."

Magdalena groaned. "Oh well, at least then all your scribbling from the last few months won't have been for nothing. In any case," she said, giving her husband a determined look, "you're not going on your own."

"Um, please don't get me wrong, but I hardly think a hangman's daughter at court—"

"Rubbish!" she cut him off. "I wasn't talking about me. I mean Peter. He'll never get another opportunity like this in his life. When the court sees what an intelligent, well-mannered boy he is, they might let him attend the Jesuit college in Munich." She narrowed her eyes. "I've always said the Schongau Latin School isn't good enough for my son. Ha! I can't wait to see the look on old Weininger's face when I tell him that Peter was accepted at the Jesuit school. Then he can recite his stupid catechism by himself."

"But, my treatise—" Simon protested.

"You're taking Peter and that's the end of it." Magdalena put her hands on her hips and glared at her husband. "That's not too much to ask. I want my sons to become something better than dishonorable hangmen. Peter, at least," she added grimly.

"Don't say anything against dishonorable hangmen," said Georg, who was now standing by the others with Barbara. "Your father, your uncle, and your brother are all hangmen. And half the guests at the tavern here."

"Which we're soon going to leave, thank God," Magdalena replied. On their walk home, her father had told her about Deibler's invitation to stay with him and his wife at the Munich executioner's house. She hadn't hesitated with her decision, and neither had Barbara. Her younger sister had been very quiet since their conversation down by the pier and the discovery of the eerie mummy. Magdalena hoped she would get the chance for a long talk with Barbara in the coming days, and not only because she worried her sister would try to run away again or harm herself. The laws against so-called frivolity had become very strict in the last few decades, especially here in Catholic Bavaria. A woman giving birth to a child out of wedlock could expect the shrew's fiddle, imprisonment on bread and water, even banishment.

But maybe they would still find a suitable husband for Barbara.

On cue, Johann Widmann stepped out through the door of the Radl Inn. He gave the Kuisl family a derisive look while twirling his moustache.

"So you've caught the wild filly?" he jeered. "Better put a bridle on her before someone gives her a whipping."

"Shut up, Widmann," Jakob Kuisl snapped. "Or I'll pluck your whiskers out one by one."

"How dare you!" Widmann flared up. "Your daughter—"

"I'm sick of sucking up to you," Kuisl interrupted him. "Everyone's had your snootiness up to here. I regretted sending you that letter the day I wrote it." He took a step toward Widmann, towering over him by more than a head. "They say you're squeamish like a little girl at beheadings. How many strokes did it take you last time? Five, six? Or did you pass out first?"

The Nuremberg hangman turned red but didn't reply. He turned to Deibler instead. "We're all waiting for the meeting to continue," he hissed, "with or without this loudmouth."

He turned around and slammed the door shut behind him. Deibler grinned broadly. "Thanks for speaking plainly. Someone should have told him off long ago."

Great, I guess we can cross out candidate number two, Magdalena thought. *The choices are getting slim.*

"I should never have written Widmann about Barbara," Kuisl said. "I was blinded by his wealth. But in truth he's nothing but an arrogant oaf, and my Barbara is much too good for him, right?"

He smiled at Barbara, but she didn't smile back. Instead, she stared straight ahead, her arms folded on her chest.

"If Master Hans is still in there, I'm not going in," she whispered. "And I don't want to see any of the other boozeheads, either, staring at me like a horse at market. I'm not spending another night in this hole."

"Speaking of Master Hans," Georg said pensively. "I was talking to Matthäus Fux earlier—you know, the Memmingen hangman, he was here last night, too." He lowered his voice. "Well, Fux swears black and blue that he saw Hans earlier last night —and he'd claimed to have just arrived from a torture in Weilheim."

"And?" Deibler said. "Perhaps he just didn't want to admit that he needed to sleep off his hangover somewhere."

"Hold on, it gets better," Georg continued. "Fux says Hans was with a girl when he saw him here in Au. A girl with reddish-blonde hair. I mean, the dead girl in the creek, she also had—"

"Are you trying to say Hans met up with the poor girl and later killed her?" Deibler laughed. "You Kuisls are all the same. You see a murderer behind every bush." He turned to Barbara and squeezed her hand. "Listen, girl, let me finish this meeting and then I'll talk to my wife. You can move in tonight, with the two lads and little Sophia. All right?"

"Yes, thank you." Barbara nodded. The warmheartedness of the Munich hangman seemed to do her good. For the first time in days, she smiled a little. Magdalena breathed a sigh of relief.

Perhaps everything is going to end well after all. For Barbara and for my Peter, too.

But something told Magdalena that it wouldn't be so easy.

A few hours later, darkness descended over Munich. Old Peter's bell chimed the seventh hour, and the busy streets and lanes became quiet. The last merchants packed away their wares on the large market square by the city hall. Several patricians hurried toward the wealthy Graggenau Quarter, their hats pulled down low. The night watchman went on his first round, and the noise and shouting of the wagon drivers ebbed away.

From the arcades on the south side of the market square the occasional lustful cry or soft moan could be heard, as so often at this time of night. Shrugging his shoulders, the night watchman left the lovers alone and moved on. He'd been young once, and the dark arcades were a popular spot for young couples and also for prostitutes going about their business. The old watchman smiled to himself, thinking of long-ago rendezvous. These days, he thought with a shiver, February would be too cold for him for such pastimes. At his age, he'd prefer a glass of hot mulled wine at one of the taverns down Sendlinger Street to amorous adventures in the cold.

Theresa Wilprecht waited until the night watchman finally disappeared around a corner, then she tied a scarf over her long blonde hair and cautiously walked toward the archways. As she scurried across the square, she kept looking left and right. If one of the old moneybags from the city hall recognized her, she'd be finished. Worst case would be running into her husband, who was always out on some kind of business and never came to bed early. When Theresa married the merchant Konrad Wilprecht two years ago, she thought her future was like a golden road leading straight to paradise. Wilprecht was one of the wealthiest patricians in Munich and even sat on the inner council, which controlled the fate of the city; becoming his wife meant a life in silks and satins, prestige, power, and a never-ending series of balls and festivities.

But twenty-year-old Theresa had soon found out that this life was nothing but a gilded cage.

Wilprecht had married her because his first wife had died of the spotted fever. After three daughters, he was hoping for a male heir, but Theresa had given him another daughter, a pale, weak thing that was always whimpering and sickly. The three older daughters despised Theresa and made no secret of it, and even the servants treated her like dirt. When she tried to speak with her husband about it, his mind was always on some contracts or the price of wheat; in bed, he was as passionate as a dead fish. Theresa's life seemed over before it had really begun.

Her only consolation was Martin.

They had met a few months ago at a ball at the city hall. Martin was young and dapper, son of the mighty Ligsalz family of Munich. He desired her, pined for her, even, and the few hours they spent together helped Theresa through this cold, dismal winter that would no doubt be followed by an equally dismal spring, summer, and autumn. With Martin at her side, she managed to forget her fat, indifferent husband, the beastly stepdaughters, and the constantly crying child at home for a little while.

With a pounding heart, Theresa approached the arcades, where merchants sold their goods in the daytime. So far, she and Martin had always met at a vegetable garden in the Hacken Quarter, in a crooked old shed, where they made love between rakes, spades, and hop crates. Perhaps not the most ideal love nest, but Martin gave the owner a few coins each time, so they were safe from discovery.

But this time, Martin had sent her a message saying he wanted to meet her at the arcades at seven o'clock, the well-known place for many young lovers in Munich. The giggling and moaning from underneath the arcades made Theresa's heart beat faster. This was so exciting! She felt like a thief in the night. Perhaps Martin would surprise her by acting like a rogue—a game she'd gladly join.

"Martin," she called softly and peered into the dark passages. "Martin? Are you there?"

"Find yourself another spot, girl," a female voice hissed at her. "This one's already taken."

Someone laughed, and Theresa quickly stumbled on. Martin could have told her where to find him. It was as dark as the woods beneath the arcades. He should have known she'd be afraid. But the thrill of anticipation made Theresa push her fear aside and she hurried on. She thought about how nice it would be to be married to young Martin instead of fat old Wilprecht. If she could only carry his child underneath her heart! But Martin's hair was black, while she and Wilprecht were both blond. The old man might smell her betrayal. He'd already been giving her suspicious looks lately. So, after each rendezvous, she rinsed her abdomen with vinegar and drank a brew of red orach, ivy, and water pepper, which was said to prevent unwanted pregnancies.

"Martin," she called out again as she made her way through the dark. "Martin? Where are you?"

Again, no reply. Theresa angrily stamped her foot on the icy ground. Was Martin leading her on? The message had already been strange enough, the handwriting barely legible, not at all like him. She was about to go back to the market square when a muffled voice called out to her from farther back.

"I'm here, Theresa. Come here."

Theresa paused. The voice sounded strange, hoarse somehow. But maybe it was just part of the game.

"Martin, is that you?" she asked.

"Of course, my white dove," the hoarse voice replied. "Come to me. I've missed you so much."

"Oh Martin!" Now Theresa was sure it was him. Only Martin called her that. She ran toward the back, where the pillars were completely swallowed up by the darkness. A single light was burning, a candle, she guessed, which Martin must have lit for their lovemaking. Perhaps there would also be a cushion and a jug of wine. It would be like heaven. Theresa hurried toward the flickering candle when she suddenly heard the crunch of footsteps behind her.

"Mar—" was all she could say before the club came down on the back of her head and she collapsed without a sound. Farther up the arcades, soft giggling and faint voices could still be heard; everything else remained silent.

Strong hands lifted Theresa up and dumped her onto a small cart like a dead beast. The dark figure spread a blanket over her body, then wheeled the screeching cart out of the arcades.

The strange merchant with the hunched back and wide coat dragged the cart across the market square. The night watchman only glanced briefly, then he called out to the citizens of Munich in their homes that all was quiet.

"How big is Deibler's house? Is it bigger than yours, Grandpa? Does he also keep his sword by the shrine, like at home in Schongau?"

Eight-year-old Paul was bouncing around at his grandfather's hand like an exuberant puppy. Since they had walked out of Au, he had been assailing Jakob Kuisl with one question after another, most of which the hangman only answered with a grunt. Both Simon and Kuisl carried bundles with the family's few belongings across their shoulders, and Georg, too, accompanied his family to their new abode at the Munich executioner's house. Afterward, he was going to return to Au with his father.

Magdalena looked over to her father and her son and couldn't help but smile. Paul loved his grandfather more than anything and dreamed of one day becoming a famous hangman—at least as famous as Jörg Abriel, their ancestor, who had made a pile of money with the notorious Schongau witch trials and used to arrive at executions by carriage with his servants.

Sometimes Magdalena found it hard to love Paul as much as Peter, her elder son. While Peter happily read, wrote, and drew pictures, Paul was almost always out in the streets, often as the loud-mouthed leader of a gang of rascals who got into mischief, pushed over buckets of dung, and beat up other boys. His entire being was wild and sometimes cruel. One time, Magdalena had watched him break a bird's neck just so he could study the little creature's dying moments.

Maybe there is something inside us Kuisls that makes us executioners after all, Magdalena thought. *Well, at least Peter is different. Perhaps Simon can do something for him at court tomorrow.*

The meeting of the executioners had lasted until late at night, so now they had to find their way around the city wall on narrow, icy paths in darkness. The house of the executioner was near the Sendlinger Gate, which was almost at the other end of town. The citizens of Munich weren't allowed to be out on the streets this late at night, and the Munich hangman didn't want to risk being stopped by a guard. He was pretty sure providing shelter to a dishonorable executioner's family from out of town was against the law.

As they walked past small farmsteads and hop poles covered in icicles, Magdalena's thoughts kept returning to the gruesome discovery at the lower raft landing. Around this area, too, called the upper raft landing, a dead girl had been found not long ago—with a stake through her heart. Since then, people had been talking about ghosts and dead bodies rising from their graves.

Magdalena tightened her hold on little Sophia, who was fast asleep in a sling across her chest. She could only hope her daughter would one day live in a time when people didn't see a witch or a ghost behind every inexplicable event.

"How much farther is it?" she asked Michael Deibler, who was walking ahead with Georg. The two men were carrying on an animated conversation; it seemed they had taken a liking to one another despite their age difference.

Deibler turned around and pointed ahead, where Magdalena

could vaguely make out a larger structure in the city wall. "That's the Sendlinger Gate. We're nearly there."

"I'm cold," Barbara complained. She was walking at the rear of their little group together with Simon and Peter. "And this area is creepy. Brooks and frozen channels everywhere, just waiting for someone to fall in. And who's to say this place isn't crawling with scoundrels at night?"

Barbara hadn't said more than just a word or two since they'd left Au, until now. Magdalena still hadn't managed to continue the conversation they had started on the raft landing. It seemed to her that Barbara was avoiding her, as though she was desperately seeking a loophole to get out of the threatened marriage.

Finally they arrived at the fortifications of the Sendlinger Gate. Like the Isar Gate, this entrance into the city was a mighty structure with three towers and a zwinger, a fortified area in between. The bridge crossing the moat that ran right around the city was empty at this time of night.

"Now we only need to ask old Lainmiller from the city guard to let us in," Deibler said with a grin as he climbed the stairs to the bridge. "But that shouldn't be a problem. Every full moon, my wife brews him a potion so he can still get it up."

He was about to step onto the bridge when the gate screeched open and a carriage came tearing out at high speed. To her horror, Magdalena saw that Paul had pulled away from his grandfather and was standing on the bridge.

The carriage was heading straight for the boy.

Kuisl dove forward, grabbed Paul, and hurled him to the other side of the road. At the last moment, Kuisl managed to roll out of the way and dodge the vehicle. Then the carriage vanished into the darkness. All that was left was the sound of the horses' hooves and the rumble of wheels.

"Bloody arrogant riffraff!" Kuisl shouted after the vehicle. "If I catch you, I'll break you on your very own wheels!"

Magdalena rushed toward Paul, her heart in her throat, but

the boy didn't seem hurt. His eyes were wide, but he was already smiling again. "Grandpa made me fly," he whispered. "Like an angel." His trousers were torn, his knees bloody, but no worse than after a brawl in the meadows outside Schongau. In her relief, Magdalena held her son tight for a long moment. She realized then that she loved Paul just as much as she loved her other children.

Each in their own special way, she thought.

"No one's supposed to leave town at this late hour," Deibler complained, still staring after the carriage that had long since gone. "God knows why the guards opened the gate for them."

"They definitely were no normal travelers," Simon said. "The carriage looked very elegant, with good horses and suspension. He frowned. "Did you notice that it was covered in black cloth? And painted black, too. Almost as if they were trying to disguise it."

"And they succeeded," Georg said grimly. "We only saw it in the last moment. I'd love to know who was sitting inside."

"My son-in-law can keep an eye out for the bastard at the oh-so-fancy court tomorrow," Kuisl mocked. "I'm sure it was just some swanky Munich youngsters with their harlots. That's all they know: galloping across freshly tilled fields with their horses or running over little children with their carriages."

"Whatever the case, they're gone now." In his blood-red coat, Michael Deibler stomped ahead toward the Sendlinger Gate, which was now closed again. He knocked at the small door on the right-hand side of the gate. "Hey, Lainmiller!" he called out. "You there? It's me, the hangman. Let me in."

A bolt was pushed aside, the door opened a crack, and a sullen, wrinkly face appeared. The watchman eyed the small group behind Deibler suspiciously from under his helmet.

"They're friends of mine who need somewhere to stay," Deibler explained. "Go on, Lainmiller, don't be like that. I know very well how late it is. I'll tell Walburga to make the next brew even stronger."

"Even stronger? Ha! The whores won't like that!" The old man grinned and opened the low door. He waved his hand for Deibler and the Kuisls to hurry. "Quick, before the other guards hear anything."

"What was that strange carriage you just let out the gate?" Michael Deibler asked. "Must have been mighty noble personages."

The watchman's face darkened. "Never you mind, hangman. You just worry about your own business."

Magdalena noticed the flicker of uncertainty in the old man's eyes—clearly, he was hiding something.

"Do you want that brew or not?" Deibler growled. "Then talk. Or I might tell Walburga to add some poisonous wolfsbane next time."

Lainmiller sighed. "What do we simple folks know about the goings-on of the noble lords and ladies? The carriage comes through once or twice a month, always covered in black. Usually it leaves town just after the gates close and comes back at dawn. We're supposed to let it pass—orders from high up. We don't ask questions."

"Especially not when you get paid for it," Michael Deibler said with a wink, pointing at the full purse dangling from Lainmiller's belt.

The guard turned red. "If you knew how little the city pays for this rotten job, damn it! This used to be a good position, once upon a time, but since the building of the fortifications gobbled up all the city's reserves, we're as poor as church mice!"

Deibler nodded and gave the old man a pat on the shoulder. "It's all right, man. We all need to get by somehow. Come around tomorrow for your brew. And now I wish you a quiet, not-too-cold night."

They left the watchman and the gate behind and turned right. Soon after, they came to a strange building. It was a two-storied,

solidly built house that stood in the middle of the street near the
city wall. It was surrounded by its own man-high wall, behind
which they could see the tops of numerous trees and bushes. The
place reminded Magdalena of one of those fortified farmsteads
that could be found scattered through the forests.

Like a small fortress, she thought. *Protected from attacks from the
outside.*

"My humble abode," Deibler said with a smile and gestured to
the house. Behind it a tower with a strangely shaped roof rose
into the night sky. "Usually executioners live outside the city
walls. But the high and mighty don't seem to mind this—a pimple on the arse of Munich."

"A rather noble pimple," Kuisl muttered approvingly. "I guess
you are the hangman of Munich, and not some obscure village
executioner like me. Widmann's home in Nuremberg is no better than this."

"It's too big for an old couple like us," Deibler said with a
shrug as he opened a small gate at the rear of the property. "Walburga and I don't have children, and my journeyman, the drunkard, lives with his old man, the knacker. A fever took my
apprentice last year." He sighed. "Hörmann from Passau wanted
to send me his son, but one drunkard on the scaffold is enough
for me."

They walked through a small garden, which now, in February, was covered with snow and wilted weeds. But Magdalena
could tell by the shrubs, trellises, and orderly rows of vegetable
beds that a loving hand was at work here. She thought of the garden at the Schongau executioner's house that her mother used to
tend. It was the same here: the premises might seem cold and
forbidding from the outside, but the garden was surprisingly
homey.

Michael Deibler knocked on the door, and it was soon opened.
The woman who greeted them was so tall that Magdalena at first
thought it was a man. Walburga Deibler's hair was black with

gray streaks and tied up neatly in a bun. Judging by her gravy-stained apron, she had come straight from the stove. Walburga Deibler was a good head taller than her husband, and while she was long and skinny, Michael Deibler was broad and stocky. Magdalena couldn't help but smile. She had never seen a more unlikely couple than the Deiblers. Five purring cats brushed around Walburga's legs, and she could hear more meowing inside.

"Come in already, you poor things," Walburga said compassionately. Her voice was soft and surprisingly deep for a woman. "No one should be outside at night in this cold." She leaned down to Peter and Paul, who were staring at her with big eyes. "My Nala has kittens. They're still very small and weak. Would you like to help me feed them?"

The children's shyness vanished instantly and they nodded enthusiastically.

Michael Deibler laughed. "Cats and children! We have too many of some and not enough of the other."

Walburga stepped aside and Magdalena and the rest followed Deibler into a tidy, warm living room that smelled of burnt honey and exotic spices. On the table stood a bowl with steaming spiced cakes and a jug of mulled wine. As at home in Schongau, the execution sword hung in the devotional corner next to the crucifix and a bunch of dried roses.

While the boys went looking for the kittens, Walburga turned to her guests with a smile. "Michael told me about your awful lodgings." She shook her head. "How could anyone think Au was an appropriate place for children and young women? But that's men for you."

"It's not that much safer here in the Anger Quarter, Burgi," Deibler grumbled. "Just now we were almost run over by a carriage on Sendlinger Bridge."

"My goodness!" Walburga exclaimed. "Aren't we even safe at night from those speeding rascals? Well, at least I can promise you there's no carriages driving through our house."

"Don't be so sure. You haven't seen my Paul on his hobby horse yet..." Magdalena grinned. Walburga's soft, pleasant voice truly seemed to be at odds with her tall body. Magdalena immediately liked the hangman's wife, who exuded a homey warmth, just like her house. "Thank you very much for having us."

"It's nothing." Walburga waved dismissively. "This house is much too big for us anyway. And I miss the sound of children in the house. I only have my cats." She gestured at Sophia, who had woken up and was crying. "May I?"

Magdalena hesitated. She seldom let anyone but herself soothe Sophia, not even Simon, but then she nodded and handed the whimpering bundle to Walburga. "You can try. If it's too much, just give her back to me."

"I think she's just hot in here." Walburga took Sophia out of her furs and the child immediately stopped crying. The hangman's wife sat Sophia on her lap and bounced and sang until the little girl squealed with pleasure and reached for Walburga's hair.

"I don't think she wants to go to bed yet." Walburga laughed while bouncing Sophia on her knees.

Magdalena smiled. "She's not usually like this with strangers. You would make a great nurse."

"All children love my wife," Michael Deibler explained with a shrug. "They run away screaming from me, but Walburga only has to wink at them and they cling to her apron strings."

"That's because you stink like a leaking barrel of beer," Walburga replied. Suddenly she paused and studied Sophia's kicking legs.

"Oh, I see the poor thing has a clubfoot," she said. "Have you tried to straighten it?"

"I try every day with bandages," Simon replied with a sigh. "But it just won't get better."

"You should try bear fat and arnica," Walburga suggested,

still rocking Sophia on her lap. "It softens the tendons. I just made a new batch yesterday. I can rub some on her foot now, if you like."

Magdalena gave her a grateful nod and Walburga took the happily giggling Sophia to the next room. Peter and Paul followed the hangman's wife together with the kittens and several of the older cats.

Magdalena saw through the open door that the room was filled with cupboards and chests. A table at the wall was laden with small bottles, jars, a mortar, and scales. Dried herbs hung from the ceiling, and Magdalena realized where the exotic smell she had noticed when entering the house stemmed from.

"It's my little kingdom!" Walburga called out to her from the chamber. "Michael does the killing, and I do the healing and look after my cats. I think that's a fair share of the workload."

Michael Deibler rolled his eyes with feigned annoyance. "She adopts every single stray cat she finds. I only wish she'd pet me like she pets her darlings!"

Magdalena laughed, then she pointed at Walburga's room. "We also have an apothecary chamber in Father's house in Schongau, but it's not nearly as big."

"Burgi truly is the best healer I know," Deibler said lovingly as he watched his wife rub the salve on Sophia's foot. "I always tell her she should write a book about all her medicines and treatments. Even our famous Jakob Kuisl could still learn a thing or two from her." He turned to his colleague. "Although we could probably use your skills in another field at the moment."

"What do you mean?" Kuisl asked. He was just about to light his pipe.

Deibler lowered his voice. "You heard the people down by the raft landing. Ghosts and living dead. Once again, common sense just goes down the drain." He snorted. "But it gets worse. Our guild meeting is a thorn in Munich's side. It was hard enough for me to get permission to hold it at Au, but now the superstitious citizens think that this many hangmen in one spot bring ill luck. They're starting to believe we dishonorable hangmen had something to do with those murders."

"What a load of rubbish," Georg said and reached for the jug of mulled wine. "We're executioners, not murderers."

"Well, three dead girls have been found in the last few days. Most likely, the cases are not connected at all, but I must admit they all look a little like executions." Deibler raised his hand and counted on his fingers: "Impaling, drowning, and walling in alive . . . and who's responsible for executions? We hangmen."

"The mummy is decades old, and the girl in the creek wasn't drowned but poisoned with deadly nightshade," Kuisl objected. "I can't see what that has to do with the Council of Twelve."

"Logic won't stop gossip," Deibler replied. He shrugged. "I have no idea who or what is behind all this. But that gruesome mummy was the final straw, especially since girls have been disappearing or turning up dead for years."

"More dead girls?" Magdalena stared at Deibler. A chill went down her spine despite the warmth of the tiled stove. "And you're only telling us now?"

Deibler thought. "Well, it's not entirely uncommon for young girls to find a tragic end in Munich. An unhappy love affair, an unwanted pregnancy, and they jump into the river. Others fall victim to drunks or other scoundrels. Most of the time they're maidservants from the country, looking for employment. People come here from all over Bavaria, especially to Au, Giesing, or Haidhausen, hoping to gain citizenship one day. Of course, this place also attracts all sorts of riffraff."

"But now people have had enough of such riffraff," Simon remarked. "They want a scapegoat. And if it's not a person, it must be a ghost. Or a dishonorable hangman, right?"

Deibler nodded glumly. They could hear the children's laughter from the next room, as if from a different world. With a serious expression, the Munich executioner turned to Jakob Kuisl.

"All I'm asking is that you keep your ears open, like you've done elsewhere before. Perhaps you'll hear something that might exonerate us hangmen before they dissolve our council—or worse."

"That's precisely what I did down at the raft landing earlier," Kuisl said. "And you didn't like it."

"That was before I knew which way the wind was blowing," Deibler sighed. "Maybe you're right after all, and all these murders are somehow connected."

"Do you really think so?" Magdalena asked her father, her curiosity aroused.

Kuisl didn't reply.

"Well, your father found a certain amulet in the mummy's mouth," Deibler replied in his stead. "Very similar to one the dead girl at Au was clutching. A Virgin Mary with an aureole."

"And what about the third girl?" Simon asked. "The impaled one? Did she have one, too?"

"It's too late to tell, unfortunately. She's already been buried." Deibler scratched his ragged beard. "I'm sure it's just a coincidence. Perhaps the girls tried to ward off evil with the amulets. But that doesn't change the fact that people might suspect the executioners."

"And what if it really was an executioner, at least for the last two murders?" Kuisl took a noisy drag on his pipe.

"How do you mean?" Deibler asked with surprise.

"Well, if Master Hans really did lie, as Georg says, we should probably look into it. Everyone knows how much he enjoys torturing people. Perhaps he happened to be in Munich at the time of the last murder, of the impaled girl. Weilheim isn't very far away. And hangman Fux reckons Master Hans met with a girl with reddish-blonde hair in Au the same day we found the body in the creek — that's enough to raise suspicion."

"Damn it, Jakob!" Deibler cursed. "I just praised your common sense, and now this. You only want to pin something on Hans because he nearly put your Barbara on the —" He broke off and glanced at Barbara, who sat in silence.

"I'm sorry," he said ruefully. "That was stupid of me."

"Already forgotten," Barbara replied softly. Her fists clenched. "I must admit, I almost wish Hans had something to do with the murders, just so Father could break his bones one by one."

No one said anything for a while, and the smoke from Kuisl's pipe floated to the ceiling in little clouds. Magdalena could tell her father was thinking. It was the same as always. If he was given a riddle, he didn't rest until he solved it.

"You're right," Kuisl eventually said to Deibler. "I can't stand Hans, and not only because he almost tortured my daughter. Things happened between us that . . . well, that shouldn't have. But revenge isn't a good counselor when you're trying to solve a murder. Hmm . . ." He chewed on his pipe. "Something else connects these murders, not just the fact that they look like executions and that two of the victims carried the same medallion. There's something else. I'll figure it out, but I need to learn more about the girls. At least about the two last ones."

"I'll see what I can do," Deibler replied and reached for the jug. "And now let's talk about pleasanter things." He smiled at Georg. "About your strapping son, for example, who is going to make a great executioner for Bamberg one day, so I hear."

"I'm afraid you'll have to excuse me." Georg rose abruptly. "I promised Uncle Bartholomäus I wouldn't be too late. And, as you know, a journeyman must obey his master in all things." He looked glum, as if the thought of his uncle had reminded him of something unpleasant.

"Then I better go, too." Jakob Kuisl got to his feet. Magdalena had a feeling that walking home with his son meant a lot to her father. Kuisl loved Georg more than anything, even if he never showed it.

"I think we'll cut through town this time. Quicker and safer." The Schongau hangman grinned. "Though I don't think anyone would be stupid enough to attempt cutting the throats of a hangman and his boy."

The two of them said their goodbyes and went out into the darkness.

Magdalena remembered too late that she still hadn't asked Georg about his future in Bamberg.

5

"IS IT THE HOUSE OF a real king, Father?"

Wide-eyed, Peter stared at the Munich Residenz, which stretched along the road to Schwabing, a small village north of the city. The palace of the Bavarian monarchs wasn't a castle as such, but more like a huge complex with its own church, numerous courtyards, stables, and a magnificent park at the north side. On the other side of the road stood the shell of an incomplete cathedral. Simon wondered how many people lived at the Residenz. More than just the electoral family, he guessed, probably even more than in Schongau.

"Um, not a king, Peter, but the Bavarian elector Ferdinand Maria," Simon told his son. "But that's very similar."

"And his wife invited *you*?" There was pride in Peter's voice, and Simon, too, felt a tingle of excitement running down his back. He had brushed out his red coat for the meeting and pinned a new feather to his hat. Peter was also wearing his best shirt, and Magdalena had combed and parted his hair and scrubbed his face with bone soap until it gleamed red.

"Well, you know, your father has a few interesting thoughts about illnesses that appear to be worth listening to," Simon replied with a little smile. "I've heard the electress is an intelligent, open-minded woman."

Father and son were standing outside a gate that was guarded by half a dozen soldiers with cuirasses, helmets, and halberds. The men stared straight ahead grimly, only stepping aside to let deliverymen pass through. For fear of being late, Simon had arrived half an hour early. In that time he had watched a merchant with a cart of wine barrels, two bakers with fresh bread, and the electoral pastry chef enter. Was all that food for the audience?

Simon listened to the bells of Old Peter announce the hour of noon. He ran his fingers through his hair one last time and adjusted his hat. "It's time for my audience."

He pulled out the permit the envoy had given him yesterday, took Peter by the hand, and strutted confidently toward the guards.

"Doctor Simon Fronwieser, I have an audience with Her Majesty, the highly esteemed electress," he introduced himself pompously.

The guard took a bored look at the letter and pointed at a wide set of stairs behind the gate. "Go upstairs and get in line," he grumbled.

Somewhat taken aback, Simon climbed the stairs with Peter. They came into a large hall decorated with halberds and other weapons. There were guards here, too, and seated on benches on the left and right were around twenty men and women who also appeared to be waiting for an audience with the electress. Simon could tell at once that the supplicants weren't noblemen but regular citizens of the lower classes. Like him, they had spruced up for the meeting with threadbare coats and polished shoes. Simon swallowed. He got the growing impression that his audience wasn't as unique as he had first thought.

Well, the main thing is that the electress listens when I tell her about my treatise. And who knows, maybe we'll even find a school for Peter.

Time passed awfully slowly, and it was so cold that Simon soon regretted not having put on a simple warm coat instead of his fashionable red one. The door at the other end of the hall opened at regular intervals, an order was shouted, and the next person was ushered into the room. Simon guessed it would be at least two hours until his audience. And the envoy had asked him to be punctual! At first, Peter sat quietly beside him, but after a while the boy grew restless.

"Can I take a look around, Father?" he asked after another quarter of an hour.

"Are you mad?" Simon hissed. "This is the electoral Residenz, not the Schongau Fair." But then he looked down the corridor to the left, which was decorated with grand paintings and stucco work. Several supplicants were standing down the hallway talking quietly. "You can go and look at those paintings," he suggested. "But not too far. I want you to be here when we're called in."

Peter nodded happily and disappeared down the corridor. Relieved, Simon took his treatise from his satchel, where he also carried the interesting book about microscoping he'd accidentally stolen the day before. By now he dared to hope that his theft would go unpunished, and he was no longer particularly worried about the counterfeit coins, either.

Simon started reading through his treatise for the hundredth time. He kept finding parts that could still be improved. When he spoke to the electress, he wanted to present his thesis in a well-formulated manner. He still wasn't entirely happy with one or two Latin sentences.

Sanitas bonum inaestimabile nec contemnendum . . .

Absorbed in his work, Simon completely forgot the time. He started with fright when his name was called out.

"Doctor Fronwieser!" one of the guards shouted. "Doctor Fronwieser to the electoral audience."

Simon packed up his papers and was about to rush over to the guards when he noticed that Peter still hadn't returned. He looked around nervously for his son but couldn't see him anywhere. Where could Peter have gone? Usually the boy could be relied upon. Had he gone outside to play?

"Doctor Simon Fronwieser!" the guard repeated with urgency. "To the audience, now!"

Simon searched the room one last time, then he gave up. Damn it! Peter would get an earful.

And I will, too . . .

Simon could only hope he'd get the chance to discuss his son's schooling with the electress. Magdalena would never forgive him if he didn't make use of this unique opportunity.

He walked over to the now rather grumpy-looking guard, who checked his permit again. Then the high double doors opened and Simon entered another hall, just as heavily decorated with paintings and Gobelin tapestries as the first. Finally Simon walked into the most magnificent room he'd ever seen.

The carvings covering the walls and ceiling were entirely gilded, and a row of paintings showed ancient rulers listening to their subjects in palatial throne rooms. There was no spot that wasn't decorated with a painting or a Gobelin. On a pedestal opposite Simon stood a gilded throne.

On the throne sat the electress.

Henriette Adelaide was in her mid-thirties. She had a thin face and brown hair, which had been curled at the sides and adorned with diamonds at the parting. Her beautifully tailored red dress was embroidered with gold thread, her eyes intelligent and friendly, albeit a little cool. Simon remembered what he had heard about Henriette: the electress came from Piedmont and had never felt fully at home in cold Bavaria, especially since she had once been intended for the future French king. She brought an entire army of Italian and French master builders to Munich, who had since been busy trying to turn the city into a second Rome.

Simon knelt down and lowered his head all the way to the floor. "Your Electoral Highness . . . I . . . it's such an honor . . . ," he croaked before his voice failed him.

If only my father could see this, he thought. *A barber's son at the electoral court.*

Henriette Adelaide raised an eyebrow at her graying court marshal, whereupon the man rapped his ceremonial staff on the floor and introduced Simon with a nasal voice. A smile darted across her face.

"Ah, so you're Doctor Fronwieser," she said with a laugh. She spoke with a strong Italian accent and her German was slow, as though she didn't use it much. "Madonna! You really are as short as they tell me."

"Er, I beg your pardon?" Simon gave her a confused look. Then he realized he still wore his hat. In his haste to take it off, it slipped from his fingers and fell onto the soft furs and rugs on the ground.

"Forgive me," he mumbled and picked it up.

"I've heard much about you, *piccolo dottore,*" the electress said with a smile. "They say you're as cunning as a fox."

Simon's confidence grew instantly. He straightened up. "Well, er, if that's what they say . . ."

"I've been told you and that Schongau hangman solved a gruesome series of murders in Oberammergau two years ago— that someone was crucified, just like our savior. *Brr!*" Henriette Adelaide shook herself with a pleasant shudder. "And you intercepted a conspiracy in Schongau that was aimed at Munich. *Bravo!*" She clapped her hands. "The stories about your deeds have turned many a boring dinner palatable to me."

Simon's jaw dropped with astonishment. This conversation was entirely different than expected. "May . . . may I ask how you . . . ," he managed eventually.

"Well, the honorable Count Sandizell is a regular guest at court. You know, the electoral representative at Schongau. While he doesn't spend a lot of time in your little town, he receives regular reports from your court clerk, Johann Lechner. The same Lechner told us that you had traveled to Munich." The electress winked at him. "You see, I know quite a lot about my flock."

Simon winced. None other than Johann Lechner, the Schongau court clerk, was behind this invitation. Lechner had also helped Simon win the position of town physician and had generally always been a positive force behind his career. And now he had even made him a topic of conversation at the court in Munich—although in a different way from what Simon had hoped and expected. It looked like the electress simply wanted to meet him, like an adorable pet one had heard much about.

Whatever the case, he knew he had to act fast. He'd never get another chance like this.

Simon nervously pulled out his treatise and almost dropped the loose pages. "I'm very pleased you've heard about my deeds," he began. "Please allow me to tell you about my latest—"

Henriette Adelaide waved dismissively. "I don't have that much time. I'm sure there are plenty more waiting outside. I asked you here because I'd like you to do me a small favor." She giggled. "I could hardly receive a dishonorable hangman, even though Count Sandizell says he's the smarter one of the two of you."

Simon turned red and couldn't say another word. The pages between his fingers suddenly felt awfully dry and brittle.

"This is what I'd like you to do," Henriette Adelaide continued. "Bring me back my dog."

Simon stared at the electress as if she'd spoken in a foreign tongue. Had she just said *dog*?

"I beg your pardon?" he finally said.

"Well, our beloved Arthur has been missing for almost a week. One of my ladies-in-waiting was taking him for a walk in the gardens when it appears Arthur spotted a cat and ran off. He's been missing ever since. I hope to God nothing happened to him. Maybe he's just hiding somewhere or someone else took him in." Henriette sighed and gave Simon a pleading look. "Arthur is the best friend of my son, Max Emanuel. The boy is beside himself. Return Arthur to us and you'll be royally rewarded. Show me that you're as clever as they say, Doctor Fronwieser."

It took a while before Simon managed to speak. "Well . . . of course, Your Highness," he mumbled. "Does he have any . . . er . . . distinctive features? That would make the search much easier."

"Arthur is a cute little spaniel, brown with white spots. When he barks, he sounds almost like a crying child. He especially likes to bark when the electoral family plays music."

"Thank you for the clues. The last one in particular will surely prove helpful."

"Oh, and he has a white blaze on his face," the electress added. "From the forehead to his nose. That will help you recognize him."

Simon stood up. Exhausted as if from a long walk, he packed his treatise back in his old leather satchel and bowed one last time while a nasty voice jeered in his head.

Doctor Simon Fronwieser. Explorer of the stinking gutters of Munich. Discoverer of the electoral family's lapdog.

"You must send me word as soon as you know anything," the electress ordered. "I expect to hear back from you in three days' time. Is that clear?"

"Of . . . of course! It will be my honor."

With his head lowered, he backed out of the audience room. Now he was glad his son hadn't witnessed this meeting.

His arms crossed at his back, Peter stood in front of the stucco painting of a grim-looking obese man with a fur collar and a gold chain, probably some king or duke. To the left and right of the painting were more portraits of equally glum-looking men.

Peter thought he saw a certain resemblance among the men.

He was a passionate and talented painter himself, but he usually only had charcoal and stained paper. These paintings glowed in the most amazing colors and had been painted directly onto the walls — a technique Peter knew from the churches in and around Schongau and admired greatly. It must have been very expensive, Peter thought. He was lucky if his father gave him a new charcoal crayon for his saint's day. If he was unlucky, his classmates broke it or used it to draw rude pictures in his notebook.

Peter sighed softly and walked among the paintings, down the corridor, moving farther and farther away from the hall where his father was waiting. This world was so different from the world he knew in Schongau. His tongue felt for the gap in his teeth the accursed Berchtholdt children had given him. He was glad to be away from the Schongau Latin School for a while. The teasing and the occasional beating were harder on him than he liked to admit in front of his parents, although he generally liked going to school. Peter soaked up the little knowledge old Weininger could give him like a sponge. Latin, arithmetic, learning Bible passages by heart — he found all those things much easier than his classmates did.

And they reminded him almost daily that he was different.

Sometimes Peter envied his younger brother, Paul, who didn't put up with anything and lashed out without warning sooner than becoming a victim himself. And Peter also sensed that his grandfather sometimes preferred his brother to him, although Peter loved his grandfather very much and admired his sharp mind and — most of all — his library, which he regularly combed for new books. But Peter knew already that he didn't want to become a hangman. He wanted to be a doctor like his father. Or a painter, but he was afraid he wouldn't be able to earn money that way. He'd heard his parents say that there might be a better school here in Munich for him. How he longed for like-minded friends who loved to learn as much and did it as quickly as he did. Maybe his father could speak with that electress? She obviously thought he was a knowledgeable man.

Deep in thought, Peter had continued down the hallway until he reached the end and stood outside another door. He was all alone, everyone else was farther up the corridor. Peter looked at the last painting, a framed picture of a young man with long black curls and a fashionably pointed beard.

He was about to turn around and head back when the man in the painting talked to him.

"Booow your head when you speak with the eleeectooor!"

Peter jumped. He must be dreaming — pictures couldn't talk. But now the man even seemed to lean forward. And he sniggered.

"Hey, silly! Do you have straw in your head?"

Peter paused. For a grown man, the voice sounded very high-pitched, almost like a . . .

child?

Now Peter saw that the man in the painting hadn't leaned forward, he had merely come a little closer, together with the entire wall. The frame wasn't a real frame, it was just painted onto a door without a doorknob, which had just opened a crack.

Peter leaned forward and knocked cautiously against the thin wood. Until then, the door had been well concealed in the wall, but now the mischievous face of a roughly ten-year-old boy appeared in the crack. He was very pale and had long dark-brown hair, almost like the man in the painting. He was still giggling.

"You really thought I was the ghost of the elector, didn't you?" he burst out. "Admit it!"

"Even if I did," Peter said, shrugging, "now I see that the ghost is just a little squirt."

"Squirt yourself." The boy stuck out his tongue. "Now don't be like that. I was just bored. I'm supposed to be at my harp lesson with Herr Kerll, but I skipped. And now I'm hiding from Maria."

"Who's Maria?" Peter asked.

The boy rolled his eyes. "Maria is my older sister. If she finds me, she'll tell on me. Big sisters are worse than the Plague."

Peter smiled. "I've got a little brother. He's not always easy, either."

Now the boy stepped out from behind the painting. He wore baggy silken trousers, a white shirt, and a blue vest. His feet were in long, pointed shoes with silver broaches. "What are you doing here, anyway?" he asked Peter. "Are you a kitchenhand or something?"

Peter looked down at himself. Until a moment ago, he had considered himself rather well dressed, but in the presence of such an elegantly dressed boy he suddenly felt awfully poor and scabby.

"I'm here with my father," he replied hesitantly. "He has an audience with the electress."

"Oh, my mother." The boy waved dismissively. "That can take ages."

Peter gaped at the boy with astonishment. "You . . . you're the son of the electress?" he stammered. "Then you must be a . . ."

"A prince, I know," the boy replied in a bored tone. "But you can call me Max. My real name is Maximilian Emanuel, but that sounds as fancy as my mother's curls." He frowned. "I can tell you one thing: when my mother gives an audience, it can take hours, days even. And it's terribly boring."

Peter sighed. "I know. That's why I went for a walk. I was sick of waiting."

"I'll tell you what we'll do." Max gave another mischievous grin, and now he wasn't looking like a prince at all but just like a normal boy. "I'll show you around the Residenz. What do you say? I know a few secret passages that'll get us past the guards."

"But what about my father?" Peter said. "He'll worry."

"Trust me, he'll be waiting till late afternoon. Do you want to sit with him and twiddle your thumbs all that time? Now come!" Max clapped his hands impatiently. Peter sensed his new friend wasn't used to asking for things. "Go on, do me a favor. Or do I have to command you? Apart from my sister there are no other children my age in the whole Residenz. And my dog, Arthur, has gone missing, too — my only playmate." Max looked at Peter with a mix of pleading and impatience. "Please! I'm dying of boredom."

"All right," Peter said, intrigued by the prospect of roaming through secret passages with this strange prince. And he really didn't feel like sitting in that cold hall with his father any longer. "But only one hour, then I have to go back." He followed Max through the crack in the door and came into a narrow, bare corridor that was only illuminated by a single candle in a holder on the wall.

"What's your name, anyway?" Max asked.

"I'm Peter Fronwieser," Peter replied. "The son of the Schongau town physician."

"Schongau?" Max scratched his nose. "Is that somewhere near Paris or Turin? Never mind." He grabbed the candle and led the way. "I'll show you my favorite places."

They followed the dark corridor until they reached a narrow spiral staircase. The two boys climbed down the stairs and walked along several other corridors. From time to time, Peter thought he could hear voices on the other side of the walls.

"Only the electoral family and a few trusted insiders know about these passages," Max whispered as they continued on. "I think they're very old. I'm not supposed to be here — if Mother finds out, I'll get a walloping."

"You're a prince and they hit you?" Peter asked, amazed.

"Oh yes, you have no idea." Max gave him a pained look. "But only the servants. My parents wouldn't lift a finger. My mother even gave Herr Kerll, my music teacher, permission to beat me. He uses an extra-long cane; it hurts like hell. *Sh!*" Suddenly he held his finger to his lips. Peter froze and heard marching footsteps just on the other side of the wall.

"The Hartschiers," Max whispered. "My mother's personal guards. If they hear us, we're done for!"

The sound of the steps faded and Max walked to a small hidden door that Peter only noticed now. The prince peered through a tiny hole and nodded with relief. "The coast is clear. Now I'll show you the Hall of Antiquities."

"The hall of what?" Peter asked, but Max had already slipped through the door.

Peter followed him and found himself in the biggest room he'd ever seen. The hall was longer than a man could throw a stone and nearly as high as a church. On a gallery at the opposite end stood a table set with silver dinnerware and crystal glasses, and a fire was burning in a large open fireplace. But the most astonishing things in the room were the countless busts of proud-looking men along the walls. Some of them wore a laurel wreath.

"I don't know who all those old fellows are," Max said with a shrug.

"Hmm. I think they're Roman emperors," Peter replied and studied one of the busts more closely. "There are Latin numbers and names. Imperator Cäsar, Divi Filius Augustus, that means—"

"You're worse than Herr Kerll," Max interrupted him, giggling. "Stop the translating. I'll show you what this place is great for." He took off his pointed shoes and slid across the polished marble floor in socks. Peter only hesitated for a moment before following the prince's lead, and before long, he was whooping with joy. This was even better than ice skating on the hangman's pond! For a long while the two boys slid across the hall floor, laughing and cheering. Then Max suddenly paused.

"Changing of the guard," he said quietly. "The Hartschiers will be coming through here again shortly. Come, let's go down to the Grottenhof yard. It's fantastic for playing hide and seek."

They slipped their shoes back on and scurried out of the room just as they heard footsteps approaching. Max ran ahead and led Peter silently through several rooms until the ceiling abruptly opened up and they were standing in a large courtyard planted with hedges and lined by shady arcades on three sides. After a few moments, Peter noticed artificial grottos decorated with shimmering minerals and seashells underneath the arcades. In the middle of the courtyard stood a gurgling fountain with a statue of a man wearing a winged helmet. He was triumphantly holding up the head of a woman with snakes for hair, and her beheaded torso lay at his feet.

"That's Perseus, a Greek hero," Max explained when he saw Peter's look of amazement. "He had to fight against Medusa — a nasty woman like my sister. If you looked into her eyes, you'd turn to stone."

"And what did Perseus do?" Peter asked curiously.

"Ha! He looked into a mirror. That way, her evil look didn't work and he could chop her head off. And, as you can see, he also has a cap of invisibility and winged sandals, which he needs for other adventures. It's a good story. My Greek teacher, Herr Battani, told me; he's much nicer than that stupid Kerll."

"We only ever learn about the Bible at my school," Peter replied sadly. Once again, he thought how much bigger the world was than Weininger's syllabus. But perhaps he'd soon learn more exciting things at his new school in Munich.

"One day I'll be a hero just like Perseus," Max said with determination. "A great general with sword and helmet. All of Europe shall tremble before me."

His expression left no doubt in Peter's mind that he was very serious. But then Max suddenly turned away and ran off. "Come on, let's play hide and seek!" he called out, laughing. "Count to ten!"

The prince ran into the yard and soon disappeared behind the tall hedges. Peter counted to ten, then followed him. The hedges were man-high and planted in a star-shaped pattern, and Peter had soon lost his bearings. He heard Max snigger from time to time but couldn't see him anywhere. He walked to the arcades at the far end, where he found a larger grotto hall with a fountain.

"I'm here!" Max called out.

The shout had definitely come from the hedges. Peter ran back into the yard, his heart beating faster with pleasure and excitement. This was so different from the brawls in the smelly lanes of Schongau. He felt the knowledge of every painting, bust, and statue speak to him. If only he could stay forever.

Max gave another shout, but this time it sounded like a cry of pain. Peter turned around the corner — and almost collided with a man. He was older, with a powdered wig and a powdered face. With his right hand he was holding Max by the collar, and the boy was squirming like a fish on dry land.

"Oh, I see Your Princely Highness found a playmate," the man said with disgust in his voice. "Evidently someone from the country, judging by the poor clothing and the smell." He grabbed Peter with his free hand and shook him like a puppy until his shirt ripped at the collar. "What are you doing here, you little rascal? Speak up!"

"Let him go, Monsieur Kerll, I command you," Max said. "He's my friend."

"Well, your mother won't be happy at all when she hears that you not only skipped my music class but also let this riffraff into the Residenz." Herr Kerll smiled maliciously. "Thankfully, your sister was able to tell me where you to like play."

"The snake," Max said. "She'll rue the day!"

"I think it's your turn to rue. I'm under strict orders from your mother to be very stern with you. And as for you, lad." The music teacher shook Peter by the collar again. "What's your name? Where do you come from?"

"My name is Peter Fronwieser," Peter gasped. "My father has an audience with the electress."

"And so you think you can just wander off and fill your pockets, you little thief? I will hand you over to the guards."

"I didn't steal anything. I — ouch!" Peter cried out when Kerll pulled his ear.

"Let him go, now!" Max shouted. "Or I'll tell my mother that you're mocking her harp playing behind her back. I heard you with my own ears."

Kerll winced and abruptly let go of Peter.

"The audience is long over," Kerll hissed into Peter's ear so he could smell the man's sickly-sweet perfume. "I hope your father will give you a good thrashing for your misconduct. And now off with you."

Dragging the two boys behind him, Kerll walked through a door in the arcades that led to an open walkway. Peter soon realized it was the same walkway he and his father had used to enter the Residenz.

"You must come back," Max whispered to Peter as they walked toward the gate to the road. "I will command my mother."

Peter looked at him with astonishment. "You command the electress?"

Max grinned. "Believe me, I'm the only one in the world who can."

Then they arrived at the gate. The guards opened it and Kerll booted Peter out onto the road.

"And don't ever show your face around here again, you thief!" Kerll shouted after him.

When the gate closed, Peter saw Max giving him one last wave goodbye.

Then his path into this wonderful new world was barred again.

• • •

Back and forth, Simon walked outside the walls of the Residenz, torn between concern for his son and the humiliation he had just experienced. He had entered this audience as Doctor Fronwieser and had come out as the town dogcatcher. Could one sink any lower? And now Peter had disappeared, too.

After Simon had been dismissed by the electress, he'd searched for his son in the great hall and the neighboring rooms and hallways. But there was no sign of Peter anywhere, and none of the guards had seen a nine-year-old boy either. In the end, they had made it very clear to him that it was time to leave the Residenz. Ever since, he'd been combing the streets and alleyways near the palace, unsure of what to do. Had Peter gone home because he was bored? The boy knew what this audience could have meant for him. Had something happened to him? But the electoral Residenz was possibly the safest place in Bavaria.

Despite his fear for Peter, the hopelessness of his situation kept returning to his thoughts. He had to find the electress's dog. How on earth was he supposed to do that? He didn't know anyone in Munich and had no idea whom to ask. In Schongau, it was the knacker's job to catch stray dogs and put them down if no one claimed them. But how did it work in Munich? He supposed he could ask Michael Deibler. That was a start, at least. And what was the worst that could happen if he didn't find the bloody dog? Surely the electress wouldn't lock him up just for that.

Or would she?

He was walking up Schwabinger Street toward the main gate when he saw a small boy with puffy eyes and a torn shirt walking toward him.

"Peter!" Simon called out. He was so relieved to see his son that he completely forgot to be angry with him. "Where have you been?" he asked and took the boy in his arms. "I've been so worried!"

"I . . . I was playing with the prince," Peter sobbed. "But then

Herr Kerll came and threw me out. And . . . and then I was looking for you."

"What is this nonsense you talk?" Now Simon became annoyed after all. "You ran away and now you're making up excuses."

"But it's the truth. I was playing with the prince. His name is Max and he wants to see me again."

"I don't want to hear another word of your lies. Let's see what your mother says when she hears you spoiled your chance of attending school in Munich." Simon grabbed Peter and dragged him along. For a while Peter protested, but then he gave up. Sulking, he followed his father across the busy market square and on toward the Anger Quarter.

Simon only slowed down when a large crowd of people appeared in front of them. They were gathered at a bay of one of the streams flowing through the city. A row of posts and chains indicated that this was a watering place for cattle and horses, called Rossschwemme. Slippery, icy steps led into the water and a rickety wooden bridge spanned the partially frozen stream. Some people in the crowd shouted excitedly, others prayed.

"I'm telling you, the devil is on the loose in Munich!" one man was shouting. "He plucks the pretty girls like ripe cherries."

"Rubbish! It's one of those accursed hangmen!" another called out, a broad-shouldered beer driver. "Sepp from Giesing told me they're holding a meeting in Au. Damned dishonorable riffraff." He pointed at the ground below him, where Simon could now make out a longish bundle that apparently had just been pulled out of the water. "Just look at it. Drowned in a sack like a cat. That's what the murderer did with a girl at Au, too, and he impaled a third one. Only hangmen do that."

"One executioner is bad enough, but a dozen is an evil number," one man called out, leading his skinny cow to the water. "You'll see, there will be more dead girls."

Simon felt his throat tighten, and his personal worries suddenly seemed far away. Holding Peter's hand, he made his way through the crowd until he stood right by the stream. Now he was able to take a closer look at the bundle.

It was a wet sack, roughly as long as a person and bound at the top with a rope. Inside, he could make out the outline of a human body. The person inside must have thrashed about in desperation, because one foot stuck out through the torn fabric.

It was a dainty foot, clean, and with carefully trimmed toenails.

With a sick feeling in his stomach, Simon turned away, his anger at Peter forgotten. "Let's go find Deibler and Grandfather," he said to his son. "I'm afraid the Council of Twelve really is in deep trouble now."

"So this is where you're hiding. I should have known."

Panting, Michael Deibler sat down heavily on the bench beside Kuisl. The Schongau hangman was sitting in front of a mug of beer at the Radl Inn, his long pipe in his mouth, the smoke enveloping him like a stinking cloud.

"I ran the whole way from my house," Deibler groaned, waving at the innkeeper to bring him a beer. "We have much to talk about."

"If it's about that damned Widmann, I'll shut up next time, I promise," Kuisl replied morosely. "He's not worth getting upset about."

The Council of Twelve had been in session all morning, mainly discussing the payment system for executioners. The council would have liked to standardize the fees for individual jobs like whipping, thumbscrewing, hanging, and burning throughout all of Bavaria, but Johann Widmann was opposed. He received the highest wages of all the hangmen. Jakob Kuisl had met Widmann's objections with some angry remarks.

"I have no idea why I ever considered giving my Barbara to that arrogant snot," Kuisl grumbled and took a long sip from his beer. "Hörmann's drunken son is out of the question, which only leaves Conrad Näher from Kaufbeuren. He puts it on a little thick for my liking. It rubs me the wrong way."

"Forget about your stupid wedding plans," Deibler scolded. "We have more important things to talk about. I've just heard they found another dead girl up by the Rossschwemme. The murderer knocked her over the head and put her in a sack. It probably happened last night, but the sack must have caught under the bridge and was only found this afternoon. The poor thing had been drowned like a kitten."

"Damn!" Kuisl put down his mug and gave Deibler his undivided attention. "From which poor suburb was this one? Au? Giesing? Haidhausen?"

"No, none of those dumps." Deibler shook his head. "That's what makes the case so interesting. The victim is Theresa Wilprecht, the young wife of a wealthy Munich patrician. Now the city council is going to take an interest in these murders as well."

"Hmm. *These* murders, you say?" Kuisl took a long drag of his pipe. "So you believe this murder is connected to the others? I thought you weren't sure."

Deibler pounded the table. "It doesn't matter what I believe. It's what the people believe. And what's worse, they think we hangmen have something to do with it." He counted on his fingers. "Impaling, drowning, walling in alive, and now drowning in a sack. Every single one is a method of execution that we hangmen use. And—"

Deibler paused when the innkeeper brought his beer. When the man had walked away again, he whispered: "You have no idea what's going on in town. Everyone's talking. And everyone suddenly remembers another strange murder from years ago. If we're not careful, they'll pin every unsolved case since Cain and Abel on us hangmen." He leaned forward. "You must do something, Jakob. They say you're so clever, now prove it."

When Kuisl didn't reply, Deibler continued: "You never said

anything, but I know it always bothered you that you hadn't been voted onto the council all those years. Now you can finally show the smug bastards, especially Widmann. Isn't that something?"

Kuisl still said nothing, the smoke from his pipe slowly rising to the ceiling. After a while he finally said: "If I must snoop around, I first need to learn more about the murder victims. You said you'd keep an ear out."

Deibler nodded with relief. "And I have. I spoke with Captain Loibl earlier. Everything he knew about the girl at Au he knew from us, but he was able to tell me more about the impaled girl. She wore a plain gray dress, typical for weavers. She carried nothing but a few pennies and a small bag with herbs. It wasn't a robbery, anyhow."

Kuisl listened up. "A bag with herbs? What herbs?"

"No idea. Perhaps something to smoke out the house — a common thing for women to do in winter. But there's something else." Deibler lowered his voice. "They kept her body in the morgue for several days in the hope of finding out who she was. One day a young girl turned up, pale, with straggly blonde hair. She reckoned the dead girl's name was Elfriede Tanninger and she used to work at the Au silk manufactory. When Loibl asked more questions, she took off."

"Silk manufactory at Au?" Kuisl frowned. "Are you joking?"

Michael Deibler laughed. "No, it's true. Our elector decided a few years ago that Bavaria ought to produce its own silk. Since then, they've bred silkworms in the electoral gardens and employ a bunch of poor girls to weave the silk at manufactories at Anger Square and Au." Deibler took a sip of his beer and wiped the foam from his beard. "No idea if the fabric is any good, but at least it gets the girls off the streets. From time to time, they send out henchmen to catch more — even children — and force them to work there. If they refuse, they get chased out of town."

"Back in the old days, women and sometimes whole families

used to toil at their own looms to earn their daily bread," Kuisl growled. "Now they get dozens to do the job and call it a manufactory—but someone else pockets the cash."

"No point pissing and moaning about it." Deibler grinned. "That's just what it's like nowadays, Jakob. We're too old to understand."

"It's idiotic, that's what it is," Kuisl said. He took another drag at his pipe before continuing. "By the way, Master Hans really did meet up with a girl at Au. And guess what? She wasn't yet eighteen, covered in freckles, with strawberry-blonde hair, just like our dead girl. Georg was right."

Deibler stared at him. "How on earth do you—"

"Do you think I just sit on my backside and drink beer until our meeting finally continues?" Kuisl cut him off. "I went and spoke to a few people in Au. You can't miss Hans, with his white hair and red eyes, after all."

"You just have it in for him because—"

"For Christ's sake, he spoke with the murder victim. Accept it, Michael. And he lied to us. If you're asking me to investigate those murders, then let me bloody well do it my way. You can't pick and choose your murderer."

Deibler shrugged. "This morning Hans was sitting at the table with us, and I saw him here last night as well. So he could hardly have murdered the patrician's wife."

"You saw him all night? You shared his bed, then, did you? No, you didn't. So—"

Kuisl stopped abruptly when the tavern door opened and a group of hangmen came in, Master Hans among them. The others walked at a distance from him, as if he carried a bad smell.

"Speak of the devil . . . ," Kuisl murmured.

When Hans spotted the Schongau hangman, he walked over to their table and bowed with a mocking smile.

"My dear friend Jakob," he said softly and brushed a strand of white hair from his face. "In all the excitement, I haven't had a chance to ask about your younger daughter. She left rather hastily yesterday."

"Don't you worry about Barbara," Kuisl replied, his fingers tightening around his mug. "She's a strong girl."

"Is that so," Master Hans nodded. "I'm glad to hear it. I've always liked her, you know? So, if you can't find a husband for her after yesterday's performance . . ." He bent down to Kuisl and winked with one of his red eyes. "There's always room for her at my house in Weilheim. I love it when women are as stroppy as young horses. Then I can break them in." Laughing, he patted Kuisl on the back and walked away.

Hans sat down at a table of his own and smiled smugly to himself, looking awfully pleased about something. Kuisl shuddered. He just couldn't read Master Hans.

"All right, I'll admit he isn't the most pleasant fellow around," Deibler said after a while, giving Hans a furtive glance. "But he does get the fastest and best confession. That is why he's on the Council of Twelve, even though I never voted for him. He's repulsive and he enjoys torturing prisoners. But a serial killer of girls? Jakob, I think you're getting carried away."

"Then we have nothing more to say to each other." Kuisl got to his feet, but Deibler pulled him back down.

"Listen, Jakob, I didn't mean to offend you," he said quietly, making sure the other hangmen couldn't hear him. "I only want you to investigate without prejudice. I need you! Or else this is going to be the last meeting of executioners for a long time, provided they don't massacre one of us first. So please"—he gave Kuisl a pleading look—"find out who's behind all this."

Kuisl hesitated. He looked over to Master Hans, who was whistling a silent song. Finally, he nodded.

"All right. I'll start at this damned silk manufactory. Just so you don't think I'm only after Hans." The hangman reached for his mug and took another long drink. "But first, let's finish our beer." Jakob Kuisl wiped the foam from his beard. "Because if

there's one thing to be said about you Munich folks—you may
be a bunch of crazy, stuck-up fools, but you sure know how to
brew beer."

Spellbound by the hustle and bustle of the big city, Barbara and
Georg drifted through the busy lanes of Munich.

Even though many shops were still closed following Candlemas, the streets were buzzing. Snorting oxen pulled carts toward
Graggenau Quarter, where the salt was stored at a large square.
Dignified Jesuits walked toward Saint Michael College in their
black robes, accompanied by a group of street children hoping
for a handout. It wasn't long before the children were chased off
by the city guards. Barbara thought Munich was even tougher on
beggars than other towns were. Any riffraff were locked out, left
to fend for themselves in the suburbs. Only a small number of
poor people were granted access to the city every morning as day
laborers. Barbara shuddered. Would she also be with the riffraff
soon? Begging with her babe in arms until the guards chased her
away?

The siblings had been strolling through town for nearly two
hours, stopping for a while at a stall with mulled wine and
doughnuts, admiring the wares of a cloth merchant in wealthy
Neuhauser Street, but most of all, they talked. The twins had
much to catch up on, not having seen each other in over two
years. In Schongau, as children, they were inseparable, sometimes even dreaming the same dreams. But the last few years had
turned Georg into a strong young man and Barbara into a
woman with her own mind. Conversation didn't flow as freely as
it used to. They had barely mentioned Barbara's pregnancy since
their first discussion. It seemed they were both afraid the subject
would only cause strife.

Just that morning, Magdalena had tried to talk to Barbara
again. Over and over she had pointed out the serious conse-

quences of not finding a husband in Munich. But of the three candidates her father had chosen, one was a useless drunkard, another an arrogant snot, and the third was her father's age. It was hopeless! Was there no other way?

And something else tormented Barbara: try as she might, she couldn't love the thing growing inside her. It was as if she harbored some foreign object that ate her flesh from within, consuming her bit by bit.

So how could I ever be a good mother?

Georg sensed that something was bothering his sister, and he squeezed her hand. "Don't worry," he tried to soothe her with an encouraging smile. "We'll find a solution."

Barbara gave a desperate laugh. Typical men, always looking for practical solutions, even in matters of the heart. As if the heart was one of those newfangled ticking clocks that could simply be repaired.

"You mean we'll find a husband for me," she said bitterly. She kicked at an icy pile of horse dung, sending it flying into one of the many streams running through the city. "Why can't I look after myself? Like Martha, the midwife in Schongau?"

"Stechlin is an old spinster. And she only helps other women give birth, she never had children of her own." Georg gave her a stern look. "Barbara, what's happened is bad enough, but you can still avoid the worst. Please, be reasonable, for your family's sake."

"Yes, it's so easy for you menfolk," Barbara said. "Plant a child in our bellies and then disappear. Leave us women alone to deal with our sorrow."

"The fellow who did this to you is a bastard," Georg replied. "No question. But maybe you . . ." He searched for the right words. "Encouraged him a little? I know you, Barbara. You like to dance, to flirt with the lads . . . The woman leads the man into temptation, so it says in the Bible."

"So now it's my fault?" Barbara flared up. Her face turned red with anger. "It still takes two to make a child. And I was so careful to . . ." She was shaken by violent sobs, and Georg held her tight.

"Whatever happens," he said gently, "we Kuisls stick together. You'll see, something good might come of all this yet. If this hadn't happened, you might have ended up a bitter, unmarried spinster like old Stechlin."

"And yet she has her own income and no man telling her what to do." Barbara sniffed and wiped the tears from her face. "Not many women are as fortunate as she is."

Georg smiled. "And what would you do for a living? Become an executioner? Well, if your sword arm is as fast as your mouth, you might just find a position. But to be honest, I've never heard of a hang*woman*." Suddenly his face turned serious. "And not even a hang*man* can always rely on his position."

Barbara stopped dead in her tracks and looked at her brother. "What is it, Georg?" she asked, glad to be changing the subject. "I could tell yesterday that something's up. Don't you want to at least tell your twin sister?" She smiled sadly. "You know my secret too, after all."

Georg wrestled with himself for a few moments, then he sighed. "To hell with it! Why shouldn't you know? The truth is . . . I can't stay in Bamberg."

"Whyever not?" Barbara frowned. "Uncle Bartholomäus always said you'd take over for him."

"But he hadn't reckoned with the city. The aldermen want someone else as his successor." Georg clenched his fists. "Widmann from Nuremberg must have paid a lot of money to get the post for his nephew. Uncle Bartholomäus had hoped to change Widmann's mind at the guild meeting." He gave a tired laugh. "But after what happened yesterday, Widmann won't be doing the Kuisls any favors."

"Oh God, Georg, I'm so sorry!" Barbara exclaimed. "I had no idea—"

"It's all right. Widmann is a bastard. He would never have

changed his mind because he hates Father." Georg took Barbara's hand again. "So you see, I don't know what the future holds for me, either."

"But you can always come back to Schongau. Father would be so pleased."

"That's the problem. I don't want to go back, not after all these years. I'd always be under the old man's thumb." Georg shook his head angrily. "Even last night, when we walked back to Au from Deibler's, he kept pushing for me to come home. If he knew there was no future for me in Bamberg, he'd move heaven and earth to get me back. But I don't want to come back."

"Just like I don't want to marry," Barbara replied. "So stop telling me what to do."

Meanwhile, they had walked down Sendlinger Street and arrived at the executioner's house by the city wall. Paul was playing with a bunch of street children with a hoop and a whip. It looked like he'd already found new friends in the Anger Quarter. When he spotted Barbara and Georg, he came running toward them.

"Uncle Georg, Uncle Georg, did you bring me something sweet?" he shouted. "You promised!"

"I knew I forgot something." Georg slapped his palm against his forehead. "Or did I . . . ?" Grinning, he pulled from inside his coat two candied apples, which Paul snatched from his hand with a cheer.

"The second one is for your brother, understood?" Georg said. "Where is he, anyway?"

"Peter came back from the Residenz with Father earlier," Paul replied between mouthfuls. "He said he played with a prince. We laughed at him. Now he's inside reading, as usual."

"And your father?" Barbara asked.

"He went to Au to find Grandpa right away. He was very excited. Apparently, there was another dead girl." Paul giggled. "They drowned her like a kitten in a sack."

"Jesus, when will it stop?" Georg swore and shook his head. "And knowing our old man, he'll already have stuck his nose in."

"And my Michael too, unfortunately. It looks like all our men have gone insane." Walburga was walking toward them from the garden, carrying Sophia on her arm. The little girl giggled happily when she recognized Barbara and held out her little arms. Walburga gave Sophia a loving look. "The world is bad, my darling. You'll find out soon enough." She turned to Barbara and Georg with an encouraging nod. "I bandaged her foot with arnica and lavender to soften the muscles. The poor girl will always have a clubfoot, but we can help make sure she won't limp too badly later on."

Barbara smiled. She liked Walburga's practical manner. And the hangman's tall wife seemed to know just as much about herbs as her own father did. Often it was the wives of executioners who looked after the apothecary's pantry at home and made sure patients were given the right medicine, but they also made talismans and love potions.

"I sent your sister on a walk," Walburga explained. "I asked her to get me a few pills at the pharmacy. But most of all, I wanted to take her mind off things for a while. There are some excellent tailors in the Graggenau Quarter, and looking is free. The fabrics are truly exquisite. Speaking of fabrics . . ." She winked at Barbara. "There is a visitor in the garden who appears to have a gift for you."

"A gift for me?" Barbara frowned. "Who would give me anything?"

"See for yourself." Walburga gestured toward the back of the garden. "He wouldn't come in. Said he wanted to wait for you outside."

Together with Georg, Barbara walked around the executioner's house and there, on a bench beneath a frozen rosebush, sat Conrad Näher, the Kaufbeuren executioner. His hair was freshly combed, and he was wearing a shirt as white as snow underneath a coat with a fur collar. His face was red from the cold. When he saw Barbara and Georg, he rose with a little bow and handed Barbara a small parcel.

"My dearest Barbara, may I offer you this little present as a token of my appreciation?" he said in a stilted tone. "You would make an old man very happy."

"Looks like Näher is serious," Georg whispered to his sister. "Give the man a chance. He's the most acceptable of Father's candidates."

Barbara sighed. "Looks like I don't have much of a choice," she replied quietly. She took the present, which was wrapped in leather. She opened it and found blue fabric shimmering at her. Barbara winced.

"That's . . . ," she began.

"Real silk," Näher finished for her. "Dyed with indigo from western India. You could sew a scarf from it." He grinned. "Of course, I realize that we dishonorable hangmen and our families aren't permitted to wear such things, but it still feels nice underneath a coat. And since the elector forbade the import of silk from abroad, a piece like that is almost as precious as silver."

Speechless, Barbara ran her hand over the fabric, which was as soft as Sophia's skin. She had never owned anything this beautiful. "Tha . . . thanks," she said after a while.

"I hoped we might take a walk together," Conrad Näher suggested. "To get to know each other. Or would you rather go to a tavern? I know a cozy place where the innkeeper doesn't look twice when a man like me turns up with a younger lady."

"Lady? No one's ever called me that before!" Suddenly, Barbara had to laugh. She looked at Näher, standing in front of her expectantly. He was at least thirty years older than she was, his belly bulging over his belt, his hair graying. But he was well groomed, had manners, and clearly knew how to make a woman happy.

"Come on, have a heart," Georg whispered to her. "Before the poor fellow dies pining for you."

Barbara stroked the soft fabric. Well, what did she have to lose? Getting to know him a little couldn't hurt.

"All right," she said eventually. "Let's go to your tavern. I could do with a mulled wine." She pointed at Näher's nose, red from the cold. "And you, too, before your sniffer freezes off."

She linked arms with Näher. His coat was warm, he smelled pleasant.

What do I have to lose? she thought again.

Then they walked out into the streets.

It was only a short walk from the Radl Inn to the Au silk manufactory, and Kuisl had been given directions by Michael Deibler. Now he was standing outside the massive three-storied building he had noticed when they first arrived.

The hangman still couldn't believe there was a manufactory of precious silk here in dirty Au, of all places. Kuisl knew that the valuable fabric was made from threads secreted by some kind of caterpillar, originally in China, later in Venice and elsewhere on the other side of the Alps. But in Bavaria? And on a large scale, with God knows how many weavers and a building almost as big as a cathedral?

Well, at the end of the day it was no skin off his nose whether they were producing silk, shoes, or hangmen's nooses in this manufactory—he was here to find out more about the impaled girl, Elfriede Tanninger.

Deibler was right, it had been bothering him that he hadn't been voted onto the Council of Twelve for all those years. Now he finally had the chance to show those narrow-minded numb-skulls that one could get further with brains and cunning than with forceps and thumbscrews.

The hangman looked up at the narrow windows, most of which were barred. The gloomy building reminded him more of a prison than a workplace. The entrance was a solid wooden door with iron hinges and a closed hatch at eye level. A bell chain hung beside it, and Kuisl pulled on it. He waited. When nothing happened, he pulled the chain again and again until the bell sounded like the Schongau parish church. Finally, he could hear shuffling footsteps.

"It's all right, I'm coming!" a female voice called out. "Whoever's outside better have a good reason for ringing like this—or else I'll pull off your skin in strips!"

Nice reception, Kuisl thought.

The hatch opened and the face of an older, heavily made-up woman appeared, eyeing him suspiciously. "What is it?" she asked harshly.

"The Munich executioner sends me," Kuisl replied. "Open up."

Jakob Kuisl knew the word *executioner* instilled fear in most people, and if it didn't, they at least became curious, which was the case here.

"What does the hangman want from us?" the woman asked, a tad milder.

"I'll tell you when you open the door."

The woman thought for a moment, then she pushed the bolt aside and the heavy door creaked open. It was hard to tell how old the woman was. She was made up like a twenty-year-old but her blonde hair was clearly a wig. Her wrinkles, the many missing teeth, and her entire grouchy appearance indicated that she was past fifty. She folded her arms over her enormous bosom and scrutinized Kuisl warily.

"So, what do you want?" she asked curtly.

Kuisl pushed past her until he stood in the entrance hall, a bare chamber with a staircase leading up. He could hear the rhythmic whirring and clattering of many individual apparatuses.

"Hey, what are you doing?" the woman protested.

"What I have to say isn't for everyone's ears, in your own interests," Kuisl said. "I'm Deibler's new assistant. He sends me because the neighbors claim your girls are earning on the side as prostitutes. You know the hangman needs to know every whore by name."

This was a blatant lie, but it had the desired effect. The woman turned red and puffed up her cheeks. "What a load of nonsense!" she exclaimed. "This is a decent establishment. And the Munich hangman isn't even responsible for Au."

"He is responsible when your girls go about their business in Munich. Like poor Elfriede Tanninger, for example, may God rest her soul."

As so often, Jakob Kuisl hadn't really planned ahead, but instinct told him he'd have to push this old bag into a corner if he wanted to get anywhere. As he'd thought, the woman winced when she heard the name of the impaled girl. He'd hit a nerve. But she soon pulled herself together and lowered her head.

"We heard what happened to poor Elfi," she purred. "Terrible story. We always warned her against going with strange men. But that's just what they're like, young girls. Never listen to good old Mother Joseffa." She peered up at Kuisl and twisted her mouth into a crooked grin. "Even though I was the one to get these girls off the streets."

And now you milk them for all they're worth, Kuisl thought.

"Did Elfi have any friends who can attest that she wasn't a whore?" he asked now.

Mother Joseffa hesitated briefly, then nodded. "Wait here," she said. She hurried up the stairs and soon returned with a young girl of about seventeen or eighteen years. She was pale and skinny with straggly blonde hair and a dirty dress. She looked very afraid, but Kuisl couldn't tell if she was scared of him or Mother Joseffa.

"This is Eva," Joseffa introduced the girl. "She knew Elfi well.

They came from the same backwater. Schrobenhausen, wasn't it, Eva?"

Eva nodded timidly, but remained silent.

Pale, with straggly blonde hair, Kuisl thought. *She could be the girl Captain Loibl was talking about.*

"You're from Schrobenhausen?" he asked in a friendly tone. "I know the place. The knacker is a cousin of mine. A pretty little town. Is the huge linden tree by the well still standing?"

A shy smile flashed across Eva's face. The memory of her hometown seemed to reassure her a little. "Yes, it . . . it's still there," she said quietly. "Where we always used to dance."

"Elfi too, I guess." Kuisl winked at her. "And there's a whole bunch of strapping young lads in Schrobenhausen. And they know how to dance. I've seen it with my own eyes."

"Yes, they do." Eva smiled again. "But—"

"Enough of this gossiping, we don't have all day," Mother Joseffa cut her off. "The shuttle won't move by itself. Go on and tell the man that Elfi was no whore." She glared at the girl. "Go on."

"Oh, no!" Eva shook her head. Her eyes were huge all of a sudden, glowing with fear. "She wasn't. She just—"

"Now go back to your place." Joseffa gave the girl a slap. With one last pleading glance at Kuisl, Eva ran back upstairs.

"That's sorted, then," Joseffa said to Kuisl when the girl had gone. "Anything else?"

Plenty, Kuisl thought, but he waved dismissively.

"That should do it for now. But watch out. I may be back."

"Yes, yes, but for now you can go to hell!" With surprising strength, Joseffa pushed the hangman out onto the street. Then the door slammed shut behind him. Kuisl stayed where he was for a moment, thinking. Things were beginning to get more interesting than he'd expected. The old hag and the girl were keeping something from him.

He was about to leave when he heard a whispering voice from above.

"Hey, I'm here!"

Kuisl looked up. It was Eva, standing behind one of the barred windows and waving timidly.

"Do you really want to know what happened to poor Elfi?" she asked quietly. "Then look for a man with red eyes and white hair."

Kuisl winced as if he'd been hit.

Master Hans, he thought. *I knew it.*

"What about this man?" he asked hoarsely.

"He hung around here following Elfi's death. One day he cornered Anni, wanted to speak about Elfi with her. I warned Anni, but she . . . she wouldn't listen." Tears were streaming down her face, and her voice broke. "I think that creepy man promised her something. I don't know what, but two days later, Anni was dead, too. They found her in Au creek."

The dead girl from the creek, Kuisl realized. *She also worked at the manufactory. And Mother Joseffa never said a word . . .*

"I'm scared I'm next," Eva whimpered. "The three of us were friends. First Elfi, then Anni, and now — me?"

"But why?" Kuisl asked. "Why would anyone want to kill you?"

"I don't know," Eva whispered. "I only know that —"

Suddenly her head disappeared from the window, and Joseffa's shrill voice rang out. "What are you doing by the window, you little bitch?" she screamed. "You're supposed to work, not look at the sky. Or were you talking to that man, hmm? Tell me, what did you say to him? Speak up, hussy!"

Kuisl heard a slapping sound, then crying.

Eva didn't come back to the window.

Deep in thought, Jakob Kuisl returned to the Radl Inn. He needed a pipe and a beer and time to think. There were so many questions, and most of them revolved around this accursed silk manufactory. Kuisl didn't think he'd find out by himself what went on behind those walls.

But he had an idea who might be able to help him.

That evening, the Kuisls sat up until late at Michael Deibler's table in the Anger Quarter.

Jakob Kuisl and Georg were also present, as there was much to talk about. Walburga had offered to look after the children. Once upon a time, the executioner's house had doubled as a whorehouse and a place for gambling, and there were countless interesting items to be found in the attic and basement of the old building—yellowed books gnawed by mice, crates full of bits and pieces, worn-out women's dresses and costumes, dice made of polished bone, and plenty of rusty forceps, chains, and thumb-screws.

The latter in particular fascinated Paul, while Peter leafed through an old prayer book that appeared to have belonged to a rueful prostitute. Occasionally Magdalena could hear Walburga humming a soothing melody to Sophia somewhere upstairs, but other than that, it was pleasantly quiet. An icy February wind swept through the streets outside, but it was warm and cozy by the tiled stove in the living room.

Magdalena had indeed enjoyed roaming the streets of Munich without Sophia that day. She and Barbara had almost fought in the morning. Her sister still didn't seem to understand the gravity of the situation and kept evading Magdalena's questions. Her stroll through town had diverted Magdalena. She had even considered buying herself a new embroidered apron, but the price of eight silver pennies had put her off. Munich was incredibly expensive!

At least there was good news about her sister now. Georg had told Magdalena that Barbara had met with Conrad Näher and hadn't run away screaming. Näher had given her a piece of real silk and Barbara now caressed it, looking visibly pleased. It was a start, at least.

But then Magdalena's good mood vanished when Simon told her about his botched audience. She had truly hoped to find a school in Munich for Peter, but instead, Simon had been appointed something like the municipal dogcatcher.

"And you're really supposed to find the lapdog of the electress?" she asked once more. They were sitting around a huge frying pan full of bacon and eggs at the large table. Sighing, Simon put down his wooden spoon. He seemed to have lost his appetite.

"The mutt's name is Arthur and a lady-in-waiting lost him," he said wearily. "I have no idea where I'm supposed to start looking for him. I think I'll just leave it. The worst that can happen is that the electress doesn't think I'm the smartest fellow in Schongau any longer." He rolled his eyes. "I've got our town clerk, Lechner, to thank. He told Count Sandizell all about us, and he in turn told the electress."

"About *us*?" Kuisl asked, frowning.

"Well, er . . . your name was mentioned."

Magdalena thought she could see her husband blush. "And then Peter had suddenly disappeared," Simon continued hastily. "And when I found him again, he made up this whole story about playing with the prince. Sometimes I think the boy's imagination runs riot. Perhaps he does read too much."

"Either way, I want you to find that lapdog," Magdalena said decisively. "If you have the mutt as a pawn, you'll be able to ask a favor of the electress, like a spot at Saint Michael College for Peter, for example."

"Wonderful!" Simon threw up his arms in despair. "And what do you suggest I do to find cute little Arthur? Put up posters with a drawing of him? Knock on every door in Munich and ask if anyone's seen a gorgeous little spaniel?"

"You could always ask Lorentz, the city dogcatcher," Michael Deibler suggested. "He might know something. Lorentz's eyes and ears are everywhere. He doesn't live far from here." He cleared his throat. "But now I'd like to discuss more pressing matters than lapdogs, namely the murders." He turned to Kuisl. "We didn't get a chance to speak at the meeting this afternoon, so now tell me: did you learn anything interesting at the silk works?"

Kuisl grinned. "Oh yes, and you won't like it at all."

With growing astonishment, Magdalena listened as their father told them about his conversation with Mother Joseffa and poor Eva. When he mentioned Master Hans, Barbara inhaled sharply.

"That devil," she hissed. "So he really is connected to the murders."

Kuisl nodded solemnly. He helped himself to a large spoonful of eggs with bacon from the pan and chewed loudly before washing it down with a swig of beer. Then he continued his story.

"Apparently, Hans spoke with Anni, the strawberry-blonde-haired girl we pulled out of Au creek. We already heard that from other witnesses. But more importantly, he hung around the silk manufactory following the death of the first girl, Elfi." Kuisl held up two fingers. "Anni and Elfi—both dead, and Hans showed interest in both of them. In my view, that makes him our main suspect."

Deibler shook his head. "I still can't believe Master Hans is supposed to have committed all those murders. What's his motive?"

Jakob Kuisl took another spoonful of egg. "I don't know yet. But something's wrong with that manufactory. Two of the murder victims worked there. And Eva wanted to tell me something before that made-up hag shut her up again."

"And what about Theresa Wilprecht, the girl they found at the Rossschwemme today?" Georg said from the far end of the table. "She certainly didn't work at the manufactory, coming from a wealthy patrician family. And the girl from the rock cellar has been dead for decades. The only thing connecting her to the other cases is a medallion."

"For God's sake, how am I supposed to know how they're all connected?" Kuisl angrily thumped the table with his spoon, sending egg flying everywhere. "But my nose tells me they are. And not just because all the murders look like executions, or because of the amulet. There's something else." He held his hand close to his face. "I'm this close. But every time I try to reach for it, it's gone. It's enough to drive a man crazy."

"It would be helpful to examine Theresa's body," Simon said. "You might find something on her. Another amulet, for example."

Deibler snorted. "Forget it. Theresa Wilprecht comes from a rich family — no hangman's going to get near her. She'll be kept at home and then taken straight to her burial."

"Well, it might be helpful to know if the murders we know of are the only ones, or if there have been more," Magdalena said placatingly. She turned to Deibler. "You mentioned once that there may have been others?"

"I wasn't sure at first. But in hindsight . . ." Deibler hesitated. Then he nodded. "Yes, there were several cases in the last few years. Drowned girls with tied hands, strangled girls . . . I remember one case in Giesing, about five years ago. Someone had dug a hole in a field and filled it up again. An arm was sticking out of the ground. The poor girl must have been buried alive and tried to dig herself out before she died."

"Jesus," Barbara gasped. "What a terrible way to die."

"How many?" Magdalena asked.

Deibler looked confused. "What do you mean?"

"For crying out loud, Michael. That wasn't a difficult question," Kuisl said angrily. "How many dead girls have there been?"

"I'm not sure." Michael Deibler shrugged. "A dozen, perhaps more. No one counts them. They're just poor young maids who come to the city from God knows where."

"And were any of them carrying amulets?" Simon asked.

"How am I supposed to know?" Deibler flared up. "I can barely even remember the girls! The knacker and I used to take them to the graveyards." He faltered. "I think there actually were amulets, on some of the girls, at least. I never took a closer look, because lots of girls wear necklaces. But by God, I think you're right, there were some Virgin Marys with aureoles."

No one said anything for a while. A wind gust rattled the shutters, as if winter himself was knocking on the windows.

"Are you thinking what I'm thinking?" Georg whispered eventually. "For decades, a crazy mass murderer has been on the loose here, killing young women and leaving an amulet. If we count the mummy in the rock cellar, then—"

"Then he's been at work for some twenty, thirty years," Jakob Kuisl finished his sentence. "As far as I know, Master Hans is in his mid-forties . . ."

"That means he would have been just a boy when he committed his first murder in Munich." Deibler laughed uneasily. "And he's from Weilheim. That's more than thirty miles away. He may have traveled to Munich from time to time, but killing someone every time? And why, anyhow?" He shook his head. "You're barking up the wrong tree, Jakob. It couldn't have been Hans. Please accept it."

"Damn it, you're right, Michael. Perhaps the walled-in mummy has nothing to do with the other cases. And maybe the amulets have no meaning at all. But if what you're saying is true, then Munich has had far too many unsolved murders in recent years." Kuisl picked at some egg in his beard. "One thing is certain: in one way or another, Hans is connected to it all. But to find out more, someone would have to pay the silk manufactory another visit."

"I hardly think Mother Joseffa's going to let you speak with her girls again," Magdalena said mockingly.

"Not me, but you," Kuisl replied with a wide grin.

Magdalena gave him a puzzled look. "What do you mean?"

"Well, I think the manufactory always needs new women to work the looms. And you girls like to chat." Kuisl leaned back and crossed his arms on his chest. "Eva might confide in you."

"Er, just so we're clear," Simon said. "You want Magdalena to work as a *weaver*?"

"Only for a few days. Just until she finds out more about this damned manufactory."

"Never," Magdalena protested. "I'm no maidservant. And who's supposed to look after the children?"

"Hmm. Burgi could, I guess," Michael Deibler said thoughtfully. "Clearly, Sophia likes her, and the boys are old enough. I don't think it's a bad idea." He gave Magdalena a pleading look. "It's only for one or two days. By then our guild meeting will be over and the hangmen will return to their hometowns. If we can prove by then that none of us had anything to do with the murders, you'll be doing our guild a great favor."

And my father once again gets his way, Magdalena thought.

She hesitated. Then she had an idea. "I'll do it under one condition."

"Which is?" Jakob Kuisl asked.

"Barbara is free to choose her own husband. She won't be forced into any wedding, neither here nor in Schongau."

Kuisl stared at his older daughter in shock. Then his eyes turned to Barbara, who smiled quietly. "For Christ's sake, you're all in on it!" he swore.

"Barbara is innocent," Magdalena replied. "It was entirely my idea."

"Do you have any idea how much work I've put into this?" her father continued. "All those letters. I almost crept up Widmann's arse."

"You've told Widmann that he's a stuck-up idiot several times since," Magdalena replied coolly. "And you can't be serious about Hörmann's ugly drunk of a son. That leaves only Conrad Näher from Kaufbeuren. And Barbara was good enough to talk to him. What more do you want?"

Jakob Kuisl didn't reply right away. Magdalena could tell he was thinking hard, grinding his teeth as if he was chewing on tough meat. Finally, he nodded. "All right. I probably wouldn't have been able to force such a stubborn woman anyway."

"Your word of honor?"

"My word of honor as a dishonorable hangman."

Magdalena smiled triumphantly. Barbara gave her hand a grateful squeeze under the table.

"That's settled, then," she said. "Tomorrow morning I'll apply for a job at the silk manufactory. I only hope I won't be too clumsy as a weaver."

6

SOMEWHERE IN THE MUNICH HACKEN QUARTER,
EARLY MORNING, 5 FEBRUARY, ANNO DOMINI 1672

COLD FOG HUNG IN THE alleyways like tobacco smoke while the rising sun struggled to push through the clouds. A few stray snowflakes tumbled from the dark sky. Here and there a rooster crowed, but other than that, the quarter lay silent at this early hour. The night watchman had finished his last round, and the countless Munich tradesmen — the carpenters, builders, brewers, linen weavers, butchers, wagon drivers, and innkeepers — hadn't risen yet. In half an hour, the city gates would open and let in the dregs of society from the suburbs, the beggars, maids, whores, and day laborers, hoping for some easy money.

During this hour, just before the floodgates opened, the silence was the most profound — and the despair the greatest.

It was the best time to hunt.

A figure emerged from the darkness of a narrow lane and silently walked across the bridges and walkways over the city stream and to the Herzogspital Church. Here, in front of the wooden statue of Our Lady of Sorrows, the hunter often found prey. Young girls liked to seek comfort beneath the Holy Virgin. In recent years, Herzogspital Church had become a popular place for those who couldn't see a way out.

Curious, the hunter opened the church door, which was never locked. The hunter's heart beat faster upon seeing a girl, all alone, praying in front of the altar. By her clothing and the whimpering and sobbing, it seemed that she might be the right girl. She wasn't yet twenty, her dress sooty, the apron stained and torn. She probably came from some village in Bavaria and now worked as a maid in one of the many taverns in the Hacken Quarter. Soon she'd stumble again through the pub in her clunky wooden clogs, carrying heavy mugs of beer in her spindly arms. Men would pat her bony backside and, at some point, one of them would promise her a bright future and take her to a stinking stable or barn. Then they'd do it like animals and the seed would be planted.

The girl's bitter weeping and her imploring prayers led the hunter to suspect the seed was already sprouting inside her.

The hunter was on the right track.

All that needed to be done now was to wait.

It took a while before the girl finally crossed herself one last time, stood up, and walked to the exit. The hunter crouched in an alcove and studied her puffed face, a face like so many others in this city. The eyes told stories of hopes dashed, of lovers gone, of childhoods in poverty. The hunter could read such faces like a book.

And there was always sin in the story.

Just like in the eyes of the young woman who scurried past and disappeared out the church door.

The hunter waited another moment before following her. The girl rushed toward the Anger Quarter, where the stinking city stream flowed along low, cowering houses until it joined Rossschwemme stream.

Good.

The Anger Quarter was one of the best hunting grounds. Lots of narrow lanes, numerous streams, a maze in which no one became suspicious. Sometimes the hunter lured the girls out to the meadows from there, where there were fewer witnesses. The hunter could be very convincing when necessary, gaining the girls' trust. And why not? A brief conversation, a walk outside the city gates, one last prayer . . . The hunter squeezed the amulet in a powerful hand. It gave the strength to do what had to be done.

The amulet with the woman in the aureole.

The hunter was about to stalk the prey when something unexpected happened. A young man — a simple laborer or stable boy, judging by his clothes — appeared from one of the alleyways. He was panting; evidently, he had been running. When he spotted the girl, he called out to her. It seemed he had been looking for her and was relieved to have found her. The girl jumped with fright at first, but after a brief hesitation, she threw her arms around the young man and cried. He stroked and soothed her, and her sobs eased. After a while, they walked off hand in hand toward Anger Square.

Disappointed, the hunter stayed behind and slipped the amulet back in a pocket. But the hunter knew that this wasn't the end of the girl's story.

The hunter had seen the sin in her eyes, and it couldn't be erased, not with stroking and soothing words. She would return to take the final step.

The hunter only needed to wait.

The bell of the parish church chimed the seventh hour of the morning when Magdalena crossed the Isar Bridge on her way to the Au silk manufactory. The city gates hadn't been open long, and now she was walking against a stream of men and women looking for work in Munich for the day or trying to earn a few pennies through begging or peddling.

Underneath her warm woolen coat Magdalena wore a simple linen dress with an apron, she hadn't bothered brushing her hair, and mud and dirt clung to the hem of her skirt. Her father had advised her to look as poor as possible so as not to arouse suspicion. But she hadn't exactly felt like a princess before her superficial disguise.

Magdalena still wasn't sure what to think of her father's plan — especially since she'd never sat at a loom before. But she guessed it probably was the easiest way to gain the trust of the weavers and find out more about the manufactory. The worst that could happen was she might get thrown out. Well, it wouldn't have been for nothing — her father promised he wouldn't force Barbara to marry.

But Barbara doesn't really have a choice, she thought glumly. *Not with a belly that grows bigger every day. At some point, even Father will notice. The only question is, will that be before the wedding or after . . .*

Magdalena had smothered little Sophia with kisses when she said her goodbyes. She knew Walburga would take good care of her and that she wasn't saying goodbye for long, but her heart still felt heavy when she thought of leaving her daughter. The fear that Sophia might fall ill or that something else might happen to her never left Magdalena — another reason she wanted to get this over and done as fast as possible.

Meanwhile, she had arrived at the three-story building. The silk manufactory looked indeed as gloomy and sinister as her father had described it. Magdalena pulled on the bell chain, and a few moments later, the hatch in the door opened. The made-up woman looking at her was probably Mother Joseffa.

"What do you want?" the old woman asked and scratched her head under the wig.

"I . . . I'm new in Au and looking for work," Magdalena replied, trying to sound shy and anxious. "I heard you're hiring."

"So, you heard, did you? Hmm. Let me see." The door opened and Mother Joseffa eyed Magdalena like a cow at the market.

"You're no spring chicken," she grumbled. "Where are you from?"

"From . . . from Schongau. The farmer I worked for threw me out. He found a younger maid."

"And I bet she keeps him warm at night, ha!" Mother Joseffa laughed maliciously. "And so you thought, I'll find something in Munich. And now you realize that no one wants a piece of filth like you in the city, so you come to Au. Am I right?"

"Please," Magdalena begged. "I don't know a soul here, and I can't go back to Schongau."

"So you're all alone, hmm?" Magdalena's last words seemed to have aroused Joseffa's interest. She looked Magdalena up and down once more. "You're not in bad shape despite your age. Can you weave?"

"No, unfortunately," Magdalena replied, her eyes lowered. "But I'm a fast learner."

"Well, we'll give it a try. But I want to make one thing clear: as an unskilled worker, you only get paid half, which is three kreuzers a week. You sleep here and get two meals a day. Understood?"

Magdalena nodded, though inwardly she was seething about the pittance. Three kreuzers a week! She knew how much weavers in Schongau were paid. This was pure exploitation. But evidently there were enough girls willing to do the job anyway.

The older woman waved her in, and Magdalena immediately heard the rhythmic rattle and clicking from upstairs. "You're lucky," Joseffa said as they climbed the narrow staircase. "Two girls left not long ago, so you can have one of their looms."

"Why did they leave?" Magdalena asked.

"That's none of your business," Joseffa snarled. "And now shut your mouth and listen while I explain the work to you."

The well-worn staircase continued on to the upper levels, but Joseffa opened a door on the second floor. Magdalena was startled by the intensity of the noise hitting her. Along the walls of a long room, around twenty girls sat in front of looms and pushed their shuttles through the vertically stretched threads. The young women wore simple linen dresses, the outlines of skeletal arms and shoulder blades clearly visible underneath. A handful of pale boys, none older than ten, scurried back and forth between the looms with bales of silk yarn that they wound around the quills, or spindles. Hardly any of the workers looked up when Magdalena and Joseffa entered the room. Most kept their eyes lowered, looking afraid. Magdalena quickly glanced around the room, hoping to spot a girl matching Eva's description, but the young women looked almost identical in their work dresses. In the center of the room stood a large chair like a throne, padded with numerous thick cushions. Magdalena guessed Mother Joseffa supervised the workers from there.

The older woman pointed at an empty loom on the left. "That's where you're going to work!" she shouted against the noise. "I'll show you how it's done. But only once. If you haven't got the hang of it by tonight, you're out."

They walked over to the loom and Mother Joseffa sat down on the seat. She picked up the shuttle, an oblong piece of wood with a quill inside that carried the silk yarn. "You have to pull the shuttle with the filling yarn through the shed in the warp yarns," she explained. "To create a shed — that's the opening between the vertical warp yarns — you push the right pedal with your foot. Like this . . ." The pedal made a clicking noise and some of the vertical yarns were pushed forward, others back, creating a kind of tunnel in between, through which Joseffa now threw the shuttle. She caught it on the other side and pushed down the fill yarn she had just laid with a batten until it sat tightly. Then she pushed the pedal again and sent the shuttle flying in the other direction. The shuttle moved back and forth so fast that Magdalena soon struggled to follow.

"It's not hard," Joseffa said. "Even the stupidest women can handle it." She stood up and handed the shuttle to Magdalena. "Now show me that you've paid attention."

Under Joseffa's watchful gaze, Magdalena slipped the shuttle with the filling yarn back and forth through the sheds, straightened the yarn with the batten, and pushed the pedals. She focused, and found that it was indeed easier than she'd first thought.

"If you continue to weave at this speed, your cloth won't be ready in a hundred years," Joseffa grumbled. "But not bad for the first time."

"And where does all this beautiful silk come from?" Magdalena asked. "Is it spun at the manufactory?"

"Didn't I tell you to keep your nosey questions to yourself?" Joseffa gave her a slap on the back of her head. "You're here to weave silk, nothing else. Now get to work before—"

She turned when a man entered the weaving room from an adjoining chamber and slammed the door noisily behind him. He was tall and haggard, with a long, lightly powdered face and bulging eyes. The frayed periwig on his head looked like a wet dog. His silken coat, his fashionably baggy trousers, and his pointed shoes made him appear like a wealthy man at first, but when she looked closer, Magdalena saw his clothes bore food stains and the seams were ripped. He held a walking stick with a silver knob and swung it about loftily.

The man moved through the room like a snake. Magdalena noticed that the girls worked even faster when he was nearby. He stopped behind one of the girls, a young, pale thing of about fifteen years, who was strikingly pretty. He brought his stick down on her back with a smack and the girl cried out.

"Do you call that weaving?" The man spat. "Hmm? Do you think I can sell such shoddy work at court?" He pulled at the fabric until it tore with an ugly noise. "The thread was crooked here, and this patch is rougher than that one. I'm going to take this cloth out of your wages."

"Please, Herr van Uffele," the girl whimpered. "I need the money. My little brother—"

The stick came down for the second time. "How dare you talk back to me!" van Uffele cried. "Is this how you thank us for dragging you out of the gutter?"

"Leave her," Joseffa said. "You know we still need the wench."

The man lowered his stick. "You're right, damn it," he growled. "Sometimes I just can't help myself." He turned to the girl again, his voice calm now. "Start again with new warp threads. I hope you at least know how to put those up."

He gave the loom a kick before walking over to Magdalena and Mother Joseffa.

"Ah, a new girl," he said, looking Magdalena up and down. "Any good?"

"Remains to be seen," Joseffa replied. She grinned. "Perhaps we'll also use her elsewhere." She winked at the man and nudged Magdalena. "You curtsy when the gentleman talks to you. Lukas van Uffele is your most generous benefactor, the director of the manufactory. His word is law. And just like me, he tolerates neither laziness nor gossiping."

"Speaking of gossiping," van Uffele said to Joseffa in a lowered voice. "The bloody investors are asking for money again. Pfundner and the others must have talked among themselves. We must appease them somehow. And we need to talk about Eva. I think we should get rid of the problem for good."

"What do you mean?" Joseffa snapped. "Isn't it enough to—"

A warning glance from van Uffele silenced her.

"I'm just going next door with the gentleman for a moment," Joseffa said loudly into the room. "Don't start thinking you can slack off. My hearing is perfect and I'll notice if your shuttles slow down. Understood?"

She followed van Uffele through the low door into the chamber. Magdalena picked up her shuttle and tried to push it through the warp yarn like before, but this time, she kept getting stuck.

"You're pushing the wrong pedal," a husky voice said next to her. It belonged to an attractive black-haired woman who seemed a little older than the other girls. Her cheeks were hollow and she kept coughing. Dark rings lay under her eyes, but Magdalena guessed she turned the heads of many men despite her illness. She threw the shuttle back and forth with nimble fingers. "You must push the pedal at the right moment, or you'll keep getting snagged," she explained. "Like this, see."

Magdalena copied her and soon found the work easier.

"Thank you," she said and smiled at the woman. "I'm Magdalena."

"I'm Agnes." The black-haired woman coughed again. She pulled out a filthy handkerchief and spat into it. "You'll see, it's not that bad here. Most girls cry for the first few nights, but it gets better. We have a roof over our heads and don't freeze to death. And you can earn a bit on the side . . ." She gave Magdalena a conspiratorial wink. "And I'll be gone by the summer, anyway."

"Where are you going?"

"Don't know." Agnes shrugged. "Maybe the Palatinate, where I've still got a sister. But then again, maybe I'll find a rich husband first." She laughed, but then started coughing again. "When I left my hometown, I thought I'd find work as a maidservant in Munich," she wheezed eventually. "But they don't let you work in the city. Now they even keep out beggars and day laborers. There's no future in Munich for me, anyhow. Nor here at Au."

"I met Eva a few days ago," Magdalena said, trying hard to sound casual. "She said I could find work here, just like herself. Do you know her?"

"Eva, you say?" Agnes suddenly seemed suspicious. She cast a cautious glance around the room. "What did she tell you about the manufactory?"

"Nothing, really. Just that they were hiring."

"Well, Eva no longer works here," Agnes replied coolly. "And now you better focus on your shuttle."

Agnes looked down and resumed her work, and Magdalena followed her example. Her thoughts were racing. Could Eva have been thrown out after speaking with her father yesterday? She had hoped fervently to be able to talk to the girl—and now it seemed she was too late.

Mother Joseffa and van Uffele hadn't returned. Two looms up from Magdalena, the girl the director had beaten was still busy tying her new warp threads. She was crying silently. Suddenly the quill with the warp yarn slipped through her fingers and rolled across the floor. Magdalena jumped up and caught the quill. When she handed it back to the girl, she stroked her dirty, straggly hair.

"It's going to be all right, love," she tried to soothe her. "You'll see. Tomorrow is another day."

The girl nodded, but then another crying fit shook her. "It's just that I need the money for my brother," she said, whimpering. "He's only five and sleeps in a stable by Au creek. He needs to eat. And Mother Joseffa doesn't want to employ him because he's too young."

Magdalena swallowed. Then she pulled a stained coin from her skirt. "It's not much," she said quietly. "But it's enough for a piece of bread."

"God bless you." The girl smiled and accepted the coin gratefully. Then her face darkened again. "I heard you talk about Eva with Agnes before. Don't believe a word Agnes says. She's just scared, like all of us. They all lie. Eva isn't gone."

"Is that so?" Magdalena asked, astonished. "And where is she?"

"Van Uffele locked her up," the girl whispered. "Somewhere in the basement. I heard her cry when I went to fetch the raw silk for the spinners. I bet the scoundrel beat her. It happened after Eva talked to that big man yesterday."

My father, Magdalena thought.

"And why did they lock her up?" she asked hoarsely.

"Because she knows too much. Eva has been here for a long time. I think they want to kill her because —"

In that moment, the door to the chamber opened and out came Mother Joseffa. When she spotted Magdalena beside the girl, her eyes narrowed.

"Didn't I tell you I don't tolerate laziness?" Joseffa hissed. "Just you wait, I'll take the rod to both of you."

"It . . . it was my fault," Magdalena implored. "I forgot which pedals to push and she showed me."

Joseffa hesitated, then nodded grumpily. "All right, just because it's your first day and I've got other problems." She raised a finger. "But if you're still here tomorrow, I won't let you get away with anything like this again!"

Like a spider in her web, she sat down in her chair in the middle of the room and watched the girls do their work.

Magdalena returned to her place and continued to weave, frantically trying to think of a way to get down to the basement of the manufactory, down where Eva awaited her fate.

Something was telling Magdalena that she didn't have much time.

Simon walked gingerly along one of the many small, slippery walkways across the stream. It was still early, but the noise of hammering and grinding, people shouting, squeaking wagon wheels, and whinnying horses was everywhere. The city had woken, and it already grated on his nerves.

He hadn't slept well the night before. Simon was worried about Magdalena, who had left at dawn to investigate the Au silk manufactory for her father and Michael Deibler. On top of that, his original plans for his stay in Munich appeared ruined. A meeting with the famous physician Doctor Malachias Geiger seemed out of the question now that he was forced to search for a barking mutt. Since Simon had no idea where to start looking for the electress's lapdog, he followed Deibler's suggestion and was on his way to the Munich dogcatcher, Lorentz. He muttered a curse. How had he gotten himself into such a mess? He might as well burn his treatise or throw it into the stinking city stream right here.

The stream ran underneath the city wall not far from the executioner's house, then it branched into several side arms through the Anger Quarter to the Cattle Market and on toward the Residenz. Especially here in the Anger Quarter, Munich's largest quarter, the countless streams formed the veins of the city. Numerous mills and the dyers' house were situated here, but also the slaughterhouse and the home of the knacker. For the tradesmen in the quarter, the streams were where they disposed of their rubbish. Now, in February, the stench was bearable, but in the dark icy water below floated plenty of things that Simon didn't want to know about. Unbidden, an image came to his mind of the dead woman at the Rossschwemme who had washed up like a piece of garbage.

After Simon had crossed another rickety bridge, he had almost reached the destination of his short walk. He followed a narrow path alongside the stream toward a crooked house that looked as though it wouldn't make it through the next winter storm. A bunch of street children were playing in the dirt outside the house, fishing with a stick in the murky water for rags that they were probably going to sell to one of the many papermills.

"Is this the house of the dogcatcher, Lorentz?" Simon asked the boys.

They looked at him and giggled. Evidently, they didn't often see someone with a halfway clean coat, vest, and hat in this part of town.

"If sir is looking for his lapdog, he's in the wrong place," one of the boys jeered. "Lorentz probably already killed and ate it."

"I think I'll go and find out for myself," Simon replied with a thin smile.

He knew dogcatchers often had an even worse reputation

than knackers and executioners. In smaller towns, the dirty task of knocking stray dogs over the head was often part of the knacker's job description, but in Munich, the number of strays had risen so much that a post had been especially created a few years ago. Sometimes they even employed a whole team of laborers who roamed the streets with cudgels for several days.

Reluctantly, Simon knocked on the door of the crooked house. When no one opened it, he walked around the corner, where a narrow path between high walls led him to a courtyard filled with crates and cages. The moment Simon entered the yard, an infernal racket set in. Simon hadn't noticed the dogs in the cages, who were now throwing themselves against the metal bars, barking and snarling at him.

Just when the medicus had recovered from his fright, an enormous mastiff came running toward him. Underneath its slobbering jowls gleamed rows of huge sharp teeth. Simon gasped. Another one or two leaps, and the beast would be upon him! He grabbed a ridiculously small rock and raised it, preparing for the inevitable.

And so ends the career of a promising doctor and scholar. As dog food . . .

Just as the mastiff was about to pounce, someone whistled loudly and then shouted: "Wastl, sit!"

The huge dog obeyed instantly. He cowered down and whimpered but eyed Simon intently, as if he hoped the command would be withdrawn at any moment.

A broad-shouldered man emerged from the back door of the house, his hair so dirty that Simon couldn't make out the color. The man had grown a wild beard, but it didn't cover the poorly healed scar that ran across the right side of his face. With his hand, he swung a heavy polished club.

Simon raised both hands. "Er, I did knock!" he shouted over the barking of the dogs. "But no one opened!"

The man looked at him blankly. Clearly, he couldn't hear a thing over the noise.

"I said, I—" Simon started again.

"Goddamnit, be quiet!" The man's roar was even louder than the barking, and he brought down his club on one of the iron cages as he shouted. The clatter was deafening, but afterward everything was silent, apart from a few soft yelps.

"Looking for any dog in particular?" the man asked without preamble. Simon assumed he was Lorentz, the dogcatcher. Now he walked slowly toward Simon, and even though he had lowered his club, he looked no less menacing.

The medicus nodded with relief. "I am indeed. I'm looking for a small spaniel, brown with white spots, and a blaze from the forehead to his nose."

"Hmm. Let me see." Lorentz walked along the crates and cages. Then he bent over one of the boxes and lifted the lid.

"There we go, here's your little runaway," he said. "And in pretty good condition, too. One silver penny and he's yours."

Grinning, Lorentz held up a whimpering spaniel by the scruff of its neck, brown with white spots. Simon couldn't believe his luck. He had found little Arthur on the first go! Beaming, he walked toward Lorentz and the dog, searching his pockets for the right coin.

"What a happy surprise," he said. "I really didn't expect—" He faltered when he noticed one small detail.

"Er, that's a female," he said. "I'm looking for a male. His name's Arthur."

Lorentz shrugged. "Just call him Arthura from now on. Sounds good, doesn't it?"

Simon squinted and took a closer look. "And this dog doesn't have a blaze, either—none that goes all the way to its nose, anyway."

"I can paint it on, no problem at all." Lorentz held the

squirming and yelping spaniel under Simon's nose like a smoked sausage. "Do you want it or not?"

"I'm afraid I can't," Simon replied with a sigh. "The dog I'm looking for belongs to a high-born lady. She'd soon notice the deceit and I'd lose my head."

"I see." Lorentz nodded and put the whimpering dog back in its cage. "I'm afraid I can't help you, then."

His hope dwindling, Simon examined the courtyard. A shed stood at the far end, probably containing more cages. Several dogs started to bark again, while others yelped or growled at one another. The large mastiff was still lying in the dirt on the ground, watching Simon with its small, murderous eyes.

"Are these all the dogs you have?" Simon asked with despair.

"These are all the dogs worth keeping alive for a little while," Lorentz replied. He ran his hand across the scabby scar on his face. "They've been looked after, so someone might claim them or I might be able to sell them. Anything else I knock over the head and take to the knacker. At least that way I get a few kreuzers for them."

Simon winced. "Perhaps you knocked the spaniel over the head, too," he said wearily.

"I'd know," Lorentz replied with a laugh. "If it's a precious lapdog, as you say, I'd be stupid to put it down." He gave his head a good scratch, studied a louse on the tip of his finger, and flicked it away. "Hmm. Still, it's strange how it's always the lapdogs at the moment."

"What do you mean?" Simon asked, confused.

"You're not the first to ask for a precious dog. Lately, I've had several footmen from wealthy homes come to ask about lost lapdogs. Must be at least a dozen spoiled mutts gone missing. I would have loved to sell them back for good money, but I just don't have them. It's jinxed."

"Can I ask you to keep your eyes peeled anyway?" Simon asked. He dug his last coins from his pocket and handed them to

Lorentz. They were all he had. Since he'd left the counterfeit coins at the bookshop, he was now completely broke. He only hoped this expense would be a good investment.

Lorentz took the coins and sniffed them as if they were food. Then he weighed them in his hand, and lastly, he bit them.

"They're good," he grumbled.

"Why shouldn't they be?" Simon asked with a smile. This fellow was truly peculiar.

"Haven't you heard?" Lorentz replied with lowered voice. "A whole lot of light silver is going around at the moment. Some kind of gang's behind it. Only two days ago they nearly caught one of them when he tried to pay for a book with false silver thalers, but he got away. And stole the book."

"Is that right?" Simon croaked.

"Yes, there are more and more counterfeit silver coins all the time. Pennies, batzen, thalers . . . They swamp Munich and ruin the prices. The elector has offered a reward for anyone who can name the counterfeiters." Lorentz grinned. "Not that I think you're one of them. But I can't take any risks. Not with silver coins. Or I'll get done myself in the end."

"Un-understandable," Simon replied. "Do they have any suspicions?"

"Well, the fellow in the bookshop was a short, dodgy sort of a fop, looked rather wealthy, apparently. Maybe he was the leader of the gang. They're still looking for him, but most of all, they're looking for their hideout. They must be minting them somewhere, after all." Lorentz winked at him. "When they catch the bastards, we'll finally get a good execution again. Like the Pappenheim family that time, or Pämb, whatever their real name was. They were impaled and then burned, but they pinched the woman's breasts first and—"

"I think it's time for me to return to my ladyship," Simon interrupted hastily. "I'll come back in a few days' time. Perhaps you'll have heard something by then." He suddenly felt like Lorentz was eyeing him a little more closely than before. But he wasn't sure.

"Um, the scar," he asked, partly in a bid to distract Lorentz. He pointed at the dogcatcher's face. "From a dog?"

Lorentz shook his head. "From a goddamn cat. They're ten times more cunning than those stupid mutts. I never caught the beast."

"Well, happy hunting, then." Simon lifted his hat in farewell and gave a strained smile.

He hurried out of the courtyard, and the moment he was back in the alleyway, the dogs behind him broke out barking and howling again.

Instinctively, Simon walked faster. It looked as though his problems were multiplying by the day.

Around the same time, Barbara was lying in bed in the house of the Munich executioner, listening to the giggling of her nephews in the next room. She smiled. It was one of the rare occasions when Peter and Paul were playing peacefully instead of fighting with each other. It sounded like the boys had carried up a box of old costumes from the basement and were trying them on. They'd even found some old masks like the ones people wore at the carnival. One of Walburga's many cats kept the brothers company. Barbara was still amazed by the sheer size of this house, so much larger than the Schongau hangman's house. But the Munich executioner simply was a little more respected than his colleague from small-town Schongau.

And the Kaufbeuren executioner? she thought involuntarily. *How well-respected would his wife be?*

Yesterday's meeting with Conrad Näher had gone much better than Barbara had expected. Näher had been very attentive. He had asked about her life in Schongau, had shown interest in her dreams and hopes. Barbara had been withdrawn at first, but then she relaxed more and more and told him about herself. The Kaufbeuren hangman was truly different than the other hangmen — in fact, he was different from any man Barbara had ever met. He appeared to be genuinely interested in her, not just in her breasts and buttocks, but in her as a person. And he listened, which was something men rarely managed. He spoke very affectionately of his dead wife.

On the other hand, he was old, almost as old as her father. And Barbara had no illusions: a marriage to him would be nothing more than a business transaction. Conrad Näher would expect children of her, and he'd pay her father a decent sum.

But did she have a choice?

Barbara's hand went to her belly. She'd felt sick several times in the last few days, just like now. So far pregnancy had been nothing but a burden — a curse, even. The rendezvous with Conrad Näher hadn't changed that. Barbara listened carefully to the signs of her body, but she found nothing that connected her to the tiny creature inside her.

She felt no love.

Suddenly she thought of little Sophia, whom Walburga had taken into the city that morning. The hangman's wife wanted to do some shopping and visit one or two elderly people and drop off some medicine. Sophia wasn't a burden to Walburga, just the opposite. Clearly, the dainty girl had put her under her spell, too. But Barbara just couldn't feel the same love she felt for Sophia for this . . . this *thing* in her belly.

My God, what am I thinking? Please forgive me!

Barbara shook herself when another wave of nausea welled up in her. She struggled to her feet to take a sip of watered-down wine when she heard a noise outside. It was the creaking of the gate to the garden. Walburga was probably back.

Barbara looked out the window but only saw that the gate stood open. She was about to call out to Walburga when she heard heavy, slow footsteps on the gravel. They walked around the house.

Heavy, slow steps . . .

Barbara breathed faster. Those weren't the steps of a woman, but of a man. It could be Deibler, her father, or her brother, but as far as she knew, the Council of Twelve was in session today. And if it was a stranger, why wasn't he knocking on the front door?

As quietly as she could, Barbara tiptoed out of her room and down the stairs into the living room. She could still hear the laughter of her nephews from upstairs, absorbed in their game. Barbara ducked behind the tiled stove and kept her eyes on the window. Again she heard footsteps, and now a shadow appeared in the window.

A large shadow.

Barbara startled. Her shock was so great she had to jam her fist into her mouth to stop herself from screaming out loud, but a short squeal slipped out nonetheless, like that of a mouse caught in a trap.

Outside the window stood Master Hans.

He gazed into the living room, his red eyes gleaming in the light of the morning sun. He hadn't spotted her yet. Scared stiff, Barbara cowered behind the stove. She closed her eyes and prayed that he hadn't heard her squeal. What on earth was that monster doing here? Was he after her? Unlike her family, Barbara had always sensed that Hans didn't view her as some kind of object, as so many others did. She had already felt it as a nine-year-old girl, when she'd met him for the first time at an executioner's meeting in Nuremberg. Already back then she'd seen the glimmer of greed in his eyes, something demanding, as if he wanted to possess Barbara, to play with her like a cat with a mouse. Two years ago, in the Schongau dungeon, he'd almost had her, and his disappointment when the torture was cut short must have been enormous. Had he come to finish the job?

Again she heard the crunching steps. Barbara risked a peek across the stove and saw that Hans was walking toward the back door. Only yesterday she had noticed how conscientiously Walburga locked both the front and back doors. Had she done so today?

Barbara held her breath and listened.

Soon she heard the door handle being pushed down. Hans rattled and pulled at it, but the door didn't open.

It was locked.

The footsteps continued. Evidently, Hans was looking for another way in. Barbara guessed he would find one sooner or later, even if he had to kick down the door. Or perhaps he'd climb up to the second floor, where the boys were playing.

The boys!

Barbara roused herself and snuck back up the stairs. She rushed into the boys' room, where she found her nephews sitting among piles of threadbare costumes. Paul wore a straw-colored wig that must have once belonged to a prostitute, while Peter teased a kitten with a moth-eaten fan. The boys were giggling merrily, but when they noticed Barbara's deathly-pale face, they fell silent.

"Listen, children," Barbara whispered breathlessly. "Master Hans is sneaking around the house. I have no idea what he wants, but I don't want to take any chances. One of you must go and get your grandfather."

"I will," Paul volunteered immediately. He tore the wig off his head and ran toward the stairs.

"Wait," Barbara hissed. "If you go out the front door you'll run right into him."

Paul grinned. "I know another way, and I'm sure Hans doesn't." The next moment, he was gone. Confused, Barbara turned to Peter.

"What was he talking about?"

"We found a secret passage that leads from the house to Little

Faust Tower," Peter explained. "That's a tower in the city wall, right behind the house. Burgi reckons the city guards used to use the passage to visit the whores. From Little Faust Tower, you can walk along the battlements all the way to the city gate." He shrugged. "You just can't get caught."

"I see." Barbara nodded as she peered out of the crown glass windows. She couldn't see anyone in the garden. She was about to turn away when the broad figure of Master Hans appeared at the gate again. He gave the executioner's house one last look before slowly walking toward the Anger Gate.

Barbara breathed a sigh of relief. "He's giving up," she whispered to Peter. "We sent Paul away for nothing. He needn't have fetched Father . . ."

She faltered when a thought struck her. The Council of Twelve was in session, and yet Hans was here in the Anger Quarter. He must have had a very good reason to skip the meeting. Perhaps he hadn't merely come for her after all? Perhaps it had something to do with his strange behavior of the last few days?

Barbara hesitated, then she walked toward the stairs.

"What are you doing, Aunt?" Peter asked.

"I'm going after that scoundrel," she replied softly. "By the time Father gets here, Hans will be long gone and we'll never find out what he was doing in the Anger Quarter."

Peter looked at her defiantly. "Then I'm going with you. I'm not leaving you alone."

"Listen, Peter. I'm not going on a nice little trip to the Residenz. Hans might be a murderer who's killed countless—"

"I'm going," Peter cut her off and reached for a small knife Paul had left behind. His eyes shone with determination. "Nobody thinks I can beat up other kids. But one thing I can do for sure, defend my aunt."

Barbara couldn't help but smile.

"All right, then, my knight in shining armor, let's go before the villain gets away."

When Barbara hurried out through the gate, holding Peter's hand, she thought at first that she'd lost track of Hans. But then she spotted him turning into a lane along the city stream. He walked slowly but resolutely, as if he knew exactly where he was going.

Barbara waited another few moments, then she began her pursuit. Peter walked beside her like a dog, clutching the knife tightly. Barbara was surprised at this new side of her gentle, bookish nephew, but he was clearly serious about being her body-guard.

Though I hope I won't need one, she thought.

It was late morning, and the lanes and streets of Munich were as busy as ever. Especially here along the city stream, countless workmen were out with their carts. An old woman emptied her stinking chamber pot at one of the many bridges, a butcher threw bucketfuls of water onto the bloody cobblestones outside his shop, sending streams of red flowing into the creek. It was easy for Barbara and Peter to follow Hans unnoticed among all the people.

That changed when the Weilheim hangman turned in to a narrow alleyway. He crossed busy Sendlinger Street and soon disappeared in the maze of the Hacken Quarter, which adjoined the Anger Quarter. For a moment Barbara feared she had lost him for good, but then she spotted his white hair down one of the winding alleys.

Many housefronts in the Hacken Quarter held statues of the Virgin Mary or saints as points of orientation for foreigners in this confusing part of town, but Barbara soon lost all sense of di-rection regardless. Where was Hans headed? Did he even have a destination in mind or was he just wandering around aimlessly?

Barbara and Peter hurried past a Virgin Mary in a half moon, squeezed past an ox cart blocking the lane, and found themselves in a wider but empty street that ran parallel to the city wall. It led to a tall church with a cemetery. Barbara was about to walk out

into the street when she saw Master Hans heading for the graveyard and entering it through a small gate. He soon disappeared
between the gravestones. The bell in the tower chimed the tenth
hour.

"What's Hans doing at a cemetery?" Peter whispered.

Barbara pulled the boy into a recess in the city wall and
thought. Peter was right. What in God's name was Master Hans
doing at a Munich cemetery? He was from Weilheim, surely
none of his family was buried here. She would have to follow
him if she wanted to find out more.

Barbara grabbed Peter's hand tightly and snuck over to the
cemetery wall, which unfortunately was too high to peer over. A
hunchbacked old woman holding a rosary walked past them, but
other than that, they were alone. When the woman had gone,
Barbara leaned against the wall and folded her fingers so she
could give Peter a leg up.

"Tell me what Hans is doing," she whispered to the boy.

He nodded silently, climbed onto her hands and then her
shoulders.

"And?" Barbara asked.

"He . . . he's walking slowly along the tombstones," Peter reported haltingly. "It looks as though he's searching for a particular one. Now he's stopped in the corner. He—oh God!"

"What is it?" Barbara asked urgently, her shoulders aching
under Peter's clunky shoes.

"He looked back," Peter gasped.

"Did he see us?"

"Not sure. He . . . he's moving again. I can't see him anymore.
I think he went behind the church."

Barbara hesitated. She would have loved to know what Master Hans was doing in the graveyard. But what if he'd become
suspicious? She decided to take the chance. She went down to
her knees so Peter could climb off. Then they walked through
the gate into the cemetery, which lay on the church's west side.

Gnarled oak trees grew everywhere, their naked branches stark against the hazy February sky. Many tombstones among the massive trunks stood askew, and Barbara saw by the inscriptions that some of them were almost two hundred years old. Others looked more recent. There were ostentatious graves with white stone crosses and statues of saints, and very plain graves, too. A cold gust of wind made Barbara shiver. There was not a soul to be seen apart from her and Paul.

"So where are the graves Hans was looking at?" she whispered at Peter.

The boy pointed toward the back of the cemetery and they hurried along the rows of tombstones and trees. Eventually, they came to a freshly dug hole, obviously intended for an impending funeral. A tall, gleaming white grave slab leaned against the pile of dirt next to the hole.

"Is this the grave—" Barbara began.

A hand shot out from behind a tombstone slab and grabbed her by the collar.

She screamed out, but the hand pulled her down relentlessly. Desperately, she waved her arms through the air but lost her balance and fell backward into the six-foot-deep hole. It smelled of fresh soil and foul water, and just slightly of something else. A sweetish smell that made Barbara gag. Evidently, the corpses in the neighboring graves were still very fresh.

Barbara sat up with difficulty, her right foot was hurt. She looked up. There was no sign of Peter, but another face appeared in her field of vision.

It was that of Master Hans.

The Weilheim hangman looked at her thoughtfully, as if studying a beetle that had fallen into a sand hole and struggled to climb back out.

"Look at that, our dear Barbara," he said flatly. "What a pleasure. Although I would have preferred a nicer place for our reunion."

The sight of Hans and the hopelessness of her situation made Barbara choke. Her heart beat so wildly that her chest ached.

"Whatever you're planning to do," she managed to croak eventually, "I'm going to scream loud enough for them to hear me in Au."

"Whatever *I'm* planning?" Master Hans frowned. He scratched his nose, considering this. He seemed to have all the time in the world. "I would rather like to know what *you* were planning, Barbara. Why were you following me? Did your father send you?"

"My . . . father?" For a moment, Barbara was confused. But then she saw her chance. "Yes, that's right," she said. "And he'll be here any moment."

Peter hadn't turned up yet, and Barbara hoped he'd run away. Maybe he'd manage to fetch help from somewhere. If not, she'd have to try her best to convince Hans that someone was on their way to her soon. She prayed he'd believe her.

"Admit it, you're scared of my father," she said. "So you better run before he gets here."

Master Hans didn't reply. Instead, he started to throw handfuls of dirt down into the grave. Barbara blinked and looked away. The soil was like cold black rain falling from the sky.

"I never understood your father," Hans muttered as the dirt continued to fall. "He's such a good executioner, quick with the sword and knowledgeable with herbs. But he's just too soft. If you want to get anywhere as a hangman, you can't show mercy." He smiled mysteriously. "There are some real treasures amongst the stammering of people at confessions. You just need to know how to retrieve them, then you'll go far in this life."

Barbara had no idea what Hans was talking about. She wondered what she should do if Peter didn't come back with help and Hans didn't buy her lie. If she screamed loudly now, how long would it take for someone to come? Would Hans shut her up first? She thought about the new tombstone leaning against the dirt. If Hans dropped it on her, she'd get squashed like a louse. Better to buy time until Peter — hopefully — returned.

"What treasures do you mean?" she asked nervously.

Hans winked at her almost cordially with his red eyes. "You'd love to know, wouldn't you? And your father too, the smart-arse. But this time, I'm the smarter one, and you're all in for a surprise." He laughed his soft, ringing chuckle that Barbara had always found creepy. "You'll see. I'm going to get far — farther yet than Widmann from Nuremberg."

Suddenly Hans became suspicious. "Has your father figured it out yet?" he hissed. "Tell me, has he? Speak up!" Now he shoveled dirt into the pit with both hands. Soon Barbara was up to her knees in soil. "Has he?"

"I have no idea what you're talking about!" she shouted. "You . . . you madman!" Her dress was torn and dirty, her face smeared with sweat and mud. She watched in horror as Hans picked up a large frozen chunk of dirt and aimed straight for her, as if he were playing a game. Barbara ducked and the chunk missed her. But Hans had already picked up the next clump.

He's trying to stone me! she thought. *Drowning, strangling, impaling, walling in alive . . . And now he chooses stoning.*

"How much does your father know?" Hans growled like a beast of prey. "Speak, before I squash your pretty little head like a rotten apple."

Barbara opened her mouth to scream.

Hans reached for the tombstone.

"By God, if it continues like this, they'll hang the lot of us like common thieves! Damn it all, how much more do we hangmen have to put up with?"

Kaspar Hörmann brought his half-empty mug down hard on the table, splattering Kuisl's last clean shirt with beer. The Passau hangman burped loudly and slumped back on his chair, almost falling off. Clearly, he'd had one too many again, even though it was still morning.

Jakob Kuisl turned away in disgust. The Council of Twelve had been in session for over an hour at the Radl Inn, the executioners as always at the long table in the center of the room with their own beer mugs, and the journeymen on chairs along the wall. Flickering black candles cast an eerie light into the room, especially since the shutters were closed to keep out the cold. The air was stuffy, the smoke from many pipes hung above the table like a dense fog. Georg had sat down next to Hörmann's snoring son, listening attentively to the hangmen's conversation, his eyes reddened from the smoke.

In the beginning they had talked about the usual topics, like better pay and the pending threat of a prohibition on healing for executioners that the German electors were pushing for. But rumors from the city had found their way into this round, too. Since the murder of the young patrician wife, Theresa Wilprecht, more and more people blamed the meeting of the executioners for the series of unhappy events.

Next to Kuisl, Philipp Teuber—his friend from Regensburg—frowned and shook his head. "Shouting at each other isn't going to help," he said in Hörmann's direction. "Let's look for a solution together, before they set this place on fire."

The other council members nodded silently and stared into their mugs. Then Bartholomäus Kuisl, who was sitting at the other end of the table, shook his head angrily. "How do the people of Munich even get the idea that we've got something to do with the murders? I've been called many things in my life—bringer of bad luck, blood guzzler, robber of souls—but never a malicious murderer."

"It must be the manner of the murders," Michael Deibler said. "Drowning in a sack, impaling, walling up alive . . . They all look like executions, and executions are our business."

"What a load of rubbish," Matthäus Fux, the red-haired Memmingen executioner, complained. He was a proud man who didn't like to be told anything. "Any stupid yokel can drown someone, and I haven't impaled anyone in my life. That hasn't been practice for years."

His colleagues from Ingolstadt and Nördlingen muttered their agreement, only Conrad Näher smiled a thin smile to himself.

"I can't see what there is to grin about," Fux snarled at him.

"Forgive me, dear cousin, I meant no disrespect," Näher replied in his typical soft, slightly unctuous tone. He brushed his graying hair from his forehead and sighed. "It's just the same old story. Can't you see that it doesn't matter at all whether we have anything to do with the murders or not? Twelve executioners." He laughed. "One alone brings ill luck. Twelve together carry enough misfortune for an entire city. That's what people are saying. I'm afraid they'll only stop talking when we end the meeting and go home."

"Impossible!" Michael Deibler pounded the table, causing the flames of the candles to flicker wildly. "It could be years before we get another permit for a meeting. And we still have so much to discuss."

"It looks like the council is dissolving already," Johann Widmann remarked pointedly. He looked around with mock astonishment. "I don't see Master Hans, do you? This is the second time he's missed a meeting."

Bartholomäus Kuisl scratched his beard and turned to Deibler. "I've been meaning to ask you about him. Where is he?"

Now everyone looked at Deibler, the chairman.

"I don't know," Deibler replied slowly. "He didn't tell me."

"Didn't tell you? Well, this never would have happened at the meeting *I* chaired in Nuremberg," Johann Widmann said smugly. "All cousins were present and I—"

"Oh, shut up already, you braggart," Jakob Kuisl cut him off.

He'd remained silent until then, but now he'd had enough. "For once it isn't just about you but about every one of us. Näher is right. Even if none of us has anything to do with the murders, people are going to try and blame us. Just because we're hangmen." He lowered his voice. "But I agree with you on one point, Widmann. Hans is taking many liberties. He's off on his own, and none of us has any idea what he's up to."

Jakob Kuisl had also been wondering why Hans wasn't at the meeting. Was the Weilheim hangman after the girls at the silk manufactory again? What was he up to? Kuisl felt deeply uncomfortable when he thought about his daughter sniffing around at the manufactory, looking for clues about a thus far unknown murderer. A murderer who was somehow connected to Hans, Kuisl felt certain about it.

If he isn't the murderer himself . . .

"Who knows, maybe the people aren't entirely wrong about blaming one of us," he said with a threatening undertone. The other executioners grumbled and exchanged annoyed looks.

"Enough!" Michael Deibler pounded the table again. "Damn it, Jakob, we agreed not to cast unnecessary suspicions. Not before we have more evidence. It's enough for people in the city to gossip about us."

"They say you're so clever, Jakob," Johann Widmann jeered, twisting his moustache between his fingers. "So, tell us, do you have any idea who the murderer is?" He pointed around the room. "If it's one of us, who's going to end up climbing the scaffold? Hans? Deibler? Your own brother, perhaps?"

Bartholomäus Kuisl jumped to his feet. He looked like he was about to launch himself at Widmann. "You dog, how dare you insult—" he began, but Deibler intervened.

"Stop it, dear cousins!" he called out. "There's no point tearing each other apart. Let's sit down and—"

In that moment, the door was flung open and Paul ran in. He struggled for breath, as though he'd been running a long way.

His small body was shaking. "Grandpa, you . . . you have to come quickly!" he gasped.

"Isn't that great," Widmann moaned. "Now the hangmen's grandchildren get a say at the meeting."

Kuisl ignored him. "What is it, Paul?" he asked with concern.

"It's . . . it's Master Hans," Paul burst out breathlessly. "He's up by the executioner's house—I think he wants to hurt Barbara."

"Ha! Finally someone's going to teach that female some manners," Widmann scoffed. "I hope he—hey!"

He winced as Conrad Näher slapped him in the face. The next moment, a full-blown brawl had broken out among the executioners. Beer mugs flew through the air, chairs shattered against heads and backs. The journeymen joined in, and Michael Deibler desperately tried to restore order.

Jakob Kuisl didn't see any of it, however, because he and Georg had already run outside.

A good mile away, Peter was running as hunched over as he could behind the tombstones toward the cemetery gate, desperately looking for someone who might be able to help.

When Master Hans dragged Barbara into the pit, Peter had fled in panic. But then love for his aunt had replaced his fear. Hadn't he sworn to protect Barbara? To be her knight in shining armor? He had snuck back and watched from behind an oak tree as Hans began throwing dirt on Barbara. Peter had soon realized that he'd have to find one or more grownups to stop this madman. He wouldn't achieve anything on his own against the Weilheim hangman.

Peter was about to rush to the exit when he passed the church's western portal and noticed that it stood ajar. On the other side of the door, he could hear the loud noise of something hitting the ground and someone cursing quietly. Someone was inside the church. Peter leapt up the few steps to the portal, opened it a crack, and to his enormous relief saw the sexton redecorating the altar. The elderly man had obviously just dropped the chalice and was now picking it back up, accompanied by more swearing. When the sexton heard the creak of the door, he turned around.

"What do you want?" he growled at Peter. "Mass won't start for a few hours yet. Make yourself scarce."

"I — I need your help," Peter gasped. "My aunt — somebody's assaulting her outside, in the cemetery. A hangman! He's thrown her into a hole, I'm sure he's going to kill her!"

"A hangman?" The sexton looked at him with red-rimmed eyes. He looked as though he'd already helped himself from the chalice that morning. "You're talking nonsense, boy. Go home and play hide and seek with your friends."

"It's the truth," Peter protested. "You have to help us or — or Barbara is going to die. Please!"

"I don't have to do anything," the sexton replied calmly while he continued his work on the altar. "How do I know you're not playing a trick on me? You probably just want me to leave the church so you can clean out the offertory box. I know what you street children are like."

"But . . . but . . ." Peter's hopes vanished. This man wouldn't help him. He'd have to run out into the streets to find a grownup after all, perhaps even a city guard. But by then it might be too late.

Then his eyes fell on an alcove behind the altar where steep winding stairs led upwards. An idea shot through his mind.

The belfry.

Without another word, Peter ran past the altar and toward the stairs.

"Hey, what do you think you're doing?" the sexton called after him. "Stop, you snot-nosed brat, in God's name!"

But Peter didn't listen. He ran up the winding staircase so fast that he became dizzy. His heart beat wildly, he gasped for breath, but he didn't slow down. Below him, the sexton's voice became farther and farther away, fading until he finally couldn't hear him at all. Up and up the stairs went, every now and then Peter passed small rectangular windows letting in the cold wind. Crows screeched somewhere above him. How much farther was it?

Finally he reached a trapdoor above his head. He pulled himself through and found he'd arrived at his destination.

The bells.

Peter had heard them when he and Barbara first entered the cemetery. They had sounded shrill and loud, and he thought people could probably hear them from very far away. Peter knew people rang the church bells in case of a fire or other emergency, and this was most definitely an emergency.

So he would ring them.

The two bells, a larger and a smaller one, hung about seven feet above him in the pointed roof of the tower. A thick rope hung from each bell. Peter decided on the smaller one. He pulled at the rope, but found to his horror that he couldn't move the bell at all. He was too weak and too light. Now he could hear the hurried steps of the sexton from below. He didn't have much time.

Once again Peter wished he was as strong as his grandfather —or at least as wild and determined as his younger brother, Paul. But all he knew was drawing, reading, and writing, and none of those skills could help him here. Only pure strength counted now.

The sexton was getting closer. "You just wait till I get my hands on you!" he shouted. "Your own mother won't recognize you."

Tears of frustration welled up in Peter's eyes. He wiped them away and was fighting back more tears when he spotted a small pile of bricks in the corner. He guessed they must have been left over from when the church was built. They were dusty red blocks, square and heavy.

Very heavy.

With desperate courage, Peter tore off his shirt, placed three bricks inside, and tied the sleeves around his neck. The weights pulled him down like millstones. Barbara's words from earlier came to his mind.

My knight in shining armor . . .

Peter jumped up as best he could, grabbed the rope and hung on, while the shirt pulled on his neck and started to tear. He tried to make himself heavier than he'd ever been in his life. Like a gallows bird he writhed on the rope as the sexton pulled himself through the hatch, cursing and swearing.

And the bell began to toll.

Jakob Kuisl, Georg, and Paul heard the bell as they hurried along the city wall toward the executioner's house. Paul had filled in his grandfather and uncle on the way.

Kuisl couldn't believe Master Hans was after his Barbara. He knew the Weilheim hangman had long been fascinated by Barbara's fierceness and beauty. Several years ago Hans had asked him bluntly if Barbara was still available. Kuisl had told the creepy fellow no, and Hans had accepted the rejection without complaint. But, apparently, the sight of Barbara at the meeting two days ago had rekindled the hangman's feelings. Kuisl wouldn't have thought Hans brazen enough to simply help himself to her, though.

People in the Anger Quarter were quick to jump aside when the huge angry man stormed past them. Even more than his size, his grim expression was menacing. The Schongau hangman was fuming with anger. When he got his hands on Hans, he'd break every bone in his body. After a while, Kuisl noticed that the bell was still ringing. Something must have happened somewhere in town, but he didn't have time to worry about that. All that mattered right now was his younger daughter.

In the meantime, the three of them had reached the executioner's house. Kuisl ran across the garden and threw himself against the front door, which flew open. He was about to run inside when he noticed Walburga at the stove. She was holding Sophia with one arm and feeding her porridge with the other. She dropped the spoon in fright when she saw the panting, furious hangman.

"My God, Jakob!" she called out, blanching. "Why do you come crashing in here like an assassin? Can't you knock?"

"I-I'm sorry, Burgi," Kuisl replied breathlessly. "But we're looking for Barbara. Apparently Master Hans was here looking for her. I wouldn't put anything past that dog."

"Master Hans?" Walburga frowned. She rocked Sophia, who had started to cry and wanted more porridge. Some of the cats began meowing, too, waiting hungrily by the stove. It was a while before the hangman's wife continued. "Well, there's no one here, anyhow. Not Master Hans, nor Barbara. Nor the two boys. I've only just come back myself and thought—" She broke off when she saw Georg and Paul behind Jakob. "At least Paul's back." She wagged a finger at him. "Is this perhaps another cheeky trick of yours?"

"No, it's true," Paul said. "Hans was here. He was sneaking around the house."

"Damn it! What if he took Barbara and Peter?" Georg said, still out of breath from the long walk. "If he hurts my sister, I . . . I . . ."

"Threats and curses don't help us now," Kuisl said. "We must figure out where Hans might have taken them."

"Where he might have taken them?" Georg gave a desperate laugh. "This is Munich, not Schongau, Father. This city is huge. He could be anywhere."

"Grandpa . . ." Paul tugged at Kuisl's hand, but he yanked it back angrily.

"Paul, can't you see that the grownups are talking? Be quiet and—"

"But I know someone who might be able to help," Paul whined. "Honest!"

"All right." The hangman groaned impatiently. "And who's that supposed to be? Saint Nicholas, perhaps?"

"No, my new friends."

When Georg, Walburga, and Kuisl merely stared at him with surprise, Paul squared his shoulders and continued with a determined voice: "I've met a few boys here. Seppi, Moser, and Schorsch, the knacker's son. They have a gang and they know everyone." He looked very impressed with himself. "They call themselves the Anger Wolves. They might have seen Barbara and Peter somewhere."

Kuisl snorted. "I can do without the help of a bunch of ragamuffins."

"The idea isn't that bad," Georg said. "I know street kids from Bamberg. They're like pushy little mutts. When they don't have to work for their parents or go to school, they roam the streets in gangs. It's at least possible they saw Barbara and Peter, and you can't miss Master Hans with his white hair and red eyes."

"Could it all be a terrible misunderstanding?" Walburga interjected. "Perhaps Hans was simply looking for my husband and Peter and Barbara left the house for an entirely different reason."

"Your husband is currently chairing a meeting in Au. Hans knows that because he was supposed to be at the meeting." Jakob Kuisl shook his head. "No, the bastard was after my Barbara." He tapped Paul on the shoulder. "Off you go, ask your friends if they saw anything. Quick!"

Paul smiled and ran outside. The hangman turned to his son, Georg. "We can't just wait here and do nothing. Perhaps you could alert Loibl from the city guard. He seems a decent sort of a fellow. I'm going to take a look around the Anger Quarter." He stomped his foot angrily. "And where the hell is my goddamned son-in-law? He's never there when you need him."

"If it's all the same to you, I'll keep looking after Sophia," Walburga said. "The girl has a very healthy appetite." She dipped a clean spoon into the barley porridge and fed it to Sophia. "I bought dried arnica at the market and want to change the bandage on her foot. And my cats need feeding. You see, there's plenty to do, even without a murderer on the loose."

Kuisl nodded and walked outside. He was about to leave through the gate when a horde of children came running toward him, his grandson Paul at the head.

"We found Barbara already," Paul said, beaming. "And Peter, too. They're walking along the city stream from the Hacken Quarter." He pointed at a tall boy with ripped trousers and matted hair who bowed to Kuisl with a grin. "Schorsch here saw them, accompanied by two guards. They say Peter rang the bell in the Church of the Holy Cross. And now they're looking for his father to give him a hefty fine."

Kuisl breathed a sigh of relief. He sat down heavily on the garden bench. Suddenly, he felt incredibly tired.

"His father isn't here," he said. "The guards will have to make do with his grandfather. I can't wait to hear what my daughter and grandson have to tell us."

7

ONCE AGAIN, WHEN SIMON GOT back to the executioner's house around noon, he learned that much had happened in his absence.

His polished leather boots and his expensive pants were filthy, one trouser leg was torn because a barking mutt had jumped up on him on his way home. After his visit at the dogcatcher's Simon had walked back and forth across the Anger and Hacken quarters, asking about the electress's dog at countless taverns and dingy inns, speaking with numerous dodgy characters. He soon realized he'd never find Arthur that way. How he hated this mission. But Simon knew it was most likely his only chance to win the favor of the electress and secure a place at a good school for Peter.

And my last opportunity to present my treatise to the public, he thought. *Because I highly doubt I'm ever going to meet Doctor Malachias Geiger if things keep going the way they are.*

Now they all sat around the big table at the executioner's house, except for Magdalena, who hadn't returned yet from the silk manufactory. It looked like they had actually employed her. Walburga had bandaged Sophia's foot with bear fat and arnica, and Simon had to admit that she was doing a fantastic job. The wife of the Munich hangman was truly an excellent healer. Now she was sitting in the apothecary chamber next door, mixing medicines, a happily squealing Sophia on her lap. Earlier she had treated Barbara, who had twisted her right foot when she fell into the hole. Simon could hardly believe what the others had just told him.

"And you really think Master Hans wanted to harm Barbara?" he asked.

"If I know the man, he didn't just want to have a friendly chat with her," Georg replied. "He knew she was staying here, and he also knew she was without male protection, since Father, Deibler, and I were at the meeting."

"And you were looking for lapdogs," Kuisl added grimly. "When we could have used you here." He shook his head. "Some crazy murderer is on the loose, the people want to see Bavaria's best hangmen hung, and what's my son-in-law doing? Looking for a goddamned mutt!"

"You know I didn't ask for the job," Simon replied curtly. "Perhaps you'll thank me one day, when your grandson goes to school in Munich."

"He's clever enough, anyway," Michael Deibler said from the head of the table. He grinned. "To just run up the belfry of the Holy Cross Church and ring the bell to catch people's attention? I wouldn't have thought of it. The sexton nearly had a heart attack. Thank God I know Loibl well enough so they dropped the fine," he said, laughing, "or I might have had to put a hangman's son in the stocks."

"I think he saved me in the very last moments," Barbara said quietly. She sat right beside the stove, listening to the conversation with her eyes closed. She had wrapped a blanket around herself despite the warmth. Her face was covered in scrapes, and she looked worn out. "Hans had already picked up the tombstone," she continued. "When the church bell rang, he must have realized people would soon show up. So he dropped it and ran away."

"What on earth was he doing at the cemetery?" Kuisl muttered, deep in thought, gazing at the smoke from his pipe. He turned to Deibler. "Do you have any idea?"

Michael Deibler puffed on his own pipe and added a few clouds of smoke to Kuisl's. "The Church of the Holy Cross is the second parish church after Saint Peter. When the cemetery at Old Peter became too full, they built another church in the Hacken Quarter. But—"

"He was looking for a particular grave." From her seat by the stove Barbara cut him off. She lowered her voice as though Master Hans were still outside. "Peter saw it. We just don't know which grave. And he said a few weird things. Asked if Father had figured it out yet." She looked at her father. "He was desperate to find out what you knew."

"I've always said it: the man's as mad as a rabid ferret." Kuisl gave a laugh, but then his expression turned serious again. "The devil knows what he meant. I know nothing."

"Just to make sure the silly physician is up to speed," Simon said tentatively, feeling a little nauseated from all the tobacco smoke. "Hans first comes here, hoping to find Barbara alone. Maybe he only wants to talk to her, maybe not. When he can't get in, he walks to the cemetery. He looks for something there. But what, and why?"

"Damn it—if only we could ask him ourselves!" Deibler swore. "But it's as if the earth swallowed the bastard up. He probably knows he can't show his face at the council after this. And they haven't seen him at the inn in Haidhausen where he'd been staying. A distant relative of his lives there, but he's a stubborn fellow and doesn't give anything away."

"We should keep an eye on that inn," Kuisl said and took another drag on his pipe.

Deibler snorted like an old dragon. "And how do you propose to do that? Georg, you, and I have to go back to the meeting this afternoon. I'm only glad I managed to stop the brawl earlier before anyone was killed. I owe the innkeeper eight kreuzers for the broken chairs." He rolled his eyes. "Of course, this is grist for Widmann's mill. The arrogant peacock thinks about nothing else but how he might push you out of the council and bring me into disrepute. He'll use any excuse." His eyes turned to Simon. "That only leaves Herr Son-in-Law to keep an eye on Hans, but he's looking for a lapdog."

Simon could feel himself blush. "Er, I think I've stressed several times that—"

"I think I know who might be able to help," Georg cut him off. "Those street children Paul hangs out with seem like a clever bunch to me. If we give them a few coins, they'll keep tabs on Hans's movements for us." He looked around the room. "Where are Peter and Paul?"

"This house is bloody big," Deibler grumbled. "Very old and very big. They probably found a new hiding place somewhere. They already found the passage to the battlements."

Kuisl scratched his large hooked nose. "I don't think Hans is going to go back to the Haidhausen tavern, anyway. The boys can try their luck. It won't do any harm." He puffed on his pipe thoughtfully. "Something's at that cemetery. I'll have to go back there myself."

"But not until after the meeting this afternoon. Perhaps your older daughter will have learned something at the silk manufactory by then." Michael Deibler knocked the cold tobacco ash into the reeds on the ground. "It's late, we have to go. The other cousins will want to hear what happened. And Widmann . . ."

"Yes, yes, I know, he has it in for me," Kuisl growled. He turned to Barbara. "Before I go, please tell me that there's still hope for Conrad Näher from Kaufbeuren. He's my last iron in the fire."

Barbara smiled a thin smile. "Well, let's say he's not as bad as the others. I've met with him once."

"And he's still alive." Georg smiled. "We have every reason to be optimistic."

He was about to head toward the door with his father and Michael Deibler when someone knocked loudly. Deibler went to the door and opened it.

Simon winced when he saw through the haze in the room who was standing outside. It was the same electoral envoy who found him two days ago. Was the electress expecting her report already? The messenger looked even more disgusted than at their last meeting in Au. He blinked his eyes repeatedly against the thick smoke and looked about suspiciously, as if he expected a robber to attack him at any moment.

"Is this where Doctor Fronwieser is staying?" he asked, his right eyebrow twitching nervously.

Simon pushed to the front. He brushed his hands down his vest, which was wrinkled and splattered with gravy. "Um, yes. I'm here."

"I've just come from Au. They told me I could find you at the"— the envoy coughed and fanned his face with his hand — "at the executioner's house. I am to ask you in the name of His Electoral Excellency to appear at the opera house at Salvator Square at six o'clock. With your son."

Simon froze. He thought he had misheard the man. "Excuse me, where?"

"At the opera house." The messenger sighed. "It appears the young crown prince wants to see your son."

"The young *crown prince?*" Simon's heart beat faster. He remembered what Peter had told him after their visit to the Residenz.

I was playing with the prince. His name is Max and he wants to see me again . . .

Evidently Peter hadn't been lying.

The envoy wrinkled his nose as he studied Simon's dirty trousers and the threadbare vest. "I'm afraid we'll have to clothe you

for the show. Peasants and simple folk aren't allowed in the opera. Neither are stinking pipe smokers," he added smugly. "You
better come to the Residenz first. Via the servants' entrance, of
course. We should be able to find something decent enough for
you. Hmm . . ." He looked Simon up and down. "Hopefully in
your size, too."

About two hours later, winter returned to Munich.

It was as if winter wanted to land one last heavy blow before
spring would finally take over. Snowflakes whirled from the sky
like goose down, and an icy northerly wind froze the first shoots
on bushes and trees. The icicles hanging from the city's belfries
like long sharp swords grew longer.

On the roads around Munich, carts and carriages battled their
way through the snowstorm toward the gates of the city. Only
one lonesome figure was headed in the opposite direction.
Dressed in a warm black woolen coat and a scarf for protection
against the wind, the stooped figure whistled a simple melody, a
nursery rhyme.

*Bumpety, bump, rider. If he falls, he cries out. If into the ditch he
falls, he'll get eaten by the crows . . .*

The hunter loved snowstorms. When the icy flakes fell thickly,
the heat inside disappeared for a little while and thoughts calmed.
And there was much to think about. The hangman and his family were closing in. How much longer before they'd piece the
mosaic together? How long before the hunter would become the
hunted?

A brief whimper slipped out through the hunter's clenched
teeth, but the wind carried it off immediately. Yes, mistakes had
been made. Moving too fast, too eagerly. On the other hand,
what else could one do when duty called? Times had changed,
there were more and more of them. So many, everywhere! There
was so much to do. Why couldn't anyone else see that they were
all running straight toward a great abyss? Were they all blind?

A wind gust hissed like a wild animal and tore off the hunter's headscarf. The hunter caught it, tied it back on firmly, and plodded on. A narrow track led from the road to a hill that could be seen from a long way away. Long poles stuck out of the snow on the hill, with a heavy wagon wheel attached to one of them. Crows and ravens circled the remains of a corpse that seemed to have been broken on the wheel months ago. The mummified joints were braided around the spokes like the artwork of the devil. The skull was lying on the ground underneath.

Next to it stood the gallows.

The body swaying in the wind from the rope was in far better condition than the one on the wheel. It belonged to the Munich tawer who had been convicted of repeated theft and was hung personally by Michael Deibler about three weeks ago. The poor fellow would be left hanging there until his limbs came off by themselves — as a warning to other thieves.

The cold temperatures had kept the corpse fresh. The crows had only eaten his eyes and other soft parts of the face so far. A thin layer of ice covered his skin and clothes, his mouth stood open in a silent scream. The stiff body swung like the pendulum of a large clock.

Back and forth, back and forth.

The steady swaying soothed the hunter. Gallows Hill near the Landsberg road always served as a reminder of the meaning of justice. God pronounced the verdict, and the hunter was His willing instrument.

Bringing purity.

As pure and white as the snow piling up on the crossbeam.

Back and forth, and back and forth . . .

The plan was taking shape.

Basically, it was simple. The others, too, were eager and greedy; greedy for news, for the truth, for the bigger picture behind the riddle. For glory, power, and money. So, the hunter would lure them with small crumbs of the truth. And they would walk into the trap.

One after the other.

The hunter smiled. Today would see the capture of the first one.

The hunter took a deep breath of the pure winter air, then turned around and headed back toward the city, humming a nursery rhyme.

The icy wind also swept across the cemetery of the Church of the Holy Cross. Jakob Kuisl clutched his hat and opened the same gate Barbara and Peter had taken a few hours earlier. He had seen few people on the way here, since the snow and cold kept most burghers of Munich in their houses or at shops and taverns. No one wanted to visit a graveyard in this weather.

Unless, of course, they were looking for one grave in particular.

Jakob Kuisl couldn't stop thinking about what Barbara had told him earlier. What in God's name had Master Hans been looking for in the cemetery? Why had he spoken of a mystery? And why did he think Kuisl might know something about it?

Jakob Kuisl had sat silently through the afternoon meeting. After the events in the city this morning, a regular meeting was hardly possible. The cousins wanted to know what happened with Master Hans. Paul and his new friends watched the inn the Weilheim hangman had been staying in. Kuisl would have preferred for his son-in-law to take on this task, but he'd rather join those arrogant Munich fops at the opera, whatever that was. And Georg was looking after his twin sister, who had a sore foot and still hadn't agreed to marry anyone. The only person Kuisl could rely upon was his elder daughter, Magdalena. He hoped she had found out more about that strange silk manufactory by now.

Angry, the hangman shut the gate behind him and stomped past the crooked tombstones on which almost a hand's breadth of fresh snow had settled. The wind howled mournfully, as if the souls were rising from their graves for judgment day. Kuisl walked down the row of tombstones in the direction Barbara had told him until he found the freshly dug grave his daughter had fallen into. The heavy stone slab was still lying beside it. When Kuisl wiped the snow aside, he saw the name of the next eternal visitor at Holy Cross cemetery.

THERESA WILPRECHT, 1652–1672, REQUIESCAT IN PACE

Jakob Kuisl nodded appreciatively. The Munich gravediggers were fast. The poor girl had only been found yesterday, and her grave was ready today. The body was probably in the nearby chapel. Had Hans been looking for this grave? But why? What had he hoped to find here? Or perhaps this was the wrong spot?

After a few moments Kuisl walked on, past oak trees swaying in the wind. The closer he got to the north end of the cemetery, the plainer the graves became. Some were merely marked with simple wooden crosses, several of them so old and rotten that the names had become illegible. Then Kuisl came to a large grave with a single, unmarked tombstone. He suspected it was a mass grave for the poorest of the poor who couldn't afford a burial. The hangman thought of the strawberry-blonde-haired girl whose body he had cut open a few days ago. What was her name again?

Anni . . .

By now she was probably lying in a grave similar to this one at Au or Giesing. How many girls like her were buried in such graves? Girls who had been searching for happiness in the big city, a city that only held misery and death for them. The hangman looked about in silent grief. Not a single wreath adorned the mass grave, not one flower by the tombstone, not even a grave candle.

Kuisl's thoughts turned to his own death. He was old. God

only knew how many years he had left. As the hangman, he had no right to a spot at the Schongau cemetery. His beloved wife, Anna-Maria, who had left him a few years ago, also lay outside the cemetery walls. At least Kuisl had managed to gain permission to bury her in a sunny spot underneath a willow. He visited her grave often, more frequently the older he became. And he always brought flowers and wreaths, even though he tried to hide it from his family.

My dear Anna-Maria, when will I see you again?

An intense longing for death suddenly took hold of the hangman. His throat tightened as though by a thick hemp rope. He needed to get away from here. He needed to leave this place of grief and anonymous dead. Kuisl tore himself away from the mass grave. He was about to walk away when he noticed a much smaller mound next to the large grave. It lay underneath a bush with frozen rowan berries, which was why he hadn't noticed it until then. A small wooden cross marked the grave, and, unlike the other graves nearby, it bore a wreath of braided fir twigs.

The needles were green and fresh, and there was hardly any snow on them, as if the wreath had just been placed there.

Frowning, Kuisl came closer. Now he also saw the grave candle, flickering inside a glass despite the wind. Only a finger's breadth of the wax had melted—someone lit this candle not long ago. The hangman looked for prints in the snow, but the heavy snowfall had covered everything in a white blanket.

Kuisl knelt down to read the inscription on the cross, which was so new that it still smelled of resin. The name startled him.

ELFRIEDE TANNINGER, 1654 TILL 1672

It was the impaled girl. Deibler had mentioned her name only yesterday.

Had Hans been looking for this grave? Deep in thought, Jakob Kuisl rose to his feet when he heard a noise behind the rowan bush. Someone was running away. Then a howling gust of wind drowned out every sound.

Kuisl didn't hesitate. He ran around the bush and peered into the whirling snow. The wind was chasing the flakes almost horizontally across the graveyard, but Kuisl thought he could make out the outline of a person. Or was it just his imagination? No, it was definitely a man in a coat or cape. He was wearing a hood or something similar that fluttered along behind him like big leathery wings.

Like a black angel.

"Stop!" Kuisl shouted, feeling odd, as if he were trying to command a ghost. He ran after the figure.

The man was fast. He was twenty or thirty paces ahead of him. Once again, Kuisl felt his age. The freezing air hurt his lungs and he was panting after just a short distance. And his legs still ached from the long run that morning. What he wouldn't give to have Georg or Simon here now. A stabbing pain cut through his chest like a knife.

The hangman gritted his teeth and suppressed the pain, running even faster. He would catch this specter, even if lightning struck him down.

The man—or whatever it was—ran toward the gate, but then he took a sharp turn and ran along the cemetery wall, which was about man-high on that side. He stopped abruptly, jumped, and grabbed hold of the top of the wall.

Then he flew.

A black angel of death . . .

Kuisl squinted. The dense snow blurred everything. For an instant, he could see the man's black outline against the white sky, like an angry goblin dancing on the wall, then he jumped down the other side.

"For Christ's sake! Stop, whatever you are!"

Kuisl went after him. Gasping, he pulled himself up the icy, snow-covered wall. Twice he slipped, then he was finally up.

But by then, the man had disappeared.

Or had he only imagined everything? An angel, calling him home to his beloved wife? Beckoning him to follow?

The street on the other side of the wall was empty. He could hear footsteps in one of the side alleys, but they soon disappeared too. Only the wind howled, high-pitched and loud.

Kuisl felt like it was mocking him.

On the other side of the city wall, Magdalena watched the dancing snowflakes through one of the small barred windows of the Au silk manufactory.

Her fingers hurt and her back ached from sitting hunched over all day, but she tried not to show it and moved the shuttle with the silk yarn through the shed, pushed the pedals and the batten again and again. The steady clicking and whirring, the constant noise around her made her both tired and restless at the same time. She studied the other twenty or so girls, hunched over at their looms, tight-lipped, their faces ashen. Magdalena thought none of the girls was older than twenty, except perhaps Agnes, who worked beside her and hadn't as much as glanced at her since their last conversation. Magdalena had no idea why Agnes had turned so cold since she asked about Eva.

There were some pretty girls among the weavers. Agnes was one of them, but also the pale fifteen-year-old Magdalena had helped out that morning. Most of them, however, looked as though they had aged before their time, cowering at their looms like lost dolls in the dim light.

Magdalena was used to working outside, searching for herbs in the forest, weeding the garden, and walking for miles through fields and meadows when she visited pregnant women together with Martha Stechlin, the midwife. The few hours she'd been locked up in this stuffy room nearly drove her insane. She didn't want to imagine what a whole lifetime at the loom would be like.

But she knew some of these young women would be doing just that for the rest of their lives.

It was late afternoon. A snowstorm was raging outside, and the large room was dark. Joseffa had put up cheap tallow candles so the work could go on, but the girls still had to strain their eyes to see what they were doing.

Mother Joseffa sat comfortably in her chair in the center of the room, nibbling on dried berries from a pouch, and kept a watchful eye on the silent weavers. Every now and again, she stood up and inspected the fabric here and there, scolding, swearing, and occasionally slapping the girls. She had only left the room once more. Magdalena had immediately tried to talk to Agnes about the dead girls, but the woman had ignored her. While Magdalena looked for someone else to speak to, Joseffa returned.

At least Magdalena found the work easier now. She could let her thoughts roam while her hands wove monotonously. She thought about Sophia, about Barbara's pregnancy and her future husband. Would it be the older, good-natured Conrad Näher from Kaufbeuren, or would they find someone else? She thought about Peter and the botched opportunity to gain a place at a Munich school for him. Most of all, however, she thought about the recent murders and how they might be connected to the silk manufactory. What was going on inside this gloomy building?

Her father had told Magdalena that three of the young weavers had been friends, Anni, Elfriede, and Eva. Two of them were dead now, and the third locked up in the basement of the manufactory. The pale girl had told Magdalena this morning that she believed Eva was going to be killed. That awful van Uffele had spoken of getting rid of the problem for good. Clearly, Eva knew something and Joseffa and van Uffele wanted to silence her.

If Eva was still alive, Magdalena needed to find her as soon as she could.

But how?

An opportunity arose in the early evening, when they fell short of yarn and Joseffa asked two skinny boys to fetch more silk from the store in the basement.

"And don't you drop the bales and get them all dirty and tangled up," Joseffa threatened the boys, who weren't older than Peter and Paul. "Or I'll beat the living daylights out of you."

"But the bales are so heavy and bulky," one of the boys replied, his voice shaking. "And we haven't eaten since this morning . . ."

"You'll get your supper soon enough, you greedy pigs," Joseffa groused. "You're eating us out of house and home already."

"I could give them a hand," Magdalena suggested timidly.

"You?" Joseffa's head shot around. "Trying to get a break, are you?"

"No, but I think we'll need more yarn very soon," Magdalena replied. She pointed to the back. "I think several other looms are running out of filling yarn, too."

Joseffa hesitated briefly, then waved dismissively. "What the hell. You're just wasting time here anyway, so you might as well be useful somewhere else." She raised a warning finger. "But no excursions, understood? The three of you go down to the storeroom, fetch the yarn, and back upstairs."

"You can rely on me, mistress."

Joseffa grinned at the word *mistress*. She made a jovial gesture and Magdalena left the room with the two boys. When they walked down the stairs, two younger, broad-shouldered men came toward them, simple tradesmen, judging by their clothes. They talked loudly, and Magdalena listened. If she wasn't mistaken, they spoke Italian. She couldn't understand a word, but it seemed the men were very upset about something.

"Who was that?" she asked the boys once the men had gone.

"The Venetians," one of the boys whispered. "There's a few of them working in rooms in the attic, where they spin raw silk into yarn. None of us is allowed in there. The Venetians are the only ones who know how to make the silk. It's a big secret."

"There seem to be a few secrets in this house," Magdalena murmured.

She noticed in passing that the bolt at the front door was secured with a heavy lock.

Like a prison, she thought.

They followed the stairs down to the basement. Behind a heavy door a long, poorly lit corridor led to the left and right. The air was damp and moldy, and it was bitter cold. Magdalena tightened her rough woolen scarf, shivering. The two boys turned left, where Magdalena could make out a number of doors. She pointed in the opposite direction.

"What's down there?" she asked.

"We don't know," the smaller of the boys said in a hushed voice. "And we're not allowed to go there, or we'll get beaten."

"When we came here yesterday, we heard a whimpering down there," the other boy whispered, looking about nervously. "It was creepy."

Magdalena's heart beat faster. The pale girl from upstairs had said the same thing. Was Eva locked in a room down the corridor?

"Listen," she whispered. "You know Eva, the girl who disappeared?"

"What about her?" the taller boy asked.

"She's a good friend of mine. I need to find out where she is. I'll go and take a quick look down the corridor, and you warn me if anyone comes, all right?"

"But van Uffele will kill us if he finds out," the younger boy whined.

"I won't be long, I promise. You keep watch. If someone comes, just whistle." She gave the boys a friendly smile. "I'll give you my supper if you do it."

That swayed the two boys. They nodded, and Magdalena turned around and hurried down the dark corridor. Unlike the left branch, no torches lit the way down this end of the passage.

Soon it was so dark that Magdalena could only just make out the outlines of doors. There seemed to be no end to the gloomy corridor, and it reeked of rot and feces. Where on earth did this passage lead?

"Eva?" she whispered into the darkness. "Eva? Are you there?"

No one answered. But then Magdalena heard a soft, barely audible whimpering from farther ahead. It sounded like the whimper of a child or a young woman. Eva! She was about to rush down the corridor when someone whistled behind her.

Someone was coming down the stairs.

Cursing softly, Magdalena stopped. She was so close to uncovering the secret and now this. What should she do? If she didn't turn around now, she wasn't just putting herself in danger but the boys, too. After hesitating for a moment, she hurried back. And not a moment too soon. Magdalena heard footsteps coming down the stairs. She didn't have much time. The torches lit the way ahead, and she saw the two boys waiting for her anxiously.

Breathlessly, Magdalena reached the bottom of the stairs as the two Venetians arrived with a lantern. They eyed Magdalena and the boys suspiciously.

"*Dove vai?*" one of them asked harshly.

Magdalena pointed down the left-hand corridor with a smile. "Um, new yarn," she said. "We're just fetching some new yarn. I took the wrong corridor. Sorry."

The two men didn't appear to understand her. They shook their heads and walked past her into the darkness of the right-hand corridor.

There goes my chance for today, Magdalena thought despairingly.

She followed the boys in the opposite direction, where they soon reached a room full of spindles, loom parts, and bundles of silk yarn. The two boys grabbed several bundles each and Magdalena followed their example. The bundles were surprisingly heavy and awkward to hold, and Magdalena feared she'd drop one and tangle the yarn. With slow steps, the three of them carried their heavy load upstairs to the weaving room. When they entered, Magdalena saw to her horror that van Uffele was standing next to Joseffa, looking agitated. Had the Venetians already said something? But when van Uffele spotted Magdalena, he broke into a sugary smile.

"Ah, there's our pretty little dove," he said. He tilted his head and looked Magdalena up and down. "Hmm. Some soap and water, a decent dress . . ." Nodding, he turned to Joseffa. "You might be right. She'll make a good replacement, even though she's a little older. I'm not sure he'll like that."

"Agnes is old, too. And this one's prettier than Agnes," Joseffa replied. "Look." She walked over to Magdalena and grabbed a handful of her hair. "Healthy black hair, full lips, large breasts . . . Her skin's not too reddened from work. And Agnes is getting sicker every day. God knows how long she's got to live. So, we'll need a new girl soon anyway." The two of them scrutinized Magdalena critically. "Let's at least try," Joseffa said eventually. "He can always throw her out."

"You're right." Van Uffele gave Magdalena one last scrutinizing look. "We have to give him something. That bloody codface is giving me a hard time because he thinks his money is going down the drain."

"And he's not entirely wrong, either," Joseffa snickered.

"Don't start!" van Uffele snapped. Then he nodded. "So we're agreed. Agnes, Carlotta, and the new one are going tomorrow." Only now did he address Magdalena directly. "What's your name again?"

"Er, Magdalena." Her hair stood on end. What was going on here? She cleared her throat. "If you'd be so kind as to tell me—"

"You'll find out soon enough," Joseffa cut her off. "Now get back to your loom. Your other work starts tomorrow morning. You'll spend the night here with us."

"But—" Magdalena protested.

"No buts," Joseffa snarled. "We have plenty to prepare for your new work. And you're not done weaving yet." She smirked. "Take good care of your pretty little fingers, darling. You're going to need them."

Bewildered, Magdalena returned to her loom. Agnes glared at her from dark-ringed eyes and another coughing fit rattled her. "Lucky you," she said quietly after a while. "Seems like you're van Uffele's new favorite. I better start packing my bags." Her smile was sad and bitter. "Looks like you're going to find out why dear Eva is no longer here after all."

Simon stood inside the huge building they called the Munich Opera House and gaped. He tried not to tremble. Never in his whole life had he felt so clearly how small and pathetic his world was. This house was as far removed from Schongau as the sun or the moon.

Entranced, Simon took in the three stories of small balconies arranged in semicircles. Nymphs and angels smiled at him from every stucco-decorated column. The domed ceiling was painted in the brightest colors with scenes from Greek mythology. Opposite Simon lay the stage, which was hung with a red velvet curtain so large and heavy that someone could probably sew dresses for every woman in Munich from it.

Almost more impressive than the opera house itself were the countless people gathered in front of the stage with Simon and Peter. The men were dressed in coats of the finest material and decorated with colorful ribbons. Their shirts bore lace collars and cuffs, and thin cloths were tied around their necks, called cravats, as Simon had heard—a new fashion from France, just like the powdered wigs the French king wore. The women wore puffy dresses with low necklines and had piled up their hair into true masterpieces.

People conversed and laughed, sometimes in French and Italian. Simon hoped fervently no one would speak to him. He guessed his slight Schongau accent would be enough to expose him as a country bumpkin.

He glanced down at himself. Before he and Peter had been driven to the wealthy Munich Kreuz Quarter by carriage, the electoral envoy had outfitted him with appropriate clothes at the Residenz. Simon wore a pair of his beloved baggy trousers, a white shirt, and a blue velvet coat. Next to him, Peter looked like a little lord in his vest and neatly combed hair. But Simon still felt like the people avoided them, as if they could smell their provincial origins. On top of that, Peter seemed to be the only child at the opera. Simon had already noticed a few surprised glances — but also displeased ones.

"Well, as for me, I'm awfully curious about Kerll's new piece," fluted a lady next to him whose hair could have held about a dozen bird's nests. "It's supposed to be very entertaining."

"I hope it's going to be better than his last opera, *L'Erinto*," a man wearing a periwig replied. "Do you remember the Italian tenor? That Macolino? I still have nightmares about his terrible bawling."

The people nearby laughed, and Simon put on a strained smile so he wouldn't look conspicuous.

"Papa," Peter whispered to him. "What is an opera?"

"Um, I think it's a play with lots of music," Simon replied quietly. "I believe it's from Italy. I'm not entirely sure either. We'll soon find out."

On the way here, the messenger had explained to them that the Munich Opera House was the first in the German Empire, an incredibly generous gift from the Bavarian electress to her subjects. Unfortunately, thought Simon, most of her subjects would never experience an opera.

The last few hours had been like a dream to Simon. He still couldn't really believe what was happening. From the scant explanations of the messenger he'd gathered that their invitation had indeed come from the young Bavarian crown prince. Apparently, Peter had run into Max Emanuel at the Residenz and the two had become friends. The envoy didn't hide the fact that he thought this invitation was a huge mistake. And Simon's own feelings were mixed, too. What if the electress asked him about her accursed lapdog? He hadn't made any headway in his search yet, and he feared the next few days would go no better. And he had plenty of other things to worry about.

"Her Electoral Excellency is taking her time," the powdered lady with the towering hair hissed. "Typical!"

"At least she's not dancing herself this time," snickered an elderly woman who had applied so much dry rouge that she had cracks in her face. "Do you remember *La Ninfa Ritrosa,* how she strutted about the stage like a peacock?" She sighed theatrically. "Soon it will be time for the first masquerades of the carnival season again, where we'll have to admire her. I'm already dreading the ball at Nymphenburg Palace. What are you going to wear?"

The two women kept gossiping shamelessly. Like many others in the room, they seemed to be courtiers, although Simon thought some of the spectators were wealthy commoners. In contrast to the nobility, the patricians wore simpler garments and stood in groups of their own. The balconies slowly filled with gentry and courtiers, while the commoners stayed down below. The powdered ladies and the gentleman with the periwig also made their way to the upper levels.

Simon immediately felt a little more comfortable. With Peter holding his hand, he walked about the large floor and admired the statues, elaborate balconies, and most of all the enormous stage, which took up a large part of the room. In front of the stage stood a raised podium with thronelike chairs, presumably for the electoral family.

While Simon waited with Peter for the show to start, he thought of Magdalena. How he would have loved to have her by his side. But for a dishonorable hangman's daughter, this world was even less accessible than it was for a simple Schongau physician. Would there ever be a time when everyone was allowed to admire such beauty? Simon hoped Magdalena had returned from the silk manufactory by now. He couldn't wait to tell her everything.

Bored, he listened to the conversations of the Munich citizens around him, the usual mix of gossip, politics, and business. But suddenly the voice of a corpulent man next to him caught his attention.

"Those bloody hangmen," he said. "Ever since they've been holding their meeting in Au, the city has been out of control. I wasn't too concerned about those murdered girls at first, but now that patricians have become victims, it's no longer tolerable."

"Apparently old Wilprecht is beside himself," said a rotund woman with an elegant bonnet and low neckline, presumably the man's wife. "He has offered a reward for anyone who can name for him the murderer of his wife."

"It's about time the city put up a reward for the arrest of those damned coin counterfeiters," the fat man grumbled. "The elector has, so I hear. It's getting worse every day. Yesterday I received thirty thalers for my three bales of cloth at the market, and when I weighed the coins at home, I found they were much too light. That's the third time already, and it's always silver coins. Thalers, batzen, pennies—those scoundrels will forge anything."

"If we're not careful, we'll end up like our fathers," an elderly man in a plain black coat said. "Remember? It was the Kipper- and Wipper time, when good coins where sorted out by weight, melted down, and mixed with cheap metals into several counterfeit coins each. And at official behest. In the end, the money was worthless and the country went to rack and ruin."

"I heard they almost caught one the counterfeiters," the corpulent man replied, dabbing at the sweat on his forehead with a silk handkerchief. "A small, sneaky fellow who told Wagner at the bookshop he was a doctor. Unfortunately, he got away."

"There must be more than one," a third man grumbled. He was wearing a stiff ruff collar and also looked like a patrician from Munich. "It has to be a very well-organized operation. They need a workshop and high-quality molds or dies. The devil knows how they do it. Their workshop must be bloody well hidden or the authorities would have found it by now."

"As I already mentioned," the older man whispered, "last time, the elector was personally responsible. You only need a few rogues to get the money among the people unnoticed. I don't want to step on anyone's toes, but it could be one of us."

The man's eyes wandered from person to person, and Simon tried to look as inconspicuous as possible. Was the fat man suddenly eyeing him strangely? Simon grabbed Peter by the hand and dragged him away from the group.

"Ouch! You're hurting me," Peter complained.

"I'm sorry," Simon whispered. "But . . . um, I think the opera is about to start and we really should . . ."

He faltered when he heard a certain name among the many conversations. Or had he been mistaken? Simon stopped and listened, and indeed, there it was again.

". . . just not getting better, Doctor Geiger."

Doctor Geiger!

Simon spun around and saw two men standing close together. One of them was around forty, balding, with soft pale lips and bulging eyes like those of a fish. The other man looked much older. His short pointed beard was silver, his hair was cropped short, his gaze was severe. He looked like a priest in his plain black coat.

"I can try again with antimony," he was just saying to fishface. "But I'm afraid the growth has progressed too far."

"And yet she just won't die," the other man moaned. "It's been like this for almost a year now."

"One could almost think you're wishing for your wife's death, Master Pfundner."

"Of course not, so God help us." Pfundner shook his head, scandalized. "I just don't want her to suffer too much."

"Then give her time and love. Those two things have healed a lot."

Fishface smiled wanly. "I don't have much of the former, and the latter melts like ice in the sunshine when your own wife stinks and wastes away. I'm sure you know what I mean, Doctor Geiger."

"I'm afraid I don't."

Simon said a silent prayer of thanks. The serious-looking man standing only a few feet away from him really was Doctor Malachias Geiger. He could hardly believe his luck. On the other hand, he wasn't surprised that the most famous physician in Munich was present at an event like this. All Simon had to do now was pluck up his courage to speak to the doctor. Unfortunately, he wasn't carrying his treatise on him, but this probably wasn't the best place to discuss it in great detail anyway.

But he might at least be able to lay the foundations for another conversation at a later date.

Simon took a deep breath. "I'll be right back," he whispered to Peter. Then he mustered all the courage he could and walked toward the two men.

"Perhaps you could at least give her more poppy syrup," fishface was just saying. "Then at least I won't have to listen to her moaning and groaning all the—"

Simon gave a little cough. "Doctor Geiger," he began. "Please forgive my intrusion."

The two men turned to him with surprise. The fishface called Pfundner raised his thin, barely visible eyebrows in annoyance.

"How dare you interrupt us?" he snarled. "And who are you?"

"Er, my name is Doctor Simon Fronwieser. I'm from Schongau and—"

"From Schongau?" Pfundner laughed maliciously. "Isn't that somewhere near the Alps? How on earth did a yokel like you get into the opera?"

I am here at the personal behest of the electress, you arrogant carp, Simon wanted to say. But he thought better of it. He didn't want to risk having to talk about his mission as the electoral family's dogcatcher.

"Schongau has a theater, too," he said proudly instead. "And not the worst, either." It was a blatant lie. Only traveling troupes of jugglers had ever performed in Schongau. But Simon couldn't bear the patrician's arrogant demeanor. "You're welcome to visit our beautiful old town sometime," he added.

"I can think of better ways to spend my time," Pfundner jeered. "And now leave us alone, please."

"You said you were a doctor?" Malachias Geiger now asked. He studied Simon carefully. "It's been a long time since I've been to Schongau. Back then, there was only a barber-surgeon, whose skills were—mildly put—not the best, and who was a little too fond of brandy."

My father, Simon thought with a pang.

"The city council appointed me town physician two years ago," he replied without mentioning his family history.

"Congratulations. And where did you study, if I may ask?"

"Ingolstadt. But that was a long time ago." Simon felt himself blush. His time at Ingolstadt University was a sore point in his life. He'd had to quit after a few semesters because he ran out of money, but also because he was lazy—a huge disappointment for his father. "I . . . I worked as a bathhouse surgeon for a few years at first," he added reluctantly.

"A bathhouse surgeon!" Pfundner smiled sardonically. "Cupping blood and money."

"Don't disregard the profession of bathhouse surgeon," Geiger said sternly. "They often have more experience than many a young medicus who knows nothing but the color of their patients' urine. And bathhouse surgeons have knowledge of the nastiest ailments." He turned to Simon with interest. "We were just speaking about a growth that ails the wife of our venerable city treasurer. It first started in the left breast, which I eventually removed. Now it has taken hold of the second breast as well and grows steadily. Tell me, dear colleague, how would you proceed?"

Simon saw Pfundner looking at him with disgust. What sort of advice could a simple bathhouse surgeon from Schongau give? He thought for a moment, then cleared his throat.

"If the growth is already as large as a pigeon egg, you will have to take off the second breast as well," he replied. "And you will have to remove it as completely as you can, so the disease can't spread any further. Cauterize the wound, bandage it, and then . . ." He hesitated.

"And then?" Geiger asked.

"Pray. Because if it is what I think — what the ancient Greeks called cancer — only God can help the dear Frau Treasurer now."

"Ha! Only God," Pfundner hissed. "So that's what a Schongau bathhouse surgeon has to say? Pray? Is that all you know?"

Simon was about to reply when a flourish was sounded, silencing all conversations. The great doors opposite the stage were opened and a group of soldiers appeared. Among the soldiers, Simon could make out the elegantly dressed electress, and beside her an equally magnificently dressed man, presumably her husband, the elector himself. A boy and a slightly older girl walked by his side, both dressed like adults. A herald appeared onstage and rapped a gilded staff on the floor.

"Dear people of Munich, bow before the electoral family!" he commanded.

Everyone on the floor knelt down, and the courtiers on the balconies bowed low. For a while, everything was silent, and Simon could hear the beating of his own heart while his forehead nearly touched the ground. How could he be so stupid and tell the most famous doctor in Bavaria to just pray? Why hadn't he recommended some kind of remedy, made up some miracle treatment? Now he could forget about speaking with the doctor again and might as well use his treatise to light the fire with. What a humiliation!

Another flourish followed, and everyone rose and went to their seats, if they had them. Musicians appeared on the stage and tuned their instruments. Simon sighed. He'd wasted his only chance.

Then he suddenly felt a hand on his shoulder. To his greatest surprise, it was Malachias Geiger. The doctor was smiling.

"I appreciate an honest opinion, young colleague," Geiger said. "It separates the true doctors from the quacks. There is no cure for cancer. If you feel like a chat, visit me tomorrow morning at the Hospice of the Holy Ghost. Then we can have a longer talk, just between doctors."

He turned away and walked toward one of balconies on the ground floor. Simon was too surprised to do or say anything.

A longer talk . . .

Only when the curtains were raised did he notice that Peter had once again disappeared.

Peter had become more and more bored listening to the conversations of the grownups. He had been excited when his father told him they were going to see some kind of play. Peter loved the theater. Two years ago he had watched rehearsals for the well-known Passion of Christ play at Oberammergau, and a man with puppets and a small wooden stage visited Schongau every now and then. But this theater seemed to be for grownups only, because Peter hadn't seen any other children.

Ever since the messenger had delivered the invitation earlier that day, Peter had been waiting to see his new friend again. No one had believed him at first when he said he knew a real prince, not his father, nor Paul, who had called him a braggart and a liar. But now they had to believe him. They were only here because Max commanded it, after all. Peter couldn't wait to see the look on that stupid music teacher Kerll's face when he saw him here. Max had promised him that they would see each other again and, evidently, he had gotten his way. He must have convinced his mother, who was something like a queen.

But now Max wasn't here, and Peter was bored.

And Peter would have loved to tell his new friend that his father was looking for his dog. The electress herself had given him the mission. He was sure his father would find little Arthur, and then Peter would be allowed to go and play at the Residenz all the time. He'd attend the new school his mother had told him about, and everything would be great.

Impatiently, Peter watched his father, who was now talking to a strict-looking elderly man and an unfriendly-looking younger one with eyes like a fish. Why was everything taking so long? Well, at least it was warm in the big room, and there were no madmen like that Master Hans who tried to hurt his aunt. Peter prayed he'd never have to see that horrible man again. How his red eyes had glowed, like the eyes of the devil. And that white hair . . .

Someone cleared his throat behind him, and Peter started. But it was only the electoral envoy, who beckoned him to follow. Peter was about to tell his father, but Simon was deep in conversation, so Peter decided to leave it. His father could get very grumpy if he was interrupted during something important.

Brimming with anticipation, Peter followed the envoy up the

stairs to the third floor of the opera house. Would he see Max again now? They walked past a few men in wigs and perfumed women who studied Peter curiously. The third floor was much emptier than down below, but every balcony door was guarded.

The envoy walked to one of the doors, opened it, and maneuvered Peter inside.

"You wait here," he ordered. "Don't you go anywhere."

He closed the door, and Peter was alone. There were only two chairs in the box, covered in blue velvet. The walls gleamed velvety as well, and the candles on either side of the box smelled wonderful, so different from the stinking tallow lights at home.

Suddenly flourishes were sounded from the stage and everyone was asked to kneel down for the electoral family. And there they were. Max was with them, but to Peter's great disappointment, he took his seat with his parents and sister downstairs. Peter would only see his friend from afar.

Disheartened, he sunk into the soft chair. In the light of the large chandeliers, he spotted his father, who seemed to be looking for him. Peter felt bad. Should he stand up and wave? But then the lights were put out and the curtain went up. Peter started when he saw Kerll, the haggard music teacher, standing on the stage and bowing. Would he throw him out again? Peter ducked instinctively, but then he realized Kerll couldn't possibly see him up there. The music teacher rearranged his wig, swung a little stick, and a single flute started to play.

The set was a grove or forest of oak trees and it looked very real. The music, gentle at first, grew increasingly intense. Peter was fascinated by the number of different instruments: he could make out violins, viols, trumpets, bugles, kettledrums, and some sounds he had never heard before.

After a while, actors wearing voluminous costumes and serious expressions appeared onstage. Some of them sang high, others low, but all very passionately, as if their lives depended on it. Peter soon noticed that there was an awful lot of long, slow dying happening onstage. The plot remained a mystery to him, especially since the actors sang in Italian. He tried to find his father every now and then, but it was too dark to make out anything but vague outlines of people.

Peter was getting tired. He wondered how much longer this opera would go on for, and what he was supposed to do here. He had hoped to see Max again, but instead he watched fat men shouting weird songs at one another.

Just when his eyes were falling shut, he heard a voice he recognized behind him.

"Phew! This is sooo boring. It can't be any more boring in a grave."

"Max!" Peter called out happily and turned around. "I thought I'd only see you from a distance."

The young prince winked at him. His crooked wig looked a little tousled. He grinned and held a finger to his lips. "*Sh!* Or my mother will arrest you! Opera is her great passion. I thought she'd never let me go."

"Do your parents know you're here?" Peter asked quietly.

"My mother said I could go upstairs as soon as it was dark." Max shrugged. "She says it doesn't do me any harm to meet with 'simpler people' every now and then, as she calls them. When I told her about you, she said I could visit you in one of the boxes — so that no one would see. Apparently, she knows your father." He gave Peter a sad look. "And she knows I have no one to play with at the Residenz. Especially now that my Arthur has disappeared."

"My father is looking for your dog," Peter said proudly. "I'm sure he'll find him. He's very clever, you know."

Max nodded. "I know. Mother told me. She also said to ask you if your father has made any progress."

"I don't think so. But I'm sure your dog will turn up soon. You couldn't have found anyone better to look for him." Peter admired his father greatly. He had helped so many people already

—as a physician, but also when he and Grandpa caught scoundrels. Surely finding a dog would be child's play to him.

"What happened to Arthur, anyway?" he asked.

"My nursemaid, Amalie, was walking him in the gardens, just
like every day," Max replied. "She said Arthur saw a cat and just
took off, ripping the lead from her hands. I found the lead near
the garden wall later." The prince sniveled. "I don't think I'll
ever see Arthur again."

Peter touched his nose in thought while three men sang a trio,
trying to outdo one another in volume. One of them had a high,
shrill voice, almost like a woman. "Hmm. At the garden wall,
you say . . . But if there's a wall, how did he get out?"

"There must be a hole somewhere. We searched for hours,
honestly!"

They couldn't talk for a while as drums and trumpets accompanied the singers. Max soon appeared to forget his grief about
his dog. He groaned when a man onstage rammed a dagger into
his heart, singing all the while. "Kerll really writes the most boring operas," he complained. "You should see one of my father's
tournaments, they're much more exciting. Or my mother's masquerades, they're funny. There's going to be one at Nymphenburg Palace soon. You should come. It's quite an event."

"I don't mind the swords," Peter said, still thinking about the
lost dog. "And the low drum. But—"

"Kerll only uses it so the spectators don't fall asleep." Max giggled and pointed at the dying actor twitching on the stage. "Now
he's singing about how he's soon going to be dead for ages, you'll
see."

"Do you speak Italian?" Peter asked, surprised.

"Do I speak Italian?" Max gave him a puzzled look. "Of
course. I speak nothing but Italian with my mother. Or French.
I only speak German with Father. Mother says it's a language for
uneducated barbarians." He grinned. "For people like you."

Embarrassed, Peter lowered his eyes. He had thought he and

Max were friends. But deep down he knew that was impossible. One small phrase had been enough to destroy this illusion.

People like you . . .

Max was a prince and Peter was just the son of a simple small-town physician. And he didn't even want to know what Max would say if he knew that his grandfather was a hangman. He'd probably laugh at him, or spit at him, as many children in Schongau did.

Max didn't seem to notice Peter's embarrassment. He pointed downstairs, where the music was reaching a climax. Only then did Peter notice the wire stretched across the stage holding up a strange, dragon-shaped contraption. Now it moved toward the actors. Peter held his breath with excitement.

"The flying machine," Max whispered. "Mother promised me Kerll would use it. Finally things are getting interesting."

"That thing really looks like a dragon," Peter said, awestruck. "Just like the monster Saint George fought." He forgot all about his gloomy thoughts from before.

Spellbound, the children watched the flying object spitting and hissing its way along the wire in front of the painted sky. Max squeezed Peter's hand when the machine wobbled menacingly.

"Later on, the dragon will disappear in hell," the prince said quietly. "You won't believe your eyes, my friend."

Peter smiled.

In that moment, the two of them were nothing but a pair of curious boys united in their love for a flapping, fire-spitting automaton.

About two miles away, the lights of the Neuhausen village tavern glowed warm and cozy into the winter night. Fresh snow covered the tavern's roof like a blanket. The muted sound of a lonesome fiddle could be heard from inside, playing the last song of the evening.

Only a handful of patrons sat at the crude tables, sipping their beer. Most of them were travelers who hadn't made it to the city before the gates closed and had to wait until tomorrow to enter. Two old drunk farmers leaned on their walking sticks, humming to the music, while the tavernkeeper washed beer mugs, waiting for everyone to go to bed.

In the farthest corner, Master Hans sat and waited.

He'd been here for over two hours now, but the person he was waiting for hadn't shown up. Hans had been thinking hard and becoming increasingly angry. So far, everything had gone according to plan, but it suddenly looked like he wasn't going to emerge as the winner in the end but a great loser. But he'd turn the tables again—oh yes, he would.

It had probably been a mistake to seek out the executioner's house and attack Barbara at the cemetery later on. But by God, the girl drove him crazy. Always had done, even as a child. How many times had he dreamed of her as his wife, submitting to him —she, the untamable wild child. Untamable by any man.

But deep down you like it, too, Barbara. You want it, don't you? You're calling for me . . .

How he would have loved to cut her white skin two years ago in the Schongau dungeon, but then her father, that unbearable smart-arse, had spoiled everything. And now Hans didn't know how close Jakob Kuisl was to solving the mystery. Did he have an inkling? Had he already figured it out?

Hans had lost control at the cemetery because of his feelings for Barbara. And now he wasn't just up against Kuisl but the entire Council of Twelve. Just because of this one stupid mistake. He'd had to hide like a thief. But enough was enough. He'd make his final devastating move and then he would be the one laughing triumphantly. The others would come crawling. He was so close.

Hans had been surprised at first when he received the message via his cousin in Haidhausen. It sounded like his adversary was handing him an olive branch. His enemy probably couldn't see

another way out because the noose was tightening. Hans had
pretended to accept the offer and agreed to meet here at the Neuhausen tavern. And now he'd been sitting here for hours and the
enemy hadn't shown up. Was someone trying to make a fool of
him?

At first Hans had looked around suspiciously, thinking the
meeting had only been arranged to arrest him. After all, he'd as-
saulted a young woman at a Munich graveyard. But no guards
turned up. And so he had grumpily emptied one mug of beer after the other, so that now—although not dead drunk—he was
feeling a little woozy.

The last song finished and Hans decided it was time to leave.
He threw a few coins on the table and left the tavern without a
word of goodbye, much to the relief of the tavernkeeper, who
had found the stranger with the white hair and red eyes more
than a bit creepy.

Outside, the moon shone brightly onto the fresh snow, which
was already turning to slush. Hans could smell a thaw in the air.
He plodded through the mud and soon passed the last houses of
the small village. In front of him, Munich was merely a few ar-
row flights away. Hans nodded grimly. Tomorrow he would
deal his final blow. He didn't have as much proof as he would
have liked; he'd been looking for further evidence and witnesses
at the Holy Cross cemetery. But at least he knew what had happened to Anni and Elfi—and what would soon also be the fate
of the third girl, Eva, unless a miracle happened. Together with
what he'd found out earlier, it would have to suffice.

And if the confession didn't come right away, he'd know what
to do.

Hans wouldn't mind applying the thumbscrews. He loved it
when the suspects screamed and writhed while he himself didn't
bat an eyelid. He didn't want people to see how much he loved
his job. How much he had always loved it, ever since he was a
child and skinned his first live cat.

Some people are born to inflict pain on others because they don't feel any pain or pity themselves. The perfect executioners. And I am a master of my trade . . .

Old linden trees lined the road to Munich, which was empty at this time of night. As Hans walked along, he realized that the three steins of beer were affecting him more than he'd thought. This Munich beer was bloody strong. He wiped sweat from his forehead and walked faster. He thought it was likely that his enemies were watching his cousin's inn, so he'd sneak in through the backyard, invisible, like smoke in the night. And first thing tomorrow he'd find Captain Loibl. Not to turn himself in but to light the fuse on the powder keg. What a triumph it was going to be.

Hans stopped to catch his breath. He felt a little nauseated. Perhaps it wasn't the beer at all, but the cold roast meat he'd eaten at the tavern. He had smothered it in mustard to cover the slightly rotten smell. Well, nothing a glass of brandy at the inn wouldn't fix.

When Hans stretched to shake off the nausea, he spotted the Munich execution site between the trees, which, unlike Gallows Hill, was near the city by Neuhausen Gate. It was a stone platform about six feet high with a pillar on top that gleamed black in the moonlight. This was where decapitations were carried out, usually in front of a large audience. Unlike at Weilheim, an execution in Munich was always a huge public spectacle, with the hangman and the poor sinner in the lead. Master Hans had always envied Michael Deibler the large audience.

Hans blinked. Had he just seen someone behind the pillar? There! The figure stepped out from behind the column and waved at him. In its hand, it held something like a scythe.

Death was waving at him.

"What the devil . . . ," Hans growled. He closed his eyes for a moment and opened them again, but the figure was still there. His imagination was playing tricks on him. Or was it the alcohol?

He swore and took a step toward the execution site, feeling dizzy. He staggered through the snow and held on to the trunk of a linden tree when he suddenly felt weak at the knees. Weak as melting snow.

Hans slid down the tree trunk until he sat on the ground. He struggled to keep his eyes open, cold sweat running down his forehead. His heart raced, the muscles in his face twitched. Slowly it dawned on him that this wasn't a normal sickness. And he hadn't had too much to drink either. Hans realized what had happened to him.

He was going to die like a poisoned rat.

"Tricked . . . me . . . ," he gasped. He tried to stick his fingers down his throat to make himself vomit, but he could no longer lift his hands. Like the muscles in his face, they started to twitch wildly. His stomach was burning as if he'd swallowed thousands of ants.

Through the cold sweat running into his eyes, he vaguely discerned the figure slowly walking toward him from the platform.

It was in no hurry.

"Go . . . to . . . hell . . . ," Hans croaked.

Boundless seething rage gave him the strength to pull himself up a little. But then he collapsed again. Leaning against the linden tree, he glared at the figure in front of him through panicked eyes.

He watched as the hunter drew a long, very sharp knife.

"No coup de grâce," the hunter murmured. "We start at the bottom."

Master Hans couldn't scream.

He could only watch as his murderer slowly cut off his feet, then his hands, and finally his head.

Magdalena stared at the ceiling of the drafty chamber. Her eyes had become accustomed to the darkness by now, but she still couldn't make out more than a few black beams above her. The night was pitch-black.

Next to her, she could hear the regular breathing of the other girls and women and occasionally Agnes's rattling cough. They were lying on straw and threadbare blankets almost directly on the cold floor somewhere above their workroom in the silk manufactory. The air smelled of sweat and thin cabbage soup, their so-called supper, which Mother Joseffa had served up with a few chunks of stale bread. As promised, Magdalena had given her bread to the two boys. Just half an hour later, the candles had been put out and Joseffa locked the door with a large key.

Since then, Magdalena had been lying in the dark with a grumbling stomach, wondering what tomorrow would bring. Agnes hadn't spoken to her since those last strange words, and the other women and girls seemed to pull away from her, too, even young Carlotta, whom Magdalena had helped earlier that day. What in God's name was going on here?

At first Magdalena had been reluctant to let herself get locked up at the manufactory overnight. But then her curiosity had won out, and also concern for all the poor young women here. She hadn't liked her father's idea to snoop around the manufactory at all, especially since she had promised Barbara to be by her side during the search for a husband. And she hated leaving Sophia behind. But one day at the loom had roused pity in Magdalena, pity for all the poor weavers and Anni and Elfi, and most of all for Eva, who was probably the only one of the three friends still alive. Magdalena simply had to find out what went on here before anyone else died. By now, she had become just as convinced as her father that the key to all the recent murders lay somewhere in this building.

She'd soon had to abandon her plan of taking another look around the basement that night. The chamber was locked, and evidently those strange Venetians were still at work. Magdalena heard the floorboards creak above her and footsteps on the stairs from time to time. Luckily, she had managed to send one of the boys to the Radl Inn during the evening to let Simon and the others know that she was all right.

Soft crying startled Magdalena from her thoughts. It came from Carlotta. Until then, Carlotta hadn't made a sound, but now she was crying like a child.

I guess you still are a child, Magdalena thought. *A poor, unhappy child in an unhappy place.*

She stood up slowly, trying not to wake the others, and tiptoed over to Carlotta. She placed a gentle hand on her shoulder. Carlotta winced, but then she calmed down a little.

"I don't want to," she whined softly.

"What don't you want?" Magdalena asked.

"What we have to do tomorrow."

Magdalena sighed. "Don't you think it's time to tell me? I'm supposed to go with you tomorrow, and I'm the only one without any idea what to expect."

"Really? You don't know?" Carlotta stared at her incredulously. "And I . . . I thought you'd done it before. You seem so mature, like you've seen it all. And you said you knew Eva. So . . ."

"What do you mean? Speak up." Magdalena was growing impatient. She had to be careful not to wake the others with her raised voice. "What am I supposed to have done before?" she asked, strained.

"Well, you know . . . worked as a prostitute."

Now it was out. Magdalena inhaled deeply. Deep down, she'd known already.

"Van Uffele always picks out the prettiest girls," Carlotta continued quietly. "Then he sends them to wealthy homes where they're supposedly working as maids for a few days. But of course, they do something else. I've never done it before, but Agnes reckons you can earn a heap of money that way."

But only a fraction of what van Uffele gets, I bet, Magdalena thought.

"You said you thought I was a prostitute because I knew Eva. Does that mean . . ."

Carlotta nodded. "Eva did it, too. And Anni and Elfi. But they're dead now. So van Uffele needs new girls. Agnes says I should be grateful for the chance to earn money. But . . . but . . ." She broke off and started to cry again.

Anni, Elfi, and Eva . . .

"Listen, Carlotta, this is important," Magdalena hissed, shaking the girl gently. "This morning you told me you knew why Eva was locked up downstairs, and that van Uffele and Mother Joseffa were going to kill her because she knew too much. Is that what you meant? That Eva knows about the deal with the whores? That those two slave-drivers are afraid she'll talk?"

Carlotta didn't reply, but her eyes said it all. Then she started sobbing again.

"Do you understand now why I didn't talk?" she whimpered. "Why none of us do? They kill us. Every girl that talks too much is simply . . . murdered."

Magdalena closed her eyes and felt her heart beat wildly.

Anni, Elfi, Eva. Two dead and one missing. All three worked as prostitutes for van Uffele and Mother Joseffa. She was on the right track. But she didn't quite understand why the girls had been murdered so brutally. Just because they were going to talk?

She'd have to work as a prostitute herself in order to find out. It was the only way of learning what really happened to the girls. And it was the only way to prevent other girls from losing their lives, too. Would she be able to do it? Magdalena hesitated briefly, then she nodded.

"It's going to be fine, Carlotta," she said and squeezed the trembling girl's hand. "I'm going to look out for you. No one's going to hurt you."

But no matter what happened, Magdalena knew one thing for certain: Simon could never find out about this part of her investigation.

8

WAKE UP, SLEEPYHEAD! WAKE UP, or they'll cut your
throat while you're asleep!"

Jakob Kuisl blinked when a sinewy, hairy hand shook him
rudely. He had just been dreaming about his wife, Anna-Maria.
She had held out her hand to him, smiling, he'd almost smelled
her hair—and now he was looking into the bearded face of Michael Deibler, who stank of stale beer and was unmistakably agitated about something. Kuisl sat up.

"What happened, damn it? Is the city burning down?" With
sleepy eyes, the hangman looked out the window of his room on
the second floor of the Radl Inn. Dawn had broken. He guessed
it was about seven in the morning. Kuisl had sat up late with his
brother, Bartholomäus, and his old friend Philipp Teuber from
Regensburg. The Kuisl brothers weren't the best of friends, but
the exceptional circumstances had brought them closer. Over
many mugs of beer, the three men had racked their brains over
the murders. Kuisl hadn't told the others about his trip to the
cemetery, however. The events of the previous day seemed foggy
in hindsight. He had woken up screaming during the night, tor-

tured by nightmares in which his wife was calling out to him from a grave. He wasn't even entirely sure if the figure at the graveyard had been a figment of his imagination.

"It's burning in the city all right," Deibler said, pacing the chamber impatiently. "But not like you think. It's about Master Hans."

Kuisl jumped to his feet. "Has he turned up? Did the boys find him?"

The previous evening Kuisl had waited for news from the Munich street children and Paul, who were watching the inn Hans had been staying at. Around nightfall, Barbara had insisted Paul return to the executioner's house and Kuisl hadn't heard anything since.

"Someone else found Hans," Michael Deibler said. "And if you don't hurry, you'll be the last person in town to see him, goddamnit."

Kuisl had a bad feeling. He walked to the wash bowl, threw a few handfuls of ice-cold water in his face, and followed Deibler down the stairs. Outside, Georg awaited them with a serious expression. Together they hurried through the Anger Quarter and the neighboring Hacken Quarter toward the Neuhausen Gate. Deibler gave them a succinct report on the way.

"Some travelers found Hans out at the execution site," he said, puffing. "There's already a crowd. I only stayed for a moment because I wanted you to take a look at the body before anyone touches it."

"Is it that bad?" Kuisl asked.

Deibler laughed grimly. "You'll see for yourself in a moment."

By now they were on the road outside the city. The air was mild, almost springlike. Wet snow was dripping from the trees or falling down in clumps; the roads were so muddy that the wagons traveling to Munich had a hard time getting through. Up ahead, Kuisl saw a large crowd gathered around the execution platform. The people jeered and hollered, and a handful of lads were throwing snowballs at the platform. Something round was lying atop a pillar.

"Bloody hell, the crowd has grown," Deibler groused. "Maybe it wasn't such a good idea to come back after all. But now it's too late."

The first few spectators had recognized Michael Deibler in his red coat. The people went quiet and made room for the three hangmen. Dozens of hostile eyes followed them. An icy snowball hit Kuisl's neck, but he didn't even blink. He knew people could smell fear just like animals. The air was laden with tension, as before a thunderstorm.

"Hey, Deibler," one of the bystanders yelled. "Are you hangmen killing each other now? That wouldn't be the worst thing for the city."

A few people laughed, but most just kept staring at them hatefully.

"The other two are next!" another young man shouted. He was wearing a bloodstained apron, probably a butcher's journeyman who had run here in a hurry. "Deibler is knocking off his cousins just like he killed the poor girls."

"How dare you, you—" Michael Deibler spun around and was about to grab the lad by his collar when Kuisl pulled him back.

"Stay calm," he whispered. "Or you'll be next."

Kuisl looked straight ahead. They were close enough to the platform now for him to see what lay on top of the column.

It was the head of Master Hans.

Cleanly separated from the body, it sat atop the pillar like a huge, bloody pearl. The white hair moved in the breeze, the red eyes stared into the distance, the mouth was twisted into a grin. It looked as though Hans was laughing, like his own death was a good joke.

Hans's torso lay in front of the pillar. Arms and legs had been neatly cut off and arranged next to the body like meat in a shop display.

And so we meet again, Jakob Kuisl thought. *Say hello to the devil, dear cousin.*

Strangely, he felt no satisfaction. Only a quiet sense of grief, much to his surprise. With the trained eye of an executioner, Kuisl studied the individual body parts. They had been cut off cleanly, with an axe or a large, sharp knife.

"My God," Georg breathed next to his father. "Like a quartered thief."

Deibler nodded. "The first travelers coming through this morning asked in town who the executed robber with the creepy red eyes and white hair was. Master Hans is somewhat well known in Munich now, and so it wasn't long before I heard about it." He sighed. "I never liked him, but no hangman should end his days like this."

"Well, at least he's done with all this," Kuisl said, "while we are up to our necks in shit, by the looks of it."

While the crowd had first kept away from them as if they were lepers, now they came closer. The butcher's journeyman raised his cleaver.

"Those hangmen only bring misfortune," he crowed. "Let's hang them and our girls will be safe again."

Jakob Kuisl sized up the crowd from the corner of his eye. He, Georg, and Michael could certainly manage a few of them, but not the whole lot. Kuisl knew executioners had been lynched by mobs before—usually when a hangman botched an execution. That's how his father had died. Was he going to share his fate now?

"Follow me," Michael Deibler hissed. "Before they pounce on us like wolves."

He ran around the platform and Kuisl and Georg followed him. Behind a small door at the back of the platform, stairs led to the top. The door could be bolted from the inside. Moments later, the three hangmen stood by the pillar atop the execution site and looked down at the raging masses.

Kuisl realized they had merely gained a short breather. The people were already picking up rocks and throwing icy snowballs. A few bold men started climbing the platform.

Kuisl had no idea what to do. He looked over to the city, whose walls and fortifications weren't far away. Then he looked again.

Several dark spots were approaching on the Neuhausen Road.

The hangman squinted. He could still rely on his eyesight, despite his ripe old age. "Talk," he whispered at Deibler.

The Munich hangman gave him a puzzled look, but Kuisl nudged him. "Go ahead and talk. Doesn't matter what, as long as you keep going."

"Um, I've never been a very good orator . . . ," Deibler replied.

"If you don't talk now, you're a dead orator, damn it," Kuisl snarled at him. "So think of something."

Deibler swallowed, then he cleared his throat. "Dear people of Munich," he began, raising his arms placatingly. "You all know me — though perhaps not as well as the gallows birds I've sent flying in the past."

An elderly farmer laughed, and Deibler continued in a steadier voice: "But most of all, you know my Burgi. Who hasn't gone to see her when they were plagued by a boil on the backside? Who hasn't bought a cough syrup from her, or something for scabies or aching limbs?"

"Or something for one very particular limb!" a man shouted from the back, and everyone hooted with laughter.

Kuisl smiled to himself. Deibler did pretty well for someone who thought he wasn't a good public speaker. He was building trust between himself and the angry mob. And he knew that while the people might not like him, his wife was very popular.

"Do you really think I did this?" Deibler shouted, pointing at Hans's dismembered body. "My Burgi knows me better than anyone else in this world—ask her. She gives me a kick up the backside if I try to drown one of her countless cats."

The people laughed again, and Deibler went on. "I'm the hangman of this city, not some kind of monster. I don't need to kill secretly at night." He pointed at Kuisl and Georg. "And the same goes for my cousins from Schongau and Bamberg."

"If it wasn't you executioners, then who was it?" a young woman with matted hair called out. "Ever since your accursed council has been meeting here, women aren't safe anymore. Ill luck sticks to you like pitch."

The crowd grumbled and swore, and the mood changed again. Some of the younger lads tried to climb the platform again.

"I'll say it again!" Michael Deibler shouted. "We hangmen are no murderers or bringers of misfortune. We're just doing our job, like all of you. And I swear by God, when I'm on this scaffold with the murderer of our girls and my cousin, I'll make sure his execution is long and slow."

Deibler's last words were drowned out by angry and disappointed shouts. Jakob Kuisl kept an eye on the road. The black dots had come closer. He could make out individual men now. To his enormous relief, he'd been right. They were city guards, a whole delegation of them, carrying muskets and halberds. Josef Loibl marched at their head, easily recognizable by his shiny cuirass.

"God in heaven," Georg sighed. "I don't think I've ever been so happy to see a bunch of zealous bailiffs."

The crowd started when they saw the guards, then people began to disperse. Some of them kept shouting for a while, a few more snowballs were thrown, then it was all over. Josef Loibl arrived at the execution site with his men and looked at Master Hans's severed head with disgust.

"What in God's name is this?" he asked eventually.

"*This* is the Weilheim hangman, who was expertly quartered

by someone last night," Michael Deibler replied after he and the two others had climbed down from the platform. He wiped the sweat off his forehead. Kuisl saw that he was trembling slightly. "The people thought we executioners had something to do with it."

"Well, I can't blame them, since the victim was quartered," Loibl said, studying the body parts. "Especially since it looks like a professional job."

"Any butcher could do that," Kuisl said. "You only need a sharp knife or an axe." He pointed at the platform. "One thing is for certain: the person who did this is also the murderer of the girls—of the last three, at least."

"Is that so?" Loibl turned to Kuisl with surprise. "What makes you think that?"

"It seems Master Hans knew something," Deibler came to his friend's aid. "He made some hints about the dead girls and acted strangely. He must have known the murderer and might have tried to blackmail him. So the murderer got rid of him."

"Hmm. But why quarter Hans?" Loibl stroked his moustache. "Wouldn't it have been enough to stick a knife in his back or cut his throat?"

"For Christ's sake, that's exactly why I'm saying it was the same murderer!" Kuisl swore. "That madman doesn't merely kill his victims, he executes them. That's what he did with the girls, and now with Hans, too."

"And with the young woman who'd been lying in a rock cellar for decades?" Loibl added mockingly. "The crazy old man probably knocked Hans over the head with his cane first."

Georg muttered something and Kuisl snarled at him, annoyed.

"What are you muttering? If you have something to say, spit it out."

Georg cleared his throat. "I said, *treason*. Quartering is the punishment for traitors."

"Treason . . . hmm. You're right." Kuisl frowned and thought.

Something had been bothering him for a while. He felt sure there was one important piece to the puzzle he had overlooked so far. But as it had every time he tried to grab hold of the thought, it slipped away.

Quartering is the punishment for traitors . . .

Before Kuisl could think any further, Loibl interrupted him. "As far as I know, this Hans was already brought to our attention yesterday. Apparently he molested your younger daughter." He eyed Jakob Kuisl suspiciously. "I might conclude you had something to do with his death. An affronted father and executioner with revenge on his mind, and now this . . ."

Deibler groaned. "Not again. Damn it, Josef, we hangmen have nothing to do with these murders!"

"Who knows . . ." Loibl's eyes were still on Kuisl. "I'll keep an eye on you, big fellow."

"Do what you want." The Schongau hangman pointed at the gruesome body parts on the platform. "But first we should get Master Hans—or what's left of him—out of here, before more curious townspeople turn up. And he can't be buried in a cemetery as an executioner, so we might as well bury him here. Even this bastard deserves that much."

Loibl nodded reluctantly. "You're probably right, hangman. I'll send a priest to say a prayer at the grave. Nobody but us is going to care two hoots about this fellow, anyhow." He turned to his guards. "Right, fellows, let's clean up this mess."

They helped the guards carry Hans's remains to a lone willow tree. They buried him silently under a pile of rocks so no animals could get to him.

While Michael Deibler and Georg waited, Jakob Kuisl used the opportunity to ask the captain a question. He wanted to clear something up that had been nagging at him. Loibl was a little surprised, but he didn't mind telling Kuisl what he wanted to know.

The hangman nodded.

Another piece of the puzzle . . .

When the last stone was placed on top, Kuisl regarded the nameless grave in silence. Hans had been a monster, he had almost tortured Barbara, and now he was lying there like a dead rabid dog. Kuisl should have been pleased, but he wasn't. Hans had been a hangman like himself, an outcast.

A cousin.

He might have committed awful acts in his life, but lying underneath this willow was no murderer, but a victim. The murderer still walked free, free to commit other cruelties.

If Kuisl was honest with himself, that's what bothered him the most.

Master Hans had taken his secret to the grave.

On busy Sendlinger Street, three women walked toward a gloomy future.

Bakers praised their bread in loud voices, a butcher whetted his knife for a squeaking pig lying bound on the dirty, muddy ground in front of him, and two Jesuit students from wealthy homes ran across the street to Saint Michael College. The three women looked like simple maids, wearing plain linen dresses, aprons, and woolen scarves around their heads and shoulders. Each of them carried a bundle of washing, like so many Munich washerwomen. Only a careful observer would have noticed that the youngest was trembling and gently pushed along by one of the older women.

And all three were subtly made up.

From the corner of her eye, Magdalena watched Agnes, who had put her arm around young Carlotta's shoulder and was talking to her in soothing tones. Magdalena felt nervous, too, but she tried not to show it.

"You'll see, it won't be as bad as you think," Agnes whispered to Carlotta. "In the beginning especially, all they want is a little kiss here and there and for you to gaze at them adoringly. And a slap on the backside never hurt no one."

"And . . . and if they want more?" Carlotta asked hesitantly.

"Then close your eyes and let it pass like a thunderstorm." Agnes smiled wanly. "It's usually over just as fast."

Magdalena touched the small knife she had hidden underneath her apron. It was from the manufactory and served to cut off leftover thread. She was determined to only use it in an absolute emergency—although she wasn't sure exactly what would qualify as one.

When van Uffele and Mother Joseffa had told her early that morning what her new task was going to be, she had pretended to be shocked, resisting at first, then nodding reluctantly. Mother Joseffa had smiled triumphantly; she'd probably seen many girls act the same way.

"Just think about it," Agnes said cheerfully to Carlotta as they passed Old Peter and its cemetery. "Weaving, you only get a few lousy kreuzers, whereas here you'll earn as much in a few days as you normally would in half a year. Men are crazy about us, especially now that whores are harder and harder to come by. And . . ." A coughing fit shook Agnes. "You're still young. Do you want to toil at the loom for the rest of your life?" She shot an angry look at Magdalena. "I'll soon be done with this, anyway. Van Uffele is always on the lookout for fresh meat for his customers."

And he makes an absolute killing, Magdalena thought. *As long as no one catches him.*

Whoring had indeed become more and more restricted in recent decades. The previous ruler of Bavaria, Duke Wilhelm V—nicknamed Wilhelm the Pious—had issued several laws banning the frowned-upon trade from the city. Even the Munich whorehouse had been shut down. Unlike the garishly made-up prostitutes who secretly searched for customers on the streets of Munich, van Uffele's girls appeared as innocent maidservants who didn't work the streets but inside the homes of wealthy men—often right under the unsuspecting wife's nose. Magdalena reckoned van Uffele's business yielded a huge profit, perhaps even more than he made with the silk manufactory.

Meanwhile, the three women had reached the Graggenau Quarter near the Residenz, where the wealthier citizens lived. The houses here were all magnificent buildings several stories high, and some of them looked like small palaces. The streets were clean and empty; no peddlers or other itinerant merchants to be seen anywhere. Numerous guards patrolled the streets instead, casting suspicious glances at Magdalena and the two others. But since they looked like maids and carried bundles of washing, the soldiers let them pass every time.

Mother Joseffa had told them that morning where they were going to spend the next few days. Agnes was going to stay with an older patrician who made his money in the cloth trade; Carlotta was destined for a young suitor from a rich house who wanted to have another adventure before getting married. Joseffa had announced Magdalena's client as the jackpot: it was no less than the city treasurer himself, Daniel Pfundner, the person responsible for Munich's finances.

"You can make a lot of money at Pfundner's," Joseffa had told Magdalena. "His wife is dying and looks awful, so I hear. Anni, who was there before you, earned plenty."

Magdalena had realized then that the last girl to work for Pfundner had been found dead in Au creek only four days ago.

Would she share Anni's fate?

Agnes was the first to leave them. She stopped outside a large house near Schwabinger Gate, gave them one last nod, then disappeared inside. Magdalena and Carlotta continued in silence until they came to an even grander house. Carlotta closed her eyes and trembled.

"You don't have to do this," Magdalena said. "You can just turn around and leave. You can go anywhere you like."

"Anywhere I like?" Carlotta laughed sadly. "That's what I thought when I arrived in this accursed city with my little brother. I'm all Basti has left. Everyone else is dead. I promised him that we'd have it better than our parents one day. And now he lives in the gutter." She nodded with determination, suddenly looking much older than her fifteen years. "I'm going to get through this, just like I've gotten through many other things. And with the money, Basti and I are moving to a warm inn where we'll eat roast, ham, and cheese for supper." She squeezed Magdalena's hand. "You've been very kind. I wish you good luck."

More luck than Anni would be good, Magdalena thought.

She gave the girl one last hug and watched her walk toward the house, praying Carlotta was right — that it wasn't going to be that bad and she'd be able to use the money for her and her brother.

But she struggled to believe it.

Lost in gloomy thoughts, Magdalena continued to the address Joseffa had given her. The house stood in a quiet lane near a church and was a three-storied whitewashed building with an ostentatious bowfront. The coat of arms on the double doors showed scales with coins, but Magdalena knew she wasn't allowed to knock here. Instead, she turned down a narrow path, barely wider than her shoulders, that led to the servants' entrance. Timidly, she used the bronze knocker. After a while, an arrogant-looking older footman in a tatty uniform opened the door.

"Yes?" he asked impatiently.

Magdalena held up her bundle of washing. "I'm the new maid the master ordered," she said with her head lowered. "I'm supposed to return the mended sheets and be of service to the master and mistress for a few days."

"Oh, the new maidservant," the footman said. He eyed Magdalena suspiciously. "Let me tell you one thing: if I catch you stealing, even if it's just a crumb of bread, I'll personally make sure the hangman whips you out of town. Is that clear?"

Magdalena nodded and the servant let her in. The corridor first led through the kitchen, then into a high-ceilinged reception room that was lined with red damask and decorated with countless paintings.

"Wait here," the footman ordered. "I'll fetch the master."

He climbed a staircase that was as wide as an entire room, and Magdalena had a chance to admire the furnishings. The handrail was made of the finest polished ebony, the marble steps gleamed white. The painting on the wall leading to the second floor didn't depict a biblical scene or a king or duke, but a patrician dressed in a black coat with an ermine collar. He was holding a quill and paper, and behind him stood a desk full of coins. The artist had clearly tried his best, but he hadn't been able to hide the fact that the man was rather ugly: short, with thin hair and watery, bulging eyes, he looked like a fish turned human.

Magdalena jumped when just this man came walking down the stairs. He smiled a thin smile, practically undressing her with his fish eyes.

"Ah, the new maid," he said happily. "Look at that, van Uffele wasn't lying. You're even prettier than the last one." He studied Magdalena appreciatively. "Truly, a good recompense for the fact that I'm still waiting for my money. Perhaps a tad old, but that doesn't matter. Age brings experience, doesn't it?" Meanwhile, the man — evidently the city treasurer Daniel Pfundner — had arrived downstairs and brushed his hand across her behind. Then he leaned forward and sniffed her décolletage. Magdalena trembled a little but kept her temper.

"You and I are going to have a lot of fun," Pfundner said and winked at her. "Just the two of us. I've taken the whole day off — they don't expect me back before tomorrow at the city hall." He giggled and pointed at the laundry in Magdalena's hands. "Van Uffele's idea with the mended sheets is brilliant. When you leave tonight, I'll give you more washing to take."

Suddenly a shaky female voice called out from upstairs. "Daniel, who is it?"

Pfundner rolled his eyes. "Don't worry, Waltraud!" he shouted back. "It's just the new maid. Josef is going to show her the kitchen and the laundry in a moment."

"I'm in so much pain, Daniel," the woman moaned. "Can't you call for the doctor again?"

"Doctor Geiger is at the hospice today," Pfundner replied. "But he might manage to squeeze in a brief visit." In a quiet, strained voice he added: "As if I hadn't spent enough on that woman already."

He turned back to Magdalena. "There's something else you can do for me today. I'm receiving a somewhat unexpected visitor in a little while. Take the pastries and wine upstairs and sweep the floor. And when he arrives, give him your best smile. He might just make use of your services, too." He gave her a more serious look. "It's important that he feels at ease, do you understand? Very important. For you, too." He giggled secretively.

"Yes, sir," Magdalena replied with a curtsy.

"Like a lady-in-waiting. I like you, you naughty thing." Laughing, Pfundner gave her a slap on the backside. "I'm going to ask Doctor Geiger to give my wife a decent portion of poppy juice." He lowered his voice and leaned close to Magdalena's neck. "And then the two of us are going to enjoy ourselves until the small hours. You like to enjoy yourself, don't you, my little dove?"

Magdalena smiled, but her hands were clenched into tight fists. She could only pray her husband would never find out about this.

Simon nervously clutched the leather satchel that held the pages of his treatise while he stood outside the doors of the Munich Hospice of the Holy Ghost.

He hadn't slept much the night before—the impressions from the previous evening had been too overwhelming. He and Peter had attended an opera with an orchestra, a painted stage set, singers, a flying machine, and other colorful props, all of it surrounded by courtiers, patricians from Munich, and the electoral family. It had been like a trip to another world—a trip that had ended abruptly when the coach had driven them back to the dirty Anger Quarter. At least Simon and Peter had been allowed to keep the borrowed clothes. Apparently, the messenger knew they—or at least Peter—would visit the Residenz again soon. His son had shared a box at the opera house with the crown prince himself, as Peter had told him excitedly on the way home. He'd already been asked to visit the palace gardens today.

Simon's happiness was marred by the fact that Magdalena hadn't been at his side through all this. Even worse—while he and Peter had worn expensive clothes and listened to Italian arias, Magdalena had spent the night in discomfort at the silk manufactory. She'd sent word to the family; evidently she was all right and she was trying to find out more.

Simon was glad Walburga and Barbara could look after Sophia and the two boys. That way he had been able to accept Doctor Geiger's invitation to visit him at the Hospice of the Holy Ghost this morning. He felt confident he'd find an opportunity to raise the subject of his treatise with Geiger, and he did his best to ignore the fact that he was supposed to be looking for the electoral lapdog.

The hospice was situated behind Old Peter and bordered the city wall to the south. Hospices like this had become widespread and generally housed the old and sick of a town. Schongau had a similar Hospice, which was why Simon had expected a single building. Instead, he was amazed to find an entire village. Even bigger: the Hospice of the Holy Ghost was almost like a city within the city.

Once he entered through the large gateway, he found himself
in a maze of lanes, houses, stables, and courtyards. The hospice
even had its own stream filled with cages of trout, lethargic from
the cold. Farther back Simon saw a large cathedral. He walked
past a brewery, a bakery, and a blacksmith, but he had no idea
where Doctor Geiger might be working. Surely there must be an
infirmary somewhere.

Simon decided to ask an elderly man who was pulling at a
stubborn cow.

"The doctor, hmm . . ." The old man scratched his nose. "I
think he might be over at the foundling house. Try your luck
there."

"And how do I find the foundling house?" Simon asked.

The man grinned. "Just follow the racket." He pointed to the
right, and indeed, Simon could hear the screaming of infants
from a low building. Simon rushed to the house, entered, and
was immediately enveloped in stink and noise. He counted at
least two dozen children, most of whom were still in cradles.
Their diapers were dirty, their faces haggard and red from
screaming. Clearly, they were hungry. A few older boys and girls
sat at a table in the center of the room, where a pinched-looking
nurse was handing out porridge with a ladle. When she noticed
Simon, she glared at him as if he were a thief.

"Hey, what are you doing here?" she mumbled between her
few remaining teeth. "Are you a sponsor or are you only bringing another squalling mouth to feed? Where am I supposed to
put all the brats, can you tell me that?"

"It's all right, Martha," a voice sounded from farther back,
where the lack of windows kept the room in relative darkness.
"The gentleman is here for me, isn't he?"

Simon was thrilled—he had actually found Malachias Geiger. Like yesterday, the doctor wore a plain black coat, and his
beard was neatly trimmed; his right eye was strangely enlarged.

Only on second look did Simon realize Geiger was wearing a monocle, which he now removed with a smile.

"I mainly wear it because the children like it," he explained and shook Simon's hand. "What was your name again, dear colleague?"

"Er, Fronwieser. D-Doctor Fronwieser from Schongau," Simon stammered. He could hardly believe that the famous doctor had called him a colleague.

"I liked your diagnosis at the opera last night," Geiger said. "Brief and honest, just the way it ought to be. I'm sorry we couldn't talk more. Treasurer Daniel Pfundner doesn't have it easy with his wife, so you must forgive his rough demeanor. He's a very good treasurer, he's done a lot for the city." He shrugged. "Being a good husband doesn't seem to be his specialty, however."

"I didn't mean to interrupt your conversation. I was just—"

"Come over here," Geiger cut him off, leading him to one of the beds. "Perhaps you can give me some advice." An approximately six-month-old baby was lying in the cradle, covered in festering pustules. The little child screamed pitifully and kept scratching its face, which was already streaked with blood.

"The poor thing was left outside the hospice church last night," Geiger said with a sad look at the infant. "It's the third child this month. The other two were newborns; evidently, the mothers didn't want them. Illegitimate, most likely." The doctor shook his head. "Ever since the old elector, Maximilian, toughened the laws against wantonness again, the number of abandoned children keeps going up. It's enough to drive you to despair."

"At least the mothers didn't kill their babies," Simon muttered, realizing this wasn't a good time to mention his treatise.

"You're right," Geiger replied. "But it's a crime nonetheless—whether committed by the mother alone or by all of us, someone else can judge." He pointed at the wailing infant in front of them. "A typical case of scabies, common among poor families, and already described by the great Avenzoar of Seville. How would you proceed, dear colleague?"

"Well, um . . ." Simon cleared his throat. He knew scabies from Schongau. The old bathhouse surgeon used to prescribe church dust, which he scraped off the Altenstadt basilica. Or he advised patients to apply a puree of ground grain. Simon had a feeling Doctor Geiger wasn't interested in such methods.

"Er, Constantin of Africa believed nature forced the bad fluids to the surface of the skin to cleanse the body," Simon scraped up his scant knowledge from university. "But I prefer the theory of Persian scholar Al-Tabari, namely that scabies is in fact caused by tiny creatures that eat into the skin. I use an ointment of sulfur and quicksilver to kill them off."

"Quicksilver, hmm . . . Interesting." Geiger frowned. "I should try it sometime. Here the children are often put in the hospice smokehouse, which usually results in temporary improvement; it also helps a bit with other undesirable vermin. Unfortunately, these creatures are so small that one can barely see them, let alone squash them."

Simon remembered the book he stole from the shop on Sendlinger Street. It was a work on magnifying lenses strong enough to make even the tiniest animals visible. He decided to take another look at the book that evening—perhaps he'd find something on scabies.

Geiger leaned over the crying child and gently rubbed cream from his bag on the sores. Simon helped him and bandaged the little hands so the infant couldn't scratch himself bloody anymore. The two doctors walked to the next bed, where an approximately one-year-old girl seemed happy and healthy. But she had a cleft lip. She beamed at Simon and Geiger with sparkling eyes.

"This child was born here," Geiger explained sadly. "But the mother didn't want to keep it. She was very poor. This poor thing will never grow up with a family, even though there's nothing really wrong with her."

Simon involuntarily thought of his own daughter, Sophia. Her clubfoot already made her an outcast, even at her young age. But at least she had parents who looked after her and she hadn't been abandoned like this little girl.

"I believe this hospice is far more than just a shelter for the old and sick," Simon said, reaching for the girl's little fingers.

Malachias Geiger nodded. "Aside from the regular hospice for the elderly, we also have a foundling house, a birthing room for homeless women, and even a lunatic asylum."

"A lunatic asylum?" Simon asked, surprised.

"Well, a place for all those who have lost control of their senses." Geiger sighed. "They need looking after, too. Once a week I fulfill my duty as a good Christian at the hospice, and I've done so for over thirty years. On all other days, I cut out the boils of the rich or treat them for gout they brought on themselves with their gluttony. The world isn't fair." He shook his head and turned to Simon. "But enough about me. Tell me, what brings you to Munich, dear colleague?"

My hour has finally arrived, Simon thought.

"Well, actually . . . ," he began, fiddling with the pages of the treatise in his leather satchel, when they suddenly heard an inhuman-sounding scream. Simon winced. The wailing came from one of the nearby houses.

"My God, what is that?" he asked, horrified. "It sounds worse than a torture chamber!"

"I'm afraid that's one of the pitiful creatures I just mentioned," Geiger replied. "Follow me. Let's go and see what's happened."

Simon hastily stuffed his treatise back in his bag and followed the doctor out the door. They ran across the lane and toward a house that looked a little like a prison with its barred windows and heavy doors. The shrill screams coming from inside sounded like someone was being flayed alive.

Just then the door opened and a broad-shouldered bald man stared at them with surprise. "Doctor, thank God you're here!" he gasped. "It's old Traudel. I just can't calm her down. I'm truly at my wits' end."

"Let me take a look." Malachias Geiger rushed past him and Simon followed. On the inside the building looked like a prison as well. To Simon's left and right were a dozen foul-smelling cells, and behind the bars cowered the most wretched-looking people he had ever seen. With their long matted hair, torn and dirty shirts, and wild eyes they seemed more like animals than humans. He couldn't tell whether some of them were man or woman. Most of them just sat apathetically in a corner, stammering silent words or merely staring straight ahead, but at the far end of the corridor an old woman threw herself against the bars of her cell again and again, screaming at the top of her lungs. Now Simon could make out some words and phrases.

"The girls…the dead girls!" the old woman screeched. "They're knocking on my ear. Take them away, they… they're knocking on my head, like a hammer."

"What in God's name is she talking about?" Simon asked the bald-headed man, evidently the lunatic warder. He just shrugged.

"I don't know. I think someone told her about the murders in the city, and now she's completely beside herself. Normally Traudel is harmless, she's been sitting in her cell for over twenty years. She's never caused me trouble before. And now this."

"For over twenty years?" Simon asked, shocked.

"Hmm. Perhaps even longer." The warder scratched his head. "We keep good records of all our cases. Traudel is definitely our oldest."

Simon shook his head in disbelief. "By God, if she wasn't crazy beforehand — she sure is now."

"The poor girls!" Traudel wailed. "All dead, dead, dead! Oh, and there's going to be more. Many more! It'll never end, no, no, *no!*"

"It's maddening!" Geiger shouted against the noise. "I'm going to give her some poppy juice. It was supposed to be for the treasurer's wife, but this seems more important." He looked at Simon. "I'll need your help, young colleague. Can you please hold the poor woman down so I can give her the juice?"

Simon nodded, and the warder cautiously opened the door. Traudel immediately launched herself at the three men like a fury. "It's you, it's your fault!" she screamed over and over. "It's all your fault!"

The warder grabbed Traudel and held her like a vise. The old woman screamed and spat, frothing like a rabid dog. "It's your fault!" she roared. "All of yours!"

"You have to hold her head," Geiger commanded. "Or I can't give her the medicine."

Simon reached for her head, but Traudel turned and bit his hand.

"Ouch! Damn it!" Cursing, Simon held his aching hand, but when he saw Geiger's look of impatience, he tried again. This time he managed to hold Traudel's head and open her mouth at the same time. Geiger rummaged in his medicine bag and produced a small bottle. Carefully, he dribbled the contents into the woman's mouth, and the warder held her nose shut so she had to swallow. Geiger gently stroked her filthy gray hair as if she were a small child.

"It's going to be fine, Traudel," he whispered. "Just calm down and then—"

Suddenly the old woman's eyes widened and she giggled. Her voice was very soft now, barely audible.

"I know who killed them," she whispered.

"Killed who?" Geiger asked.

"The girls, of course. All those sweet young girls. I know who killed them. Who's always been killing them in this cursed city."

"And who is that supposed to be?" Simon asked, feeling a tingle of excitement. Suddenly, the old woman didn't seem insane anymore. Her voice sounded calm and composed.

"I can't tell," she hissed. "I promised. A long time ago." She was almost pleading now. "If I tell you, I'm next. I beg you, stop this monster."

"Who killed those girls?" Simon tried again. "If you really know, you—"

"It's your fault!" she shouted again, shaking herself like a wet dog. "Yours! Yours! Yours!"

Malachias Geiger turned away with a sigh. "She's truly out of her mind. I hope the poppy juice brings her some relief."

"But if she really knows something about the murders?" Simon objected.

"You aren't serious, are you?" Geiger looked almost mockingly at Simon. "You heard who she thinks the murderer is—all of us! It's a shame someone told her about it in the first place. Now she's completely confused. At least the medicine seems to be working now."

Old Traudel had stopped screaming and thrashing about. Her head sank to her chest and her muscles relaxed. The warder placed her gently in the dirty straw on the ground, and the three men left her cell.

"You're right, it was foolish of me to take her seriously," Simon said sheepishly. "She just sounded so . . . so normal. If you hadn't given her the treasurer's wife's—"

"The treasurer's wife!" Malachias Geiger slapped his forehead. "In all the excitement, I completely forgot that I was supposed to visit the Pfundners at nine o'clock. Please excuse me." With a curt nod, he turned to leave.

"But . . . ," Simon started.

"We can continue our conversation next week, dear colleague," Geiger called out as he hurried toward the exit. "And thanks again for your help."

"You're . . . you're welcome," Simon stammered.

He felt like punching himself. For the second time he'd missed his chance to talk about his treatise. And now Geiger thought he believed the rantings of an old lunatic. He'd made such a fool of himself.

And yet, Simon couldn't stop thinking about old Traudel's words.

I know who killed the girls . . . It's your fault . . . yours, yours, yours . . .

Who in God's name was she talking about?

Simon sighed and suddenly felt the urgent need to leave this godforsaken place. Behind him, several of the pitiable lunatics banged their heads against the bars of their cells. Most likely, Traudel's raving had been nothing but the spawn of her insane imagination.

"Bloody hell—has everyone in this town gone mad?" Bartholomäus jumped to his feet and punched the table so hard the pewter mugs clattered. "In good old Bamberg, folks still appreciate a hangman and don't chop off his hands and feet."

"In good old Bamberg, folks were hunting for a werewolf only a few years ago," Kuisl said, sitting next to his brother in the backroom of the Radl Inn. "Remember? When people are afraid, they turn nasty like wasps at the end of summer. Everywhere. Sit back down so we can talk calmly."

Reluctantly, Bartholomäus sat down again, cursing under his breath. The other executioners were visibly upset, too, swearing and interrupting one another. Michael Deibler had asked them to another meeting at the Au tavern that morning, but just as at the last session, they weren't discussing wages and electoral mandates but the latest gruesome discovery in the city. A discovery that shook the hangmen more than any previous one.

The death of Master Hans, a member of their council.

"Quiet!" Deibler shouted into the smoky room. The journeymen and apprentices had once again taken their seats along the wall. "Jakob is right. We must talk calmly about how to proceed from here."

"How to proceed?" the Nuremberg executioner, Johann Widmann, jeered. "I can tell you how we're going to proceed, Deibler. We're going to dissolve this council, pack our bags, and get the hell out of here before the next one of us gets lynched." Several other hangmen nodded their agreement.

"But it's not even certain that Hans was killed by an angry mob," Philipp Teuber interjected. Kuisl had always known the Regensburg hangman to be a quiet man, and now that he spoke up, he seemed composed. "If I understand Deibler and Jakob correctly, they reckon it was the same serial killer who's been murdering girls in Munich."

"And why should he kill Hans?" replied Jörg Defner from Nördlingen, an old, experienced executioner with an eyepatch who generally held back his opinions. "So far, he's only been after young, attractive women. And Hans was neither."

Jakob Kuisl took his pipe from his mouth and cleared his throat. He knew it was crucial to convince the others now. "I believe Hans knew something," he said firmly. "He probably knew the murderer. I don't know why, but he dropped some hints. It appears he came to Munich a couple of days before the rest of us and made some inquiries. Fux will confirm that."

Matthäus Fux, the Memmingen executioner, nodded. "I saw him with my own eyes. Hans was looking for a strawberry-blonde-haired girl—a girl who may have been the same one who was found dead in Au creek the next day."

"And he was going on about some kind of secret at the Holy Cross cemetery," Kuisl said. "He must have been looking for something there. Evidence, most likely. Something that would pin down the murderer." He didn't mention that he himself had returned to the cemetery in the hope of finding something. Kuisl still couldn't figure out what Hans had been doing at Elfi's grave and who the mysterious figure fleeing from him had been. "I think Hans wanted to blackmail the murderer," he continued thoughtfully. "But it backfired on him."

"Nothing but guesswork," Johann Widmann replied with a shake of his head. "To me, the case is crystal clear. The people of Munich wanted to blame us executioners for the murders from the start. Now they caught the first one of us they could find and lynched him."

"Arms and legs cleanly taken off, the head sitting on a pillar —someone had plenty of time." Kuisl leaned back with his arms folded, staring at Widmann defiantly. "I say this was no mob. This was a solitary murderer who relished this execution like a feast."

"I've heard something else entirely," Passau hangman Kaspar Hörmann chimed in. He seemed relatively sober compared to the previous days, though his bulbous red nose glowed in his excitement. He turned to Kuisl with a malicious grin. "Let's not beat around the bush. You hated Hans. Even here in Munich they say that he'd always had a thing for your daughter. Perhaps you had enough one day, huh? So you decided to shut him up for good."

"Kaspar, please!" Deibler called out. "You can't accuse Jakob of murdering someone just because his daughter doesn't want to marry your son."

"Whyever not?" Johann Widmann came to Hörmann's aid. "Jakob is well known for his temper. And he's jammed spokes in Hans's wheel before. Maybe he's just trying to divert suspicion from himself with his absurd theories."

A commotion broke out at Widmann's words and several of the men jumped up, ready to fight one another. Some of them, like Kaspar Hörmann, were clearly on Widmann's side, together with the hangmen from Ingolstadt and Ansbach. Kuisl hadn't made many friends with his grumpy, forbidding manner in recent years. Of all the men present, he could only truly rely on Philipp Teuber, Michael Deibler, and — probably — his brother.

And indeed, Bartholomäus sprang to his feet angrily. "If you insult my brother, you insult me!" he yelled, and Philipp Teuber struggled to stop him from attacking Widmann and Hörmann. The only hangman not joining in the argument was Conrad Näher from Kaufbeuren. He sat in silence at the far end of the table, watching his colleagues shout at one another. Kuisl still hadn't figured out what sort of a person Näher was. And there was a good chance this man, who was roughly the same age as himself, would soon become his son-in-law.

"Quiet, goddamnit!" Michael Deibler shouted against the noise. "I said *quiet*! In the name of the council!" When no one listened, he picked up his pewter mug and threw it against the wall. The ensuing clash of tin shut the hangmen up for a moment.

Deibler took a deep breath. "I didn't call a meeting so we could bash each other's heads in," he said eventually. "Although I must admit that a normal meeting isn't possible in these circumstances." He lowered his head. "Unfortunately, I have to agree with my cousin from Nuremberg. Dissolving the council is probably for the best."

"Told you." Widmann smiled triumphantly. "I'll immediately advise the servants to pack my —"

"But if we leave now, none of us is safe."

"Huh?" Widmann's head spun to the right, where Conrad Näher was sitting. It was the first time the Kaufbeuren hangman had spoken that day.

"What do you mean?" Widmann asked his colleague.

"Hans was on his own outside the city, and someone killed him," Näher replied. "Who's to say it won't happen to us? It doesn't matter if it's just a solitary lunatic or an angry mob, we're weak on our own. They'll think we've got something to hide and are running away. I say we stay together until all this is over."

"And what if it's never over?" Philipp Teuber asked. "What then?"

"I suggest we stay in Munich for two more days," Näher replied. "Two days—no more, no less. Let Jakob try to find out what really happened to Hans in that time. I think we owe as much to our cousin."

The noise level around the table rose again. Kuisl couldn't suppress a thin smile. Näher was absolutely right, but he suspected the Kaufbeuren executioner was after something else entirely: he wanted to woo Barbara for a while longer. If the council was dissolved now, the Kuisl family would go home—and their younger daughter hadn't yet made up her mind whom to marry. After all the fighting of the last few days, Kuisl wasn't so sure he still wanted Barbara to marry an executioner.

We're outcasts, the lot of us, he thought. *Loneliness has turned us into angry, hateful beasts.*

As his eyes scanned the executioners, Jakob Kuisl thought that perhaps the people of Munich were right after all. Maybe the murderer really was one of the Council of Twelve. Kuisl had suspected Master Hans because he arrived earlier than the others. But who was to say that none of the others had traveled to Munich even earlier? And that one of their own hadn't visited the capital repeatedly in the past?

Or that murders like these didn't occur elsewhere in Bavaria?

Hangmen traveled a lot. Not every town could afford its own executioner, so hangmen often came from other cities. If possible, such towns didn't employ the next butcher that came around but one of the best—one of the Council of Twelve.

Kuisl winced.

A traveling hangman . . . The perfect murderer . . .

Was that what Master Hans found out and had to die for?

Suddenly Jakob Kuisl saw the loudly arguing cousins with different eyes, and a chill ran down his back.

Angry, hateful beasts . . .

"We'll take a vote," Deibler announced, tearing Kuisl from his thoughts. The Munich hangman rapped his knuckles on the table. "Who's in favor of Näher's suggestion to stay put for two more days in the hope of solving the case? As the chairman, I'm going to abstain, as our rules demand."

After some hesitation, six executioners raised their hands. The hands of Johann Widmann, Kaspar Hörmann, and the Ingolstadt and Ansbach executioners stayed down.

"Six to four," Michael Deibler declared. "It's decided. We're staying until Sunday." He sighed and folded his hands. "And now let us do what we ought to have done to begin with. Let's pray for our dead cousin. O Lord, hear my voice. Let your ears be attentive to the voice of my supplication," he began, and the others slowly joined in.

With lowered heads, the hangmen murmured the penitential psalm in honor of Master Hans.

But from the corner of his eye, Jakob Kuisl saw how they all looked at one another suspiciously.

Peter sat on one of the benches in the court gardens with his eyes closed and enjoyed the sun on his face. His forehead was sweaty, his breathing heavy. He'd been running through the expansive park with Max, playing catch and hide and seek. Now they were both out of breath and took a break in the noon sunshine, which had melted the snow as fast as it had fallen the day before.

When they sat together like this, Peter managed to forget for a moment that he was only the son of a simple doctor and Max was a prince. But as soon as he opened his eyes again, he saw all the pomp around him, saw this fairy-tale-like place that was so different from his playgrounds at home, the meadows by the Lech River, the dark forests, or the fields near the Schongau Tanners' Quarter.

The court gardens were an elaborately designed park that bordered the Residenz on the north. There were tall trees, strangely cut hedges, and countless fountains, thin sheets of ice still floating in some of them. Then there were marble statues like the ones Peter had already seen at the Residenz. In the center of the park, where the white graveled paths met, stood a stone pavilion.

Peter regretted not having brought his drawing supplies. He would have loved to capture this view, and to be able to show his father later. But he didn't know what Max would think of that. The crown prince had made it very clear that he didn't think much of Latin and music classes. Perhaps he had his own drawing teacher? Did that even exist?

From time to time, courtiers strolled past the two boys and bowed at the sight of the prince. Just then, another made-up dandy with a periwig came by, bowing especially low. Max giggled when the man had gone.

"Sometimes they bow so low that their wigs get dirty," he said, laughing. "Or it comes off, and you see their bald heads."

"And if someone doesn't bow?" Peter asked.

"Then the hangman chops their head off," Max replied as casually as if he was talking about the weather. "I'm the son of the Bavarian elector, after all."

Peter flinched. Once again he was pleased his new friend didn't know whose grandson he was.

"Mother always holds balls in the court gardens," Max said. "Everyone wears masks and they play catch just like children. And on Lake Würm, we have a big ship, the bucentaur, which is like a floating hunting lodge. The best part are the cannons, but other than that it's pretty boring for children."

Peter couldn't imagine anything boring about a floating hunting lodge. But then again, he was no prince.

"Tomorrow night, Mother is holding a huge masquerade at Nymphenburg Palace, our new summer residence," Max said, balancing on the bench seat's backrest while some of the courtiers watched him shyly. "So far, it's nothing but a freezing cold box of stone, but Mother loves the place. You must come, or it's going to be so boring again. Promise you'll come?"

"If . . . if my parents let me, sure," Peter replied. Max waved dismissively.

"I'm the prince. I order you to come. It's that easy."

Peter looked over to the high wall that separated the gardens from Schwabinger Road. "Commoners aren't allowed in here, are they?" he asked.

"Of course not." Max laughed and jumped off the backrest. "I had to beg and plead so they'd let you in." His face turned glum. "Only till lunchtime, though, then you have to leave again. I've got violin class with Kerll this afternoon. How I hate it!"

"And if you don't go? You're the prince, you can do what you want."

"Bah! As if!" Max made a rude noise. "I think I've got more chores than a peasant boy. Boring receptions from morning till night, getting dressed alone takes an hour, and then all those classes. Latin, theology, arithmetic, geography, violin, harp, and flute . . ." He groaned. "Most of all, I hate Latin and violin class with Kerll. At least when Arthur was still here he'd bark and howl during class until Kerll went crazy. But now Arthur's gone. And God knows if he'll ever come back to me." Max quickly wiped a tear from the corner of his eye.

Peter would have loved to tell Max that his father was hot on the dog's trail, but he didn't know if Simon was making any progress. Peter was increasingly worried his father wouldn't find Max's dog after all. That would probably mean the end of his friendship with Max — and he wouldn't be allowed to attend the Jesuit college, either.

"Arthur is probably playing with a bunch of stray dogs as we speak," Peter tried to reassure his friend. "And when he gets bored of it, he'll come back."

"I think he's dead," Max said sadly. "Someone knocked him over the head or drowned him, like they do with strays. The groom told me about it. And he knows lots about animals."

Peter looked around the park. Laughing courtiers strolled through the gardens in their open fur coats and padded vests, enjoying the weak February sun. "This is where Arthur disappeared, right?" he asked. "How exactly did it happen?"

"I already told you," Max replied dejectedly. "My nursemaid, Amalie, was walking him on his lead. He must have seen a cat and broke free."

Thoughtfully, Peter looked at the high walls. "But how did he get out of the gardens?"

"There must be a hole somewhere. We searched for hours but found no trace of him anywhere." Max wiped another tear from his eye. "Amalie was very upset, but she says it wasn't her fault. The lead tore at the collar because Arthur pulled too hard."

"Tore?" Peter gave Max a look of disbelief. "But Arthur is just a small dog, isn't he? Not a huge mastiff. Hmm . . ." He touched his nose, as he always did when he thought hard. Suddenly he had an idea. If his father couldn't or wouldn't solve this case, perhaps he might think of something.

But what?

"Is the lead still around?" he asked eventually.

Max shrugged. "Not sure. I think Lohmiller, the head groom, took it. He was going to stitch it up because the collar is very precious. It's studded with pearls and small diamonds."

Peter frowned. "Do you think we could take a look at it?"

"I have no idea what good that's supposed to do, but all right. I can show you the electoral stables at the same time." Max stood up and Peter followed him down several paths to a more remote part of the park, and from there to the electoral stables, situated behind the Residenz. This part of the complex wasn't as splendid and ostentatious. The plain houses contained haylofts under the roofs and Peter heard horses whinnying behind large wooden doors. The air smelled of dung and animal sweat. In the center, between the houses, several horses trotted around in a muddy corral under the supervision of servants.

A man was just leading a gray horse out from the end of a long building, and the horse was larger than any Peter had ever seen. It snorted and reared, but the strong, broad-shouldered man held the reins firmly and spoke to the animal soothingly.

"That's the head groom I told you about, Lohmiller," Max said admiringly. "They say he can speak with horses, and he rides like the devil. He always picks out the most beautiful foals for me to break in."

As they walked toward Lohmiller, Peter stared at all the horses in the stables with amazement. There were enough to equip a whole army. He himself had only ridden once in his life, on a skinny old carthorse that belonged to a Schongau wagon driver and had been taken to the knacker soon after. By comparison, the horses here all looked like imperial destriers.

"Ah, Your Excellency!" Lohmiller greeted the prince when he saw him. He bowed, too, but not as low as the courtiers in the park. "Do you want to ride out with your young friend before your violin lesson?"

"I'd love to," Max sighed. "And ideally, I'd break my arm while riding out, then I wouldn't have to attend stupid Kerll's music class." He shook himself. "But no, we're here for something else. Do you still have Arthur's lead? You were going to fix it."

"The lead from your dog?" Lohmiller scratched his head. "Hmm. I'm very sorry, young sir. I haven't fixed it yet. But I'm sure you can have a new one—"

"You don't need to fix it," Peter interjected. "We just want to take a quick look at it."

"Look at it?" Lohmiller stared at Peter as if he only just noticed him properly. Then he shrugged. "I think it's somewhere by the other leather things that need to be fixed in my room.

Wait here." He walked over to the long building and soon returned with a lead. It was about six feet long, made of leather,
and the collar was decorated with pearls and tiny diamonds.
Peter guessed this lead alone was worth as much as two destriers.

"There you go," Lohmiller said and handed the lead to Peter.
"Although I don't really understand what you want with it." He
waited, curious to see what happened next.

Peter looked at the collar, which was indeed torn in one place.

"Like I told you," Max said quietly. "Arthur tore himself free.
There's nothing special about it."

Thoughtfully, Peter ran his finger over the tear. The lead was
made of the finest calf leather and had been greased well, every
pearl and diamond was still in its place. No precious stone had
fallen out. Peter handed the lead back to Lohmiller.

"Could you do us a favor?" he asked. "Could you please pull
on both ends as hard as you can?"

The head groom laughed. "Your requests are becoming
stranger and stranger." He looked at Max, and when the prince
nodded, he pulled on the lead so the muscles on his arms bulged
under his shirt.

"Is that enough?" he gasped after a while.

"Yes, that's enough," Peter replied. "Thank you very much.
You can take the lead back now."

"As you wish. Always a pleasure, young sirs." Shaking his
head, the groom disappeared in the stables, and Max stared at
Peter uncomprehendingly.

"If that was some kind of trick, you'll have to explain."

Peter smiled. "Not a trick, just an experiment. That's what
you do in science, I read about it. You make observations and
draw conclusions."

"And what conclusions did you draw?" Max asked with
interest.

"Well, the leather is strong enough that not even that bear of a head groom can break it. And something else." Peter paused dramatically.

"Stop keeping me in suspense like this," Max complained. "What else?"

"The tear in the collar is smooth. When leather rips, the edge is soft and fibrous. I know that from the Schongau tanneries. This lead didn't tear, it was cut."

"Cut?" Max's jaw dropped for a moment. "But . . . but . . . that means . . ."

"That means your nursemaid was lying. She or someone else cut the collar and abducted the dog." Peter contentedly crossed his arms on his chest. "*Quod erat demonstrandum.* That's Latin, and it means: *which was to be proven.*"

Max turned purple with rage. "Amalie is going to regret this, I swear! I'm going to tell my father and he'll throw her into the deepest hole where worms and bugs can eat her, and—"

"Is that really what you want?" Peter interrupted him. "Because that's probably exactly what's going to happen."

"No, damn it, that's not what I want." Max groaned. "Amalie is really nice, I've known her longer than I can remember. I have no idea why she'd do something like that. She loved Arthur almost as much as I do." He clenched his fists. "But if I *don't* tell my father, I'll never get Arthur back. What a quagmire! What are we supposed to do?"

"I tell you what we'll do," Peter said. "We'll watch Amalie. That's what you do when you're trying to catch a thief. I know that from my father. He says they all make a mistake sooner or later."

"But I can't watch her," Max objected. "She knows me. She'd become suspicious right away. And I'm not allowed to leave the Residenz, and she always goes into town for something or other."

"Hmm. Yes, she knows you . . . But . . ." Peter thought. Suddenly, his face brightened. "I know who's going to watch Amalie for us when she goes to town."

"And who's that?"

Peter grinned. "It's a surprise. I don't think you could find any better noses for the job."

He felt a pleasant tingle spreading from his scalp to his toes. They had found a lead, just like dogs following a scent. For the first time, Peter understood why his father and grandfather kept chasing rogues.

It was incredibly fun.

Barbara also enjoyed the almost springlike sun while she tried to forget about her uncertain future for a few hours.

Together with Conrad Näher she stood on a rise outside Munich and gazed at the panorama of the city, with its churches, patrician palaces, tall stone buildings, and the fortifications surrounding the angular city wall. In the center stood the huge church with two domed towers; it could be seen far into the countryside on clear days like today. Barbara wondered if the tall church could be seen from Hoher Peißenberg, the mountain that marked the border of her home around Schongau.

Around noon, Näher had turned up at the executioner's house with a bunch of dried flowers and invited her to join him for a walk. Apparently, the guild meeting finished earlier than expected, and she could imagine why.

Barbara had felt like declining. The pregnancy was making her nauseated, and she was still sore from her fall at the cemetery the day before. Michael Deibler had told her about Hans's death, that he had been executed like a traitor. Strangely, she hadn't been filled with happiness at the news, but more with a sense of dread. Like Deibler and her father, she didn't believe an angry mob of citizens was responsible for Hans's death. Someone was lurking out there, and she wondered who the next victim was going to be.

Apart from that, she just didn't know what to do. Marry Conrad Näher, this friendly, gallant executioner from Kaufbeuren, who was almost as old as her father? Or simply run away? Because her sister was right on one point: she couldn't go back to Schongau. Only a few more weeks and she wouldn't be able to hide the pregnancy any longer, and Barbara didn't want to put her family and herself through what would inevitably follow.

Conrad Näher had been standing next to her in silence for a while. Something seemed to be on his mind, and Barbara suspected it had something to do with Hans's death and the meeting of the council that morning. Suddenly, he squeezed her hand, and she gave a start. A cold breeze made her shiver. Barbara had made Näher's gift of blue silk into a scarf; out here, with hardly anyone around, she had dared to wear it.

"A beautiful view, isn't it?" Näher said with a gesture at the city in front of them. "When you see Munich on a sunny day like this, it's hard to imagine the suffering that went on here only a few decades ago."

"What do you mean?" Barbara asked, glad for the distraction.

"Well, the Swedes didn't manage to storm the city, but Munich had to pay a huge ransom. The countryside around the city was ravaged. And then came the Plague. More than half the people of Munich died." Näher sighed. "But now that Elector Ferdinand Maria and his foreign wife rule the country, Munich is blossoming like a rose in May. It's almost a miracle."

Barbara thought of all the young maids, the traveling journeymen, the rag collectors, peddlers, old mercenaries, orphans, and beggars in the suburbs, who would love to smell that rose but weren't allowed to. The dead girls had belonged to that group, too. She was about to make a reply when Näher spoke again with a timid voice.

"My dear Barbara," he began awkwardly. "I want to be honest with you. I . . . I understand the decision to marry isn't an easy one for you. I'm not the youngest man, and I can't promise you heaven on earth. And also, the last few days . . ." He smiled sadly. "Well, I'm sure you've noticed that we hangmen don't have the best reputation, but you already know that from home." He squared his shoulders. "I'm not the worst prospect as the Kaufbeuren executioner. I have money and a big house that's waiting to be filled with the patter of children's feet."

Barbara blushed and turned away, but Conrad Näher continued, more eagerly now. "I know your father wants to force you to marry, but I don't believe in that. A wife that bawls her eyes out all day long only brings a man the ridicule of his neighbors. I don't need a wife like that. You have to want it, Barbara. But we don't have much time. The city is raging because of those damned murders, trying to blame us hangmen for them. They already lynched Master Hans, and no one knows what's going to happen next. Deibler and Widmann wanted to dissolve the council today. I asked them to wait two more days. Two days, then we all go our separate ways again." Conrad Näher looked at her intently. "I'm afraid you must decide now, Barbara. Do you want to come to Kaufbeuren with me?"

Barbara felt nausea rising up in her again. She needed to sit down. But there was no bench on the rise, not even a tree trunk. Only a faded wayside cross and a stone that marked the border of a village called Sendling. A handful of farmhouses stood on either side of the village street, and farther down was a little church and a tavern next to it. Barbara could hear faint music coming from inside.

"Can we go there?" she asked with a trembling voice and pointed at the tavern. "I . . . feel a little faint. And it's still quite cold when the sun disappears behind a cloud."

Näher eyed her closely. Did he suspect something? But then he nodded and gently placed his coat around her shoulders. "Of course. It's better to discuss such matters in the warmth, over a jug of beer or some mulled wine, anyway."

They walked down to the tavern. Its shutters had been freshly painted, smoke rose from the chimney, two horses tied to a post chewed on oats from a feeding trough. Inside, the tavern smelled deliciously of freshly baked bread and smoked sausages.

Few patrons sat at the tables at this time of day, most of them farmers who didn't have much to do this time of the year. Three musicians played a fast folk song. They were a young violinist, an older man with a wheel fiddle, and a flute player with a dark complexion who also played the tambourine. They didn't seem to play so much for their sparse audience as for themselves, laughing out loud in the middle of the song or taking breaks for sips of beer. They were cheerful, boyish men, and Barbara particularly liked the young blond violinist—a jaunty lad whose teeth gleamed white and whose eyes had an intelligent and curious look about them.

When Barbara and Näher sat down at a table near the musicians, the violinist gave her a cheeky smile and fiddled a wild series of notes. For a brief moment, Barbara felt like he played only for her. She returned the smile bashfully.

Conrad Näher ordered a beer for himself and a cup of mulled wine for Barbara, which really did make her feel better. The nausea disappeared and a warm feeling spread in her chest. But Conrad Näher's serious expression told her that she couldn't put off this conversation any longer.

"Barbara, if you've got something to tell me, you should do it now." His hand reached for hers, and she winced again. "I'm not blind, girl. My late wife wasn't so fortunate as to have children of her own, but many young women sought us out for help, some desperate, others joyful. If you know what I mean . . ." He paused, and Barbara swallowed hard. She'd been right, Näher did suspect something. But she also knew there was no way back once she confessed. If she told the Kaufbeuren hangman about her pregnancy, she was at his mercy. Who was to say he wouldn't tell her father right away?

"I, er . . . ," she began, clearing her throat. "Well . . ." She desperately searched for the right words.

Just then, a younger man who appeared to have been sitting somewhere at the back of the room stepped to their table. He was about thirty, although his face had something childlike about it. With his tight red vest, his fur-collared coat, and the jauntily tilted hat, he looked like a typical dandy from the city. He was unquestionably attractive, but Barbara didn't like the arrogant smile on his fleshy lips.

"What a surprise!" he exclaimed, spreading his arms. "It's good old Conrad. How small the world is."

Näher winced noticeably when he saw the man. Then he nodded reluctantly.

"Greetings, Johann," he grumbled. "What brings you to Sendling?"

"My father's business dealings. Fustian is expensive, especially here in Munich, where the foreigners ruin the prices. So, I'm looking for weavers in the wider region who can offer us a better price." The man winked at Barbara. "And if the business talks end in a good game of dice and a glass of wine, I'm not one to complain."

"Well, then, good luck with your gambling and business talks." Näher turned away, clearly eager to end the conversation. But the other man wasn't fobbed off that easily.

"What a pretty girl you have there," he said with a smile. "You aren't trying to find yourself a wife, are you?"

Barbara thought Näher grew a little paler. "Her father is the Schongau hangman," he said quietly. "As you might have heard, we hangmen are holding a meeting at Munich."

"Oh, and of course there's always enough time for a little fun," the stranger said with a grin. "And why not?" He turned to Barbara. "Especially if the hangman's girl is so young and pretty. How old are you, darling?"

"I can't see how that's any of your business," said Barbara, who increasingly disliked the man's tone. She thought she detected a silent threat. "And now please leave us alone."

"Of course, I didn't mean to disturb your cozy rendezvous. Pardon my intrusion." The young man took a bow. "I was about to leave anyhow. I'll be back in Munich this evening — perhaps I'll see you around." Chuckling, he walked to the door.

"Who in God's name was that?" Barbara asked Conrad Näher with disgust when they were alone again. "Do you know that man well?"

Näher shook his head. He clearly felt uncomfortable, biting his lip nervously.

"No, it's . . . more of a superficial acquaintance. Nothing that . . ." He faltered, then he suddenly stood up. "Please excuse me. I must speak privately with Johann. You know the way back to Munich."

Barbara stared at him with shock. "But—" she started.

"It's not about you," Näher cut her off. "It's something between men. An old story. But I don't know how long this conversation is going to take, so you might as well head back to the city." His eyes flickered and he rummaged in his pockets. He pulled out a few coins and put them on the table. "That should be enough for the beer and wine. I will send you word when we can meet again. God bless you."

With his coat billowing behind him, Conrad Näher rushed after the stranger. The door slammed shut and Barbara was alone. She had been too stunned to even say goodbye to Näher. What had come over him? Just a moment ago he had urged her to choose a life with him in Kaufbeuren, and now he was running away like a thief in the night. What on earth did he and that strange dandy have to talk about?

The musicians now played a slow song with a mournful melody that put Barbara in a melancholy mood. She had almost confided in Näher and revealed her secret. She had probably been close to agreeing to marry him. But now she was no longer sure what was right and what was wrong. She put her head in her hands and started to cry, silently at first, then sobbing as the tears fell into her cup of mulled wine. How she longed for her older sister right now. But Magdalena had her own problems, and at the end of the day, she couldn't help her either.

No one could.

Barbara was so lost in her misery that she didn't notice the music stop. She jumped with fright when she looked up. The young violin player had sat down at her table and was looking at her sympathetically.

"Whatever happened, there's no reason to cry so much," he said. "Was it our music? If it was too sad, I can easily rectify that. Do you know the song about dumb Augustus?" He picked up his fiddle and played a cheerful tune, moving his head from side to side like a little dog. He looked so funny that Barbara couldn't help but smile.

"There you go, that's better." The young man put his violin aside. "But don't you dare start crying again or I'll play all thirty-three verses of the song. It makes you awfully dizzy. I always do it when a robber tries to attack me. I make the scoundrel spin round and round until he spins right into the Isar River."

Now Barbara laughed out loud. She wiped the tears from her face and took a closer look at the young man. Again, she noticed the lively eyes, his small frame, the fine features of his face, and the soft fluff growing on his chin. His hair was flaxen, and his nose covered in freckles despite it being winter, which gave him a slightly mischievous look. Barbara guessed he was about the same age as her.

"Your music was beautiful," she said. "Do you often play here?"

The violin player shrugged and pointed at the two other musicians, who were just packing away their instruments. "Hans and Ludwig are from around here, I usually play in Munich. Today was just a rehearsal. A wealthy Sendling farmer is getting married in two weeks, and we're providing the music. We need enough songs for the whole night and half the day."

"So you . . . you're a traveling musician?" Barbara asked curiously. She knew this kind of musician from Schongau. They traveled from place to place together with jugglers and other itinerant artists and played for a few coins and somewhere to sleep.

"A pauper musician?" The young man raised his eyebrows with indignation. "Oh no! I'm a Munich town musician. I'm officially permitted to play at weddings and other celebrations for money. I have a steady income and a roof over my head. Not like those roaming rogues."

"I . . . I'm sorry, I meant no offense," Barbara said haltingly. For a moment she'd been tempted to tell the violinist that she was an outcast just like the traveling folks, a dishonorable hangman's daughter.

He waved dismissively. "Who cares? Music is music." He held out his hand. "I'm Valentin."

"And I'm Barbara," she replied. Suddenly, she felt terribly nervous and happy at the same time, a strange combination she'd never felt in the presence of men before.

"And I guess the man just then was your father, wasn't he?" Valentin said and pointed toward the door. "It looked like you had a fight."

Barbara laughed. "No, no fight, and he isn't my father, either. He's . . ." She broke off.

Probably soon my husband, she thought, but didn't say anything. Instead, she stood up.

"It was nice meeting you," she mumbled. "But I've got to head back to the city."

"To Munich?" Valentin laughed, his white teeth gleamed. "So you're from Munich, like me? How come I've never seen you before? I would have noticed someone like you."

"No, I'm just visiting," Barbara replied. "Um, I'm staying with my uncle. The man before was my uncle."

She couldn't think of a better lie, and she didn't dare tell Valentin that she was the daughter of the Schongau hangman. It was probably safer not to be related to an executioner in Munich at the moment. And she didn't want to admit that she was being courted by a man so much older than her.

"May I walk to Munich with you?" Valentin asked. "Hans and Ludwig live in Sendling and the walk to Munich is much less boring with company. I can even play a couple of songs if you like."

Barbara hesitated briefly, but then nodded. It was strange, but she didn't feel uncomfortable around the young violinist at all, unlike the way she felt around other men lately. It hadn't been too bad with Conrad Näher, but Valentin radiated an energy and vivacity she found contagious.

"All right," she said with a smile. "I could use some company."

Together they left the Sendling tavern. It wasn't long before Valentin picked up his fiddle and played a merry tune, dancing and skipping ahead of her like a young colt. Without meaning to, Barbara soon clapped to the beat of the music.

And with every beat, her gloomy thoughts became a little lighter.

9

Followed by the footman's watchful eyes, Magdalena carried the last silver platter of food up to the second floor of the patrician palace.

She could sense that the servant was just waiting for her to drop the platter. For the last few hours he had done nothing but bully, watch, and correct her. Right now Magdalena didn't know what she disliked more: sitting at the loom from dawn till dusk or playing the maidservant in the house of the Munich treasurer. She had cooked with the grumpy housekeeper downstairs, she had cleaned, swept, waxed the floors, and polished the silverware —all for the mysterious visitor Pfundner eagerly awaited. Magdalena constantly expected Daniel Pfundner to pounce on her, his new wench—she still wasn't sure how she'd react. But it didn't come to that, mainly thanks to Pfundner's wife.

If the treasurer hadn't been such a toad, Magdalena would have felt a little sorry for him. His wife called for him nonstop. She was in pain, and her moaning could be heard throughout the entire house. She needed her pillows to be fluffed, her windows opened and closed again, a pan with dried herbs lit, the chamber pot emptied . . . Mostly, Pfundner sent the footman up, but sometimes he went himself.

At first Magdalena had been surprised he didn't ask her to attend to his wife, but then she realized that he probably didn't want to arouse her suspicion. His wife might have a hunch that he amused himself with other women, and a pretty maidservant could raise all sorts of unpleasant questions.

Magdalena never even saw the doctor, whose brief visit had brought no relief. The promised poppy juice hadn't been available for some reason. Pfundner's wife kept moaning and groaning, and so Magdalena was spared any romantic advances for the time being.

When she placed the last platter on the table in the parlor, she heard footsteps on the stairs and the treasurer walked in the room. He looked visibly pleased at the sight of all the food and the full jugs of wine.

"Very good," he said with a nod. "The wine is especially important. The wine is going to put him in a friendly mood. And you, too, perhaps." He winked at Magdalena. Then he signaled to the footman. "You can go now, Johann. We're finished."

"As you wish, sir." With one last poisonous glance at Magdalena, the servant left the parlor. Daniel Pfundner licked his meaty lips and looked Magdalena up and down.

"Look at you," he complained. "You look like a washerwoman. You can't possibly serve our guest like this." Magdalena looked down at herself. Her apron was stained from cooking, and her skirt was smeared with ash and soot.

"We must find something better for you to wear," Pfundner commanded. "Come with me."

He opened one of the tall side doors, which led to a corridor hung with tapestries and paintings. Magdalena followed him to a room filled with chests and a Venetian mirror on the wall.

"This is where my wife keeps her dresses," Pfundner said. "They're all gathering dust since she can't leave her bed anymore. You two should be around the same size, so pick something. Nothing too grand, God forbid. Something modest yet elegant. My wife is a plain woman, so I'm sure you'll find something."

Magdalena reluctantly opened one of the chests and pulled out a dress of the finest silk. She thought of all the poor, hungry girls who had probably woven this silk. Disgusted, she put the dress back and picked up a simpler one made of gray fustian.

Suddenly she felt Pfundner's hand on her behind.

"Go on, take off your clothes, I can't wait to see what you look like," he whispered in her ear so she could smell his sour breath. "I like women best in Eve's costume, anyhow." He snickered, and his fingers wandered up to her neckline. "It's time to show me you're worth the money."

Magdalena froze. The moment she'd feared had finally arrived. Pfundner had paid for a prostitute and now he was claiming his goods. Magdalena knew that if she made a fuss now or refused outright, Pfundner would throw her out. And she'd never find out what happened to Anni and the other girls.

"Come on," Pfundner urged. "Don't act coy." He pulled up her skirts. "We don't have much time."

"And . . . and what if your wife hears us?" Magdalena asked.

The treasurer narrowed his eyes. "Let her wail and moan, I'm sick of it. If I didn't know that she tells her father everything, I'd take you right in front of her, damn it. But I need his money. Though not for much longer."

"Not . . . not for much longer?" Magdalena squirmed in Pfundner's hands. "How do you mean?"

Pfundner laughed. "As if that's any of your business, wench." He fumbled with his belt, a bulge growing beneath it. "Your job is to spread your legs, nothing else."

Magdalena trembled. She thought about what happened to her sister two years ago. Barbara never spoke about it, but the wound in her soul had never fully healed. Would it be the same for her now? Would she ever be able to look Simon in the eye again?

Her fingers instinctively felt for the small knife underneath her skirt. The blade felt smooth and sharp.

"Daaaniel!" the mournful voice of his wife suddenly rang out. She sounded close, almost as if she was in the same room. Magdalena stiffened and looked up. The bedroom of the treasurer's wife must have been directly above them.

"Daaaniel! I need you, it's so stuffy in here. Daaaniel, where are you?"

"The devil take her." Pfundner swore and paused groping Magdalena. "I'm going to kill that woman, I swear by God. If the disease doesn't take her soon, I'm going to kill her."

"I'll be right there, darling," he called upstairs. Then he shoved Magdalena against the wall and pushed up her apron and skirt.

"I don't pay van Uffele for you to clean my house," he panted. "It'll just have to be quick."

Magdalena closed her eyes and waited for the inevitable. Her fingers clasped the knife again.

In that moment, someone knocked on the front door.

"I can't believe it," Pfundner groused. "First the wife, then the visitor arrives early. Goddamnit!"

As he turned away from Magdalena, his feet got caught in the dresses on the floor and he crashed to the ground.

"Daaaniel, is everything all right?" his wife's voice sounded from upstairs.

"We . . . we're having visitors, Agathe," Pfundner stammered. "I told you." He scrambled to his feet and did up his belt. "I'll send Johann up. I have to go and welcome our guest."

Daniel Pfundner gave Magdalena one last look of desire. "We'll just have to do it later," he said. "And this is what I stayed home for today. Bugger it all!" He gestured at the rumpled clothes on the floor. "Put something on and wait on our guest."

He rushed out of the room. Magdalena closed her eyes and took a deep breath. She still didn't know what she would have done if Pfundner had raped her. At least now she'd gained a short reprieve.

Magdalena could hear male voices downstairs and the servant's footsteps above her. A window was opened. She reached for the dress of fustian and got changed. Pfundner's wife and she were indeed roughly the same size. The dress was a loose cut and plain gray in color. It was a tidy garment without unnecessary frills and embellishments, as would have been appropriate for a higher maid or nurse.

Magdalena looked in the mirror. It had been a long time since she'd last seen her own reflection, and that had been in a polished copper plate at home, not in a mirror of expensive Venetian glass. She was looking at a mature woman. A woman who had learned to fight in recent years, who had overcome countless dangers and wouldn't be taken by any lewd fop.

Not unless it was absolutely necessary.

She turned away and walked out into the corridor, and from there to the closed parlor door. She could hear quiet voices inside; the men must have already sat down. She was about to enter when she caught snippets of the conversation behind the door.

". . . must do it tonight."

Curious, she held her ear against the door. Now she could hear better.

". . . can't waste any time," a slightly nasal voice said, probably that of the guest. The voice sounded concerned, anxious even. "We have to bring this to an end tonight. We must take them away before we're found out. Everything must go."

Magdalena froze.

We must take them away . . .

Was he talking about the girls at the silk manufactory, girls like Eva?

"And how do you propose we do that?" Daniel Pfundner asked angrily. "It's not that simple. I was planning on tomorrow night."

"But I'm telling you: tomorrow night's too late," the other man pleaded. "I heard it from the horse's mouth. That accursed ball spoils everything. It's now or never."

"Then . . . why don't you do it by yourself," Pfundner suggested. "I can give you everything you need. I can even —"

"Out of the question. I've done your dirty work for long enough. We're doing it together or not at all, and that's my final word."

No one said anything for a while. Magdalena heard someone get up and pace the room.

"Very well," Pfundner said eventually, his voice sounding awfully close to the door. "If we must. Even though I had other . . . er . . . plans for tonight. I need some time to prepare everything."

"We'll meet behind your house when the bells chime ten, as always. We must be fast. And then I never want to hear about this damned business again, understood? We ought to be glad we haven't climbed the scaffold yet. The hangman would boil us in oil for this."

"It's a bit late for such qualms." Daniel Pfundner laughed sardonically. "You have done very well out of our little business. And now please excuse me."

The door handle was pushed down. Magdalena took a step back and tried to look inconspicuous. Then the door opened and Daniel Pfundner came out. The treasurer seemed confused for a moment but appeared too preoccupied to suspect anything.

"Oh, there you are," he said absentmindedly. "I won't require your services today. Come back tomorrow." His eyes went down Magdalena's chastely covered chest and he sighed. "Truly, a shame, but business comes first."

"Who is that?" the man behind him asked suspiciously. "I've never seen her here before."

For the first time, Magdalena could see the strange visitor. He was short and squat, with a bald head, bull neck, and large, hairy hands. If he hadn't been wearing such a fine black coat, Magdalena would have thought he was a simple tradesman, a blacksmith, perhaps, or a wagon driver. Fear was in his small eyes as he studied Magdalena.

"You have nothing to worry about," Pfundner said. "She's a dumb girl from the country, nothing more. No one who could pose any danger to you. And she's going to keep her mouth shut, isn't she?" He placed his hand on Magdalena's shoulder and his fingers pressed hard on her collarbone. "If anyone asks, I had no visitors today," he whispered in her ear. "Understood? Or I'll personally make sure that van Uffele takes care of you, if you know what I mean . . ."

Magdalena nodded silently, and the pain eased. Daniel Pfundner gave her a companionable pat on the back. "I'll see you tomorrow. You can keep the dress—at least until I tell you to take it off," he added with a grin. He gave her one last slap on the backside, then Magdalena turned around and walked down the stairs. She thought she could still feel the eyes of the bullnecked guest on her back, but she walked slowly and confidently, as if she hadn't a care in the world.

Once outside on the street, she ran as if the devil was behind her.

"And you really think that nursemaid stole the dog?"

Paul looked at his brother with wide eyes while chewing excitedly on a piece of licorice. They were sitting in the attic of the executioner's house, the wind blowing through the roof tiles. From time to time, they heard Walburga's footsteps from downstairs and the meowing of one of the many cats living in the house. All the other grownups were out. But even if they had been home, they would have struggled to find the boys. This house was huge and old, with cellars and secret passages. The siblings still hadn't explored every room.

Even though it was bitter cold, the boys loved this magical place they had only discovered the day before. A retractable ladder led here, to the upper story underneath the roof. Between cobwebs, broken bricks, and all kinds of rubbish, the children felt as safe as in a fortress. Safe and undisturbed.

Especially if one had secrets to discuss.

Peter nodded and continued his report. "I took a good look at the collar. It was cut. But the nursemaid said the dog had run away. So she's lying. I don't know why, but it's a fact."

"And you want me to watch her?" Paul asked. "Me and the Anger Wolves?" He couldn't contain his excitement. He jumped up, climbed onto one of the rafters, and started to balance on it. Suddenly he stopped and turned to Peter. "And what do we get for it, hmm?"

Peter sighed. His younger brother was very keen on money for his eight years. Paul was very quick at adding—a gift that left him abruptly whenever he walked into school. Peter never understood that.

The two brothers were different in many ways. Paul thought learning to read and draw was a waste of time, but he could build tiny millwheels from willow branches, whittle beautiful dolls, and he usually emerged victorious from street fights, even against older kids. But what Peter couldn't understand was Paul's passion for executions and tortures, which he sometimes enacted on animals. Paul already felt certain that he would be a renowned executioner one day. Peter's dream, on the other hand, was to become a successful physician, or a painter, like those who decorated the walls and ceilings of churches.

Peter was all the happier that Paul and he finally shared an interest.

"I can't promise you anything," he said to his brother up on the rafter. "But the dog belongs to the prince. I'm sure Max will reward us generously when we return his favorite pet to him."

"Max, Max, Max!" Paul parroted his brother. "Soon you'll be wearing one of those ridiculous wigs and wide pants that look like girls' skirts."

"Stop it," Peter said. "It's not Max's fault that he's a prince. And he's actually quite nice."

"Ooohh, Max is nice." Paul giggled. "Do you know what the boys on the street say? They say his mother is a foreign harlot who can't even speak German."

"Leave his mother out of it. Father met her and he said she's an intelligent woman."

"I thought it was Father's job to find that mutt?" Paul said. "Didn't he promise the electress that he would? What's he going to say if you're doing it instead of him?"

"I . . . I think Father is going to be glad if we help him," Peter replied hesitantly. "He's got a lot on his mind. Grandpa needs him because of those murders. He doesn't have time to search for a lapdog."

"Yes, yes, you and Father. You always stick together. You even *read* together." Paul spat out the word *read* as if it were something indecent. "Father loves you more, anyway," he sulked. "Just because I don't know Latin." He sat down on the rafter dejectedly.

"That's not true." Peter climbed up to Paul, and the two boys dangled their legs and looked out a small hatch in the roof. They could see the two towers of the Frauenkirche. The Jesuit college wasn't far from there, Peter now knew, the school that was still unreachable for him. But perhaps, if he managed to return Arthur, that door might open.

"Father loves you just as much as me and Sophia," Peter said after a while. But deep down he knew it wasn't true. Their father had always felt closer to him, the eldest child, because they were more similar. Paul, on the other hand, spent much more time with their grandfather.

"What do you say, are you going to help me watch the nurse-maid?" Peter asked eventually to distract his brother. "That is one thing you can do much better than me. Perhaps she'll give herself away when we find out where she's going in town. You and those Anger Wolves, you're the best for a job like this. No one can hide as well and follow someone unnoticed."

Paul was visibly flattered. His mood improved dramatically. "All right, I'll ask the boys," he said with importance. "But only on one condition."

"Which is?" Peter asked.

"I decide how we're going to do it. Not you. For once, you don't get a say in what I do, all right?"

Peter smiled. "All right, I promise. The main thing is that we find the dog." He held out his hand to Paul. "So we're agreed?"

"Agreed." Paul spat into his right hand and squeezed it against Peter's. "That's how the Anger Wolves do it," he said. "Now the promise is sealed." Then he hesitated. "And what if Father doesn't want us to help him? What then?"

"Well, he doesn't have to find out." Peter winked at his brother. "When we find Arthur, we just hand him over like a present. Then he can't get mad at us."

They could hear voices from downstairs now. Evidently, the grownups were back.

"Let's stay up here a while longer," Paul whispered. "I whittled a little man and a cart with proper wheels — here, I'll show you!"

Soon the two boys were sitting on the dusty floor of the attic, absorbed in their play. The grownups' conversation sounded muffled through the stories of the house.

And so they didn't hear their mother make a momentous decision.

. . .

"They're up to something, this very night. And it's got something to do with the girls from the silk manufactory, I'm sure of it."

Simon squeezed his wife's hand. She sat next to him in the Munich executioner's house and was still agitated. She shivered as though she was freezing, but the fire in the tiled stove kept the room pleasantly warm. Magdalena wore a plain dress of good quality that Simon had never seen on her before, but in all the excitement, he hadn't had a chance to ask her about it. It was late afternoon, the mild February sun had already disappeared behind the city walls.

Following his visit to the hospice and the unsettling encounter with the madwoman in the lunatic asylum, Simon had wandered the lanes of the city, thinking. He couldn't get old Traudel's words off his mind.

I know who killed them . . . All those sweet young girls . . .

That sentence had triggered something in him, but he just couldn't figure out what. Perhaps he would pay the crazy old woman another visit sometime.

Once again Simon cursed himself for constantly forgetting to look for his beloved coffee beans. There was nothing that stimulated his thoughts better than coffee. But with everything that had been happening, he just hadn't had the time.

On his way home, Simon had called in at Lorentz the dog-catcher's in the hope of learning something new about that damned dog. But, as expected, there was no news, although Lorentz once again mentioned that other dogs of ladies and gentlemen had also vanished. At the end of the day, Simon thought, this entire search was utter nonsense.

Much more important was what just happened to his wife.

"Now, why don't you start from the beginning," Simon asked Magdalena. On the other side of the table sat his father-in-law, Michael Deibler, and Georg. Walburga held little Sophia in her arms and walked up and down the living room, humming softly.

The men looked expectantly at Magdalena. So far, her news had come pouring out so fast, everyone struggled to make sense of it.

"So you were sent to the house of a patrician this morning," Simon said slowly. "Why? I thought you were working as a weaver."

"Because . . . because I was supposed to take mended sheets to the posh gentleman and lend a hand in the household," Magdalena replied. "Van Uffele and Mother Joseffa sometimes hire out girls as maidservants. It pays well and it's a chance to get a break from the loom. I thought I might find out more that way." Simon had the strange feeling that his wife wasn't telling him everything.

"And who was that posh gentleman?" he asked.

"His name is Daniel Pfundner. He's the city treasurer."

"Pfundner?" Simon jumped to his feet. "I know that fishface. He's an arrogant snob I met at the opera. I don't want my wife to—"

"For Christ's sake, let Magdalena finish," Jakob Kuisl cut him off and pulled Simon back down on his seat. "You can always tell her off afterward." He looked at his daughter. "Well? What happened at the treasurer's house?"

"A bald-headed man visited Pfundner. I listened in on them. They were discussing something that was supposed to happen tonight instead of tomorrow night. The bald one was very agitated. He said something about taking *them* away." Magdalena sighed. "I couldn't find out who he was talking about, but I'm worried it has something to do with the girls at the manufactory."

"And what makes you think that?" Georg asked.

Magdalena hesitated, clearly grappling with something. Eventually, she took a deep breath and started to talk. "The silk weaving is just a pretense. In actual fact, van Uffele and Mother Joseffa hire out young girls as prostitutes to rich men. The dead girls,

Anni and Elfi, also were such prostitutes. Anni used to be at Pfundner's, too. And I'm afraid that's what Eva was going to tell me and now they want to silence her. And maybe other girls, too. *They* must be taken away. I'm sure that's what the bald visitor meant."

"Hang on a moment." Simon stared at his wife, suddenly seeing her through different eyes. "Are you trying to say you and that arrogant snob . . . you . . . as a prostitute . . .?" He couldn't go on.

Magdalena shook her head. "It never came to that."

"I bloody hope not," her father grumbled. "My daughter's no whore, I won't have it."

Georg nodded seriously. "I may not be your father, but I'm still your brother. And as such I can only tell you: it's shameful what those women do. A Kuisl doesn't do that."

"Um, perhaps the husband gets a say in this, too," Simon said. "I really don't approve of my—"

"For crying out loud! Do you menfolk want to hear what I found out or do you just want to make stupid comments?" Magdalena groused. "You men are all the same. Point your fingers at the wenches but still want to have your fun. Isn't that right?"

"Well, maybe I did visit Rosengasse Lane in Bamberg once or twice," Georg admitted. "But it's different when your own sister—"

"This is about the lives of young women and not about honor or shame," Magdalena snapped. "Can you get that through your thick skulls?"

No one said anything for a while. The only sound came from Walburga, who tried to soothe Sophia with a song.

Eventually, Michael Deibler cleared his throat. "You're right, Magdalena. We men can be muttonheads from time to time. Please continue."

The men listened attentively as Magdalena told them about

what she'd learned. She described the terrible conditions in the manufactory, the girls' fear, and the trade in prostitutes. She also mentioned her strange experience in the basement.

"I heard a soft whimpering," she told them, concluding her report. "It's highly likely that Eva and perhaps other girls are locked up down there. Those Venetian silk weavers are probably in on it and act as guards."

"Hmm. If it's true what you're saying, the two of them are running a truly clever business," Michael Deibler said with a frown. "Whoring has been prohibited in Munich since Duke Wilhelm the Pious. Anyone who gets caught is put in the stocks, which is the worst nightmare of the high and mighty gentlemen. But this way, they get their hands on young girls without having to fear anything. Van Uffele and Joseffa must be making a fortune."

"But then why did Anni and Elfi have to die?" Simon asked.

"Perhaps they were going to talk?" Georg said. "That would be a motive, at least."

"Maybe those disgusting men do much worse things to the girls, and they want to keep it secret," Magdalena suggested. "Have you ever thought of that?"

"I don't know. Something seems odd . . ." Simon tilted his head to one side. "What does all this have to do with the murder of Theresa Wilprecht, the patrician's wife? Not to mention the mummy in the rock cellar. It just doesn't fit."

"Master Hans probably knew how it all fit together," Jakob Kuisl said. "And he knew the murderer. But now he's dead." He pounded the table angrily. "Goddamnit! I feel like we're so close to solving the riddle. What connects all the cases? What? Jesus bloody Christ and—"

"*Sh!*" Walburga hushed from the corner. "Or you're going to wake Sophia. She only just nodded off in my arms. And the poor thing truly isn't to blame for any of those gruesome crimes you're talking about."

Simon saw Magdalena smile for the first time since she'd returned to the executioner's house. He was glad Walburga was in the room with them, even if only in the background. The hangman's wife's kind and caring nature clearly helped his wife to forget the day's disturbing events.

"You're right, Burgi," Magdalena said. "And I'm very grateful for everything you do for Sophia. I couldn't have done any of this without your help." She turned back to the men at the table. "I'm certain van Uffele and Mother Joseffa have something to do with the murders. Two of the victims worked for them as prostitutes."

"What if that young patrician woman, Wilprecht, also worked as a whore?" Georg thought out loud. "Not for the money, but just to get one over on her old man?"

"A whore killer? Hmm. I don't know." Deibler scratched his head. "They say the young Wilprecht woman may have had a lover. And again, how does our mummy fit into all this? Her murder happened decades ago."

"The amulets," Kuisl said suddenly.

Michael Deibler gave him an irritated look. "What do you mean?"

"The amulets. He always marks his victims with those amulets. That's what he did back then, and that's what he's still doing today. Anni and the mummy had one. I bet you anything Elfi had one, too. Even if we can no longer prove it." Jakob Kuisl took out his tobacco to prepare a new pipe. "This morning, when we buried Hans, I asked Loibl if he noticed any medallions on Theresa Wilprecht. And voilà, she had one. It was in the sack her murderer had stuffed her into. Loibl couldn't remember exactly, but he thought the amulet showed a Virgin Mary with halo, just like the others."

"So that means we were right," Magdalena whispered and tightened her scarf around her shoulders, shivering. "This madman has been going around for decades."

Jakob Kuisl leaned over the table and chopped a lump of tobacco into tiny pieces that he put into his pipe. Then he held a
burning pine chip to the pipe bowl. "The executions, the amulets . . . ," he muttered, puffing on his pipe between phrases to
keep the embers glowing. "The murderer always follows the
same pattern. But we still don't know why he does it. No one
kills without reason. What's his motivation? Once we know that,
we're a hell of a lot closer to catching him." The hangman blew
a cloud of tobacco smoke up to the ceiling, from where it spread
through the entire room. "There must be witnesses. It's impossible for something like this to go unnoticed for such a long time.
Hans might have found one of those witnesses. And apart from
that, I don't really believe that van Uffele and his whore are behind all those murders."

"And what do you believe instead?" Georg asked.

But Jakob Kuisl remained silent and sent another cloud of
smoke to the ceiling.

Simon cleared his throat. "There's something I've been meaning to tell you about. I went to the lunatic asylum in the Hospice
of the Holy Ghost today. There's a crazy old woman who's been
there for over twenty years. Today, she was completely beside
herself, reckoned she knew the murderer."

"And you think she could be one of those witnesses Father is
talking about?" Georg asked skeptically. "Isn't it far more likely
that she has no idea what she's saying, after all those years? Did
she say anything that might help us?"

"No, not really. But there was one moment when she didn't
seem crazy at all. She said it was the fault of all of us."

Deibler looked at him with disbelief. "All of us?"

"Yes, that's what she said. I'm thinking about going—"

Suddenly, Sophia started to cry. Walburga gave the men a
withering look. "Now you woke her with your scary stories after
all," she admonished. "And she'd been sleeping so nicely."

Magdalena stood up and the two women tended to the child.

Georg, Simon, and Jakob Kuisl watched them in silence, as it was impossible to hold a conversation over Sophia's screaming. All at once Simon felt silly for even considering paying old Traudel another visit. She was insane, and that was that.

Michael Deibler stared out the small, barred living room window. Outside, night had fallen. He shook himself.

"In any case," he said with a sigh, "I think Magdalena's theory is the best we have at the moment. If what she heard is true, the treasurer and that other man are planning some kind of villainy. And Anni, the last girl to work for Pfundner, is dead. It definitely looks like Pfundner is somehow tangled up in this."

"If they're going to do away with some of the girls tonight, I must get Eva out of that cellar," Magdalena said. Sophia was falling asleep on her chest.

"And how are you going to do that?" Simon asked.

"By spending another night at the manufactory. And this time I'm going to the basement no matter what."

"Have you lost your mind?" Simon stared at his wife in horror. "I thank God that you made it out of that hole alive. There's no way I'm letting you go back."

"It's about the life of a girl, don't you understand? Maybe even several. It could be me or Barbara awaiting our death in that basement."

"And what about Sophia?" Simon pointed at their sleeping daughter. "Are you going to leave her already again? Walburga can't look after her forever. You're her mother."

Magdalena pinched her lips, and Simon realized he'd hurt her. He regretted his comment immediately. He was about to apologize when Walburga placed her hand on his arm.

"It's all right, Simon. Sophia and I get on well. And it's nice to have someone other than my cats around for a change. Let Magdalena go." The hangman's wife nodded. "She's right, you know. When the lives of innocent people are at stake, we're sometimes forced to do things we don't like. But they must be done."

"Very . . . well," Simon replied after some time. "Looks like I'm the only one who believes my wife is putting herself in danger."

"We're here, too," Georg tried to reassure him. "If anything happens, we'll give van Uffele hell."

If it's not too late by then, Simon thought gloomily. He still had a bad feeling.

"Where is Barbara?" Jakob Kuisl suddenly asked. "I haven't seen her all afternoon. It's quite enough for just one of my daughters to spend the night somewhere else . . ."

"As far as I know, she was meeting with Conrad Näher again," Deibler replied with a grin. "Another rendezvous, so to speak. Näher left the meeting early. Who knows, perhaps you'll be greeted by your future son-in-law tonight."

With a smile on her face, Barbara took a sip of mulled wine as she listened to another one of Valentin's stories. They had been sitting in one of the many taverns on Sendlinger Street for more than two hours now, talking, eating a steaming stew, and watching the other patrons who gradually filled the room. Much to her astonishment, Barbara realized that, for the first time in a long time, she didn't feel utterly unhappy. On the contrary, she felt like she had a new lease on life.

And that was entirely thanks to the young violinist in whose blue eyes she was about to drown once more.

Valentin had played and danced for her the whole way from Sendling, and he had made her laugh — something Barbara thought she had forgotten how to do. Valentin was an expert at making her forget her gloomy future. Once they had reached Munich, Valentin had taken her to several shops. They had tried on expensive clothes at a dressmaker's, pretending they could afford them. At a girdle maker's, Valentin had looked for cheap jewelry and haggled until the master had thrown them out. Now they were warming themselves in the tavern, and Valentin was telling her about his life as the son of a street musician.

"I could play the fiddle before I could walk," he said with a laugh. "My father put me on the stage and made me dance like a monkey. I plucked the strings at the same time. It sounded so god-awful that people ran away in droves. After that, my father gave me a tambourine."

"And did that go any better?" Barbara asked and took another sip of her mulled wine.

"Well, depends how you look at it. One of the spectators took pity and gave my father three kreuzers so I would stop." Valentin raised his mug to her with a smile. "We only talked about me again. You're extremely good at keeping silent about yourself. But I'm not letting you get away with it." He continued with mock severity: "It's time to confess. What are you doing here in Munich?"

Barbara hesitated. She had known this moment would come sooner or later. "If I tell you, promise you won't run away?" she asked eventually.

Valentin laughed. "Sure, as long as you aren't a man in disguise."

"Very well." Barbara took a deep breath. "I'm the daughter of the Schongau executioner. You might have heard that the hangmen are holding a meeting just outside town. The whole family came to Munich with my father."

She didn't mention her true reason for coming to Munich, or why she had been at the tavern with Conrad Näher. She still didn't understand why the Kaufbeuren executioner had run off the way he had.

To her surprise, Valentin didn't seem particularly shocked. He merely raised one eyebrow, then a wide grin spread across his face.

"So, a dishonorable hangman's daughter," he said. "God save me! Where is your devil's tail? Have you hidden it under your skirt? Well, at least your hair is as black as the coals of hell." Then he turned serious. "My father was also dishonorable as a street musician. We've gained citizenship since, but we had to pay dearly for it. And to most people, I'm still nothing but a rakish fiddler, just good enough to play at weddings. They cheer the musicians, give them a few coins, and tell them to go. It's always been that way."

"At least you're allowed to live in the city," Barbara said. "In Schongau, the hangman has to live in the stinking Tanners' Quarter, and he's only allowed at the tavern if all the guests agree, and—" She broke off when she heard the sound of Old Peter's bell.

"Jesus!" she called out. "Is it five in the evening already? I must go home before my father gets too mad. I've been gone for hours."

"What a shame." Valentin looked sad. "Can I see you again before you leave town?"

Barbara felt a warm wave wash through her. His question made her strangely nervous and happy. "I hope so . . . um, I mean, I think so," she said haltingly. "Let's say, tomorrow morning at the Sendling Gate?"

Valentin winked at her. "You don't want your family to meet me?"

"You'd understand if you knew my father," Barbara replied with a sigh. "He's not always easy."

She stood up and squeezed his hand. "Thank you," she said softly.

Valentin looked surprised. "What for?"

"For making me laugh. And for . . . letting me forget my worries for a while."

"Is it because of your uncle?" Valentin asked sympathetically. "Did he make you cry like that earlier?"

"He . . . he isn't my uncle. He's . . ." Barbara hesitated, then she turned away. "See you tomorrow," she said hoarsely and left the tavern.

Outside, she didn't know whether to laugh or cry. For the first time in her life, she had met a man who understood her. Even more, someone she could laugh with, someone who listened . . .

And someone her own age.

She thought of Conrad Näher, who was nearly her father's age. What would it be like in ten or twenty years' time, living at his side in Kaufbeuren? With a dotard! Would he still be as kind and understanding? She thought of the strange encounter at the Sendling tavern. How could she marry a man she didn't even know? Meeting Valentin had changed everything.

Suddenly Barbara knew she could never marry Conrad Näher.

With a guilty feeling, she touched the silk scarf under her woolen coat. It felt as soft and smooth as the day he had given her the rich fabric, but something had changed: the scarf seemed to weigh a thousand tons. It reminded her of a duty she no longer wanted to fulfill.

She pulled the scarf off with a jerk, crumpled it up like a rag, and threw it in the gutter.

Deep in thought, Barbara walked through the narrow busy lanes of the Anger Quarter, where tradesmen were just closing up their shops for the day. She had almost reached the executioner's house when Georg came walking toward her.

"There you are," he called out with relief. "We were all getting worried." He gave her a lewd grin. "So, it got a little late with Näher? They say you took a *very* long walk."

"Oh, just leave me alone," Barbara hissed at him. "Stupid menfolk! What do you know about women?"

She stormed past him, leaving him gaping.

Georg didn't see the tears streaming down her face.

The hunter stood at the window and looked out into the darkness and the fog enveloping the city.

Despite the icy temperatures the hunter felt warm inside. There was always a lot to do during the colder months. People huddled close like animals, and then it happened. It might be happening right now behind every one of the small illuminated squares out there, behind all these windows. The hunter could almost hear the hot breath, the groaning and panting. A steady, shrill cacophony that was carried by the wind and hurt the ears.

The amulet felt warm between the hunter's fingers, providing the surge of strength needed to fulfill the mission. How many of these amulets, how many medallions and pendants had been distributed in the last two decades? The hunter had lost count. Every single medallion had been meant as a warning to other sinful women, but also as protection for those who would be shepherded. The hunter nodded. Yes, truly, both a hunter and a shepherd. A shepherd tending a peacefully grazing, innocent flock and keeping away the wolves. Suddenly the hunter trembled and began to recite the psalm that never failed to soothe.

The Lord is my shepherd; I shall not want. He maketh me to lie down in green pastures; He leadeth me beside the still waters . . .

They were closing in, it was clear. The hunter could almost feel their breath. And that even though Master Hans had been dealt his just punishment before he could reveal anything. But it was like an avalanche. Sooner or later it would sweep down the valley. The hunter's head would shatter eventually.

The only question was, how soon?

Well, there was one way of slowing them down. But the hunter had some qualms about it. The divine mission had to be weighed against the lives of innocents. It hadn't been hard to make the decision in the case of Master Hans, because the scoundrel had been guilty. But in this case?

O Lord, give me strength.

Again, the hunter squeezed the amulet, and indeed, the Lord sent strength. This task was too important. God was showing the way.

So the hunter would kill to preserve the good. And to save lives.

But suspicion needed to be avoided under any circumstances. The hunter would have to be smart about it, couldn't afford another mistake. Who should die first? Who was the most dangerous? Who was the closest in their pursuit?

O Lord, give me strength.

The hunter threw the amulet.

Heads or silver . . .

The medallion landed on the floor with a soft *clink.*

Heads.

The Lord had decided. The victim was chosen. Now all that was needed was a plan.

The hunter thought . . . and smiled.

Around the same time, Magdalena went on her way to the Au silk manufactory.

It was completely dark by now, and a light northerly wind was bringing back winter. Magdalena had taken off the dress Pfundner had given her that afternoon and put on the plain outfit she had worn to the manufactory the day before instead. The rough woolen scarf was poor protection against the cold.

Just before she'd left, Barbara had finally returned. Her sister had been withdrawn and went upstairs to her room immediately. It appeared the walk with Conrad Näher hadn't gone as well as expected. Magdalena hoped she'd get the chance for a long talk with her sister tomorrow.

Tonight, she had to try to save another girl.

As Magdalena hurried through the Isar Gate toward Au with some of the last day laborers, she thought about her decision again. Of course it was dangerous to return to the silk manufactory. And it was possible she wouldn't even make it down to the basement. But she had to at least try.

She was still convinced that van Uffele and Joseffa were to blame for the deaths of Anni and Elfi. The girls had probably been killed because, like Eva, they had talked. But Magdalena couldn't figure out how those two murders were connected with the other brutal killings. Had this trade in girls been going on for a very long time? Could van Uffele and Joseffa merely be the most recent in a long row of scoundrels who abused and killed young women? What was really going on at that manufactory?

Suddenly Magdalena doubted her decision to go back. But then she was already at the door. The sound of music and laughter from the taverns seemed far away now; the street outside the manufactory was dark and empty. Magdalena hesitated for a moment, then she rang the bell.

She heard footsteps, then Mother Joseffa opened the door. She pulled Magdalena into the hallway and gave her a resounding slap.

"Where have you been, you hussy?" she hissed. "The other two came back hours ago. Speak up, what have you been up to all this time?"

"Pf-Pfundner wouldn't let me go," Magdalena whined, keeping her head down. "He couldn't get enough of me. He . . . he reckoned you owed him that much." She had just remembered that Joseffa and van Uffele were somehow indebted to Pfundner. And it worked — her last sentence appeared to dampen Joseffa's anger a little.

"We owe him, bah!" She spat. "He'll get twice, three times as much money back. But all right, let him have his fun." She gave Magdalena a sour look. "But don't think you'll get paid extra for those hours. You don't get paid till the end of the month, then we'll see if you're worth your money."

Magdalena nodded in silence.

"And he didn't give you back the laundry," Joseffa groused. "You're lucky the guards didn't stop you. The washing is your cover, understood? You're just a simple maidservant, nothing else."

"I . . . I'm sorry," Magdalena said quietly.

"Well, you'll have to pick up the laundry tomorrow. And now it's time for bed. The candles have already been put out. And you won't get any supper. Your own fault."

I wouldn't even feed your supper to the pigs, Magdalena thought angrily.

But she kept acting intimidated and followed Joseffa up to the dormitory, where everything was quiet. The girls lay on their sacks of straw and snoozed, only a few looking up when Magdalena came in.

"Tomorrow morning you start on the loom," Joseffa said harshly. "Then you can go back to Pfundner later on." She grinned. "And tomorrow night, we have something special planned for you. But that's a surprise." She slammed the door shut and walked away.

Magdalena tiptoed over to her sleeping place. She was about to lie down when Agnes nudged her.

"Hey, sunshine," she said mockingly. She lifted her blanket and revealed a small, flickering candle. "How was your day at the honorable treasurer's house? Did he spoil you with wine and white bread and slip a few coins in your pocket? Go on, let's hear it."

"His wife spoiled everything," Magdalena whispered in reply. "I think she suspects something. She called for him all the time."

Agnes giggled. "At least you didn't have to spread your legs." She paused and nodded to the left. "Unlike others, who weren't so lucky."

Only now did Magdalena notice Carlotta lying not far away. The fifteen-year-old girl had hidden her face under a thin, holey blanket and trembled all over. Now Magdalena also heard her muffled sobs.

"The bastard was rough with her," Agnes whispered. "Apparently he enjoyed nailing a virgin. I couldn't get more than a few words out of the poor thing."

Magdalena thought about what Carlotta had said this morning, that she and her brother would soon lead a better life than their parents.

Is the price too high? Raped and then thrown away like trash . . .

Magdalena's eyes had become accustomed to the dark now, and she studied Agnes's once beautiful face. In the flickering of the tiny candle it almost looked like the face of a very old woman.

"She'll get used to it," Agnes said. "We all get used to it."

"Have you heard anything else about Eva?" Magdalena asked suddenly.

"Damn it—forget Eva! Do you hear me? What happened to her will happen to us if we don't shut up."

"That's it, isn't it?" Magdalena grabbed Agnes by the shoulders and shook her. "Eva was going to talk, and now she's waiting for her death in the basement, if she hasn't already been murdered. Just like Anni and Elfi." She squeezed Agnes so hard that she gave a little cry. Some of the other weavers groaned in their sleep, others lifted their heads and looked over at them. "Tell me, how many other girls have disappeared since you've been here?" Magdalena hissed. "How many?"

"I . . . I don't know," Agnes coughed. "Three or four, perhaps, maybe more. Who can keep track of all the girls that come and go here? But . . . there are stories."

"What stories?"

"Stories about balls. Van Uffele sends entire groups of girls to the balls. Anni and Elfi went to them, too, and Eva. Everyone wears masks, and they play games. Evil games." Agnes swallowed. "They never spoke about it."

Magdalena abruptly let go of Agnes's shoulders. She remembered what the bald-headed man had said this afternoon at the treasurer's house.

That accursed ball spoils everything . . .

Was he talking about one of those balls? A ball where evil games cost the girls their lives?

"What . . . what kind of balls are you talking about?" she asked hesitantly.

"Masquerades." Agnes's mouth was very close to her ear now. "I heard there's another one tomorrow night at Nymphenburg Palace. Van Uffele was talking to Joseffa about it. The three of us are supposed to go, they don't have anyone else at the moment. By God, I'm scared."

"What if we run away?" Magdalena said. "You, Carlotta, and me?"

Agnes laughed sadly. "That's what Eva tried to do, and now she's dead or locked up in the basement."

"Listen," Magdalena hissed, "you have to help me, Agnes. If Eva's still down there, we must get her out tonight."

"But how? The dormitory door is locked, and then there's the Venetians who probably stand guard. It's impossible."

Magdalena thought frantically. There must be a solution, damn it, there always was. But this time she had no father or husband to help her. She was on her own.

Or was she?

Magdalena bit her lip, then she nodded.

"It's possible," she said with grim determination. "But only if all us girls work together. We'll show those bastards! And now, listen carefully."

Torn between happiness and despair, Barbara lay on her bed in the Munich executioner's house and listened. She could hear her nephews whispering excitedly in their bed next door and the muted conversation of the men downstairs. A soft whimpering came from the apothecary chamber, together with Walburga's gentle lullaby.

How Barbara longed to have Magdalena at her side now. She was bursting to tell her what had happened. She had met a young man, and suddenly everything she had known as true and right had gone out the window. She had tried to be reasonable, but then she'd crossed paths with love.

Love.

"Valentin." Her lips formed the name all by themselves. "Valentin, Valentin . . ." A shiver ran through her.

Barbara remembered something similar happening to her in Bamberg a few years ago. She had visited her Uncle Bartholomäus and met a handsome young lad she wanted to run away with. But she had only been fifteen then, a naïve thing, and the passion had soon ebbed away. It was different this time, much more powerful. Invincible.

But most of all, she knew that she could no longer marry Conrad Näher. Moreover, the encounter in the Sendling tavern had had something uncanny about it. Who was that stranger who had unsettled Näher so much that he had to break off their conversation? She had wanted to discuss all those things with Magdalena, her joy and her sorrow, but her sister had left for the silk manufactory as soon as she'd arrived home. Now Barbara was alone with her worries and didn't know who she could talk to.

She placed a hand on her belly, which grumbled and growled as if a nasty little goblin lived inside. That's exactly what she felt like: a woman with a goblin in her tummy. Would she ever learn to love this . . . this thing? She winced.

Oh God, Barbara, you can't think like that. Never! God hears everything.

She heard footsteps coming up the stairs, then someone knocked timidly. She didn't answer, but the door opened nonetheless and her brother's concerned face appeared.

"Are . . . are you all right?" he asked.

Barbara wished she could tell Georg about Valentin. He was her twin brother—they always used to share their secrets. But he was also a man. How could he understand what she was going through? But then she decided to tell him at least part of her sorrows.

"Come in before you grow roots." She sighed.

Georg sat down on her bed and took her hand. It was almost like when they were children and stayed up late. "There's so much going on at the moment," he said tiredly. "All those murders and nightmares. And we just wanted to find a nice husband for you in Munich." He smiled. "Well, perhaps you've found one, now."

"Listen," Barbara began hesitantly. "Something's up with Näher. I'm not sure what, but there's something he's not telling us."

Georg frowned. "How do you mean?"

She told her brother about the incident at the Sendling tavern. Georg listened in silence, then he shook his head with disapproval.

"Don't you start suspecting people now," he groused. "Your sister, father, and Simon already do too much of that. I mean, is it really that bad? Näher met an acquaintance and wanted to speak with him in private. Men do that from time to time."

"Oh, and it upsets him so much that he leaves his future wife to walk home alone with a murderer about? You should have seen his face. He was pale as a ghost." Beseechingly, Barbara continued, "I'm telling you, something's not right with Näher and that young fop. They're up to something."

Georg looked at her suspiciously. "One could almost think you found someone else and are frantically looking for reasons to get rid of Näher. Am I right?" He squeezed her hand. "I'm your twin, Barbara. You can't keep a secret from me. I can tell there's something else."

"Even if I have, it's none of your business," Barbara snapped. She could feel herself blush. "We all have our secrets. You still haven't told Father that you have to leave Bamberg."

Georg groaned. "Because he'll pester me about going back to Schongau with him. But I don't want to. I'm glad to have turned my back on Schongau once and for all."

"And I don't want to marry a man I can't trust," Barbara said. "Is that so difficult to understand?"

"Barbara," Georg pleaded. "Don't destroy what Father built up so carefully just because you suddenly like some fellow who just happened along." When Barbara opened her mouth to object, he cut her off: "You can't fool me, I can tell there's someone else. But marriage has nothing to do with love. It's about family, about making a living. Can't you understand that? You carry a child who is going to need a father. Not a juggler or similar kind of dreamer."

"Father said I don't have to marry if I absolutely don't want to," Barbara said defiantly. "I have his word. So, are you going to help me or not?"

Georg didn't say anything for a while, then he stood up. "All right, I'll make you a deal," he said. "I'll keep an eye on Näher after the meeting tomorrow. Can't hurt to take a closer look at a future brother-in-law, after all. But if I don't find anything out of the ordinary, you'll stop this nonsense, all right? We truly have enough problems as it is."

"How could I deny my dear brother anything?" Barbara replied with a tired smile. "And believe me, Conrad Näher's strange behavior isn't my biggest concern right now either."

When Georg left her room, she could at least say she hadn't lied.

The screams were so loud that Magdalena thought they'd wake all of Au.

The girls ran up and down the dormitory and squealed, whined, and moaned as if the devil himself had taken hold of them. Agnes screamed the loudest, while casting a conspiratorial glance at Magdalena. The older woman had hesitated a long time before agreeing to Magdalena's plan. But eventually, anger and a sense of honor had won out over her fear. With Agnes at her side, it had been easy to convince the other girls to join the charade. Only Carlotta had retreated to a corner, watching the chaos out of wide eyes. She still wasn't back to herself.

In another corner, a small fire was burning, fueled by blankets and straw. The women got it started with Agnes's candle, and now they needed to keep it under control. They didn't want anyone to get hurt, after all. They only wanted to create confusion.

And that's exactly what happened.

It wasn't long before they heard loud footsteps on the stairs. The door was pushed open and Mother Joseffa and the two Venetians came running in. Van Uffele followed more slowly, still tying up his codpiece. Evidently, he had already gone to bed, and he seemed a little drunk.

"Jesus, what have you done, you stupid girls?" Joseffa screamed. She coughed and waved her arms to dispel the smoke. "Didn't I forbid you to light candles at night?" She ran over to the closed shutters and opened them to let fresh air in. The two Venetians were busy trying to put out the fire. Van Uffele alone was still outside the door, too bewildered to do anything. No one noticed that Magdalena stood right behind the door.

Come on, she thought, watching van Uffele through the crack. *For Christ's sake, come on in.*

"Are you going to help me with the windows or not, you muttonhead?" Joseffa shouted and waved impatiently at van Uffele. "Or we'll suffocate like rats."

Magdalena's silent pleading hadn't fallen on deaf ears. Van Uffele started from his trance and rushed toward the shutters. Magdalena shot a glance at the Venetians, who were still busy with the fire. She uttered a quick prayer, then she darted out from behind the door and toward the stairs.

No one called after her. As she ran down the stairs, she still heard Joseffa scolding and shouting at the girls. Then the cries became quieter and quieter, until they stopped. It seemed her escape had gone unnoticed.

Finally Magdalena arrived at the basement. She listened in the darkness but couldn't hear any whimpering. Was Eva dead? Had she come too late?

Her heart racing, she turned right, where—like last time— no torches lit the way. Again she smelled mold and feces.

Cautiously, struggling to see anything, Magdalena made her way down the corridor, passing several low doors. She opened one of them at random and squinted inside. It appeared to be a kind of storeroom, as she could vaguely make out crates and parts of looms. She closed the door as softly as she could and walked on.

"Eva?" she whispered. "Eva? Are you there?"

Nothing.

"Eva!" Magdalena tried again. "If you can hear me, I'm one of the weavers. I want to help you."

There, in the distance, a whimper. It sounded just like last time. What in God's name was it? It almost sounded as if someone was in terrible pain. Magdalena clenched her fists angrily, then she hurried on.

Eva, what did they do to you?

The corridor went around a bend, then she came to a fork. Which way should she go? Magdalena heard another whimper, and she thought it came from the left. She felt her way down the next corridor, the stench getting worse and worse. Then the passage ended abruptly in a solid wall. The darkness was almost thick enough to cut.

Damn!

She must have taken the wrong turn, Eva must be down the other corridor. Magdalena was about to turn around when she stepped on something metallic. She bent down and felt the ground until her hands found a grate. The stench seemed to come from down there. And Magdalena could feel the slightest draft that carried the smell of rot up to her. She listened intently. There it was again, the whimpering, closer this time. Her fingers pulled at the grate. Maybe she could lift it, then—

A hand grabbed Magdalena by the shoulder and spun her around. She screamed, but another hairy hand clamped down on her mouth immediately. Strong arms lifted her and dragged her back down the corridor. She struggled as hard as she could, but it was useless, her opponents were much too strong. When they neared the torches by the stairs, Magdalena could see who had captured her.

The two Venetians.

They threw Magdalena to the ground like a sack. One of them gave her a kick in the head and everything went black for a moment. Magdalena fought to stay conscious. When the dizzy spell eased, she saw van Uffele and Joseffa leaning over her.

"Didn't I tell you something was wrong with her?" Joseffa was saying. "This is no simple girl from the country. But no, you only stare at her breasts. You men are all the same." She snorted derisively. "If I hadn't suspected her from the beginning, she would surely have gotten away. Lucky I sent the Venetians down as soon as I noticed someone was missing."

"Hmm. But if she isn't a runaway maid, then who is she?" van Uffele asked.

He gave Magdalena a kick in the stomach that made her gag. "Speak up, you whore! Who sent you?"

"Perhaps she's spying for one of our backers?" Joseffa surmised, looking at the groaning Magdalena as if she were a disgusting bug. "Or maybe even for the Augsburgers. They're dying to know our secrets."

"It doesn't matter who, she has to go," van Uffele growled. "We can't afford any mistakes right now. *Andiamo, portala via.*"

The last words were meant for the Venetians, who picked Magdalena up as if she were a lifeless puppet and dragged her into the left-hand corridor. They opened the door to a chamber full of bales of silk yarn and dragged her inside. Then one of the men grabbed her and held her in a viselike grip. Magdalena was still foggy from the beating, and she watched through a haze as van Uffele opened a bulbous bottle. A moment later, Joseffa grabbed Magdalena's nose and pinched it shut.

"You pigs!" Magdalena shouted. "You . . . you . . ."

She didn't get any further because a burning liquid was poured down her throat. It was strong alcohol. Magdalena coughed and spluttered, but in the end, she had to swallow to avoid suffocating.

"Drink up, pretty girl," Joseffa giggled as van Uffele rammed the bottleneck deep into her mouth. "One sip for our dear Uffele and one for me, and one for every damned hungry mouth to feed upstairs. What a nice little plan you hatched there. By God, you're going to long for the day you worked at the loom for me."

While the alcohol ran down her throat like hot wax, Magdalena thought of Simon, her beloved husband. He had been right, this manufactory was the gateway to hell.

She would never see him again.

IO

𝕴 THINK WE WAITED LONG ENOUGH. No one else is going to show up."

Tired and sad, Michael Deibler looked at the gathered council
at the Radl Inn, or rather, what was left of it. Several seats around
the table had remained empty, only the engraved pewter mugs
were left. A number of chairs along the walls were also missing
their apprentices and journeymen. The remaining men started
muttering quietly as they realized that some of the executioners
had made off during the night. Fear of ending on the scaffold
like Master Hans must have been stronger than their promise to
stay.

Jakob Kuisl was the last one to arrive. He had hoped to the last
that Magdalena would return from the silk manufactory. He
wasn't overly concerned yet, as they had agreed she'd send word
at some point during the morning. Nonetheless Kuisl decided to
stay sober at today's meeting. He might need a clear head later on.

"Missing are Michael Rosner from Ingolstadt and Ludwig
Hamberger from Ansbach," Deibler said, scanning the pitiful
congregation. "And Conrad Näher hasn't turned up either. So
now there's only eight of us."

Johann Widmann from Nuremberg gave a sardonic laugh. "Ha! It was Näher who urged us to stay for two more days. And now he's slunk off with his tail between his legs."

"That's strange indeed," Deibler replied quietly. "Let's hope nothing's happened to him."

"What do you mean?" asked Bartholomäus Kuisl, on Deibler's right. He set down the mug he had been about to drink from. "By God, do you think—"

"How's he supposed to mean it?" Kaspar Hörmann chimed in. The Passau hangman looked even worse than usual—his bulbous nose was practically glowing. Jakob Kuisl guessed he'd been on the booze the entire night with his son. He slurred his speech as he went on: "I tell you what happened: the people of Munich killed off another one of us. Goddamnit, we should have left like Rosner and Hamberger. Who knows which one of us is next?" Swaying, he stood up and raised his right hand like a drunk prophet. "I'm telling you, cousins, it's going to be . . ." With a loud crash, Hörmann swiped his full mug off the table with his left hand. Annoyed, he tried to soak up the puddle of beer with his shirt sleeve. Then he started licking it off the table. Jakob Kuisl, who was sitting next to him, moved his chair away in disgust.

"Filthy hole of a town," Hörmann grumbled, wiping his lips. "What a goddamn hole of a town this Munich is. Nothing but noise, snobs, and crazy people. The only good thing is the beer, and that's getting more expensive all the time . . ."

"I'd be very grateful if you drank a little less," Deibler scolded. "You're an embarrassment to the entire council, Hörmann."

"Well, the council isn't very large anymore," red-haired Matthäus Fux said. "Now that Näher's probably burning in hell, too."

"Rubbish! If the people of Munich had lynched another one of us, we'd have heard of it by now," Philipp Teuber remarked, sitting next to Fux. The Regensburg hangman scratched his shaggy beard. "No, I think Näher simply went home."

"Or someone else has finished him," Johann Widmann added

maliciously. He looked at Jakob Kuisl, who hadn't said anything yet. "Well, Jakob? Perhaps Näher found out that you killed Hans, and now it was his turn? Who's next, eh?"

Bartholomäus Kuisl jumped up and leaned across the table. He grabbed Widmann by the collar with both hands. "Don't you dare call my brother a murderer again," he hissed. "We might not be the best of friends, but no one insults a Kuisl, understood? Least of all a snot-nosed, stuck-up would-be hangman from Nuremberg."

"Leave him be, brother," Jakob Kuisl grumbled. "Don't waste your energy on that idiot." He pulled Bartholomäus back onto his chair and Widmann sank back, gasping.

"We should think about what might have happened to Näher," Kuisl continued. He turned to the seven remaining hangmen. "I had a hunch Rosner and Hamberger might run off. They voted against staying two more days. But Näher? He was so keen to stay on, not least because of my Barbara." He shook his head and muttered, more to himself, "And I thought he was going to be my son-in-law."

"If I may say something . . ." Georg stood up from his chair on the side, and the eight executioners turned to regard him with annoyance.

Deibler was about to make a harsh reply, but then he waved dismissively. "It's not usual for a journeyman to speak up at the Council of Twelve without invitation, but this meeting's a farce, anyhow."

"I . . . I spoke with my sister last night," Georg began, uncertain. "She said Näher acted very strangely on their walk together. Apparently, he met a stranger who frightened him. And then he just took off and didn't come back."

"What do you mean, didn't come back?" Kuisl asked impatiently.

"Well, he just vanished," Georg replied. "Left Barbara where she was and never came back."

Bartholomäus tore at what was left of his hair. "This is getting better all the time. Now it isn't the angry mob of citizens but the mysterious stranger who might have done away with Näher."

"If our murderer has taken Conrad Näher, who's next?" Matthäus Fux said and looked around suspiciously. "First Hans, then Näher . . ."

Loud murmuring set in at the table and from the chairs along the wall. Some of the hangmen and apprentices spat over their shoulders, others reached for amulets and crucifixes. Kuisl used the opportunity to walk over to Georg.

"I want you to go looking for Näher, all right?" he whispered to him. "I don't believe he went home to Kaufbeuren. It's not like him. Ask in the taverns and at the gates, or ask the whores if you like. Someone must have seen him."

Georg nodded reluctantly. He seemed to want to say something else.

"What is it?" Kuisl asked.

"Er, nothing, really. It's just . . . Barbara reckons she doesn't trust Näher any longer. She's certain he's hiding something."

"Ha! Believe me, everyone in this council is hiding something. And now go, before Näher really does leave town." Kuisl gave his son one last pat on the shoulder. Then he returned to his seat, while Georg quietly slipped out the door.

"Quiet, for pity's sake!" Michael Deibler roared against the noise of the others. "By the thrice-knotted hangman's noose, are we here to talk or to bash each other's heads in? My dear cousins, that's not going to get us anywhere." He stood up and spread his arms in a desperate attempt to calm the men down. And indeed, the noise level gradually subsided.

"We don't even know for certain if anything has happened to Näher," Deibler continued. "Maybe he went home, or perhaps he's sick in bed. Let's just wait and see."

"He's not in his room," Philipp Teuber said with a shrug.

"He's staying here at the Radl Inn, like most of us. I knocked on his door earlier to check on him, but he wasn't there."

"I'm not going to shed a tear over Näher," Matthäus Fux grumbled and shook his matted red hair. "The way he was dressed and how he talked—as if he's better than us."

"I know someone else like that," Jörg Defner from Nördlingen jeered. He winked at the Nuremberg executioner with his good eye and made a gesture that was supposed to be feminine. "Widmann always looks like he's bathed in violet perfume."

"Bah! Just because I'm a hangman doesn't mean I have to stink like carrion. Be careful, Defner, or I'll—" A loud thud cut Widmann off. It was Kaspar Hörmann, who had collapsed onto the table. His filthy hair floated in a new puddle of beer.

"Damn it, Hörmann, I've well and truly had enough!" Michael Deibler flared up. "You old drunkard, I'll throw you—"

Suddenly, Hörmann started to twitch and his arms flailed about wildly. His head jerked up, and the other seven executioners jumped with fright. Saliva and vomit ran out of the Passau hangman's mouth, his forehead was wet with cold sweat. He gargled incoherently.

"My God, poison!" Matthäus Fux screamed and shot up from his chair. "Someone poisoned Hörmann!"

Kaspar Hörmann crashed to the ground. He gasped as if he was suffocating, his tongue hanging out, and he shivered like he was freezing. He still twitched, but his movements became weaker and weaker. A jerk went through his body, then he lay still, strangely twisted like a broken doll. Only his eyes still moved, staring up at the ceiling as if something infinitely evil lurked there.

"Father! What's the matter with you?" Hörmann's son, Lothar, sobered up quickly. He dove to his father's side, knelt down beside him, and shook him as though he could bring him back that way. "Help him! Lord in heaven, someone help him!" he screamed.

The other hangmen and apprentices had also jumped to their feet and were now approaching cautiously, almost as if the curse might be contagious.

"Is . . . is he dead?" Johann Widmann asked fearfully. Young Lothar was holding his father by the collar, moaning and sobbing pitifully, drowning out Widmann's question.

"Out of the way." Jakob Kuisl pushed the crying journeyman aside and knelt down beside Hörmann. He held his ear against his chest, felt his pulse, and finally stood up with a serious expression.

"There's nothing more we can do for him," he said and squeezed Lothar's shoulder. The boy broke down whimpering next to his father.

"Is he dead or not?" Widmann asked again, holding a handkerchief over his mouth as if he was trying to keep out dangerous vapors. Evidently he wasn't brimming with compassion but rather appeared repulsed.

"Not quite," Jakob Kuisl replied. "But it won't be long. If it is what I fear it is, I hope for his sake that death will come soon."

Kaspar Hörmann started to twitch again like a fish on dry land. His body was racked by convulsions. When Kuisl wiped the sweat off his forehead, he seemed to relax a little.

"Can't you help him?" Lothar Hörmann begged. "Anything? Is there no antidote?" Kuisl shook his head.

"He's already on his final journey. I don't think he can feel much. At least I hope he can't."

"Jesus, not even a dog deserves to die like this," said Bartholomäus Kuisl, who, like the others, watched the dying hangman with horror. "Not even a rat." He turned to his brother. "What do you think it is? You know more about this sort of stuff than any of us."

"I believe it's wolfsbane." Kuisl bent down to Hörmann once more and smelled his mouth, which was still dripping with saliva and vomit. "Not hemlock, because that smells of mouse piss. Nor arsenic, because it wouldn't have worked so fast."

"Oh God, oh God, wolfsbane!" Lothar screamed. "Maybe the people of Munich are right and an evil beast is roaming the streets. We must protect ourselves, we must . . ."

"Get him out of here, goddamnit," Michael Deibler said. "He's not helping his father with all that screaming."

Two journeymen led the sobbing, whimpering Lothar out the door. They'd pour brandy down his throat to help him forget for a while.

When the room was quiet again, Kuisl addressed the others once more.

"Wolfsbane is the most potent poison I know. I heard that once upon a time, dangerous criminals were executed that way. It's not an easy death."

"It must have been in his mug," Michael Deibler said, turning away from the twitching body with horror. Like everyone else in this room, he had seen many men die in his life. But this one was hard to watch even for the Munich hangman. He was pale, clearly shaken by the death of a cousin.

"But how can that be?" Bartholomäus Kuisl replied. "How can he have poisoned himself with his own mug? Hörmann knocked his mug over right at the start of the meeting, remember?"

"Strange," Philipp Teuber said. "I clearly remember him drinking from a mug afterward. Could he have . . . ?"

Everyone's eyes turned to Hörmann's seat, and indeed, there were two pewter mugs. Deibler rushed over to the table and lifted both drinking vessels in the air for everyone to see. Then he studied the engraved names.

"This one's Hörmann's," he said loudly. "But his mug is empty.

He must have spilled all his beer when he knocked it over. And when he felt thirsty again, he simply reached for the nearest full mug."

"And?" Matthäus Fux asked excitedly. "Whose name is on the mug?"

"You all know who was sitting next to him." Michael Deibler took a deep breath, then he looked Jakob Kuisl straight in the eyes.

"It's yours, Jakob. You were supposed to be the next victim."

Lost in gloomy thoughts, Simon walked along Sendlinger Street, which was already congested with wagons and carts this morning. Everyone was headed to the market square, where farmers and merchants offered their goods for sale today, Saturday. There were exotic, strong-smelling spices from East India, candied fruits, and even costly sugar, which had come to Munich all the way from the distant West Indies. In the last few days Simon had occasionally kept an eye out for coffee beans, but today he wasn't in the mood.

He had hardly slept that night, sick with worry about Magdalena. Now it was already after ten o'clock, and still no news from her. Had something happened to her at the silk manufactory? Had Magdalena been able to free Eva from the basement, or had her ruse been uncovered?

Simon cursed himself for letting his wife go in the first place. But Magdalena always got her way. When the bells had chimed the tenth hour, Simon had decided to go and find out what had happened. Perhaps everything would turn out to be just fine when he got there.

But there was something else Simon wanted to do on his way to Au. Something to do with those strange murders.

Soon after, he arrived at the house of Malachias Geiger on Sendlinger Street. Simon carried a letter he had composed the night before. Another thought had kept him awake—a crazy idea, admittedly, but he just couldn't shake it. He hoped the visit at Doctor Geiger's would bring him peace of mind.

Like last time, he ascended the wide steps to the entrance and rang the bell. Again, it was Geiger's assistant who opened the door. When the young man recognized Simon, he twisted his mouth mockingly.

"Ah, it's Herr *Colleague*," he said venomously. "You're persistent. But I must disappoint you once again, Herr Doktor is attending to a patient in the Kreuz Quarter. I'm afraid you—"

"Thank you, I already met with Doctor Geiger yesterday," Simon interrupted him. "We had a very interesting conversation at the Hospice of the Holy Ghost."

The assistant looked confused. "Oh, you did? Very well . . . But then why are you here?"

"Because I have an important letter for the doctor," Simon replied and produced a small sealed envelope from his vest. "Would you be so kind as to make sure he receives it today?"

Simon had expected the doctor to be out this time of day, which was why he had written the letter he now handed to the assistant.

"I'll see what I can do," the young man muttered and took the letter. "The doctor is a very busy man."

With a jerk, Simon grabbed the assistant's hand and pulled him close. "This letter concerns a very important patient," he said with a threatening undertone. "I will see the doctor tomorrow. If I find out he still hasn't received the letter, there are going to be very tragic consequences. For the patient—and for yourself," he added with a thin smile. "Do we have an understanding?"

"I . . . I think so." The assistant nodded reluctantly and Simon let go of his hand.

"Wonderful. Then I bid you a good day and happy urine sampling."

Without another word, Simon turned around and walked

down the stairs while the door behind him was shut softly. The story about the patient was a blatant lie, but it had the desired effect. Now Simon could only wait and see. But, most likely, anyhow, he was wrong.

Simon hurried along Sendlinger Street and crossed the market square, which was so crowded that he made slow progress. Merchants praised their wares in loud voices, giggling street children ran into him followed by a cursing bailiff, and a group of nuns walked toward the Anger Nunnery as leisurely as a herd of cows, blocking Simon's way. He walked past the city hall and followed the plastered street to the Isar Gate, where it was a little less busy.

When he finally arrived at Au, another half hour had passed. He felt his fear growing. What had happened to Magdalena? Would he find her alive and well at the manufactory? Simon still hoped everything would turn out just fine, but the bad feeling that had been with him since the previous evening grew stronger with every step.

Damn it, Magdalena, I should never have let you go. Why do I let myself get talked into these suicide missions every time?

When he reached the silk manufactory, Simon paused and studied the barred windows. He could hear the clicking and squeaking of looms upstairs, but no voices. Simon rang the bell, but no one answered, and no footsteps approached. He pulled the chain a second time, then once more as hard as he could, then he knocked on the door. When there was still no reaction, he started to call out.

"Hey, open up! Open up right this moment!"

He kicked the door with his foot several times before the hatch at eye level finally opened. A rough-looking, unshaved fellow glared at him.

"*Cosa c'è?*" he growled in Italian.

"I . . . I'm looking for a woman," Simon said, surprised by the man's sudden appearance. "Her name is Magdalena. Where is she?"

"*Non capisco,*" the man replied and shut the hatch. But Simon didn't give up. He kicked the solid timber again and again until a bolt was pushed back and the door opened with great force.

"*Vattene!*" the man roared at him. "*Subito!*"

"No subito, damn it!" Simon shouted back. "It's about my wife. Don't you understand, you foreign idiot? My wife, Magdalena. She's somewhere in there. And if you don't let me in right this moment, I'll fetch the hangman. He happens to be my father-in-law."

But the threat didn't work. The man kicked Simon in the shins until he stumbled and fell into the mud on the lane. The door slammed shut with a loud bang and this time three bolts rattled across.

Simon threw himself against the door and pounded it with his fists while he ranted and raved. "Whatever you've done to my Magdalena, I swear by God I'll get you strung up. Open this damned door right now!"

But nothing happened.

One last time Simon kicked the door, then he gave up. Panting hard, he sat down on the dirty ground. His shins hurt like hell, but even worse was his nagging fear. What had van Uffele and Mother Joseffa done with Magdalena? And what in God's name was he supposed to do now?

Where are you, Magdalena?

"Hey, you! Yes, you."

Simon started when a soft voice spoke from somewhere underneath him, as if directly from hell. He looked around and eventually spotted a narrow light shaft that led to a barred window in the basement of the manufactory. Behind the bars, he could make out the face of a woman. She had clearly taken a terrible beating. The right side of her face was badly swollen and streaked with blood, her bruised eye was completely shut, and she was missing several teeth.

"You're looking for Magdalena?" she mumbled.

"Yes, for heaven's sake." Excited, Simon knelt over the light shaft. "Do you know where she is? She's my wife."

"That's why I'm talking to you," the woman whispered and wiped some dried blood off her lip. "Your wife was very brave. If there were more like her, this world would be a different place. But God always takes back early those he loves most."

"Do you know where Magdalena is?" Simon persisted, ignoring her last remark.

"Don't you understand? She's . . ." The woman hesitated, then she said quietly, "I'm so sorry, but I believe your wife is dead."

Simon felt like someone was pulling the ground out from under his feet. His hands searched the wall for support. "What . . . what did you say?" he gasped.

"They took her away very early this morning. On a cart, covered with a few old rags. But I got a glimpse of her feet from here —they were definitely her shoes." The woman coughed. "My name is Agnes. Yesterday I helped Magdalena get down to the basement. She wanted to help another girl—"

"Eva," Simon whispered, petrified.

Agnes seemed surprised. "Yes, Eva. I should never have agreed to it. Now we're all paying for it!"

"The people with the cart, that would have been van Uffele and Joseffa, right?" Simon croaked.

Agnes nodded. "I'm guessing they dumped her body in some ditch this morning. One more dead girl from the country. Who cares?"

"I do," Simon said quietly. "I care." His voice became louder. "What is going on in this house? What happened to the other girls? Why . . . why did Magdalena . . ." He couldn't go on as tears of anger and grief welled up in his eyes.

"Listen, I'm not telling you anything else," Agnes replied. Her lips became thin. "I only called out to you because you say you're her husband. I sure wonder what she was doing in this hole, then. And now you better go before the Venetians come back."

"Where did they take Magdalena?" Simon pleaded. "Where did van Uffele and Joseffa go?"

"They won't come back today. And anyway, what good would it do you to see her now. Your wife is dead. Anyone who gets in their way is silenced." Agnes rattled the bars on her window. "All I wanted was to earn some money, damn it. One, two more weeks and I would have left this accursed city. And now look at me. Go away, goddamnit." She hissed at him like a snake. "Go, before they beat me to death like they did to your wife. Go!"

Simon shrank back. He sensed Agnes wouldn't tell him anything else. And now he heard footsteps somewhere in the depths of the basement.

"Magdalena isn't dead," he said softly as he slowly pulled himself up using the wall of the building. "No, she isn't dead, no way." But doubts were like small nasty creatures climbing up inside him. "No way," he repeated flatly.

Simon turned around. He staggered down the empty lane like a drunk, unable to decide what to do next.

In the backroom of the Radl Inn, the remaining seven executioners cowered in their seats and watched their cousin Kaspar Hörmann on his last, difficult voyage.

The Passau hangman only twitched weakly now, and his breathing was so shallow that Kuisl almost hadn't been able to detect it on his last examination. Hörmann's eyes flickered wildly like two candles in the wind, darting to and fro as though they were looking for his murderer. The journeymen and apprentices had been sent outside. The remaining men sat in silence, no one had touched their beer mugs again. They couldn't help Hörmann, so the seven cousins paid their last respects through silence. They were all men of death, it was their way of dealing with it.

"Jesus Christ, can't anyone put an end to it?" Johann Widmann said, looking ghostly pale as he stared at Hörmann's twitching body. Nervously, he chewed on his fingernails. "It's unbearable to watch."

"It's almost over," Kuisl said, sniffing at a puddle of beer on the table with his huge hooked nose. "Wolfsbane works fast. But if it's too slow for you, Johann, feel free to cut his throat yourself."

Widmann didn't reply and focused on his fingernails again.

After having sniffed the puddle almost like a dog, Jakob Kuisl stood up and walked over to Hörmann. As before, he bent down to wipe the cold sweat off the dying man's forehead. Then he held his ear against Hörmann's chest. "His heartbeat is extremely weak," he said. "I doubt he feels anything now."

"But those eyes," Matthäus Fux whispered. "Just look at his eyes — they're terrifying."

"There's nothing more we can do for him," Michael Deibler sighed, still sitting at the head of the table. "But we can avenge him by finding his murderer. Here and now." He paused meaningfully. "Because one thing is for certain: the murderer is still here in this room."

"Are you saying one of us is to blame for Hörmann's death?" Jörg Defner asked. The one-eyed hangman from Nördlingen hadn't said much until then, but now he was getting visibly upset. His good eye twitched nervously.

"Numbskull." Bartholomäus Kuisl snorted derisively. "Who else could have done it? The beer was poisoned. So, someone must have poured the poison into the mug during the meeting. And since the victim was supposed to be my brother, I wonder who in this room might be after the Kuisls." He looked straight at Johann Widmann. "You've always had something against us — admit it. For years you refused to elect Jakob onto the council.

And now that his daughter put you in your place in front of everyone, you retaliate by poisoning him. Isn't that right?"

"How . . . how dare you!" Widmann flared up. "That's nothing but nasty slander. My journeyman will whip you through the city for that."

"You're not in your beloved Nuremberg where everyone kisses your arse, but in Munich," Philipp Teuber intervened. "So pull yourself together, Johann." He turned to Bartholomäus Kuisl. "Although I must agree, we should be careful with accusations."

"But it's the truth," Bartholomäus insisted. "For days now Widmann's been trying to pin something or other on Jakob. When that didn't work, he used poison."

"Enough!" Michael Deibler barked at him. "Once and for all!" He jumped to his feet and pounded the table angrily. "You've all been acting like a bunch of vipers for days. People call us dishonorable, and I must say they're right. We're an embarrassment to our profession. Even in the presence of a dying cousin—"

"He's dead," Jakob Kuisl said.

"What did you say?" Deibler's anger evaporated as quickly as it had arrived. He turned his full attention to the Schongau hangman, who knelt beside Hörmann.

"I said he's dead. His heart finally stopped beating."

Indeed, Kaspar Hörmann now lay still, and his eyes had stopped moving. Jakob Kuisl pushed his eyelids closed and wiped the vomit from the corner of his mouth. Hörmann almost looked as though he was sleeping.

"Thank God!" Johann Widmann burst out. "Those eyes were truly unbearable."

"Maybe because they kept looking at the murderer," Bartholomäus Kuisl snarled.

"It's all right, brother." Jakob Kuisl stood up and walked over to the table, where he picked up the mug with his name on it. "Squabbling and bickering won't unmask this murderer." The hangman stuck his nose deep down into the mug and sniffed, making loud panting and even smacking noises.

"I'll never get used to that kind of examination," Michael Deibler muttered. The other executioners also watched Kuisl with a mix of fascination and disgust.

Shortly thereafter, the Schongau hangman concluded his examination. "Wolfsbane, as I suspected," he said. "Also known as monkshood or women's bane. Even touching it is dangerous, not to mention guzzling it down like a cow drinks water." He tilted the mug, and a tiny stream trickled out. "He drank the lot, but something remained in the mug."

"What do you mean?" Jörg Defner asked.

Kuisl held the mug on its side so the other hangmen could see inside. "Can you see the dark sticky spot at the bottom? Judging by the smell, I'd say it's forest honey mixed with the poison. The murderer smeared it on the inside of the mug. It's made of pewter, so you can't see it from the outside. Later, the poison dissolves in the beer." Kuisl grinned. "And thanks to the honey, you can't really taste it, especially not in the so very quaffable Munich brew. Hops, malt, and monkshood—cheers!"

"Hang on," Philipp Teuber said. "Something like that would have taken time. Are you saying the murderer prepared the mug in advance?"

Jakob Kuisl nodded, then he turned to Deibler. "Every day we hand our mugs to you so you look after them between meetings. They're the symbol that we belong to the Council of Twelve. Where have you been storing them?"

"Hmm. To be honest, I just leave them in here," Deibler replied with a shrug. "No one touches the mug of a hangman, it's bad luck. I never worried about theft."

"Damn it!" Matthäus Fux cursed. "That means anyone could have come in here during the night and prepared the mug."

"Conrad Näher, for example," Jörg Defner said, his one eye darting back and forth. "Maybe now we know why he disappeared so quietly."

"Yes, it could have been Conrad Näher," Kuisl said, "or any one of us. Everyone except for Michael is staying at the Radl Inn. All they had to do was sneak down here at night and smear the poisoned honey into the mug. It's not hard." He scratched his nose. "So perhaps we shouldn't be asking *who* just yet, but *why*. And I think I know the answer."

Jakob Kuisl pointed at dead Hörmann, still lying where he had passed away. "But I think it's time to call the guards before the innkeeper comes in and we all land on the scaffold as poisoners."

"And you really think she's going to come out here?" Paul asked his brother while he played with the small knife he had taken from the executioner's house.

Together with half a dozen other boys, the two brothers stood at a corner of Schwabinger Street, not far from the gate to the Residenz. The guards had tried to shoo them away several times, but the boys merely moved to another spot each time until the soldiers finally gave up.

"The prince told me that his nursemaid is going to town today," Peter replied with a shrug. "Apparently she's going to a tailor in Graggenau Quarter and to a goldsmith."

"Did you hear that?" giggled Seppi, a small, freckled boy. "The prince himself told him."

"Sure, and I watched the emperor take a shit yesterday," replied a thin, tall boy whom everyone called Moser and who was well known for his sarcasm.

The other children laughed until a sharp whistle cut them off. It was Paul, who glowered angrily at the street boys.

"If my brother says he knows the prince, then it's the truth," he said with a steady voice. "Does anyone not believe him? Out

with it!" He held out the knife, ready to fight, and the boys involuntarily stepped back. Peter was always amazed how easily Paul
put older kids in their place. It was as if the others could sense
that this scrawny eight-year-old wasn't bluffing, that he would
use the knife if he had to.

His posture looked as if he'd done it many times.

And the children from the Anger Quarter knew that Peter
and Paul were the grandsons of a proper executioner, and a huge
and grim-looking one on top of that. At least in Paul's case, it was
enough to instill the necessary respect.

As he had promised, Paul had talked to the Anger Wolves,
who had been more than happy to help the brothers with the sur-
veillance of the nursemaid. Peter suspected it had something to
do with the huge reward Paul had promised the kids if they
found the prince's dog. Nevertheless, some of the boys didn't
seem entirely convinced that Peter wasn't simply bragging. But
they'd never say it in front of Paul.

"Calm down, little fellow, no one's insulting you or your
brother," said Schorsch, the knacker's son and leader of their
gang. "But it's bloody freezing, and we've been standing here
since early morning. If your nursemaid doesn't come out soon,
we'll freeze to death. I say we stay till the bells strike noon, then
we go home."

The other children muttered their agreement, and Paul didn't
object. He shot his brother a warning glance, and Peter swallowed hard. If Paul lost face in front of these boys, he'd never
help him again. Max had told him about Amalie's shopping rou-
tine at their last meeting, and Peter could only hope the prince
was right. And Peter had promised him he'd go to the strange
masquerade that night, where he was supposed to report to Max
what he found out about his dog.

The next half-hour passed in silence. Some of the boys picked
up stones for their slingshots, but other than that, they just stared
at the gate to the Residenz. Several footmen rushed by, some

tradesmen entered the gate, but not a single woman. Peter was about to admit defeat when the double doors opened once more and an elegantly dressed woman came out. She carried a muff and wore a green dress that was a little longer than her fur coat. Most noticeable was her hair. It was as blonde as wheat in the sun and braided into an elaborate artwork, topped with a tiny hat. Peter let out a small cry of joy. That was exactly how Max had described his nursemaid.

The woman outside the Residenz was clearly Amalie.

"That's her," he whispered, and the other boys gathered around him and stared across the road.

"Don't stare," Schorsch said. He bent down as if he was picking up some horse dung, and the others followed his example. Only Peter kept watching the nursemaid.

Until then, he hadn't really thought about what they would do if Amalie actually turned up. Now he realized an elegant lady like her would probably take a carriage. But to his relief, Amalie kept walking. She turned left toward the Graggenau Quarter, and the boys followed her at some distance.

It turned out that following her was easier than he had thought. Amalie never looked back, she walked fast, and the lanes and alleys were so busy that the boys could always hide behind vehicles or merge with the crowd. As the prince had predicted, Amalie's first stop was a tailor, where she stayed for some time. Then she continued on to a goldsmith near the Alter Hof, where the Bavarian dukes used to reside. The boys waited in the narrow gaps between houses on the opposite side of the road and passed the time throwing snowballs and sucking on icicles.

Their initial euphoria soon vanished, as everyone, including Peter, had imagined a pursuit like this would be much more exciting. But all they really did was watch a court lady running her boring errands. After a while, some of the boys had to go home. In the end, the only Anger Wolves left were Schorsch, Seppi, and Moser.

"What is she doing in there for so long?" Seppi grumbled and rubbed his shivering arms. "Seriously, she's nice and warm while we're freezing our arses off."

"She's probably buying a toy for the noble prince," Moser jeered. "A golden spinning top or one of those small automatons that clap their hands. I saw one at the Jakobi Fair. A thing like that costs as much as the whole Anger Quarter together."

"If you've really met the prince, he must have given you something," Seppi said to Peter. "Go on, give it here before—"

"*Shush!* She's coming out!" Paul hissed.

"Yes, and now she's going to return to her bed of gold and we go back to our stinking quarter," Schorsch said in a bored tone of voice. "Well, at least we won't have to be cold any longer."

But to their surprise, Amalie didn't turn left toward the Residenz but walked down one of the narrow lanes. It led to a much less prosperous area. Tawers and tanners had their workshops here, the air reeked of urine and feces that floated down a nearby stream. Seppi wrinkled his nose. "I would have preferred the streets back to the Residenz," he complained. But even he seemed curious about what the nursemaid was doing in such a disreputable place.

Amalie soon turned left and followed an alley that led to an open square with a fountain. On the right-hand side stood a large stone building with a gate, through which carts laden with barrels of beer jolted in regular intervals.

"Look at that, the Hofbräuhaus," Moser said with raised eyebrows. "That's a little strange indeed. What's a lady like her doing at a brewery?"

"Maybe she's picking up the beer for the noble prince?" Seppi said with a grin. "Only question is, how's she going to carry the barrel. On her pretty little hat?"

Schorsch frowned. "This is where they brew the elector's beer. The high and mighty are crazy about frothy wheat beer. Perhaps the lady really is making inquiries for the court. Maybe she's placing an order for a celebration or something."

"A nursemaid? I don't know ..." Like the others, Peter had ducked behind the fountain and watched Amalie approach the gate. "And something else is strange," he continued. "She's looking around. Almost as if she doesn't want to be seen here."

"You're right, damn it," Schorsch said. "The whole way she didn't care at all if anyone followed her, and now she's suddenly acting like a thief in the night. Something's not right."

After looking around cautiously one more time, Amalie walked to the gate, where she exchanged a few words with one of the wagon drivers. Moments later, the nursemaid had disappeared into the inner courtyard.

"Damn, now that things are getting interesting, we can't follow her," Moser swore. "They'll never let a bunch of dirty street kids into the Hofbräuhaus."

"There must be another way. But how ...?" Peter desperately tried to think of a solution. He knew the boys had merely viewed him as an annoying attachment to his brother so far, even though the plan had been his. If only he could show them that sometimes brains could get you further than fists. Peter had no idea what Amalie might be up to in the brewery, but whatever it was, it was bound to be something illegal. What could it be?

Another cart with barrels rattled past them. Tired and bored, the driver waited for the wide gate to open. His head sagged forward, as if he was having a little snooze. And Peter still thought hard.

Another way ...

An idea struck him.

"The barrels on the cart," he whispered excitedly. "They're empty and open at the top. See?"

"Damn it, you're right," Schorsch said. "We might actually get in that way. Follow me."

Without waiting for the others, Schorsch jumped onto the cart and climbed in one of the barrels. The driver didn't notice a thing. The other boys followed his lead, Peter last. He shared a barrel with Schorsch, his back pressed against the wet staves. The strong smell of old beer almost made him drunk. Peter heard the gate squeak open, then the cart started to move.

Soon they stopped again. The horses whinnied, something creaked and groaned; Peter thought it was the driver climbing off the cart and walking away. From a little farther away, they could hear the laughter of other drivers. Steins clanked, someone burped. Evidently, some of the men were sitting down to their lunch beers at the taproom.

But there was also another sound.

Peter held his breath. A woman was crying.

Amalie . . .

Schorsch had also heard the sobbing. Very slowly, the two boys straightened up until their heads stuck up from the top of the barrel by a hand's breadth. Peter cautiously looked around the courtyard. Numerous carts were parked beside them, burly men lifted barrels off the wagons and replaced them with new ones. On the other side of the boys' cart, in a shady corner, Peter spotted Amalie deep in conversation with a young man. He had thick black hair and black eyes, his back was wide, and his arms showed that he had carried countless barrels of beer in his life.

"You promised," Amalie whined. "You said he wasn't going to get hurt."

"Jesus Christ, what was I supposed to do?" the man snarled at her. "I couldn't keep him here any longer. He's in good hands now."

"In good hands, bah! I know the fellow. I've heard only bad things about him. He's probably drowned him in the Isar by now."

"That would be stupid of him. He knows how much money that dog's going to make."

Peter winced. There couldn't be any doubt. Amalie and the man were talking about Arthur, the electoral family's lapdog. He'd been right. They were on to something.

"I can't sleep at night," Amalie wailed, shaken by another cry-ing fit. "Every time his electoral highness looks at me, I feel cer-tain he knows what I've done."

"Amalie, we didn't have a choice." The man placed an arm around the nursemaid's shoulder. The pair was hidden from the view of the drivers in their quiet corner behind the carts. The man continued softly: "And you didn't kill the dog. So you don't have to feel bad."

"Oh Markus, you . . . you shouldn't have given him away." Amalie collapsed against the man's broad chest and cried uncon-trollably. "If this ever gets out . . ."

"Hey, you!"

The loud, deep voice was very close. Peter thought at first someone had called out to the young couple, but then someone started to shake their barrel, sending the boys flying back and forth. "Rotten riffraff, what are you doing in my barrels?" the angry voice continued. "You just wait! I'll teach you a lesson."

Peter didn't want to know what exactly the man out there was going to do to them. With a deep breath, he jumped out of the barrel and found himself face-to-face with the angry driver who had carted them into the brewery. Now he raised his whip.

"Bloody vermin!" he shouted. "I bet you're from Au or an-other hole like that. What are you useless rabble doing in the city, huh? What were you going to steal?"

Peter didn't reply. Together with the other boys he jumped off the cart and headed for the open gate. The whip whirred some-where above him but missed.

"Stop them!" the driver screamed. "They're thieves!"

Other drivers tried to block their way. Schorsch and Seppi threw snowballs that smacked into angry red faces. Paul spun his slingshot, and a menacing hiss followed. From the corner of his eye, Peter saw one of the men grab his head in agony and sink to his knees. Meanwhile, two other boys had knocked over some of the barrels, which now rolled toward their cursing pursuers. A strong arm reached for Peter from the right, but he managed to dodge it at the last moment and raced toward the exit, where the gate was slowly closing. He slipped through the shrinking crack and stumbled out into the square. With the other boys he ran through the lanes of the Graggenau Quarter, the shouts of their pursuers growing faint and finally stopping completely.

Even though his heart was about to burst with fear and exhaustion, Peter couldn't suppress a smile. His observations had actually led them somewhere. They had found the culprits. As with an equation with several unknown variables, he had managed to come up with a solution — with brain power alone, not muscles.

His father would be proud of him.

"Just wonderful! If it goes on like this, soon there won't be any hangmen left in Bavaria."

Josef Loibl, the captain of the guard, leaned back in his chair and folded his arms. Jakob Kuisl thought he saw a mischievous twinkle in his eyes. Together with Michael Deibler, he was sitting in the headquarters of the city guard at the market square, not far from Schwabinger Street. Loibl had asked them here to find out more about the murder of Kaspar Hörmann. His body had been taken away by now and was being kept at the knacker's since the church refused to bury a hangman in a consecrated cemetery.

"First the Weilheim executioner quartered, and now poison at your guild meeting," Loibl continued. "What's next? Breaking on the wheel or boiling in oil?"

"I can do without your mockery," Kuisl replied grumpily. "Your time would be better spent helping us find out who's responsible for the murders of the hangmen as well as the girls in your city. Because there's a connection, that's as clear as pear schnapps."

"That's what you say, hangman," Loibl said. "Where's your evidence?"

"For heaven's sake, Master Hans knew the murderer of the girls and had to die for it. And I was supposed to be next because I'm on to the fellow." Kuisl leaned across the table. "We are looking for the same culprit, is that so hard to understand? Where am I, at the Munich city guard or the madhouse?"

Josef Loibl gave Kuisl a cold look. "Watch your tongue, hangman. You may be strong and clever, but in this city you're nothing but a dishonorable foreigner who's getting very close to having himself thrown into the Falken Tower for insult."

Michael Deibler touched Kuisl's arm. "He's right, Jakob. Shouting at people won't help. Why don't you tell Loibl everything you've found out about the dead girls so far."

Josef Loibl made an encouraging gesture. "Be my guest. Why not? We're grateful for any information, even if it comes from a hangman."

Kuisl cleared his throat, then he began to talk. "I'm convinced by now that our murderer has been at work for a very long time. Poor girls have been getting murdered in and around Munich for years. The culprit always follows the same pattern: he executes them like a hangman and leaves an amulet."

"An amulet?" Loibl asked.

"It's some kind of Virgin Mary pendant," Deibler came to his friend's aid. "I spoke to the knacker yesterday. He often brings back dead bodies from the nearby villages. He remembers seeing such amulets, too, and also that some girls suffered strange deaths. Drowned, strangled, buried alive . . . Only no one's ever really given a toss about those poor things. Most of them had no relatives and came from far away to find employment in the city. That's why there's never been an investigation."

"You told me yourself that one of those amulets was found

with the body of the young patrician woman, Theresa Wil-precht," Kuisl said to the captain. "The mummy had one, too. The amulets are the link between all these cases. The amulets and the manner of killing."

"Nonsense," Loibl replied. "Pious young women simply like wearing religious pendants. And every now and then a poor girl gets strangled or drowned by some bastard—it happens. What am I supposed to do with such vague suspicions? Mysterious am-ulets, alleged murders that happened years ago . . . What I need is solid evidence or witnesses." He turned to Michael Deibler. "What about this Näher, the Kaufbeuren executioner? I hear he's gone missing. Could he have something to do with the poi-soning? Perhaps even the other murders, too? Or is he the next victim?"

"We . . . we're still looking for him," Deibler replied haltingly. "We'll let you know when we find him."

They still hadn't heard back from Georg, whom Kuisl had sent looking for Näher. Kuisl knew how big this accursed Mu-nich was. Searching for Näher was like trying to find the prover-bial needle in the haystack.

"Have you by any chance tried to find out if the dead girls knew anyone in town?" he grumbled. "I saw a new cross at Elfi's grave over at Holy Cross cemetery, and a wreath. Someone must have put them there. And Elfi wasn't buried in the paupers' grave like Anni, but on her own. Who paid for that?"

Kuisl had pushed the memory of the eerie encounter in the cemetery aside in the last couple of days, mostly because it re-minded him of his wife's death and his own longing for death. He still didn't know how much of what happened in the Holy Cross cemetery had been his imagination and how much had been real, but now he remembered the wreath of fresh pine twigs, the cross that still smelled of sap . . .

Josef Loibl shrugged. "As far as I know, the money for the burial came from an anonymous donor—"

"An anonymous donor?" Kuisl brought his fist down hard on the table. "Bloody hell! A girl is impaled, someone decorates her grave, and no one wonders who this unknown person is. Is the entire Munich city guard drunk?"

"That's enough!" Loibl shouted back. "I'm not going to let a hangman speak to me like this. Get out before—"

He was interrupted by a commotion outside the office. Loibl rose and yanked open the door. "What's going on here?" he roared. "Didn't I say I don't want to be disturbed?"

"But I must speak with the captain," a voice called out, evidently someone being restrained by the guards. "It's about my wife, she's missing. She might even be dead. I need the help of the city guard, now."

Jakob Kuisl started when he recognized the voice outside the door. The hair on his neck stood on end and a chill ran down his spine. What he'd just heard concerned someone he knew very well.

My wife . . . she's missing . . . might even be dead . . .

The man pleading so desperately for help outside was undoubtedly his son-in-law.

A short while later, Jakob Kuisl, Deibler, and the captain listened to Simon's story as he struggled to find the right words. The slender medicus was as white as a sheet, his breathing rapid, his shirt torn from the run-in with the guards. His hat had fallen off and was lying on the ground, dirty and squashed. Kuisl felt his throat dry out like a puddle in the sun. As always when he was afraid, he was overcome by a strong urge to drink. And right now he was very thirsty and afraid.

Afraid for his daughter.

"That woman named Agnes said van Uffele and Joseffa had taken Magdalena away on . . . on a cart, like a dead cow," Simon concluded his report. "She thought she recognized her under the rags. My wife must have found something out at the manufactory and they silenced her." He looked at his father-in-law. "We should never have let her go."

"There is no proof Magdalena is dead," Kuisl replied in a monotone. He felt like he was listening to someone else speak. "She . . . she might have just been unconscious or tied and gagged."

"Van Uffele didn't waste any time with the other girls," Simon persisted. "Why should it be any different this time?"

"Because I know that my daughter isn't dead, all right?" Kuisl shouted at him. "I *know* she isn't."

"In any case, the city guard must search the manufactory immediately, from top to bottom," Michael Deibler said, squeezing Kuisl's callused hand reassuringly. "We must find out what's going on in there, right now."

"That's . . . not that easy." Josef Loibl bit his lip.

"What do you mean, it's not that easy?" Kuisl growled. "Send your guards to Au and take the damned house apart."

"Well, we hardly have more than a suspicion so far," Loibl explained hesitantly. Clearly, there was something he wasn't telling them. "Some girl said something —"

"Out with it, Captain," Deibler said. "Why don't you want to search the silk manufactory?"

"Because we'd need personal permission from the elector." Loibl sighed. "The manufactory is under his direct jurisdiction. The silk production is highly secret — they want to avoid foreign powers learning of the trade. Van Uffele might be a sleazy character, but his connections go right to the top. There is no way we can search the building unless the order comes from the elector himself. And that takes time. As far as I know, His Excellency is out hunting, and later on he's joining the electress at some ball or other." Josef Loibl shrugged and turned to Simon. "I'm sorry. All I can offer you is for my guards to keep an eye out for your wife in the city. You never know, they might just find her."

"This is about the life of my daughter, you ox, not about a lost puppy!" Kuisl thundered. He clenched his fists hard, making them crack like broken twigs. "And all you're going to do is ask a drunken night watchman to keep an eye out? You just wait, I'll . . . I'll . . ."

The hangman was about to jump up, hot rage welling up in him. Loibl's muscles tensed, he reached for his sword.

Then someone knocked on the door.

"What is it this time?" Josef Loibl grumbled, not taking his eyes off the hangman.

A guard stepped into the office and saluted. "Um, you said we should report anything out of the ordinary," he said uncertainly. "Anything that might be connected to those murders. Well, I'm not sure if—"

"Spit it out," Loibl barked. "What do you know?"

"A merchant on horseback just arrived in town from Freising. He's spreading some disturbing rumors on the market square."

"And what is it this time?" Loibl asked with a sigh. He put his sword aside but kept his eyes on Kuisl.

The guard looked down and made the sign of the cross. "Apparently someone buried a woman alive in the Bogenhausen cemetery. The farmers swear they saw a woman's arm reaching out from under the earth. By the mother of God! Like a living dead . . ."

For a moment, everyone was stunned and horrified. No one spoke. Then Jakob Kuisl sprang to his feet, his chair crashing to the ground.

"How far to Bogenhausen?" he asked Loibl.

"About . . . about four miles. You don't think . . ."

But Kuisl wasn't listening anymore. He ran outside, followed closely by Simon, who was as pale as the living dead himself.

"I have to admit, you were right."

Still breathless from the long run, Schorsch leaned against the drystone wall of a small, overgrown vegetable garden in the

Graggenau Quarter. The leader of the Anger Wolves had a wide grin on his face. "Now I can tell you, smart-arse. I actually thought you were telling fibs and just trying to sound important."

"I told you my brother doesn't lie," Paul said proudly. "And I knew he'd find the dog thief. He's pretty smart, you know. He can even read Latin, and not just the Paternoster."

Peter smiled. A compliment from the mouth of his own brother felt especially good. Suddenly he felt like the Anger lads viewed him differently. They were loitering in the deserted backyard of a workman's house. A handful of chickens pecked for grain in the muddy snow, and the hammering of a black-smith echoed through the air. Their exciting escape from the Munich Hofbräuhaus suddenly seemed very far away.

"I don't want to be a spoilsport," Moser muttered, "but we aren't really any further than before. All right, we know now that the nursemaid stole the prince's dog, but we still don't know where the mutt is. And no dog—no reward. Am I right?"

"The oh-so-elegant lady said the dog had most likely already been drowned," Seppi added, aiming his slingshot at one of the chickens. "If she's right, we can forget about the reward. Damn it!"

The stone hit the ground inches from the chicken, which ran away cackling loudly. Seppi cursed, and Peter's feeling of tri-umph vanished. The boys were right. What good was it know-ing who took the dog if they didn't have the dog? And something else bothered Peter: whenever his father or grandfather talked about their hunts for thieves and murderers, the culprits always were scoundrels. But Amalie just didn't seem like a scoundrel to him. The nursemaid had cried earlier; she truly appeared to care for Arthur. And that black-haired man who must have been her boyfriend, he said they didn't have a choice. The whole thing didn't sound so evil after all.

But why then did Amalie kidnap Arthur?

"So what should we do now?" Schorsch asked. "Go back home? I don't think there's anything else we can do here."

Peter realized everyone was looking at him, even his brother. Evidently, the boys expected some sort of decision from him. He cleared his throat.

"You're right," he admitted. "The case isn't solved yet, but we made great progress. Now we have to question the kidnapper about the location of her victim."

"Huh? I don't understand a word." Seppi scratched his lice-infested head.

"I think he means we should torture Amalie," Paul said. "That's what Grandpa does when people don't want to talk."

Peter sighed. People could be so slow sometimes . . . "Of course we're not going to torture her," he replied patiently. "We won't need to, because we know her secret. If she doesn't tell us where the dog is, we threaten to tell the prince."

"You mean *you* tell the prince," Schorsch said. "For us he's as far away as the moon. And where could you talk to the lady, anyway? She's bound to be back at the Residenz by now."

"I don't think so," Peter replied. "She was a mess, her makeup was smudged everywhere from the crying. She can't go back looking like that or someone will ask questions. And she can't go to the brewer's or the driver's houses either; that would be too conspicuous." He frowned. More to himself, he said, "So she's still somewhere out there. But it's too cold to stay outside for long. Hmm. So she's somewhere indoors, where no one bothers her . . . Somewhere you'd go to find consolation."

"A tavern?" Paul surmised. "Grandfather says that's where he finds consolation."

Peter smiled. "Grandpa, perhaps, but not an elegant lady." He nodded. "I think she's in a church. It's the only place where you can be completely alone in the daytime, even among many other people. Maybe she's confessing." He stood up with determination. "Let's go look for her in the churches. If we haven't found her in two hours, we give up. Agreed?"

The boys nodded, and to his enormous surprise, Peter realized they had actually listened. For the first time in his life, other children weren't meeting him with contempt, mockery, or envy, but with respect. More than that, he was their leader, if only for a brief time.

And all that without yelling and punching—he had convinced them with words alone.

It was like a miracle.

They found Amalie in the Frauenkirche.

Paul and Seppi had spotted her toward the end of their search. The nursemaid had just emerged from the confessional box, stooped with sorrow like an old woman, a woolen scarf draped over her hat, so the boys almost hadn't recognized her. When the rest of them finally entered the huge church, Amalie still sat in one of the pews, praying with her eyes closed. There weren't a lot of people in church at this time of day. The sexton was lighting candles in the side altars and chapels. When he caught sight of the dirty street children, he paused and started walking toward them, eyeing them suspiciously.

"Quick, the pews," Schorsch hissed. "If we pray, he won't dare kick us out."

The boys slipped into the pews, knelt down, and folded their hands in prayer. The sexton slowed his pace and walked past them without saying anything.

From the corner of his eye, Peter studied the massive church, which seemed as long to him as the main road of a village. The early afternoon light fell through the tall windows onto the colorful patterns on the ground. Numerous side altars were decorated with carvings and paintings. Peter decided he'd have to visit the Frauenkirche again. Perhaps he could even bring his drawing equipment.

"And now?" Moser whispered, pulling him back to reality. "What do we do now?"

Peter thought for a moment. "I'm going to go and talk to her," he said eventually.

"To a lady from court?" Seppi stared at him with astonishment. "Do you even know how to?"

"My brother knows the prince of Bavaria; of course he can talk to a nursemaid," Paul hissed. "And now shut up already, you lice-ridden good-for-nothing."

"Lice-ridden good-for-nothing yourself," Seppi muttered.

They watched in silence as Peter waited for the sexton to turn his back. Then he stood up and snuck over to Amalie's pew. He moved close to her, lowered his head and folded his hands, as though he was praying, too. He gathered all his courage.

"I'm sorry about the dog," he said softly.

Amalie gave a start. Apparently, she had been too absorbed in her grief to notice anything around her. Her face was wet with tears and streaked with makeup.

"I . . . I beg your pardon?" she asked, confused. When she realized the person talking to her was only a small boy off the street, her eyes narrowed. "Who do you think you are, you dirty rascal? Do you know who you're talking to?"

"You're Amalie, lady-in-waiting and nursemaid to His Highness the prince," Peter replied calmly. "And you stole his dog."

"How . . . how dare you . . . ," Amalie flared up. She flushed bright red and was about to jump up indignantly, but Peter held her back with a gentle grip.

"There's no point in lying. We overheard your conversation with the man at the Hofbräuhaus."

"We?" Amalie looked around anxiously. Then she understood. "Of course, you're the boys who ran away from the wagon drivers before." She gave him a haughty look, her pride returning. "What makes you think we were talking about the prince's dog? That's nonsense."

"It isn't nonsense," Peter insisted. "You cut the collar in the palace gardens and gave Arthur to that man, and he passed him on to someone else. We have evidence."

"Evidence . . . collar . . . gardens?" Slowly, it appeared to dawn on Amalie that the boy next to her wasn't just some random, filthy kid off the street.

"How do you know all this?" she asked eventually.

"Listen," Peter replied, ignoring her question. "I don't want Max to be angry with you. He said you're a nice nursemaid."

"Max said that, did he?" Amalie replied weakly. She seemed close to fainting.

"Yes, he did. But he really wants his dog back. So why don't you just tell us where he is, and I promise we won't say a word."

"But I don't know," Amalie whined. "That horrible man has Arthur now and—" She faltered when the sexton looked over to them.

"Take my hand, as if you were my mother or aunt," Peter commanded. "I want him to think we're together."

As if in a trance, the nursemaid reached for his hand. "I . . . I didn't want any of this," she stammered once the sexton had turned away again, after casting one last suspicious glance at them. "But as God is my witness, I didn't have a choice."

"Why?" Peter asked, curious.

"M . . . Markus and I, we've been a couple for over half a year now. But no one at court can find out," she said haltingly. "Markus is just a simple brewer's journeyman and I'm a lady from court. But that repulsive Kerll must have found out somehow."

"Max's music teacher," Peter said with a nod.

"Yes." Amalie sighed. "You really are well informed. Well, Kerll blackmailed me. He told me to get rid of the dog or he'd tell the elector. I would have lost my position, and they would probably have transferred Markus into the woods, to Straubing or even farther away."

"But why did Kerll want to get rid of the dog?" Peter asked. "What did he ever do to him?"

"Arthur always barked and howled when the prince played the violin," Amalie whispered. "It truly was unbearable. Both the violin playing and the howling." She gave a desperate laugh. "The two together almost drove Kerll insane. But His Highness Prince Max insisted Arthur stay with him during music lessons. So Kerll decided the dog had to go. I . . . I was supposed to drown him, but I couldn't. So I gave him to Markus at the Hofbräuhaus, who took good care of him."

"But then Markus gave Arthur to another man," Peter said with a bad feeling in his stomach. "Someone who's not as good to him."

Amalie nodded. "That monster steals precious dogs from wealthy homes and sells them on. Markus told me about it. He was hoping Arthur would find a new home that way. But I'm afraid that nasty man won't manage to sell Arthur. No one wants such a whimpering, annoying mutt. So he'll probably knock him dead, if he hasn't already. I'm sure he's capable of it. He truly is a god-awful man."

"And who is this horrible person?" Peter asked.

Amalie told him.

II

THE MAN ONSTAGE JUGGLED THREE golden apples and whistled a merry soldiers' tune, as if he were going to war.

He wore a tousled wig that looked like birds were nesting in it. On top of the wig sat a wooden crown, and a holey coat served as a royal cape, barely keeping out the cold. The young man shivered all over, but nonetheless he wore a mischievous smile on his face. When she looked again, Barbara realized the golden apples were merely painted balls of wood.

"See here Emperor Leopold juggling his countries," a bearded man with a drum proclaimed, standing next to the juggler on the stage. "Bohemia, Hungary, and the German Empire. And every year a new country." The man beat his drum and announced in his sonorous voice: "Croatia! Slavonia! And, with God's help, the southern countries." With each beat of the drum, someone threw another golden apple to the juggler from behind the stage, and the crowd laughed and applauded. Now the drummer launched into a clattering drumroll. "But oh dear!" he called out despairingly. "See for yourself. The sinister Mussulman cometh."

Barbara held her breath and watched as another juggler, dressed in the exotic garb of an Ottoman and carrying a saber, climbed the rough-hewn stage. Together with Valentin, she stood in the large crowd gathered on the square outside the Anger monastery and watched the exciting play. The troupe of jugglers had first entertained the audience with farces, then with a moresca dance, where the dancers wore tight pants and carried tambourines, jumping about like wild Moors. Now they enacted the growing threat of the Ottomans to the German Empire. The grim-looking Mussulman swung his wooden saber and hit the juggler until he stumbled, almost dropping his balls. The audience shrieked with fright—including Barbara, so that Valentin gave her a reassuring smile.

"I think all ends well for the German Empire. The emperor won't let himself be chased away by such a clumsy dervish."

Barbara smiled back, and indeed, the juggler managed to keep all his balls in the air.

That morning, Georg had told her that Magdalena had stayed at the silk manufactory for another night because she wanted to find out more about the murders. Barbara had listened and looked abashed, but her thoughts had already been with Valentin. As arranged, she had met Valentin at the Sendling Gate later that morning. Like the day before, they had roamed the lanes of Munich, occasionally stopping to warm up at a tavern, and eventually ended up on Anger Square. If Saint Peter hadn't chimed the hours, Barbara would have completely forgotten the time. But even so she had managed to push her gloomy thoughts aside for a while.

She felt happier than she had in a long time when she was with Valentin. She glanced at him furtively, and her heart glowed. The flaxen hair, the freckles, the cheeky smile as he watched the jugglers . . . Barbara imagined what it would be like if Valentin, not some dishonorable hangman, asked for her hand. She didn't even know if Valentin already had a sweetheart. He was almost twenty, he must have thought about marriage. But he hadn't given much away about himself so far.

Barbara only knew that Valentin's father had passed away a few years ago. There were two younger sisters and his mother, and he only just managed to feed the three of them with his music. Valentin got paid to play at weddings, funerals, christenings, church fairs, and anywhere else a quick bow and fiddle were required. He was no dishonorable itinerant musician but a municipal one, which meant he had permission from the city to earn his daily bread within the city boundaries with his music. But Valentin's threadbare clothes and his hollow cheeks showed Barbara that business wasn't going overwhelmingly well.

Despite the repeated, increasingly aggressive attacks of the Mussulman, the juggling emperor had so far managed to keep the balls in the air. But now the drummer started a new roll, and the audience held its breath.

"Watch as the faithful German countries finish off the saber-rattling heathen," he announced in a loud voice. "Behold the power of the emperor!"

The juggler abruptly lowered his hands and the hard wooden balls rained down like hailstones on the Mussulman, who fled amidst loud wailing and cursing. Everyone clapped and cheered, and a young girl in a colorful costume walked through the crowd with a purse.

"Next time, use silver thalers instead of golden apples," someone from the audience shouted. "They aren't as heavy — they get lighter by the day."

The crowd laughed, and Barbara gave Valentin a puzzled look.

"Apparently there's a gang of counterfeiters at work in town," he explained with a shrug. "They turn good silver coins into bad ones and pocket the difference. The merchants especially complain that there are more and more of those coins." He sighed. "I'd be glad for one single silver thaler in my pocket, even a light one. But the likes of us get paid nothing but rusty kreuzers."

Barbara smiled. "At least you don't have to chop anyone's head off. You make your living by making people dance."

"Well, your father makes them dance, too—only on the gallows." Valentin pulled a face, and Barbara shuddered. She looked away.

Valentin reached for her hand. "I'm sorry," he said. "No one can help where God places them. The Lord gave me the fiddle and your father the sword."

"Does that mean we can't choose our own path?" Barbara asked bitterly.

"I think we can try," Valentin replied after pondering for a while. "I think God means well with us. Sometimes he shows us a different path, but that doesn't necessarily mean happiness lies at the end of it. That's for us to find out. As for me, I don't want to trade places with a king or an emperor for anything." He grinned. "What use would all the gold in the world be to me if I had to marry a princess as ugly as a toad just to serve my country? Or even my own niece, like our venerable emperor Leopold."

"But even we poor folks must marry because our parents or some reeve or high-and-mighty lord says so," Barbara replied flatly.

"You're right. But at least no one gets beheaded over it." Valentin pointed at the jugglers, who had set up a wooden crate to serve as a stage for puppets. Now they enacted the sad story of some English king who ended up being executed like a common thief. A tiny puppet hangman with a mask swung his sword, and the king's wooden head fell to the ground amidst the roaring laughter of the crowd.

Barbara thought of Conrad Näher, the Kaufbeuren executioner she was being pressured to marry. How could she explain to her father that she'd never take Näher as her husband, ever? Especially because she didn't trust him.

And because you're in love with someone else, she thought secretly. *Admit it.*

Perhaps by now Georg had found out something about Conrad Näher and his strange behavior in the Sendling tavern yesterday. But who was to say she could trust Valentin? So many men had betrayed and disappointed her—lastly a juggler in Schongau who, just like the jugglers here, had made her laugh.

Just like Valentin . . .

Why shouldn't he betray her, too? Barbara's hands went to her belly, which once again rumbled as if some kind of beast was living inside.

Who can I trust at all?

While the people around her continued to roar and applaud, Barbara suddenly felt tears running down her cheeks. Valentin took her hands in his and gave her a concerned look.

"Barbara, what's the matter? There's something you're not telling me, isn't there?"

She remembered that her brother had asked the same thing the night before. She hadn't told him about Valentin because she knew Georg would only try to talk her out of her foolishness. And then he might tell Father about Valentin—her father, who was doing everything in his power for her to marry a well-to-do executioner and definitely not some obscure town musician without any money.

Barbara noticed some of the people around them staring at her. Probably because she was crying when everyone else was laughing. But perhaps also because of something else. They were in the Anger Quarter, not far away from the executioner's house. By now word was bound to have gone around that the Munich executioner was harboring some strange guests. If her father found out about her meeting with Valentin, he'd explode like a barrel of gunpowder.

Who can I trust? she thought again. *Valentin?*

"I . . . I can't talk about it," Barbara said quietly. "Not here, anyway."

Valentin thought for a moment, then winked at her. "I know a good place to talk. You'll like it, I promise."

He took her by the hand and led her away from the howling masses, away from the suspicious looks. And Barbara felt poignantly how good it was to simply follow him.

"Van Uffele? What sort of a name is that? Sounds like someone from the jungle. *Uff, uff, uff!*" Seppi danced across Neuhauser Street like a monkey, and the other children laughed. Even Peter couldn't help but grin.

They were standing outside the large complex of the Jesuit monastery, not far from the Frauenkirche. Many homes of the nobility and houses of worship were situated here in the Kreuz Quarter. In the nearby Augustiner monastery, mass was coming to an end; the bells tolled, and men in black clothes and women with austere bonnets walked past, giving the boys admonishing glances. This part of town was too posh for beggars and peddlers. It most likely wouldn't be long before the guards chased the children away.

"So, this, er . . . van Uffele has the prince's dog now, right?" Moser summed up Peter's conversation with Amalie in the Frauenkirche earlier. "If he hasn't already killed him and sold his pelt to the knacker, that is."

Peter nodded. "Van Uffele must be a pretty sinister sort of a fellow, but he's still highly esteemed at court. He has dealings with just about everyone there. Amalie says he has stolen dogs off wealthy people before and sold them back to their owners or others at horrendous prices."

"So why isn't he doing it with Arthur?" Schorsch asked, while a group of Jesuits in black regalia and hats as large as wagon wheels walked past.

"I'm guessing he doesn't dare blackmail the electoral family," Peter replied thoughtfully. "That's too big, even for him. And he can't get rid of the dog elsewhere. Apparently, Arthur barks and whimpers and is a right pain in the backside, Amalie says."

"If van Uffele is so high up, we probably don't have a chance of getting the dog back," Paul said, disappointed. As so often, he was playing with his knife, which he handled very nimbly by now. "He probably lives in a palace or something like that. To hell with all those arrogant snots! Grandpa should chop off all their heads." He hurled the knife at an old barrel by the side of the road, where it lodged with a *hum*.

Peter smiled smugly. He had saved his best news for last. "Well, I happen to know where the arrogant snot lives," he announced triumphantly. "And it sure isn't a palace."

All eyes were on him. Peter paused a moment longer, then he turned to his brother: "Do you remember the grownups talking about the silk manufactory?"

Paul nodded. "You mean the house where Mother has been working for the last two days because she's trying to find out more about the dead girls?"

"That's the one. It belongs to van Uffele, or at least Mother was talking about him being there."

"Hang on a minute." Schorsch cut him off. "Are you saying this monster not only abducts dogs but also murders girls? The same girls everyone has been talking about lately?"

"I don't know what he does exactly," Peter replied with a shrug. "But he sounds like a really nasty fellow."

"Ha!" Paul clapped his hands. "We'll show him! Imagine if *we* catch him, not the adults. Grandpa would give us licorice every day for the rest of our lives."

"It's not that easy," Peter said. "And very dangerous. If Mother is right, then van Uffele is a murderer. And he has helpers, a woman and a bunch of tough Venetians."

"Are you chickening out?" Paul gave his older brother a defiant look. "Now that we finally know where the dog is?"

"Your brother may be clever, but he still wets his pants when it gets down to it," Moser jeered. "He'd rather play catch with the prince in the court gardens." He made a feminine gesture and imitated Peter: "Oh Max, I'm so scared, I think I peed my pants." The boys giggled, and Peter felt himself flush.

"We could ask the prince for help," Seppi suggested.

Peter shook his head. "I told you, van Uffele is well known at court. Someone would tip him off. And Max's nursemaid would get in trouble. And I don't think that's what he wants—he likes Amalie a lot."

"Well, looks like our adventure ends here." Schorsch brushed the dirt off his trousers and turned toward the Anger Quarter. "We do it together or not at all. That's how it works with the Anger Wolves."

Peter felt the piercing looks of the others, especially his brother, who regarded him with disappointment. He saw contempt in the eyes of the boys, so soon after they'd celebrated him as a kind of leader. Didn't they realize how dangerous and, yes, hopeless this undertaking was? For all they knew, van Uffele was a cold-blooded murderer. Peter had helpers, too, but they were no more than a gang of scrawny, half-starved boys. And Peter didn't know for certain if Arthur really was at the silk manufactory, let alone if he was still alive or hadn't already gone to the knacker's as a piece of fur.

Embarrassed, Peter looked away. He gazed at the Jesuit monastery where, presumably, the Latin school his mother had told him about was also located. Just then some students dressed in fine garments walked over to mass. They were no older than him, and yet they seemed to be from another world, a world he'd been allowed to glimpse through Max. If he brought back the dog, he might become part of this world—or at least it might increase his chances of getting into a better school. Peter bit his lips.

The others were still looking at him.

"All right, let's do it," he said eventually. The boys clapped their hands and cheered, but he raised his hands, asking for silence. "Although it's going to be difficult to get into the manufactory in the first place. It's like a prison. Anyone have any ideas?"

"Ha! We're prison experts," Paul exclaimed excitedly. "Our grandfather is the Schongau jailer, after all."

"I might know someone who could help us," Seppi said. "I've met a few boys from Au before. They know the place better than anyone."

"Brrr, the Au lads are bloody fierce," Moser said, shaking himself. "If they catch you, you're done for. They call themselves the Au Dogs, but if someone else calls them that, they cut his throat."

"Oh rubbish, they're not that bad." Seppi waved dismissively. "And we'll tell them they won't go empty-handed if they help us break into the silk manufactory." He winked at them. "Silk is very precious, they say."

"We're doing this for the dog," Peter reprimanded him. "We're not thieves."

"Yes, yes, and my grandfather is the pope in Rome." Schorsch gave Peter a disparaging look. "You have much to learn if you want to become a true Anger Wolf." He smiled suddenly. "But you are very clever, I have to hand it to you. If you were as cunning as your brother, you'd be a born leader."

Disappointed and thoughtful, Georg walked down the wide main street of Au toward the Radl Inn.

The whole morning and half the afternoon he had combed the quarters of Munich. He'd been to the knacker's, countless taverns, the raft landing, even the Munich dungeons below the city hall and the Falken Tower. It was as if the earth had swallowed up Conrad Näher. No one had seen the graying older man with—for a hangman—elegant clothes and refined speech. On his way back to Au, Georg had called in at the executioner's house in the hope of finding Barbara and the others there. But to his surprise, only Walburga had been home, together with little Sophia and half a dozen meowing cats. The hangman's wife didn't know where everyone else was either. Where on earth could they all be?

A short while later, Georg was back outside the Radl Inn, where he'd begun his search for Näher that morning. He entered the pub and was on his way to the backroom when the innkeeper blocked his way.

"What do you want here?" the potbellied bald man barked.

"What do you think? I want to go to the guild meeting of the executioners," Georg replied, astonished. "I'm one of the journeymen. You know me."

"There is no more guild meeting, and there's never going to be another one in this tavern." The innkeeper crossed his thick arms on his chest. "I've had enough. You kill others, and now you're killing each other as well. I should never have agreed to this. I'll be lucky if people don't set fire to this place now."

"What happened?" Georg asked.

"What happened? Ha! The guards carried one of you out this afternoon—dead! Poisoned, they say."

"Jesus!" Georg grew pale. He thought of Master Hans and what had happened to him because he stuck his nose in somebody else's business.

Just like my father. O Mary, Mother of God, don't let it be my father.

"Who was it?" he breathed.

"That drunkard from Passau." The innkeeper snorted derisively. "At first I thought he simply drank himself to death. At least he won't spew in my chamber again." He eyed Georg suspiciously. "Did you know him well? You're all related, aren't you?

Then you can pay his bill. His son fled town as fast as he could run."

We almost would have been related, Georg thought, remembering how his father had considered Hörmann's son as a suitor for Barbara. A wave of relief washed over Georg; his father had been spared.

"I'd never seen him before this meeting," he replied truthfully. Then he remembered something else. A question he'd forgotten to ask that morning in all the excitement.

"I'm actually looking for someone," he started. "Conrad Näher from Kaufbeuren. You know, the graying man from the second floor? Do you happen to know where he went?"

"For Christ's sake, didn't you hear me? I want nothing more to do with you hangmen. That's what I told the others and threw them out. You have until tonight to pack your bags and be gone." The innkeeper shrugged. "Most of you have already left. First of all that snot from Nuremberg together with his flashy servants. He was going to skip out on the bill, but I stopped him." The innkeeper tapped Georg on the chest. "Tell that Kaufbeuren hangman, Näher, if he doesn't fetch his things by tonight, I'll burn them. Anything you godless executioners have touched brings misfortune."

He turned around without another word and left Georg standing there alone. Some of the patrons gave him sullen glances, but when Georg returned them, they all stared into their mugs. No one wanted to speak with a hangman's journeyman. It was always the same story. They needed him if someone was to be hung, but they didn't want to share a beer with him. On the contrary, if he wasn't careful, they would spit in his mug.

In that moment, Georg was more than glad that at least Barbara, Magdalena, and her family had found shelter in the executioner's house. It looked like the Council of Twelve was finished. He'd have to find somewhere else to stay that night, and tomorrow he'd return to Bamberg with Bartholomäus. He couldn't imagine his uncle would have left without him. He was probably out looking for a new place to stay, too.

He didn't know what the future held for him, Barbara, and the other Kuisls. But their task in Munich was finished. Even Father would have to accept that. There wouldn't be any more investigating. Let Deibler and that Captain Loibl solve those murders. It had nothing more to do with the Kuisl family. But Georg had to at least find out what happened to Conrad Näher. After all, he might be his future brother-in-law.

Georg nodded, deep in thought. It would be best if Barbara and Näher got engaged this very day. Everything else could be settled from Schongau.

If Näher is still alive, Georg thought. *Perhaps he also fell victim to that madman.*

He was about to leave the inn when he heard someone snigger in the corner. A little old man sat there, almost toothless, a plate of steaming bread soup in front of him.

"You want to know where the Kaufbeuren hangman went?" the little man croaked and sniggered again. "Well, I might just know."

Georg paused. The old man must have listened to his conversation with the innkeeper. Maybe he had noticed something or saw where Näher went. His curiosity aroused, Georg sat down at the old man's table. "Well, then," he said. "Let's hear it."

"Hey, hey, not so fast." The man grinned. "Nothing's free in this life—only death. What do I get if I tell you?"

Georg sighed. "I'd get you a beer, but I'm afraid I don't get served here any longer."

"And I'm afraid a beer isn't enough for my information. I want money, understood?"

Georg hesitated. Then he reached into his pocket, cursing. He could only hope his future brother-in-law would pay him back one day. Grumpily, he pushed a few stained coins to the center of the table. "Here, that's all I have left. But you only get it once you've talked and I agree that your information was worth it."

"You sure that's all you've got left? Well, at least they aren't false silver coins." The old man eyed the handful of pennies, then he shrugged. "To heck with it! An old mason must take what he can get. I worked hard under Elector Maximilian, building the Munich fortifications, but now no one gives two hoots—"

"I don't have time for your moaning," Georg cut him off. "Tell me, where is the Kaufbeuren hangman?"

The little man grinned broadly, revealing his only tooth. "The innkeeper doesn't know, because he's only been here for a year. But I remember well. The man you're looking for has been here before. Graying hair, good clothes, from the Allgäu, judging by his speech . . . I know because I've been sitting here for over thirty years, always in the same place. Back when I was a young man, I used to dance here and—"

"Where did he go?" Georg cut him off again.

"All right, all right. I know, no one cares about the stories of an old mason." The man sulked and slurped a spoonful of his soup. Then he continued: "I used to see him here several times a year. And I think I know where he went. If I were you, I'd try the Thürlbath."

"The Thürlbath?" Georg gave him a puzzled look. "Where in God's name is that?"

"Near the Isar Gate. I'm sure you'll find it. Knock on the door and say you want your fiery red beard shaved."

"But I don't have a fiery red beard."

The little man sighed. "Just do as I say. You'll understand. Tell them Jonas sent you, that should help." The old man giggled and pulled the coins over nearer to him. "And now I'd like to eat my soup in peace. Don't take it badly, but the company of a hangman always spoils my appetite." He bent over his soup; evidently, he considered their conversation over.

"Shave my fiery red beard," Georg muttered, rising to his feet. "What a load of nonsense. God have mercy on you if you're having me on. I'll find you."

He turned to the door. As he walked out, he heard the little man snigger once more like an evil sprite.

Simon gasped, and his lungs hurt with every breath he took, but he clenched his teeth and pressed on. Ahead of him, Jakob Kuisl ran along a narrow icy path that led through a dense forest close to the banks of the Isar River. According to several travelers they had passed along the way, this was the fastest route to Bogenhausen, a small village several miles northeast of Munich. As the two men hurried along, Simon's thoughts kept returning to the words of the guard earlier on.

Apparently, someone buried a woman alive in Bogenhausen cemetery . . .

Simon prayed it wasn't Magdalena. He knew it wasn't necessarily his wife, but he couldn't suppress his fear. Magdalena had been taken from the manufactory on a cart that morning, Agnes told him — dead, or at least unconscious — by two dodgy characters who had probably killed young women before: van Uffele and Mother Joseffa. Simon still couldn't explain how the two of them were connected to the older murders. But he was sure there was a connection.

Burying a woman alive fit perfectly with the other murders. The culprit always killed his victims in ways used by executioners. He had drowned, strangled, quartered, walled in, impaled, and buried alive. As far as Simon knew, the last wasn't used anymore nowadays because it was considered too horrible. The convict used to be tied and placed on his back so he would have to watch the dirt slowly covering him, from the feet to, finally, the head. The sentence was considered more lenient if a stake was first driven through the heart, but often enough, the unhappy man or woman would simply be left to suffocate under the soil.

Evidently, the buried woman in Bogenhausen had tried to free herself. The guard had spoken of an arm sticking up out of the ground. Had the poor woman managed to escape death in the end?

Was that woman Magdalena?

"Faster!" Jakob Kuisl ordered harshly and looked around for Simon. "Why are you so slow? If that unfortunate woman really is my daughter, every moment counts."

The hangman waved impatiently and kept running, dodging icy roots and fallen branches. Simon was amazed at the speed and strength of his aging father-in-law. He found himself involuntarily slowing down the harder he thought. He struggled to keep up with his father-in-law, and he finally caught up with him when they reached the edge of the forest another quarter of an hour later. On their left, the Isar River rushed through the valley below. Above the steep slope lay several fallow fields with patches of snow, and beyond them a small village church and about a dozen houses. Simon breathed a sigh of relief.

Bogenhausen. Finally.

One last time he increased his pace. They had been running nonstop for almost an hour since their hasty departure from the guards' headquarters. Simon was more stumbling than running by now. Together with his father-in-law he crossed the village street and ran toward the church. A crowd had gathered in the cemetery beside it.

The people watched the two running men suspiciously. Simon regretted that they hadn't brought Michael Deibler along. The Munich executioner would have commanded respect from the farmers. On the other hand, it was probably for the best if the well-known hangman didn't talk to the people, not when it was about an alleged living dead. And Deibler was not particularly fast; he would have only slowed them down.

As they got closer, Simon saw that the villagers stood around a hole in the ground. A mound of fresh soil was right next to it.

Jakob Kuisl had already opened the cemetery gate and rushed toward the hole without paying any attention to the crowd.

"Magdalena!" Jakob Kuisl shouted as he ran. "Are you there?"

Simon stumbled after him with a thumping heart — and looked down into the hole.

It was empty.

"Where is she?" Kuisl gasped and pushed through the crowd with his huge body, almost shoving several people into the hole. His eyes searched the crowd desperately. "Tell me already!"

"Hey, who do you think you are?" a corpulent farmer with a wide-brimmed hat asked. He stepped in front of the hangman with his arms folded. "You from Munich? Think you can do what you like here?"

"I asked where the woman who was buried alive is," Jakob Kuisl repeated harshly. He straightened up, towering over everyone present. "For God's sake, out with it or there'll be another funeral here shortly." Something in Kuisl's voice told the farmer that he was deadly serious.

"The priest took her to his house," he replied, pointing at a house at the edge of the cemetery. "He said he didn't know whether she'd make it. Do you know her?"

"So she's still alive?" Simon asked with relief, ignoring the question.

"Bah! How can she be alive when she crawled out of a grave?" an old woman muttered, bent over her walking stick. She raised a finger in warning. "I'm telling you, it was a living dead. Just went and took the freshly dug grave of my good friend Grete. And now Grete has to wait for her funeral in her cold coffin. But this was just the start. There's going to be more dead rising from—"

But Simon was no longer listening. Together with his father-in-law, he ran across the cemetery to the rectory and banged against the door. After a few moments, the priest opened up, dressed in his official regalia.

"What in God's name—" he began, astonished.

But Kuisl pushed past him and ran into the living room, and from there into the bedchamber.

A woman lay on the bed.

She was as pale as a shroud, her eyes were closed, but a slight trembling all over her body showed that she wasn't dead. But with her torn, dirty dress and clumps of clay in her matted hair she really did look like someone risen from the dead. Simon felt the tension from the last few hours drain from his body. Exhausted, he leaned on one of the bedposts.

The woman on the bed wasn't Magdalena.

Simon didn't know whether to be relieved or disappointed. On their way here, he had felt increasingly certain that the buried woman must be his wife. At the same time, he hadn't given up hope of finding Magdalena alive and well in Bogenhausen. Now he was looking at a perfect stranger. The young woman on the bed was about seventeen, eighteen years old, with blonde hair and a pretty face, albeit haggard and drained of blood.

"Eva," Jakob Kuisl whispered beside him.

"You . . . you know her?" The priest had entered the chamber behind them. "Does that mean you're her father?" he asked gently. Evidently, he had already forgiven Kuisl his forceful entry.

The hangman shook his head. "I only saw her once at Au. She works at the silk manufactory there."

Simon looked at the girl on the bed in astonishment. So this was Eva, the third of the three friends, two of whom were dead. The young woman Magdalena had set out to rescue.

"Did she say anything?" he asked the priest. "I mean, about who did this to her?"

"At this point I don't even know if she's going to live." The priest sighed. "We were supposed to have a funeral today. Someone must have thrown the poor thing into the grave last night or early this morning and buried her with the fresh soil. Who would do such a thing?" He looked down on the skinny, trembling body with sadness. "The girl is strong, even if she doesn't look it at the moment. She dug herself out. By God, if I hadn't . . . if I hadn't intervened, the villagers would have killed her. They came for a funeral, and then an arm emerges from the grave. Of course people think she's a walking dead—no thanks to the gruesome stories we've been hearing from Munich lately. Mysterious murders and a meeting of twelve dishonorable hangmen at once." He shook himself. "May God protect our little village from such evil. Only god-fearing folk live here."

Simon refrained from commenting. Instead, he leaned down to Eva and examined her superficially. The girl appeared to be deeply unconscious. Her lips quivered but no sound came out. Her entire body was covered in scratches and grazes, probably from the fall into the hole. On a thin string around her neck hung an amulet depicting a woman with an aureole. Simon cast a meaningful glance at Kuisl, who nodded in silence.

"The wound on the back of her head," Simon said eventually and pointed at a blood-crusted swelling. "Could that have been your virtuous, god-fearing flock?"

The priest appeared not to notice the mocking tone. "I don't think so. I got there in time. The wound must be from earlier."

"The bastard knocked her over the head and chucked her in the grave," Jakob Kuisl growled. He clenched his fists. "If only she could tell us who did this to her. Then we'd finally have the murderer of Anni, Elfi, and all the others. She might even know where my Magdalena is. It's enough to make you crazy."

"You seem to know more about her after all," the priest said in a pinched tone. "Perhaps now is the time to tell me what's going on here."

"It was a heavy blow," Simon said without answering the question. He continued his examination. When he reached her fingers, he saw that all the nails were broken off. Blood had mixed with dirt, and in a few places, Simon could see bone.

"Jesus!" Simon gasped. "She really did dig herself out with

her own hands. No wonder she's barely alive now." He looked at Jakob Kuisl. "If we want to find out who did this and where Magdalena is, Eva needs better care and proper medicine as soon as possible. Shepherd's purse, arnica, perhaps a brew of linden flowers and lavender to relax the cramping . . ."

"This is a rectory, not a bathhouse," the priest replied with a shrug. "All I can give her are my prayers. And now I'd really like to know—"

"That's why we're going to take her with us," Jakob Kuisl interrupted the priest and gave him a pat on the back. "Nothing against your prayers, but she's better off with us."

"Us?" The priest eyed Simon and Kuisl distrustfully. "Who are you two, anyhow? I can tell you one thing for certain: I'm not going to give the poor girl to a pair of gallows birds who just happened along."

"You can rest assured that we're no gallows birds," Simon replied with a tired smile. "More like men who know a lot about death as well as life. I'll tell you everything else in just a moment." He stood up and wiped the dirt from his hands. "But first I'd like to ask you to find us a stretcher. Fast as you can. I promise you we'll keep this woman safe."

About four miles away, Georg set out to solve the mysterious disappearance of Conrad Näher once and for all.

This late in the afternoon the smaller lanes were almost empty, the shops in the Graggenau Quarter were closed, and a cold damp fog crept across the cobblestones. Georg tightened his coat around him and turned into Lederer Lane, a narrow alleyway only a bow's shot away from the Isar Gate. When he'd walked down Tal Street a few moments ago, he had still passed a few carts and pedestrians, but now he was suddenly as alone as in a dark forest.

Of the three people he had asked for directions on the way to the mysterious Thürlbath, two had given him evasive replies.

The third one had finally told him where to go, but not without giving him very strange looks, which Georg hadn't understood. Something was up with this bathhouse the old man at the Radl Inn had told him about.

Georg had heard about bathhouses before. They used to have several in Schongau, too. They were places where men and women climbed into large tubs filled with hot water together, just the way God had made them. There was a bathhouse surgeon who shaved beards, pulled bad teeth, or bled people as required, but more often than not, such bathhouses were mainly for pleasure. Many an innocent child had been conceived in those wooden tubs. The accursed French disease and also the Protestant hatred of anything uncouth had caused bathhouses to die out gradually. Apparently there still was one in Munich, and Georg was curious to see it.

At a dark street corner, a rusty tin sign above a doorway showed a bathtub and a snake. The crooked two-storied building looked like it had seen better times. The shutters were nailed shut, plaster crumbled off the walls, but Georg saw light gleaming through the cracks in the windows and from time to time laughter and the amused shrieks of women could be heard from inside.

Slowly it dawned on Georg what this ominous Thürlbath was about and why the man he'd asked for directions had given him a queer look. Once upon a time this might have been a place for honorable citizens, but now it was a dive where a little money got you a cheap girl or two.

The Thürlbath was nothing more than a brothel.

Georg remembered his conversation with Magdalena about whores the day before. He had acted indignant, but the truth was he had visited the prostitutes in the Bamberg Rosengasse Lane plenty of times. Neither men nor women were allowed carnal pleasures until wedlock, but you needed money and permission from the city or overlord for a wedding, which was why many journeymen didn't marry until later in life. Until then, they had to see to their needs.

Like Georg.

He assumed the goings-on at the Thürlbath were known to the guards. Brothels had been banned in Munich for several decades, but evidently the officials tolerated this establishment as long as it didn't attract too much attention. Some of the guards probably frequented this house themselves.

Georg knocked timidly, and a small barred hatch opened.

"It's after five," a voice behind it growled. "The bath is closed. Come back tomorrow."

"I . . . I've come for a shave," Georg replied hesitantly.

"And what sort of a shave is that?" the other one asked, a little more attentive now.

"I . . . want to shave my red beard," Georg said, remembering the old man's words.

"Your red beard, you say. Let me take a look."

The door opened, and Georg found himself face-to-face with a wide, bullnecked man in a leather apron, sweat running down his forehead in streams. Georg felt a warm rush of air that smelled of spruce resin, and somewhere down the dark corridor behind the man a woman screamed.

"I'm the bathhouse owner," the man grunted and glared at Georg. "And who are you? I've never seen you here before."

Georg swallowed. "Jonas sent me."

The bathhouse owner's face lifted instantly. He grinned. "Old Jonas! Is he still alive or did he speak to you from the grave?"

"He's in the best of health and sends his greetings," Georg fibbed without batting an eyelash.

"Come in, come in." The bathhouse owner pulled him across the threshold and Georg entered a narrow hallway with a stove. On the right was the empty bathing room, and on the left an equally empty chamber. But where had the screams come from? At the end of the hallway stood a large, man-high wardrobe. The bathhouse owner opened its doors and steam billowed out. Georg's eyebrows went up when he saw what the piece of furniture had concealed.

On the other side of the wardrobe was another corridor.

Georg followed the man into the dimly lit darkness. He immediately became too hot in his winter coat. The air was as muggy and warm as right before a thunderstorm in summer. Georg heard shrieks and moans behind doors to his left and right, but the bathhouse owner didn't seem perturbed.

They turned left and walked down a few stairs to a longish, low-ceilinged room filled with smoke and steam. At the far end stood a large tiled stove that gave off both intense heat and the smoke. Benches holding several men and women stood along the walls. Everyone was naked except for a few who wore loosely wrapped towels that barely concealed anything. Two couples amused themselves in a large tub in the middle. When Georg entered the room with the bathhouse owner, the women's eyes turned to the young hangman's journeyman.

"Oh, who's this handsome one?" a fat woman cooed, her bosom bulging over the towel like warm bread dough. She patted the bench next to her and winked at Georg. "Come to Trude, darling, and we'll have so much fun."

Georg felt himself tense up. He looked around for Conrad Näher, but couldn't find him anywhere.

"He's not for you, Trude," the bathhouse man said. "Jonas sends him. He wants to shave his red beard."

"His red beard? Oh, what a shame," the fat woman sulked. "Such a waste."

Accompanied by the giggles and laughs of the other visitors, Georg followed the man through the room. They took another narrow, slippery staircase to another chamber, where the steam was too dense for Georg to see anything at first. After a while, he made out benches and tubs and hazy figures in close embrace.

And, in one of the tubs, Conrad Näher.

Georg recognized him immediately, even without his clothes on. His graying hair hung in his face in wet strands. He had his eyes closed, and the water in front of him bubbled and stirred. Georg could see a shadow under the water's surface. Then a figure slowly emerged.

In that moment, he knew that there was no way Barbara could marry the Kaufbeuren hangman.

12

WHILE IN THE CEMETERY OUTSIDE people were still talking, cursing, and praying, gathered around the empty grave, Simon and Jakob Kuisl desperately waited for a stretcher on which to carry Eva back to Munich.

Simon used the time to convince the priest that they meant no harm to the girl and that he, a doctor, would take good care of her. Simon prudently decided not to mention that the tall, sullen man by his side was actually an executioner. Nonetheless, the priest remained skeptical. In the end, however, he was probably glad to be rid of the strangers and for peace to return to his village.

Simon was in equal parts relieved and worried about not having found Magdalena in Bogenhausen. He still didn't know where his wife was, but at least she might still be alive. The woman on the cart Agnes was talking about must have been Eva, not Magdalena. Agnes had been mistaken. That's what must have happened. But then where was Magdalena? Was she still at the manufactory? But wouldn't Agnes have known? In any case, it was vitally important for them to return to Munich as fast as possible.

Finally, two farmers brought a stretcher made of coarse linen and rough-sawn timber poles. They set the construction down outside the door and disappeared quickly, as though they feared the living dead might attack them at any moment.

"Superstitious rabble," Kuisl muttered, lifting Eva onto the stretcher as gently as if she were his own granddaughter. "They'd probably burn the body of their own grandmother just because a black raven flew over her tombstone." Carefully, he draped his coat over the girl.

Followed by the suspicious gaze of the priest, the hangman and Simon finally carried the girl over to the main road. Eva didn't weigh more than a child, but Simon was utterly exhausted from the long run, and the villagers kept trying to block their way.

"She's a living dead!" screamed the same old woman who had ranted so loudly earlier. "You must drive a stake through her heart, it's the only way to put unhappy souls like hers to rest."

"Who's to say those two aren't a pair of warlocks who're going to bring this godforsaken corpse back to life?" one farmer asked, swinging his scythe. Others had armed themselves with pitchforks and flails but stayed in the background, as if they wanted to wait and see whether Eva would reawaken and hurl curses at them.

Some of the braver ones tried to take the stretcher off Kuisl and Simon, but after the hangman gave one of them a bloody nose, the others slowly retreated, muttering angrily, like hungry wolves who found themselves robbed of their prey. Once again, Simon thought that humans weren't that different from animals.

Worse, actually, he couldn't help thinking. *Animals don't know superstition, only hunger.*

When they reached the edge of the forest, they were finally left alone. The crowd gradually stopped following them, and after the villagers gave a few last angry shouts, the forest enveloped them in silence. Panting, Simon stopped.

"It's going to take us hours to get back to Munich this way," he moaned. "If I don't break my back first."

"Idiot!" Kuisl snarled. "Do you think I feel like trudging through the snow for hours? I just wanted to get away from those crazy people." He gestured ahead, where Simon could make out a fork in the path. "The main road to Freising isn't far away. I'm sure we can find a kindly driver who hasn't heard about the living dead from Bogenhausen yet and is willing to give us a ride."

And indeed, it wasn't long before a wagon laden with barrels and bales of cloth appeared between the trees. Kuisl stood in the middle of the road and held up both hands, signaling he meant no harm. The driver hastily picked up a loaded crossbow, but relaxed when he saw the stretcher.

"My daughter has a fever," Kuisl explained to the old driver, who was wrapped in furs from head to toe. "Would you be so kind as to take us to Munich? She needs a barber surgeon, urgently. My son-in-law is beside himself with worry."

The old man nodded and helped them to stow the stretcher between the barrels. "Got a girl around that age myself," he said. "May God keep our children alive."

As the cart creaked toward Munich, Simon watched the still unconscious Eva, who, as if plagued by evil nightmares, gave small shrieks from time to time. Her face was bathed in sweat despite the cold. Most likely, she had already been ill before someone buried her. The exertion of digging herself out had stoked the fever inside her like a fire in a stove.

Simon tried to imagine someone covering him in soil, shovelful by shovelful, until his face was covered and he could no longer breathe. How the wet dirt and clay became heavier and heavier, almost crushing him. How he strained and squirmed but couldn't move an inch. He shuddered—it was just too horrible.

"I should have helped her sooner," Jakob Kuisl said next to

him. "When I saw her face behind the barred windows that last time. I should have kicked the bloody door in, thrown that old bitch against the wall, and gotten the girl out of there, all the girls."

"Well, at least there's still hope for Magdalena now," Simon said quietly. "She must be somewhere else."

He tried to think. If Eva was the girl van Uffele and Joseffa had carted away, more questions arose. Why had the two of them buried Eva alive, and in a village several miles away from Munich? If all they wanted was to silence Eva, then why not simply knock her dead and throw her in the river? It would have been much less conspicuous. So why this terrible execution?

"Do you think Magdalena is still in the manufactory?" Simon asked his father-in-law, as the wagon slowly rolled through snow and mud. Night had fallen by now, and the forest stood like a black, silent wall that slowly closed in on them from both sides of the road.

Jakob Kuisl took his time with his reply. Eventually he said: "By God, I don't know. Van Uffele and Joseffa might have carted other girls away, too. But then again, Magdalena might simply be locked up in the basement."

"We'd first have to get into that accursed manufactory," Simon said with a sigh. "But it's obviously closely guarded by those Venetians, and Loibl can't help us either because van Uffele has powerful friends. It's hopeless." He lifted both hands. "Sometimes I really wonder what our family has done to deserve such punishment."

"Women's punishments," Jakob Kuisl said all of a sudden.

Simon gave him an irritated look. "Beg your pardon?"

Kuisl suddenly seemed very agitated, his fingers nervously drumming against the wooden side of the cart. "The whole time we've been saying these murders are classic executions," he said with urgency. "But we never thought any further than that. The murderer executes his victims in ways traditionally used for women. Drowning, drowning in a sack, and strangulation are classic punishments for women, just like burying alive. Why?"

"But Elfi was impaled, and the woman in the rock cellar walled in," Simon replied. "And Master Hans was quartered. How does that fit in?"

"Hans was executed as a traitor, and the punishment for high treason is quartering. But I'm not sure about the impaling and walling in. We'd have to research old books to find out what their meanings used to be. But we don't have enough time . . . Goddamnit!" Kuisl angrily punched the side of the cart. "Why can't all the killing finally come to an end? Why am I, the hangman, always condemned to solve it?" He groaned quietly, and Simon suddenly saw how old his father-in-law had become. In the dusky light, his hair and beard seemed even grayer, the wrinkles in his face even deeper.

Simon thought about how much they had gone through together in recent years. They had lost loved ones, gained many scars and wounds, and Jakob Kuisl had reached an age where most people sat by the stove and watched their grandchildren play in the snow outside the window.

Instead, he had to search for his daughter, who was possibly trapped in the hands of a deranged murderer.

"It's the executions and those damned amulets," Kuisl grumbled eventually. "They're like encrypted messages. What in God's name is he trying to tell us? Why is he always going for the same kinds of punishments?"

"Because he wants to punish women in particular?" Simon asked.

"That's obvious. But why?"

Jakob Kuisl bent over Eva, picked up the leather string around her neck, and untied it. He looked at the Virgin Mary amulet in his hand.

"What are you doing in this cold, dirty world, Holy Virgin?" the hangman asked. "What is your secret, gentle Mother?"

Kuisl stared at the amulet for a long time before putting it away.

It was still a good hour before the cart finally rolled through the Isar Gate into the city. The gates had long been shut, but the driver seemed to have connections. A few coins changed hands, and the guard opened the gate once more. Simon thought of the black-clad carriage that had raced through Sendling Gate a few days ago. The guards had been paid then, too, probably much more than this time.

This city is like a vain, greedy whore, he thought. *She only smiles at those who pay her well.*

At this time of the year, the lanes behind the gate were as black as the bottom of a lake by seven o'clock at night. The bigger streets were partially illuminated by lanterns outside taverns. The night watchman was just calling the last hour before closing time, and soon the only people on the streets would be thieves and other shady characters.

Simon and Jakob carefully lifted the stretcher off the cart and carried Eva through narrow alleyways to the Anger Quarter. A few meowing cats greeted them in the garden of the execution-er's house. Kuisl knocked, and soon a very agitated Michael Deibler opened the door.

"So?" the Munich hangman asked with a husky voice. His eyes darted to the stretcher. "Did you find her?"

Simon shook his head. "That's not Magdalena, but the girl ur-gently needs care and medicines."

"Is she alive? Let me take a look," Walburga called out from behind her husband. When she saw Eva on the stretcher, she seemed speechless. She held one hand to her chest and squeezed a tiny medallion on her necklace, as though she was praying si-lently.

"Michael told me about this awful business," she said eventually, turning to Simon. "What do you think? Is she going to make it?"

"I don't think she's going to die," Simon replied. "But she's extremely weak. After all, she was buried alive and dug herself out."

"Jesus," Deibler said. "Buried alive..." He looked visibly shaken, his hands trembled as he took a step back.

"Can she talk?" Walburga asked.

"Unfortunately not," Simon said. "Or we'd already know who did this. But we're relatively certain that it's the same madman who's been killing people in Munich for years."

"Bring the poor thing inside before she freezes to death," Walburga commanded in a gentle voice. "I'll take care of her."

Jakob Kuisl carefully lifted Eva from the stretcher and carried her to the bed in the apothecary chamber. As soon as he put Eva down, Walburga began rummaging in the cupboards for herbs and medicines. "Linden blossoms with willow bark, dissolved in strong brandy...," she muttered. "That should get her back on her feet. First of all, we must lower her fever and make sure the wounds on her fingers don't become infected." She picked up a small pouch and turned to Simon. "I almost forgot. Your wife told me you loved coffee more than anything. I brought you a handful of those beans from the market yesterday. Would you like me to brew a cup for you? You look like you need it."

Simon nodded absentmindedly. "I assume Magdalena hasn't turned up yet?" he asked without much hope.

Walburga shook her head as she ground the coffee beans in her mortar. "No, sadly. Neither have Peter and Paul. But I wouldn't worry too much about those two. They'll be somewhere outside with the Anger boys." She looked up briefly and smiled. "By the way, that strange envoy from the Residenz called in again earlier. He wanted to pick up you and Peter for some kind of ball. But you weren't here, so I sent him away."

"And just as well," Kuisl said and nodded grimly. "We really have enough on our plates without playing the fool for those fops at the moment. I never liked my grandson going there in the first place, and my son-in-law searching for a bloody lapdog."

Simon would have liked to object, but he had to concede that they had more important things to worry about right now.

"Perhaps it's better the boys aren't here right now," he said. "Their mother is missing, after all, and it's enough that we worry about her. But Barbara and Georg should know. Are they here?"

"Um, I haven't seen Barbara today," Michael Deibler replied. He was still standing on the threshold, lost in thought. "Bloody cold!" He rubbed his arms and closed the door behind him. "But Georg is here, he arrived home about half an hour ago. I told him about Magdalena, and he's been sitting in the living room ever since, downing one beer after another."

In that moment, Georg staggered into the hallway. He looked questioningly at Simon and Kuisl, his face ashen. "And? Is she . . ."

"The woman in the grave wasn't Magdalena," Kuisl said. "That's the good news. The bad news is, we still don't know where she is or how she's doing."

They all went into the warm living room while Walburga continued to care for the unconscious Eva in the apothecary's chamber.

In the corner of the room, below the family shrine, stood a cradle painted with colorful though slightly faded flowers. Inside, Sophia slept peacefully. Simon breathed a sigh of relief. It felt good to see that at least one member of the Kuisl family was well looked after.

"I found the cradle in the attic," Deibler explained with a tired smile. "Walburga and I weren't fortunate enough to have children of our own. Once, many years ago, God gave us a beautiful little baby, but He took it back soon after birth." He shook himself, as though trying to get rid of unhappy memories. "The Lord moves in mysterious ways. Well, the cradle is from back then. I'm glad to see it used for your Sophia."

"Luckily she's too little to understand what's going on." With a nod, Simon turned back to his brother-in-law, who was sitting at the table in silence again. Georg's eyes were slightly reddened, and he clung to his beer mug like a drowning man. Simon thought of the coffee next door. He hoped Walburga was brewing him a cupful. He needed to think, and he preferred to do so with coffee, not with alcohol.

"We don't know where Magdalena is," Kuisl said once everyone was seated. "But perhaps a different lead might help us." He looked at Georg. "Speak, son. What about Näher? Did you find him? Could he know something about Magdalena?"

Georg took another sip of his beer, then he said in a monotone: "Näher won't marry Barbara."

Kuisl looked at him with surprise. "Why not? Everything was going well, they went for a walk, he gave her a present, did all the right things. And Barbara didn't seem disinclined. At least she wasn't crying afterward." His face darkened. "Or has she changed her mind again? This girl really is the most pigheaded—"

"Näher won't marry Barbara because he's a sodomite."

The room fell silent. It took a while before everyone grasped the meaning of Georg's words.

"He . . . he's what?" Simon asked eventually.

Georg sighed. "He's a sodomite. He does it with other men, not just here in Munich, but in Kaufbeuren as well." He wiped the foam from his mouth, then continued. "Conrad Näher would have married Barbara, and they might even have had children. But the marriage would have just been a front. Apparently, there have been rumors about him for a while, so when his wife died, he quickly needed to find someone new so the gossiping would stop."

"And my Barbara was supposed to be that new wife." Kuisl's eyes narrowed. "That . . . that dirty bastard."

Simon was about to reply when the door opened.

"Sorry to disturb," Walburga said, carrying a steaming cup that smelled delicious to Simon. Despite their desperate situation, he couldn't help but smile. "You really made coffee. Thank you so much, that's much appreciated."

Walburga shrugged. "If only I could heal Eva with coffee. But I'm afraid it'll take more than that. At least she seems to sleep quite peacefully now. I better stay with her for a while longer."

She closed the door behind her and Simon took a long drink. The coffee was excellent. Perhaps a tad bitter, but he was hardly going to ask for expensive sugar in a hangman's house. The brew helped him digest the news he'd just heard.

"At the end of the day, Näher is a poor wretch," Georg continued. "He has two lives, a real one and a false one. And when he's unlucky, the two of them mix. When he was in Sendling with Barbara, he ran into a former lover of his who threatened to tell on him. Näher had to pay him a large sum, and he couldn't be sure if the other man would ask for more. He was going to leave town at first, but then he stopped by a certain Munich bathhouse. He got hopelessly drunk and stayed longer than he'd planned."

"And how do you know all this?" Simon asked. He could already feel the revitalizing effect of the coffee spreading through his body as his exhaustion disappeared.

"Because I found him in that bathhouse, damn it, and he told me," Georg replied bitterly. "There's a password that gets you into the chamber where men in bathtubs . . ." He shook himself. "It was awful."

"We shouldn't judge those men," Simon said. "God created everyone in their own way. I read somewhere that it wasn't uncommon in ancient Greece for men to love men."

"Well, these days it's punished by death," Kuisl growled. "Sodomites are burned or boiled in oil. It's understandable that

Näher needed to cover himself, but I can't forgive him for wanting to use my daughter."

"Where is he now?" Michael Deibler asked.

"He left town. I just couldn't bring myself to hand him in. He's not a bad fellow—I feel kind of sorry for him." Georg looked at the others. "By the way, Näher isn't the only hangman who has skipped town. Widmann's gone back to Nuremberg, and the others are leaving tomorrow at the latest. Uncle Bartholomäus is going to return to Bamberg in the morning, too, and he'll want me to come." His expression grew even darker, and he raised his mug to his lips again.

"Now stop drowning in self-pity," Kuisl said, taking the mug from his son's hand. "We need clear heads if we want to find Magdalena. Provided she's still alive . . . ," he added glumly.

Georg shook his head. "Magdalena isn't dead. I'd feel it. She was always like a mother to Barbara and me."

"I don't think she's dead either," Simon said. "But we have no idea where she might be. And we can't get into the manufactory."

"Eva would know," Georg replied thoughtfully. "Are you sure she can't talk?"

"She'd have to wake up first," Kuisl said. "And that—"

He stopped when Walburga burst into the room again. She was very agitated, her wide chest heaved as she tried to compose herself.

"Eva!" she called out. "I . . . I think she's waking up."

The meeting between the Anger Wolves and the Au Dogs took place at eight in the evening.

The bells of nearby St. Mary's Church tolled loudly as the members of both gangs assembled. Peter tried not to let his nerves show, but it was difficult in view of the tall dirty lads staring at him from partly pockmarked, partly blood-encrusted faces like he was a rare, delicate insect they could easily squash between two fingers. Peter had to agree with Moser: the Au Dogs really did look scary, even though most were no older than twelve.

Seppi had arranged the meeting at the overgrown garden of the Paulaner monastery east of Au. The garden used to belong to a castle, but now it was part of the Paulaner monks' property, and apparently they were better brewers than gardeners.

The monastery garden was a veritable maze of overgrown hedges and bushes. The once neatly maintained gravel paths were covered in mud and ice, and the wall had collapsed in many places, making it easy for the boys to get in.

Peter had considered calling in at the executioner's house before the meeting, since they hadn't been back all day. But Paul convinced him that their mother wouldn't let them go out again once they returned. Paul had a good nose for parental reactions.

To the Au Dogs, the Paulaner garden was a second home. Here, just a stone's throw away from the taverns of Au, they met to play, to fight, to punish traitors, or share loot. Torches lit up a rotten pavilion that probably used to be surrounded by roses. The two gang leaders sat in the center, Schorsch and a strong-looking lad of about fourteen whom everyone called Luki. Despite his young age, a long scar ran across his face, and the story went that a wagon driver from Haidhausen had given it to him. Apparently — people whispered on the quiet — the driver was found in a ditch with his throat cut the next day.

Schorsch had asked Peter to sit beside him so he could explain his plan to the Au boys. The rest of the children sat stony-faced behind their respective leaders. All in all, there were about thirty boys.

A proper army, Peter thought. *With slingshots instead of muskets and sticks instead of swords.*

"And you really think the prince's dog is inside the manufactory?" Luki growled, sounding like a hoarse mutt himself.

Peter nodded. He tried to sound calm but wasn't entirely successful. "Someone called van Uffele stole the dog in order to extort money from the electoral family," he told them. "We're reasonably certain he's got the dog locked up in there somewhere."

"We're reasonably certain . . ." Luki grinned and winked at Schorsch. "Where did you find this one? In church? The fellow sounds like a goddammned Jesuit."

"He's the grandson of the Schongau executioner," Schorsch replied succinctly. "His grandfather wields the sword like no other."

Loud murmuring broke out among the Au Dogs and some nodded respectfully. It was one of the few times Peter was proud of his heritage. He turned to Paul, who sat a few paces behind him, jutting out his chin with confidence. His knife gleamed in the light from the torches.

"And what makes you think we'd help you get into the manufactory?" Luki asked after a while. "There may be peace between the Anger Wolves and the Au Dogs—unlike with the Giesing Bastards or the Haidhausen Scoundrels—but that doesn't mean we wipe your asses."

"If we find the dog, we'll get richly rewarded," Schorsch explained. "We'd divide it evenly between the two gangs. And there's much to be gotten at the manufactory, silk especially. You can take it all—we just want our share of the reward."

Peter had made the suggestion to the Anger Wolves earlier on. They hadn't liked it at first, but Peter had convinced them that they needed to have something to offer the Au Dogs.

Luki clearly liked the idea. He nodded slowly, as though he was thinking hard, but Peter had a feeling Luki's strength lay in his fists rather than his brains.

"How do you propose to hand the dog back to the prince and cash in the reward?" a haggard boy asked from the second row. "Even if it is the right dog, the guards are never going to let you into the Residenz."

The other boys grumbled and talked quietly among themselves, while Luki shot the boy who had asked an angry glance.
Apparently, it wasn't customary for anyone but the leader to
speak at a meeting of the Au Dogs. But eventually Luki nodded,
just as if it had been his idea. "Yes, how are you going to do that,
huh? You didn't think that far, did you?"

"I can get into the Residenz," Peter said. "Trust me."

"He knows the prince," Paul called out and looked around triumphantly. "My brother knows the prince."

"Son of an executioner and pet of a prince." Luki grinned and
tapped on Peter's narrow chest. "Either you're brilliant or nothing but a liar and a braggart. I think you're the latter. If I'm right,
I'm really going to enjoy turning your pretty little face to pulp."

Peter swallowed and didn't reply. He had no doubt Luki
would be true to his word. And he didn't feel right about having
stood Max up today. He was supposed to accompany the prince
to that strange masquerade. He'd promised. Instead he was
meeting up with a bunch of cutthroats in an overgrown garden.
But it was about Arthur. If he could give Max back his beloved
lapdog in the morning, the prince was bound to forgive him.

Luki narrowed his eyes. "All right," he said finally, making
his voice sound as benevolent as that of a priest at confession.
"You can count on the help of the Au Dogs." He cracked his
knuckles while sizing up Schorsch. "But let me tell you one
thing: if we find out you're leading us on, that there's no dog at
the manufactory at all and you told us a load of rubbish, it's war
between the Anger Quarter and Au. Is that clear?"

"As clear as the electress's piss." Schorsch nodded. He glanced
at Peter, who realized how great the responsibility on his shoulders was. If his plan failed, blood would flow—and not just his
own.

"Shake on it, then." Luki drew his knife, ran the blade across
the palm of his hand until it bled, and Schorsch did the same.
The two leaders pressed their hands together, staring each other

down as if they were going to pounce like a pair of rabid dogs. Neither wanted to avert their eyes. Luki gave a sudden laugh and brought his hand down hard on Schorsch's shoulder.

"You Anger Wolves are cut from tough cloth, not like the Hacken kids, those girlish wimps. Or those Giesing Bastards. It's good to do business with you."

"So what do you propose?" Schorsch asked. "Do you know how to get into the manufactory?"

Luki laughed again and turned to look at his boys. "Hey, Dogs! He's asking if we know how to get into the manufactory. What do you reckon? Should we tell them?"

The others laughed and hooted until Luki signaled them to be quiet.

"Now listen carefully, Anger lads," he began. He winked at Peter. "And I hope your little prince's pet brought his rosewater, because what I'm about to tell you reeks to the high heavens."

"The girl opened her eyes and mumbled something," Walburga said, still standing in the middle of the living room. She wore a dirt- and bloodstained apron and held a strip of linen in one hand. "I just finished washing her and was about to put fresh bandages on when she spoke."

Simon jumped to his feet and ran into the apothecary's chamber next door, where Eva still lay on the bed. She looked just as pale as before, her eyes still closed. But her face was clean, the blood was washed off, and her hands were bandaged. Simon gently touched Eva's shoulder and leaned down to her. He smelled alcohol and herbs. Walburga probably gave the girl one of her legendary tinctures.

"Eva?" he said softly. "Can you hear me?" When she didn't answer, he shook her by the shoulder. "Eva, can you hear me? We want to help you, you're safe. Do you know where Magdalena is?"

"If you keep shaking her like that, you'll break her neck," Jakob Kuisl grumbled from behind him. The others had come into the chamber, too.

"Hmm. Looks like she's fast asleep," Georg said, clearly disappointed. He turned to Walburga. "And you're sure she said something?"

"I might be old but I'm not deaf," Walburga replied. "She spoke. And she opened her eyes for a moment, too. But she must have lost consciousness again immediately."

"Damn!" Simon swore. "And I really hoped she'd be able to tell us something about Magdalena or the murderer."

"I . . . I think she mentioned your wife's name," Walburga said thoughtfully. "It was only a few words, but . . ."

"For heaven's sake, woman, speak up," Jakob Kuisl implored. "What did she say?"

Walburga tried to concentrate. "I believe one of the words was Magdalena. And then another word, which didn't really fit with it." The hangman's wife frowned. "It sounded like . . . ball. She said it over and over and squeezed my hand. Ball, ball, ball . . ."

"Nothing useful, anyhow." Georg shrugged. "Perhaps she's dreaming she's a child again and playing with a ball, or—"

"Ball!" Simon shouted suddenly. "Of course! A ball."

Deibler gave him an astonished look. "Now he's starting, too. Seems to be contagious. Maybe it's that strange coffee brew—"

"A ball," Simon cut him off excitedly. "Don't you understand? It must be some kind of feast, a ball, here in Munich. Eva is trying to tell us that Magdalena is at that ball."

"But . . . but that doesn't make any sense," Georg said. "Why would Magdalena be at a ball?"

"Because they're using my daughter as a goddamned whore." Jakob Kuisl had spoken quietly, but everyone turned to look at him. The hangman ground his teeth.

"I hate to admit it, but my son-in-law is right. We should have listened more closely. Van Uffele hires out girls as prostitutes. Not just to the houses of the high and mighty, but also for balls and festivities. I'm guessing the girls get slightly sedated, with poppy syrup or devil's trumpet or something similar. Or they get them drunk if they don't do as they're told. And then men use them as they please. It's possible Magdalena has been taken to a party like that."

"Is there a ball somewhere in Munich tonight?" Simon asked Michael Deibler, but he seemed lost in thought again and didn't reply. Simon nervously turned to Walburga. "Have you heard anything?"

"Hmm. The envoy from earlier was talking about a ball," Walburga replied. "Maybe that's what everyone at the market was talking about today. Apparently they're celebrating the completion of that new palace outside the city. The electress herself is going to be there, she asked her husband to build the place for her, after all, and she gave it its fairy-tale name."

"And what's this palace called?" Simon asked with growing impatience.

"The electress named it Nymphenburg Palace, after nymphs, the mythical creatures that haunt forests and streams. They say everyone attending tonight is dressing up—there will be nymphs, fauns, satyrs, elves." Walburga shook her head. "Everyone wears masks and costumes, just like carnival. And the likes of us have to try to make it through winter somehow."

"Masks and costumes?" Simon thought frantically. There must be a solution, there always was one. If he wanted to save Magdalena, he had to think of something right now. Time was running out.

Masks and costumes . . .

A thin smile spread across Simon's face. He turned to Walburga.

"How long would it take you to alter a few costumes?"

The lights were everywhere, twinkling above and below her. Barbara pulled her woolen scarf tighter and watched the tiny dots that spread around them. At the edge of a large circle they merged with the blackness of night. She felt like she was on the roof of the world.

"Do you like it?" Valentin took a step closer and placed one arm around her shoulders. Unlike every other time a man had touched her in the last few years, Barbara didn't wince.

"It's . . . it's beautiful," she breathed.

Valentin laughed. "I told you I'd take you to a special place. We just can't forget to keep an eye out for fires, or Gustl won't let me up here again."

They stood at the top of the tower of Old Peter, almost fifty paces above the rooftops of Munich. Valentin was friends with the watchman, who kindly let them enjoy the view for a little while. A pan with glowing embers in the center of the watchman's aerie exuded a little heat, but the night was freezing nonetheless, with an icy northerly wind howling around the tower.

They had already been up here that afternoon, when Valentin had led Barbara away from the jugglers' show at Anger Square. The view had been spectacular in the daytime as well, with the snow-covered mountains so close Barbara felt she could almost touch them. Now, at night, the stars sparkled above them and the lights of the city below, candles in the houses of patricians, open fires in the taverns, and lanterns of night watchmen making their rounds in their respective quarters. Behind the city walls, the surrounding countryside was completely dark. Munich was like a glittering island in a sea of black.

In that moment, Barbara understood all those poor young men and women who were drawn to Munich by the hope of finding work in a city that promised glamour, freedom, and new beginnings, one that was very different from all the stinking, dingy backwaters surrounding it. Backwaters like Schongau.

In the last few hours, Valentin had shown her this glamorous side of Munich. They had meandered down Neuhauser Street, past the better taverns of town, past churches and monasteries; they had admired the electoral Residenz and also the new fortifications, surrounding the city in the shape of a star. Valentin had shown her hidden gardens and palaces, men with powdered wigs and women with fancy muffs and fur coats, and explained to her how Electress Henriette Adelaide was responsible for Munich's blossoming culture.

With his warm and kind ways, Valentin had once again managed to help Barbara forget her worries for a while. Not once had he pressed her or steered the conversation in a certain direction. But now she sensed the moment had come to tell him everything. About Conrad Näher, the marriage her father demanded, but most of all about the child she carried in her belly and didn't want. So far, she had only really spoken to Magdalena about it. She felt that she needed to open up to someone else if she didn't want to burst with fear and sorrow.

"After Frauenkirche, Old Peter is the second-highest point in Munich," Valentin explained, leaning closer, and she could smell his cold sweat. She didn't mind it—on the contrary, it was beguiling.

"You could probably tell by the countless steps we had to climb," he continued. "From up here, the watchman looks out for fires. But his first task is to ring the bells." He pointed at the bells behind them, hanging on a massive beam in order of their size. Some of them looked like they weighed over a thousand pounds.

"We should go back down before the next ringing," Valentin said with a smile. "People have gone deaf up here when the eleven o'clock bells toll."

"I like the smallest one, right at the back," Barbara said and pointed at a tiny bell in the corner. "When do they ring that one?"

Valentin's expression turned serious. "That's the poor sinner's bell. The watchman only rings it when there's an execution. It announces someone's final hour. But I'm sure you know the custom from your father."

Barbara didn't say anything. She wondered how many more times she'd hear the ringing of a poor sinner's bell in her life.

Every time my future husband walks to the scaffold with his sword. Is there no way out?

If she confided in Valentin now and told him about the pregnancy, it would almost be the same as standing naked in front of him. There would be no way back. How would he react? Would he take his arm off her shoulder and view her differently? Barbara knew: once the words were out, they'd be like a wall between them, forever and ever.

"When . . . when I told you my father and our family came to Munich for the guild meeting, it was only half of the truth," she said after a while. "I had to accompany them for a very specific reason . . ." She faltered, but when Valentin gave her a questioning look, she gathered all her courage and went on: "I'm supposed to marry one of the hangmen from the council, Conrad Näher, the man you saw in Sendling. He isn't my uncle, he's my fiancé—at least if my father has his way."

"But you don't want to?" Valentin asked gently.

Barbara gave a desperate laugh. "Since when do we womenfolk get a say? My father promised I could refuse—but the disgrace would be irrevocable."

"Just because you didn't get married?" Valentin looked at her in disbelief.

"No, damn it! Because . . . because I'm pregnant and the bloody scoundrel of a father is over the hills and far away."

Barbara wished the bells would chime loud enough to erase everything inside her, but the words kept pouring out of her mouth. "Yes, I'm pregnant. And if I give birth to the child without a husband, I'll be put in the stocks or worse. And my father is the hangman who's supposed to carry out the punishments. Do you know what that means? He'll refuse, and . . . we'll get chased out of town. All of us. My innocent young nephews, my niece, everyone." She cried, and Valentin placed his arm around her shoulders again.

"Does your father know about the baby?" he asked.

Barbara shook her head, sniveling. "Only my sister and brother know. If . . . if Father finds out . . ." She paused. "You don't know him. He's a kind man normally, but when he gets angry . . ."

"The sun goes down in the middle of the day," Valentin finished the sentence for her. He smiled. "I think I've got a fair idea of your father by now. But I still think he'll forgive you."

"But that's beside the point," Barbara said. "The point is that I don't want the child in my belly. I know it's a sin. But it was made with force, not love. Every time I think of it, every time I touch my body I feel nothing but disgust. And I'm ashamed. By God, I know I'll burn in hell for it, for many thousands of years. I'm ashamed of my thoughts, but I can't help them."

Crying, she collapsed. It was out. The feeling that had increasingly taken over her mind and body in the last few days, this hatred of the thing growing inside her, she hadn't even confessed to Magdalena. Her older sister might have an idea of how she felt, but Barbara had not told her. Nonetheless, she stood alone with her guilt. No one could help her.

Not even Valentin.

For a while, the only sound was the howling of the wind sweeping around the tower. Then Valentin suddenly asked into the silence: "How far?"

Barbara gave him a confused look and wiped the tears from her cheeks. "What do you mean, 'how far'?"

"How far along are you?"

She shrugged. "Over three months. Too long to do anything

about it, anyhow. Not without the risk of dying in the process. It's too late."

Valentin thought. "There might be a way," he said eventually. "But you must really want it. Do you want it?"

A spark of hope flared up inside Barbara. "Believe me, if there's any way I can undo all this, I'll try it. I'm not afraid." She gave him a determined look. "What are you thinking?"

13

UNDER COVER OF DARKNESS, three men rode through the forest west of Munich. Wrapped in heavy coats against the cold, they bent low over the necks of their mounts. Two of them were broad-shouldered and tall, the third one delicate and short. The last kept cursing and swearing and seemed to be highly uncomfortable in the saddle. At a closer look, an observer would notice that he didn't even have a saddle—and the animal he rode was no horse.

"I really don't understand why I have to ride Deibler's donkey," Simon complained. "The darned animal bucks and bites. A hangman could deal with it much better."

"At least if you fall off the ass you won't break your neck," Jakob Kuisl said, unable to suppress a thin smile. "Falling off mine would be like falling from a church tower."

Kuisl was riding a solid draft horse that stood more than five feet tall; it usually pulled carts laden with beer barrels. A friend of Michael Deibler's had loaned them the gentle but very slow horse without asking too many questions. Georg rode a skinny old mare that belonged to the Anger knacker. The scrawny gray looked like it was nothing but skin and bones and might collapse at any moment under the hangman's son's weight. But they hadn't been able to find any other mounts in a hurry, and Nymphenburg Palace was too far away to walk. It was late enough already.

"Three oh-so-terrible riders of the apocalypse," Georg jeered. "If we'd brought Deibler along, the four bringers of ill fortune would have been complete."

"Deibler is holding the fort at home in case there's any news," Kuisl said. "And the murders really seem to have hit him hard. He's not the same. He'd only have been in the way on this mad undertaking of ours."

Kuisl still wasn't sure what to think of his son-in-law's ludicrous plan. Simon had remembered that the boys had been playing with masks and costumes at the executioner's house. In the last hour, Walburga had rummaged through the attic and found a few suitable garments. There hadn't been enough time for proper alterations, but at least she'd found old carnival masks in another chest; their former owners had probably rotted away in their graves a long time ago.

Kuisl hadn't even taken a proper look at their costumes yet. The whole thing was just too ridiculous. But he couldn't think of a better plan either. If Magdalena really was at the masquerade at Nymphenburg Palace, they had no choice but to dress up. They weren't invited, not he and Georg, at least. Kuisl doubted executioners would ever be invited to balls at court.

They rode along a narrow forest track that ran parallel to a new wide avenue leading to the palace. Apparently the plan was to clear the woodland on both sides of the avenue to give the electress an unobstructed view of Munich. Simon had also heard that the new palace wasn't finished yet, but enough of it had been built to hold balls and other festivities.

Kuisl felt sick at the thought of Magdalena being at the mercy of some rogues from court right at this moment. But at least that would also mean that she wasn't dead or seriously injured. Why else would van Uffele and Joseffa go to the trouble of taking her to the palace? But what if Walburga had misheard Eva's mumbled words and Magdalena wasn't at Nymphenburg Palace at all, but somewhere else? And if she was at the ball, how were they supposed to find her among all the masked people?

Meanwhile, they had left the forest behind and were crossing a snow-covered field, at the end of which they saw a brightly lit building several stories tall. On the left were outlines of other houses; on the right stood a small church. And in between, tiny dots of light danced like will-o'-the-wisps and Kuisl heard soft music.

"Nymphenburg Palace," Simon said, while his donkey jumped and veered to the right. "I think we've arrived."

"I'll never understand those courtiers," Georg said, shivering. "Why in God's name would anyone dance around in this cold dressed like a fool when they could be at home by the stove?"

"I think the ball will mainly be held inside," Simon replied. "And the nobility is grateful for any kind of distraction. If you don't have to work, life can get very boring."

"Let's quit talking and go inside to look for Magdalena." Kuisl kicked his horse's sides, and it broke into a reluctant trot. The others followed.

The avenue ended at a newly built wooden fence guarded by several soldiers. The music sounded much closer now. Kuisl could make out the sounds of violins and trumpets mixed with the laughter of many guests. Several carriages with gleaming black and white horses stood nearby, even two sleds padded with furs were parked in the flickering torchlight. A group of masked ball guests was just alighting from one of the sleds and were led toward the great building by the guards.

"What now?" Georg asked his brother-in-law. "What's your plan? We put our costumes on and introduce ourselves as the Barons of Thunderfist?"

"We must avoid talking at all cost," Simon said, ignoring

Georg's mocking tone. "Or we'll get tangled up in lies. And we don't have an invitation. I was supposed to attend with Peter, but he didn't come home." He pointed to the right, where the small church bordered directly on the forest. "We should make use of the fact that the walls haven't been completed yet. We'll just walk around to the back."

"And if they've put up guards there, too?" Georg asked.

"Then tough luck for the guards," Kuisl growled. "And now let's go before my horse freezes to the spot."

Out of view of the guards, they rode around the large building and the church, and were soon back in dense forest. They tied the horses and the donkey to trees and Simon opened the sack with the costumes that had been tied to the back of Kuisl's saddle. The medicus reached for a black robe and an equally black hangman's hood and handed it to his father-in-law.

Kuisl couldn't believe his eyes.

"I'm going as a *hangman?*" he asked incredulously and stared at the hood. "Are you serious?"

"Well," Simon replied, "I heard courtiers like to dress up as commoners. Shepherds, tavernkeepers, butlers . . ."

"And hangmen?"

"I couldn't whip up a nymph costume for you in a hurry," Simon said tersely. "To be honest, I'm just glad Walburga found something in your size at all."

Kuisl accepted his costume without another word, while Simon handed Georg a coat made of colorful patches of cloth and a black eye mask. "You're a harlequin," Simon explained.

Georg frowned. "A what?"

Simon sighed. "A kind of Italian buffoon. You can't really go wrong. Just jump in the air from time to time and move as awkwardly as you can. I'm sure you'll be fine. And the advantage of the harlequin disguise is that you can go armed." He handed Georg a short, wide wooden sword that looked more like a plank. "This is the harlequin's weapon."

"Great," Georg groaned and waved the sword through the air. "When it comes down to it, I can at least swat some flies." Curious, he watched Simon pull the last costume from the sack. "And what will you be going as?"

"Er, I'm the dottore," Simon replied. "That's Italian for doctor. I thought it was appropriate for me. Also, both the harlequin and the dottore are popular disguises at the carnival and don't require much effort. We should be fairly inconspicuous."

Simon's costume consisted of a black coat, a white ruff collar, and a mask with a bulbous nose and bulging forehead. When he tied it on, Georg took an involuntary step back. "*Brr!* You look more like the devil to me!"

"Some doctors are nothing but devils," Simon replied in a nasal voice, pushing the mask into place. "And now let's hurry before the guards find us here."

Visibly uncomfortable, Georg and Jakob Kuisl put on their costumes. Then they stepped out of the cover of the forest together and walked toward the palace from the rear.

Suddenly, the hangman paused.

In front of them, a clearing surrounded by Greek statues was bathed in the flickering, eerie light of several large fires. Countless candles in tiny boats floated on a pond, torches in the snow guided the way through the grounds. Farther back, a park had been partially landscaped but looked unfinished with its overgrown groves of trees and shapeless bushes.

Between the fires pranced the strangest creatures Kuisl had ever seen. There were forest sprites wrapped in green garments and wearing masks of tree bark, fauns with horns and tails, and amazons in gleaming armor. There were moors with black masks of ebony, Saracens with tin sabers, red-haired gypsies, Roman soldiers, and three Chinese emperors. The creatures laughed and chatted while footmen with serious faces served wine in paper-thin blue glasses.

Jakob Kuisl was completely dumbstruck.

"My God," he said eventually. "Has everyone here gone insane?"

Kuisl's idea of carnival consisted of a handful of journeymen roaming the streets in fools' costumes and drinking plenty of beer along the way. In the twelve nights after Christmas, people in Bavarian villages wore devil masks and joined processions to banish winter. But this was like a disturbing dream in which noblemen acted like animals and children at the same time, spending a heap of money in the process.

"How are we ever supposed to find Magdalena in this madhouse?" asked Georg, just as stunned as his father. "What if she's also in disguise? She could be anywhere."

"We must at least try," Simon replied. "If Walburga heard correctly, my wife is here somewhere. And by God, I'm going to find her." He rearranged his mask, raised his chin, and strutted toward the palace with the confident posture of the courtiers.

As Jakob Kuisl followed him cautiously, he realized that they indeed blended in rather well. The handful of guards positioned in the garden were visibly cold and gave them no more than a tired glance. The masquerade guests didn't pay them any particular attention either. Kuisl thought about how often people looked askance at him, the hangman, just because he wanted to drink a beer at the tavern. But here he was nothing but one fool among many.

His initial anxiety evaporated with every step, and he became increasingly bold. He helped himself to one of the small blue glasses from the tray of a passing footman, walked past two French-speaking moors, raised his drink to a Greek philosopher whose teeth chattered in his thin toga, and eventually followed Simon and Georg up a wide flight of stairs that led into the palace from two sides. No one stopped them.

The stairs led them up to the second floor, and the sight in front of them took Kuisl's breath away.

He was standing inside the biggest hall he'd ever seen. The

ceiling was dizzyingly high, and the lights of countless chandeliers reflected in the polished marble floor. Over a hundred masked guests crowded the room like exotic animals in an enormous menagerie. On the opposite side, around two dozen musicians played atop a stage, among them violinists, flutists, and a dainty harpist, together with an older man with a wig who was bent over a wooden crate, punching some sort of keys.

"That's the electress's concertmaster," Simon said in a low voice. "A certain Johann Caspar von Kerll. I saw him at the opera. Apparently, he's the best conductor in all of Europe."

"If he's the best, I don't want to know what the others sound like," Kuisl replied. "If you played like that in Schongau I'd put you in the stocks."

The piece of music was indeed a little strange. It sounded very slow and solemn, almost like a funeral march. The ball guests performed a kind of processional dance, in which Venetians, Muscovites, nymphs, Arabs, and tree sprites held each other's hands and twisted and turned in complicated ways.

"If this is how they dance at court, I'm glad for our simple folk dances at the tavern," Georg murmured behind his mask. "What a ridiculous mummery."

"How about Georg and I take a look through any nearby chambers," Kuisl whispered. "If whores are part of this feast, they'll probably be somewhere more private. My son-in-law can keep his eye on the dance floor."

"All right." Simon nodded. "And remember, Magdalena may be sedated or not entirely herself. Take a close look at every girl."

The two Kuisls walked through a side portal while Simon mingled with the crowd. The other ball guests readily made way for the hangman and the harlequin, and Jakob Kuisl especially was met with respectful glances. The music, the flickering torches, and the bizarre costumes made Kuisl feel more and more like he was dreaming. Any moment he expected someone to shake him awake.

Several smaller halls branched off the stucco-walled corridor. In the light of more sparkling chandeliers, Kuisl saw his own reflection multiplied by countless mirrors on the walls, as if the world was full of executioners. Giggling couples lolled on divans and furs, most of them masked shepherdesses and shepherds or farmer's wives and farmers in plain garb that was much too clean, feeding each other sweets. Kuisl ran his eyes over each couple. When he passed yet another shepherd couple, the fur-clad courtier grinned and winked at him. The young woman at his side seemed very drunk. Her almost naked body was covered with blankets, and a mass of hair flowed out from under her mask.

Black hair, like Magdalena's.

"I swear, my compliments on your costume," the shepherd called out to Kuisl with a laugh. "I haven't seen anything like it in all my years. Who are you going to drag up the scaffold tonight, Herr Hangman? The electress? Or a pretty wench you'd like to marry?"

"You, if you don't shut up," Kuisl said, too softly for the other man to hear. Instead, he took a step toward the couple, leaned down, and lifted the girl's mask in one swift movement.

Drunk eyes stared at him. The girl was heavily made up, very young, and definitely not Magdalena.

"Hey, what do you think you're doing?" the courtier flared up. "This is my playmate. Go find your own."

"Forgive me, I thought it was mine," Kuisl grumbled and quickly walked off. He would have liked to beat the fellow to a pulp, but he doubted that was permitted at the elector's masquerade. This feast repulsed him more and more.

He crossed the room as fast as he could, scanning the other masked women from the corner of his eye. None looked even remotely like Magdalena. He was no luckier in the next room. He began to doubt they were even in the right place.

Walburga must have been mistaken.

Jakob Kuisl and Georg were about to go into another room when Simon came toward them, visibly agitated.

"I saw Pfundner," he hissed. "You know, the Munich treasurer Magdalena worked for. He's wearing a Pantaloon costume, but I'm sure it's him. We must find out what he's up to."

"Do you mean he's our kidnapper?" Georg asked. "Or even the murderer?"

"Maybe," Simon replied with a shrug. "Or at least he's got something to do with it. I'm sure of it. Remember what Magdalena told us after she eavesdropped on Pfundner and the other man? They were talking about a ball. Those two are up to something. It's no coincidence that he's here tonight."

The three of them rushed back down the corridor to one of the side portals overlooking the dance floor. Simon furtively pointed at a man in a red waistcoat and red tights. A bulging purse dangled out from under his black coat, and his long fake beard hung crooked on his face. He stood a little to the side of the dance floor, talking to a bald Roman soldier.

"That might be the man Pfundner met two days ago," Simon guessed. "We must find out what they—"

"Where is Peter?"

Simon winced at the sound of the high boyish voice behind them. Jakob Kuisl turned around and saw a boy of about ten years in front of them. Instead of a shirt and waistcoat, he only wore a fur and held panpipes in one hand. Evidently, he was supposed to be some shepherd boy from Greek mythology.

"Where is Peter?" the boy asked again.

Simon groaned. "Your ... Your Electoral Highness ..." he stammered. "I, er ... I'm so sorry ..." He struggled for words.

When Kuisl saw the fury in the boy's eyes, he knew they had a problem.

"We're supposed to go down *there*?"

Disgusted, Schorsch stared down into the hole that stank like the devil's arse. Peter was feeling sick from the smell, and he struggled to breathe through his nose. Together with Luki, they stood in a small shack that leaned against a paper mill right by Au creek. The tiny den appeared to be the miller's outhouse. A wooden beam served as the seat across a feces-smeared hole in the ground about as wide as a man's hips. Luki grinned as though this hole was the best joke in the world.

"This is most likely the only way to get into the manufactory unnoticed," he explained. "We've only known about it for a few weeks ourselves. One of our boys dropped his knife down there while he was you know what, and he wanted it back, so he gritted his teeth and climbed down. The shaft ends in an underground stream. My grandpa once told me that there used to be many streams in Au, but most of them were buried or diverted when more and more houses were built."

"And you think this stream runs underneath the manufactory?" Peter asked, revolted by the thought of climbing down into the hole.

"Well, it flows into the right direction, and the manufactory is only a stone's throw away from the mill."

"And why didn't you try it yourself?" Schorsch asked. "There's much to be had, isn't there?"

"Well, um . . . ," Luki began uncertainly. "The boy who fetched his knife reckoned it was pretty spooky down there. He heard this scary whining . . ."

"Just like my mother," Peter remembered excitedly. "She thinks it's a girl locked up in the basement. So you might be right, the stream does lead to the manufactory."

"But maybe it's a howling ghost," Schorsch jeered, looking at Luki. *"Boooo . . ."*

Luki swiftly grabbed Schorsch by the collar and pulled him close. "Are you trying to say I'm scared?" he asked. "You just wait, I'll throw you down this shithole, you filthy Anger —"

Peter tried to separate them. "No reason to fight," he said.

"We'll all climb down there together and find out where the stream leads. Together we're strong, we have nothing to fear."

"I don't fear anyone or anything, understood?" Luki snarled but let go of Schorsch. "But don't start thinking you can hide behind me down there," he growled at the leader of the Anger Wolves. "The two of us will lead the way, is that clear?"

"Clear." Schorsch nodded. "And how do we get down there?"

"With a rope, of course, numbskull." Luki produced a coil of rope and tied one end around the beam over the hole. Then he whistled softly.

A good dozen boys scurried over to them from the creek. They had previously decided that only the bravest and fittest of each gang should come along. Seppi, Moser, and Paul were part of the party, although Paul had only been allowed to come after lengthy discussions. In the end, he had convinced the others by shooting the hat of an Au Dog clean off his head with his slingshot—at nighttime and twenty paces. The explosive mix of anger and determination in Paul's eyes had silenced the last doubters.

The end of the rope disappeared in the darkness, Luki handed out a few burning torches, then he climbed down into the stinking hole, his torch between his teeth. Peter could tell by Luki's eyes that he was afraid. But he wasn't going to be stupid and say anything—he might as well ram a knife into his own stomach.

Schorsch followed Luki, then two Au boys climbed down, and finally Peter. He held his breath and slowly slid down the rope.

The walls of the shaft were smeared in feces and so slippery that he struggled to find footholds. For a moment, a torch lit up the corridor about five paces below him, but it disappeared again. Where had the others gone? Even though Peter breathed through his mouth, the stench was so awful that he felt like vomiting. His eyes watered as he slid farther down the rope. Now he could hear a soft trickle below him. Peter imagined letting go of the rope and falling into a huge pile of shit—would it be up to his neck?

I only hope we find Arthur, he thought. *If I really get to go to school in Munich one day, all this trouble will have been worth it. I'll even crawl through poo and rubbish for that.*

When Peter finally reached the bottom, he found there wasn't nearly as much muck as he'd feared—probably thanks to the small stream he could hear flowing under his feet, washing away the excrement. Soon his feet were wet and cold. But that wasn't the worst.

The worst was that he was alone.

None of the other boys had yet started the descent after him, and he hadn't taken a torch, so everything around him was pitch-black. Repulsed, Peter felt his way to the left and right, touching slimy feces with his hands. Slowly he crouched down and finally saw light again. At the bottom of the shaft was a knee-high passage carved out of the hard rock. It went slightly downhill, and Peter could see torches flickering at the other end.

Peter was about to call out to the others but then decided against it. He didn't want them to think he was scared. Instead, he went down on his knees and crawled toward the lights, which kept moving farther away from him. Feces and dirt became less and less, and the smell was getting better, too, but now he heard squeaking and scurrying around him.

A moment later small, scratchy feet ran across his hands and piercing little red eyes glared at him from writhing black bodies. Peter winced.

Rats! Huge rats!

Ever since a rat had paid him a visit in bed one night and bitten him on the cheek, Peter was terrified of the beasts—especially when they were as large and fat as these. His father said rats carried diseases, but even if that wasn't true, they were disgusting, devilish creatures.

The boys in front of him must have seen the rats, too. Luki

was probably just waiting for him to scream out like a little girl, but he wasn't going to do him the favor. Instead, Peter continued to crawl toward the torches, which — thankfully — seemed to have stopped moving. The corridor widened until he could almost stand upright. Peter suspected this stream roared with water in springtime, but now it was nothing but a trickle.

Luki, Schorsch, and the others stood waiting at a particularly wide spot. Now the boys who had climbed down the shaft behind him started to arrive, too. They were covered in mud and feces, and they stank as if they'd climbed out of a pigpen. One of the boys vomited noisily into the stream.

"Did you meet the rats, too?" Luki maliciously asked Peter, who still looked rather pale. "I love it when they nibble on my feet. It tickles so nicely and—"

"Forget the rats and help me open this thing," Schorsch cut him off. He pointed to a rusty grate in the ceiling.

"And what makes you think this leads into the manufactory?" Luki asked, frowning.

"Probably the fact that he counted the steps from the mill to the manufactory earlier," Peter said quietly. "And then down here, too. It's called *math*."

Schorsch winked at Peter. During their talks at the monastery gardens, Peter had noticed that the leader of the Anger Wolves was smarter than he'd initially thought — smarter than most other street kids. Perhaps they'd end up proper friends in the end. Peter longed to be fully accepted as a friend by the Anger Wolves, as they had done with Paul. So far — he could tell — they merely respected him for his brains.

Luki was about to make a reply, but Schorsch slapped him on the shoulder.

"Kneel down," he said. Luki didn't seem to understand at first, but then he knelt down, glaring at Peter. But he was probably glad Schorsch would be the first to climb up.

Schorsch climbed on Luki's back and grabbed hold of the

grate. He tried to move it, bracing himself against it as hard as he could, but it wouldn't budge.

"Damn it!" he said. "It's locked. Hold the torch here."

Indeed, a heavy and quite new-looking lock hung on one side of the grate.

"Would have been too easy," Schorsch sighed. "Of course the basement of the manufactory is locked. We should have known." He jumped off Luki's back and shrugged his shoulders. "Any ideas?"

"I can get it open," Paul said, raising his little knife. "Grandpa showed me how to pick the shackles and locks in the dungeon. It's not hard."

"Shut it, ragamuffin." Luki growled. "The grownups are talking."

"He could at least try," said Seppi, who had joined the others. "He's pretty quick with his knife."

Luki rolled his eyes but didn't object, and Schorsch gave Paul a signal. Quick as a weasel the little boy climbed onto the shoulders of the Anger Wolves' leader, pulled out his knife, and went to work. The others held their breath in anticipation.

"Like I thought," Luki said after a while. "He can't do it. He's just a showoff like his brother."

"Give him time," Schorsch replied. "Or do you have a better idea?"

Luki didn't reply, a sullen look on his face.

All at once the lock clicked and Paul cheered triumphantly.

"Told you," he boasted. "I knew I could do it. Ha! I can pick any lock, I'm the best lock-picker in all of Bavaria!" He pushed against the grate and it squeaked open. "Please come in," he said with a grin, still lording it on Schorsch's shoulders like a little king. "Entry just one kreuzer per person . . ."

Moser shushed him suddenly. "Do you hear that?"

Peter and the others listened. And indeed, there it was!

A howl.

Loud and mournful, as if from the depths of hell.

"Jesus," Seppi whispered. "That sounds like someone who's been dead for a while."

Still struggling for words, Simon stood in front of the young prince, who asked his question for the third time. The coffee Walburga had brewed for Simon earlier must have been strong, because his heart was racing like crazy.

"Where is Peter?" Max Emanuel stamped his foot angrily. "He promised he would come. I sent a messenger. Why were my orders disregarded?"

Simon couldn't understand how the prince had recognized him so fast with his mask on. He looked down at himself and saw his snow- and mud-stained leather boots, which looked rather different from the polished shoes of the other guests. They were the same boots he had worn at the opera. Evidently, the prince was a keen observer. He had probably been looking for Simon and Peter for a while.

"Um . . . Peter couldn't come, unfortunately," Simon said. "He . . . he's inconsolable. But he's ill. A slight fever, he must stay in bed."

"Ill?" Max Emanuel eyed him suspiciously. "Then why don't you heal him? You're a doctor, aren't you?"

"Er, yes, sure. But he must stay in bed nonetheless." Simon put on a strained smile. "I'm sure he'll be better tomorrow."

Several guards came over now, presumably the prince's bodyguards. Simon groaned and gave Jakob Kuisl and Georg an inconspicuous signal to move away. The last thing they needed right now was attention. Kuisl immediately understood, and he and Georg mingled with the crowd—just in time, as Simon heard another familiar voice.

"May I ask what's going on here?"

The guards immediately stepped aside and bowed low at the cutting sound of the voice, and the electress herself appeared between them. She wore a Roman toga, and her hair was pinned up with so many dried flowers that she looked like a mountain meadow in summer. The quiver and bow slung over her shoulder told Simon that Henriette Adelaide was supposed to be the Roman goddess of the hunt, Diana. She held a fawn wearing a blue ribbon on a golden leash, and it peacefully nibbled on the wall damask.

Simon took off his mask and Henriette Adelaide recognized him right away. "Oh, the medicus from Schongau!" she called out, pleased. "So you did get the invitation in time. My son told me about his friendship with your son. I'm happy for Max to mingle with children from the simpler classes from time to time. It molds the character. I'm glad you could both make it." She looked around. "Where is the boy?"

"Er, as I was just telling your handsome son here," Simon replied, now on his knees with his head bowed. "He's ill, unfortunately. A fever, Your Excellency. Nothing serious, but I wanted him to stay in bed."

"Oh dear, the poor thing." Henriette Adelaide turned to Max and raised an admonishing finger. "There you go, that's what happens when you don't dress warmly enough in winter. I told you not to come wearing nothing but a fur."

"But *Maman*," he whinged, automatically switching to French. "*C'est injuste!* I must always spend hours in the dressing room. It's so much more comfortable just wearing a fur."

"Still," Henriette Adelaide said, shaking her head disapprovingly. "Even Pan's shepherd boys have more sense. At least put on a fox fur coat over the top. How many times have I told you . . ."

While the electress admonished her son, Simon desperately scanned the room for Daniel Pfundner and the bald-headed man. But they seemed to have vanished, just like Jakob Kuisl and Georg. This whole operation was getting out of control. Simon's forehead was damp with sweat and his heart was racing.

He needed to get away. But that was only possible if the electress dismissed him.

Meanwhile, a crowd of courtiers had gathered around Simon, Henriette, and Prince Max Emanuel. They whispered and put their heads together. Simon cursed softly. The electoral family attracted courtiers like raw meat attracted a cloud of blowflies.

Suddenly, everyone bowed even lower when a haggard man joined them. He was dressed as a shepherd, with plain woolen leggings, a tattered linen shirt, and a hat with carefully sewn-on patches. Despite the costume, Simon recognized his well-known, somewhat sheepish-looking face from the paintings.

The elector, Simon realized. *Just wonderful . . . I'm spared nothing today.*

Simon bowed until his forehead touched the cold marble floor. The electress's fawn happily licked his face.

"Your Highness," he stammered. "It is such an honor . . . "

"This is the doctor from Schongau I told you about, Ferdinand," Henriette Adelaide said to her husband. "You know, the one I asked to find the dog."

"What dog?" the elector asked with surprise.

"Arthur, of course. Your son's lapdog. How many times do I have to tell you that he's run away? Madonna! Where is your head, Ferdl?"

"Oh yes, of course, Arthur." Ferdinand Maria nodded and fumbled with his hat. "And, er . . . have you found it?" he asked Simon, who was still getting licked by the fawn. Finally, the animal stopped.

"I . . . have a good lead," Simon lied. "I have already been offered several dogs, but they all turned out to be . . . well, falsifications. Everyone wants to be the prince's dog. Ha-ha." He smiled cheerfully. "I'm sure I'll be able to tell you more in just a few days' time."

Once I've left this city for good.

Simon had completely lost sight of his dog mission. The devil knew if the mutt was even alive or if it had long since been turned to leather. He didn't care. It saddened Simon that all hope for a place at school in Munich was lost for his son, but something else was much more important right now—his wife's life.

Simon briefly considered using the opportunity to tell the electoral couple about Magdalena's disappearance, but he knew van Uffele had powerful friends at court, and Pfundner was an important man as the municipal treasurer. Who would believe a simple physician from Schongau?

"What a shame," the electress said, visibly disappointed. "I truly thought you would have found Arthur by now. Weren't you going to report back to me?"

"Well, unfortunately it isn't easy to get an audience with—"

"Peter is finding Arthur, not his father," Max Emanuel suddenly piped up. He had been standing next to his mother with a defiant look on his face. "You'll see."

"What did you say?" Henriette Adelaide asked with surprise. Simon gave Max an astonished look, too. The boy sounded very sure of himself.

"I know Peter is going to find my dog," Max insisted. "He's on the right track," he added mysteriously. "And he promised. And a friend keeps his promises." He played a few low notes on his pan pipes, then darted between the guards and disappeared in the crowd.

"I see, he promised." Henriette winked at Simon while fanning herself. "My son thinks very highly of yours. I hear the boy isn't silly." She smiled. "The apple doesn't fall far from the tree, right?"

"He is rather bright, that's true," Simon replied, seeing his chance. "That's why we've been thinking about sending him to another school—"

The electress cut him off with a gesture. "I'm afraid we'll have to continue our conversation some other time," she said with a shrug. "The roundup of the rams is about to begin in the park, and my husband and I have to be there as the first shepherd and the goddess of the hunt. I'm sure you understand. *Au revoir.*" She held out her hand to Simon, a diamond ring on each finger. Simon kissed one of the rings and kept his head down, still confused about Max's last statement about Peter.

He's on the right track . . .

Was that why Peter and Paul hadn't come home? Were they looking for that godforsaken mutt? Well, he didn't really have time to worry about that now. He needed to find Pfundner. And where had his father-in-law and Georg gone?

While the musicians struck up a folk tune and Moors, shepherds, Turks, and giggling peasants with powdered wigs assumed their positions for the dance, Simon hurried through the corridors and chambers of Nymphenburg Palace.

But no matter how hard he looked, he couldn't find Jakob Kuisl or Georg anywhere.

And he found no trace of Magdalena either.

"Crikey, that howling really gives me the creeps," Seppi whispered as he and the other boys stood in the stinking corridor below the silk manufactory.

Together they listened to the rising and falling of the mournful wailing. It seemed to come from far away and yet nearby at the same time. They only knew that it came from somewhere above them. The boys exchanged anxious looks.

Peter wondered whether it wouldn't have been better to tell their mother after all. But most likely she would have forbidden Peter from going to search for the prince's lapdog with his friends when he needed this success so badly. For Max, for his chance at a place at school in Munich, but also to impress the other boys and show them that he was more than a pale bookworm.

The howling started again. Peter felt fear creep up inside him. Fear, but also doubt.

"If we want to know what it is, we'll have to go and see, won't we?" Schorsch said into the silence and pulled himself up on the edges of the trapdoor.

"Hey, wait a minute! You're not going *in* there, are you?" Luki gasped, white as a sheet. "What . . . what if the basement is haunted? You know I never shy away from a fight, but a ghost . . ."

"Then just stay here with your boys," Schorsch said from above them, his torch illuminating his face. "The Anger Wolves won't be intimated by anything. We're afraid of nothing."

The Au Dogs looked expectantly at their leader, who was clearly wrestling with himself.

"To hell with it," Luki said eventually. "No one can say the Au Dogs chickened out." He jumped up and pulled himself through the hole in one swift movement. The other boys followed more hesitantly, helping both Peter and Paul climb up.

Once he was up, Peter saw that they were standing in a dark basement corridor with doors on either side. It smelled musty, but far better than downstairs. The howling had stopped for a while, but suddenly they heard it again. It seemed to come from farther back, where the corridor disappeared into the darkness.

"By God, that's not human," one of the Au Dogs groaned. "No mortal can make such sounds."

"Don't say that," said Paul, who seemed to be the only one not afraid at all. Or at least he didn't show it. "When Grandpa puts someone on the rack, they sometimes sound like that," he continued cheerfully. "Sometimes you can hear the screams on the street outside, even all the way to the Tanners' Quarter, where—"

"*Sh!*" Peter said. "Listen!"

Together with the others, he listened to the howling down the corridor. It sounded like a ghostly whimper, followed by a scratching and knocking as if someone were trying to dig their way through the wall.

Howling, scratching, knocking . . .

Peter's heart beat faster. Down in the sewer a suspicion had sprouted in his mind. Fear and exhaustion had prevented him from thinking straight earlier, but now he was almost certain: the boy was right.

No human could howl like this.

He took the torch from Moser, who was too surprised to object, and ran down the corridor without waiting for the others. The howling and scratching became louder.

"Hey, where are you going?" Schorsch called after him. "Watch out! We don't know what's down there. Wait for us!"

But Peter didn't reply. He kept going past several doors until he reached the end of the corridor. The last heavy door was merely secured by a bolt. Behind it, the scratching, whimpering, moaning, and howling sounded like a thousand furies. Without hesitation, Peter braced himself against the bolt, and it screeched across. The door opened.

And a black shadow leapt at him.

In the light of the torches in the park of Nymphenburg Palace, a hangman and a harlequin pursued a bald Roman and a man in a mask.

Jakob Kuisl squinted and tried to see more in the dim light. After Prince Max Emanuel had recognized Simon, he and Georg had disappeared as fast as they could. Kuisl realized that they only had a chance of finding Magdalena if they remained unrecognized. So he and his son had mingled with the other guests on the dance floor, and when they saw Daniel Pfundner and the bald-headed man leave the room, they had followed. Now they were back in the park behind the palace, where a flock of rams was being herded in the snow. The animals bleated anxiously and tried to break out, but the guards kept chasing them back. Each ram wore colorful ribbons, and some of them had wreaths of flowers tied around their horns. A crowd of masked guests surrounded them, laughing expectantly.

Jakob Kuisl had given up wondering about the strange customs of Munich courtiers. Evidently, the curiosities were just about to reach a new climax.

Damn these Munich fops, he thought.

All he wanted was to find his daughter — or at least find out what happened to her. And that dodgy Pfundner was their only lead right now.

Kuisl spotted Daniel Pfundner and the bald man dressed as a Roman on the other side of the heaving herd. The two men were about to sneak off into the adjacent woods. Kuisl frowned. Whatever those fellows were up to, it wasn't anything good. Why else would they leave this feast so stealthily? And not in the direction of Munich, but through the park to the west? Simon must have been right. The two of them were definitely up to something.

Kuisl tried to make his way around the flock of sheep, but the stupid rams ran from side to side, blocking his way every time. After several futile attempts at walking around the flock, the hangman muttered a curse and stormed right through the middle. Georg followed him, sending the animals into an even greater panic. Shouts of surprise rose from the crowd as the rams broke free, several of them running up the back stairs and right into the ballroom, where they appeared to cause great turmoil. The music stopped, women screamed. One ram with lowered horns chased a shrieking elderly lady.

The hangman was unperturbed. Like a reaper in a meadow, he ploughed through the bleating herd, kicking out of the way any ram that didn't jump aside quickly enough. Once he reached the other side, he pulled a torch out of the ground and rushed into the forest with Georg.

As soon as Jakob and Georg Kuisl were among the trees, the shouting, bleating, and turmoil behind them became much quieter. The glow of the fires in the park lit their way for a little while, but Kuisl still felt like they were entering another world

—one in which, unlike at the palace, nymphs, fairies, and forest sprites actually existed. Snow covered the trees and bushes like icing sugar. A deer flitted underneath a low-hanging branch, raising a white cloud. All sounds were strangely muffled, as if by thick fabric.

Father and son walked past a well, the moon reflected on its frozen surface. Three statues on the edge of the well seemed to watch their every movement, icicles hanging from their stone limbs. They appeared to be some sort of ancient gods whose powers had long gone.

Or had they? Kuisl thought. He looked around cautiously, half expecting an angry god to jump out of the bushes at any moment. Then he called himself a fool. That stupid masquerade was messing with his head.

"And now?" Georg whispered, looking around helplessly. "Where have they gone?"

Jakob Kuisl held the torch to the ground and pointed to prints in the snow. The two men hadn't tried to cover their tracks. Maybe they were in a hurry, but they probably didn't expect to be watched or followed. The hangman signaled to his son and together they followed the tracks.

The footprints led past the well, back into the forest, and not long thereafter ended at a clearing with an unfinished temple. Only the columns were still standing, reaching into the night sky like black fingers. A large hole had been dug out beside them, probably intended as a pond. On the other side of the pond, massive rocks formed a more-than-seven-foot-high hill.

The steps led directly toward it.

Kuisl followed the prints until he stood in front of the hill, where they ended abruptly. As though a meteorite had fallen from the sky and buried the men.

"What the devil . . . ," the hangman cursed.

Georg stopped beside him, just as astonished.

"They can't have vanished into thin air," he mumbled and leaned down to search the ground. He walked a few steps to the left and then to the right, but couldn't find anything.

Kuisl knelt down in the snow and held the torch close to the ground. The footprints definitely belonged to two men. On closer examination, Kuisl noticed the last print was only half visible, disappearing underneath a rock about the size of a door at the front of the hill. Kuisl frowned.

A door . . .

He pushed against the rock, and it gave way almost instantly, swinging open without a sound.

"What in God's name is that?" Georg asked, surprised.

"A proper nymph grotto." Kuisl grinned. "Let's go and see where our two pretty elves are hiding."

Now the hangman noticed that the hidden entrance wasn't made of rock but plaster that had been painted gray, just like the narrow corridor starting on the other side of the door. Stalactites hung from the ceiling like drooping tears. Kuisl broke a piece off one and crumbled it between his fingers.

"An artificial grotto," he muttered. "Probably for future masquerades. You'd almost think the nobility had nothing better to do than prance through the woods in costume jumping each other's bones."

Now they could hear groaning and the sound of something dragging on the ground from inside the mountain, together with the echoing voices of two men. There was a pungent stench in the air.

"I told you we should have gotten rid of the stuff yesterday, damn it," one of the voices hissed from below. "Now half of Munich's out there."

"No one saw us," the other one said reassuringly. "The carriage will be here soon, and then we're out of here. If we'd carted everything away last night, we would have ended up empty-handed. Now you're going to lead a very pleasant life with your share. Isn't that right?"

"Not if this life ends in a barrel of boiling oil. If I'm lucky, the hangman will gut me first. If not, I'll be cooked alive. I should never have agreed to this. What we're doing is worse than high treason."

The first man continued to curse under his breath, and Kuisl and Georg could hear clattering as if from metal. Then something crashed to the ground noisily.

"Watch out," the second man snapped. "If anyone hears us . . ."

Meanwhile, Jakob and Georg had crept down the corridor. The ground was slippery with ice, and a handful of steps led farther down. Now they saw the flickering of several torches or lanterns ahead, the noise grew louder, and the stench stronger. Kuisl struggled to suppress the urge to cough. The hangman stopped his son before a bend in the corridor.

"Let me go first," he whispered. "I'm older."

"That's exactly why I should—" Georg started, but his father's angry glare silenced him. Jakob Kuisl cautiously peered out from behind a plaster rock . . .

And froze.

"By all the saints!" he exclaimed quietly.

What the hangman saw was so strange that he forgot to breathe for a moment.

The shadow jumped at Peter—and licked his face.

Then the barking, yelping, and howling around him grew as loud as if he was surrounded by a pack of wolves. Hairy creatures shot past Peter and a foul-smelling cloud enveloped him, almost as bad as down in the sewage canal. He could hear the other boys call out behind him.

"Damn, where are all these dogs coming from all of a sudden?" Luki cursed. "Hey, Peter, what's happening down there?"

Peter didn't reply, although he knew by now what was going on. The terrible whimpering they and his mother had heard hadn't come from a person but from a whole bunch of locked-up dogs who were now looking for a way out. Peter had already had a hunch when he first heard the sound while they were crawling through the passageway below, but Luki's palaver about ghosts had distracted him.

Peter estimated that at least a dozen dogs had just run past him. Their whining had sounded like the eerie howling of ghosts through the thick door and the maze of underground corridors. They had most likely been locked up for many days—weeks, even—in terrible conditions, hence the awful smell.

Peter finally managed to pull the slobbering dog off his face. The animal yelped happily and started to bark in a pitch and volume that made Peter jump. He remembered what Max had said about Arthur—*he'd bark and howl during class until Kerll went crazy.*

Peter couldn't blame the music teacher.

Even though it was too dark to see much, he felt reasonably certain he was holding the right dog.

"Arthur!" he said while the dog continued to howl, whine, and lick him. "Stop it! You're not acting like a dog of noble birth at all."

Meanwhile, the other boys had arrived at the open door as well. Peter's last remaining doubts disappeared in the light of the torches. The dog in his arms was a small spaniel with brown fur and white spots—just as Max described him.

They had found Arthur.

"*That* is the dog of the prince?" Luki asked with disbelief. "It looks totally normal. Could be any stray dog from the street."

"And yet this one's worth a pile of money," Moser replied with a grin. "Lucky Lorentz the dogcatcher hasn't turned him into soap. What a waste that would have been."

"At least he'd have smelled better," Seppi remarked, wrinkling his nose.

"I'm guessing the other dogs also belong to wealthy people," Peter said. "Van Uffele stole them in order to sell them back to their owners. But he must have been busy with other things lately."

Peter's face darkened when he thought about what those other things might be. Murdering innocent girls, as his mother suspected? A chill crept up his neck. Kidnapping dogs was one thing, but brutally killing people . . . Peter shuddered. They ought to get out of here as fast as they could now that they'd found Arthur. No one knew what else lurked in this place.

"The poor mutts that ran past us didn't look too good," Seppi said and gave the spaniel a look of pity. "They would have starved soon or started to eat each other." He pointed at Arthur. "That one still looks somewhat all right, and he's the friendliest. Probably because the prince fed him treats all his life. Now he thinks you're going to give him one."

Arthur, too, was so skinny that his bones were clearly visible under the fur. He appeared to have accepted Peter not only as his liberator, but also as his new owner. The boy struggled to hold the squirming and barking dog in his arms. On top of the barking, Arthur made shrill high-pitched noises that vaguely sounded like human screams. The boys' ears started to ache.

"If the mutt doesn't shut up soon, van Uffele and the Venetians are bound to show up, damn it," Schorsch said. He looked at Peter. "Make him stop!"

"Me?" Peter cried. "Why me?"

"He likes you," Paul said from beside his brother. "It's obvious. He'll listen to you. Animals always like you — in Schongau, too."

"Because I don't torture them like you," Peter replied. "But that doesn't mean—"

"Enough of this!" a nasal voice suddenly barked from the darkness of the corridor. "You're no better than those lousy mutts and at least as irritating. And that's why you're going to get locked up like them until your parents pay a decent price for you."

Peter spun around with fright and saw four figures slowly approaching from the darkness. Two of them were holding pistols aimed at the children. Between them stood an older woman and a haggard man in a patchy silk coat, a malicious grin on his face.

Peter groaned quietly. His worst fear had come true: van Uffele and his henchmen had heard the barking.

"Shoo, shoo! Back into the hole, you smelly little rats," the director of the manufactory said and gestured toward the open cell door. "Now you're going to be my precious mutts." He pointed at the two gloomy-looking fellows at his side. "And no wrong movements or my Venetians will blow a few holes in your heads. Understood?"

Peter was about to retreat into the cell with his head hung low when he noticed Schorsch and Luki exchange a brief glance, like generals before a battle. Fear gleamed in their eyes, but only for an instant.

"No one locks up the Au Dogs," Luki whispered.

"Nor the Anger Wolves," Schorsch replied quietly. "Even if it means blood will be shed. On three. One, two . . . THREE!"

The two gangs of boys hurled themselves against their enemies. Screams and the barking of dogs mingled in the narrow corridor, together with Joseffa's screeching and van Uffele's cursing.

And then Peter heard the earsplitting bang of a pistol.

Magdalena was in hell.

Screaming devils buzzed around her, howling demonically and pricking her with their forks. Their points pierced her skull like needles and hurt hellishly. The howling became louder, now they were also yelping and barking. Then screaming. Magdalena started up.

Yelping and barking? Since when did devils bark?

Where am I?

She opened her eyes with great difficulty, and all she saw was black. Then, gradually, outlines became visible, and she could make out several objects. Her memory returned, too. She had looked for Eva in the basement of the manufactory and van Uffele and Mother Joseffa had caught her. The two Venetians had poured brandy down her throat, lots of it, and perhaps it had even been spiked with something else. The last thing she remembered was the sound of a bolt sliding shut.

Magdalena struggled to sit up, her head ached as if she'd boozed for several nights in a row. How long had she been asleep? She staggered through the darkness, bumping into old looms and other junk, until she felt something like a door handle. She rattled it but, as expected, it was locked. They had locked her up to deal with later. Well, at least they hadn't killed her yet.

That was the good news.

Now she heard more screaming and the barking of a dog. The strange, shrill bark must have pulled her back to reality. From another direction she could hear the barking of several dogs, then the screaming became louder and a shot rang out, probably from a pistol. What in God's name was going on out there?

Magdalena hesitated briefly, then she started banging against the door.

"Help!" she screamed as loud as she could. "I'm locked up in here! Can anybody hear me? Help!"

She knew she might attract the attention of the wrong people, but she didn't care. Magdalena thought of the dead girls, of Eva. Had she spent her final hours in this cell, too?

"Help me!" she screamed again and kicked the door. "I'm in here!" But no one seemed to hear her.

A wave of nausea overcame her and she crouched down. Pain

throbbed in her head, getting worse and worse. Another shot was fired.

And then something happened that made her blood run cold.

A single scream rang out, high and shrill. Magdalena froze. She could pick out this scream from among a thousand others, probably even if it came from the other side of the ocean.

It was the scream of one of her children.

She couldn't have been mistaken. She'd heard Peter. Or was it Paul? It had been a scream of enormous pain mixed with anger. Magdalena had no idea what one of her sons might be doing out there. Had Peter and Paul come to free her? But then where were her father, Simon, and Georg? Then another scream, and again Magdalena was certain it was one of her sons.

He was screaming for his life.

"Peter! Paul! Your mother is here!" Desperately Magdalena threw herself against the solid door and pounded it with her fists, her pain and nausea forgotten.

But as much as she called out and cried, the door didn't open.

One of her children was in mortal danger, and she couldn't do anything to help him.

14

It was as if summer had suddenly appeared in the middle of winter—only deep underground.

Jakob Kuisl gaped at the sea of colorful flowers growing from the walls of the approximately seven-foot-high grotto, out of cracks, gray plaster rocks, and the ground as well. Some even hung from the ceiling, as though they'd accidentally sprouted into the mountain instead of outside into the light. They shimmered red, blue, green, purple, and yellow in the light of three lanterns hanging on the wall, like a meadow of summer flowers. Only on second glance did Kuisl realize they were made of tin. Still, they lent something fairylike to the grotto, as if tiny, winged fairies would flutter out from the flowers at any moment.

But the smell didn't fit with the picture at all.

It was caustic and pungent and probably had something to do with the rather earthly objects standing around a well in the center of the grotto. Kuisl saw countless firepans and crucibles, several large pots and wooden tubs with a white substance on their edges. Pokers and ladles leaned against their sides. A wooden case containing long shiny molds of metal sat atop a rustic wooden table.

The whole scene looked like the subterranean forge of Hephaestus, the Greek god of blacksmiths.

Between the firepans, Daniel Pfundner and the bald man were busy throwing the crucibles into a chest, and more empty crates and containers suggested they were going to pack up the remaining objects as well. The two men seemed to be in a hurry. Pfundner's mask and the other man's Roman helmet lay in the corner. The bald man was sweating heavily under his armor and beads of sweat stood on his hairless head as he packed more crucibles and pots into a crate.

"The electress might come here any day now that the palace is officially open—tomorrow, if we're unlucky," he gasped. "Or some other curious courtier. We'll never get everything out of here in time."

"The dies and crucibles should suffice, Master Frießhammer," the treasurer replied. "We can leave anything that won't lead them to us."

"What about the tubs? You can still see the remains of acid," the man called Frießhammer objected. "And the molds? Anyone with half a brain knows what they're for. It won't even take a day until the guards suspect me. Who else would have taken the dies from the mint? But I can tell you one thing: I'm not climbing the scaffold alone."

"No one is going to climb the scaffold if we clean up after ourselves," Pfundner said calmly. "And now quit whining and hurry up before any of the guests choose this place for a love nest. The door upstairs is shut, but the electress and several courtiers know of this grotto."

Slowly it dawned on Kuisl what was going on here. He remembered Simon and various citizens talking about coin counterfeiters who were flooding the market in and around Munich with cheap silver coins. He looked again at the wooden case, into which Pfundner was just throwing several longish metal bolts.

Coin dies. Those bastards actually stole the electoral coin dies.

The dies for minting coins were more closely guarded than many treasures. Every electorate had their own, and they never left the mint. Anyone holding the dies could create far superior counterfeits than with just molds.

Kuisl nodded grimly. They added copper to the silver to make the coins as cheaply as possible. The tubs were probably filled with acid and used to turn the added copper white like silver. This grotto was nothing but a well-hidden counterfeiting operation.

Pfundner and the bald man probably chose this place for its seclusion. Kuisl remembered the carriage that had raced through Sendling Gate a few nights ago. The guard had spoken of wealthy people who were paying a ton of money to leave and enter the city after the gates were shut without being asked questions. Hadn't Pfundner spoken about a carriage that would soon await them outside?

"If the dies aren't back at the mint by tomorrow, it's too late," Master Frießhammer continued to complain. "I've told you a hundred times that the warden of the mint is paying me a visit tomorrow. I have to show him the dies."

"And that's why we're taking them back tonight," Pfundner said, carefully closing one of the chests. "The money's going back to city hall, and the dies to the mint, just like always. No reason to get upset."

From their hiding place behind the artificial rock, Kuisl and Georg watched the proceedings for a while. Georg gently tapped his father's shoulder.

"So, if I understand correctly," he whispered, "those two fops are forging money?"

"They probably turn one good silver coin into two bad ones," Kuisl replied. "One they keep, and the other goes back into the city treasury, and no one notices a thing. If it wasn't such a nasty thing to do, I'd congratulate them on their cunning."

When he was a child, the hangman remembered, many merchants, tradesmen, and mercenaries had been ruined that way. These two scoundrels were getting rich through the misery of others. And it was no coincidence that one of them was the Munich city treasurer. And that Frießhammer appeared to work at the electoral mint, perhaps as the mint master or die maker.

Money from the treasurer and dies from the mint master, Kuisl thought. *And a secret hideout not far from Munich. An almost perfect crime—but only almost . . .*

"But there's one thing I don't understand," Georg whispered into his father's ear. "We thought those two would lead us to Magdalena. But what does Magdalena have to do with counterfeiters? Can you explain?"

Jakob Kuisl didn't reply, but deep down he knew they'd made a big mistake.

They had followed the wrong villains.

Simon stood at the edge of the dance floor in the great hall of Nymphenburg Palace and stared at the masked ball guests twirling endlessly to the music. Gypsies danced with mermen, amazons with Greek philosophers, and forest sprites with made-up shepherdesses and flower girls. The feast was definitely nearing its climax.

Silent despair took hold of him. Three times he had searched through every room in the palace, as well as the park and the main entrance where carriages came and went, but he'd found no sign of Jakob Kuisl and Georg anywhere. Nor of Magdalena, even though he'd seen several women he felt sure were prostitutes. Some of them looked like very young girls. Once he tore the mask off a very drunk fairy in the hope of finding the face of his beloved wife. Instead, a lady-in-waiting with a large nose and a beauty spot had slapped him across the face. He'd only just managed to evade her lover's revenge.

After studying the guests on the dance floor one last time, Simon gave up. No hangman, no harlequin, and no Magdalena . . .

And Pfundner and the bald man hadn't returned either. Something must have happened. And he could do nothing but stand around watching a bunch of crazy court people woo each other. Simon had rarely felt so helpless. He had taken off his mask, disgusted at this whole charade.

He was about to turn away when someone tapped him on the shoulder.

Probably a guard taking me back to the electress, he thought. *She probably wants to know exactly what I'm planning to do about her accursed mutt. I wish Magdalena and I had never traveled to this city full of fops and dandies.*

It was no guard, however, but someone he knew reasonably well by now.

"Doctor Geiger!" Simon exclaimed with surprise. "You're here, too?"

Malachias Geiger, his mask off, too, smiled at Simon. The rest of his costume, like Simon's, consisted of a black coat and a white ruff collar. Geiger looked practically the same as always.

The doctor shrugged. "Part of my duties," he said unhappily. "I hate these balls. But if I don't make an appearance, everyone talks. I can't afford that." He pointed at Simon's costume. "I see we both went for the dottore. How appropriate."

Simon didn't know if Geiger's last remark had been ironic or serious. But he was probably glad to find a like-minded person among all these crazy courtiers.

"I already saw one of your patients," Simon said to the doctor, raising his voice above the music. "Daniel Pfundner, the treasurer. I don't suppose you know where he went?"

"No, I'm sorry." Malachias Geiger shook his head. "Though I don't complain if I don't constantly run into patients at occasions like these." He looked cautiously around, but no one was paying them any attention. "It's very exhausting to be on duty all the time."

Simon gave a tired smile. "Then you should have picked a different costume. A shepherd, perhaps, like the elector? People rarely approach shepherds regarding urinary tract infections or boils."

"Ha-ha! Touché!" Malachias Geiger smirked, an expression that seemed strangely foreign on his face. "You're right. I'll think of something else next time." Then he turned serious again. "Anyhow, I'm pleased to run into you here, because now I can tell you what I found out for you."

"For me . . . ?" Simon was puzzled for a moment, but then he realized what the doctor meant. In all the excitement of the last few hours, he had forgotten that he'd stopped by at Geiger's house earlier that day to ask him a favor. There was something he just couldn't get out of his mind.

"So my letter reached you?" he asked, feeling increasingly restless. That damned coffee had been awfully strong. The music was picking up tempo, and the couples spun round and round like windmills.

Geiger nodded. "Yes, it did. And I set off immediately." He sighed. "It was the perfect excuse not to look for a better costume. My wife always wants me to dress up more originally, but—"

"And?" Simon interrupted him hoarsely. "Did you find anything?"

"I don't think so." Geiger shrugged apologetically, and Simon's hopes were dashed. It would have been too good. But evidently, he'd been carried away by the idea, as so often in recent days.

But then the doctor hesitated. "Hmm. But there's one name I found rather interesting. Let's say I wouldn't have expected it—not on this list."

Simon listened up. "And the name is . . . ?"

"Well, as I said, I'm sure it means nothing . . ."

"For Christ's sake, speak up." Simon forgot all his manners in his agitation. "Please," he added quietly.

Doctor Malachias told him the name.

And a piece in Simon's mental mosaic fell into just the right place.

It was as if he'd been looking too closely at a chaotic picture and had now taken a step back. Everything made sense all of a sudden. Simon held his breath, his thoughts racing.

How could we have been so stupid? It was right in front of us all along, and we didn't see it. Didn't want to see it.

The dance ended with a final flourish, and the couples fell into one another's arms, laughing.

"Thank you," Simon breathed. "That name is . . . interesting indeed." He squeezed Geiger's hand, then he remembered something.

"Um, I'm sorry to bother you with this, but you don't happen to have a carriage I could borrow? I'm afraid it's rather urgent."

When the second shot was fired, Peter threw himself to the ground. He heard a whistling noise directly above him, then someone screamed. Peter winced. The boy who had screamed was Paul, his brother. And it had been a scream of pain.

From the corner of his eye he saw Schorsch and Seppi jump on one of the Venetians, trying to wrestle his pistol from him. But the huge man struck Seppi on the head with the butt, making Schorsch even angrier. Meanwhile, Luki and two other boys wrestled with the second Venetian on the ground. Several of the imprisoned dogs had returned and tore at the sleeves of their former jailers or snapped at their throats.

Van Uffele and Mother Joseffa were barely visible among a throng of children and dogs. Where was Paul? Peter desperately searched the corridor with his eyes. There! His brother lay in a dark corner, his body strangely twisted. Peter saw in the light of a torch that a dark pool was growing underneath the eight-year-old.

"Paul!" he screamed. "Jesus, Paul!"

Without checking whether one of the Venetians was about to

shoot again, he ran over to his brother. Paul had been among the first to hurl himself at the scoundrels. The men had been taken completely by surprise but still managed to fire two shots.

The second shot must have hit Paul.

His eyes were closed and he was breathing heavily. Peter ripped off his brother's shirt to see where the bullet had hit him. He wiped away the blood with his sleeve until he found the hole. The bullet had struck his left upper arm, just above the elbow. The wound was bleeding heavily. Most likely Paul was in shock, but soon the pain would set in, and he'd scream much louder than before.

While the battle raged around Peter, he tried to focus on what his father had taught him. He needed to stop the bleeding, that was the most important thing. He clenched his teeth and tore his own shirt into strips, tying one of them tightly around Paul's arm above the wound and the others loosely around the bullet hole. Then he grabbed a torch that had gone out, broke off the lower half, and pushed the stick under the loose bandage. He turned the stick until the bandage was so tight that no more blood came out of the wound, but he also knew that this was merely a temporary solution. He needed medicine to stanch the bleeding for good. If the arm stayed tied off for too long—his father had told him—it would die and need to be amputated.

And his brother would be a cripple for the rest of his life, if he didn't die of gangrene in the next few days.

Paul groaned, but he didn't seem to be fully conscious. His small knife lay next to him. Boundless rage took hold of Peter. He grabbed the knife and threw himself at the Venetian wrestling with Schorsch. The fellow was holding his pistol in his right hand, aiming for the leader of the Anger Wolves.

"You pigs!" Peter screamed deliriously. "You goddamned pigs! Shooting at my little brother! To hell with all of you!"

He stabbed the Venetian with the knife, and the man dropped his pistol with a shout of pain. But Peter didn't stop, stabbing the

Venetian again and again. The knife was only small, but the sharp point dug into the man's arms and chest and cut open his cheek. Peter had never felt such rage. The anger helped him conquer his fear. Perhaps it was the same kind of anger that fueled his brother to commit all sorts of mischief?

"Finite!" the Venetian screamed in panic while trying to fend off the knife. *"Mi arrendo!"*

In the meantime, several of the other boys had rushed to Peter's and Schorsch's aid. They held the large, whimpering man to the ground and tied him with ropes they had found in a nearby chamber. Peter attacked until someone touched him on the shoulder and pulled him back. It was Moser.

"He can't hurt us anymore, Peter," he said gently. "You can stop now. Do you hear me? It's over."

Peter started up with fright and looked at his bloodstained hands. He felt as though he was waking up from a nightmare. Rage had carried him away and nearly turned him into a murderer. Sobbing, he threw the knife to the ground while the Venetian moaned quietly.

"He . . . he shot my brother," Peter whimpered. "If Paul dies . . ."

"I don't think he'll die," Schorsch tried to reassure him. "He just needs a doctor as soon as possible." He gave the man on the ground a grim look. "Just like that Venetian scoundrel you taught more than one lesson."

Peter looked around. The battle was over. The two Venetians, van Uffele, and Mother Joseffa lay on the ground, tied up. A good dozen boys and a bunch of mangy dogs had won over four armed grownup villains; the prince's dog was found; and a healthy reward was on the horizon.

And yet Peter felt no triumph, only a deep sense of despair. How many times had he cursed his little brother, who had so little compassion for animals and people, who didn't care about reading and writing and preferred to pick fights instead. But now that Paul was lying on the ground in front of him, pale and bleeding, Peter realized how much he needed his brother. They were like two halves of one being.

Only together were they whole.

The dogs were barking so wildly that it was difficult to hear one's own words. Peter thought he could hear someone thumping against a door and shouting. Were there people locked up down here as well? Perhaps that Eva his mother had spoken about? It wouldn't take long for any inhabitants of the manufactory and the neighboring houses to wake up with this racket.

"You're making a grave mistake," van Uffele said, pulling on his fetters. "A very grave mistake. I have friends in the city, everywhere. If you don't untie me right away, you won't live to see the next few days."

"You . . . you dirty little thieves!" Mother Joseffa hissed. Her makeup was smeared and she had lost her blonde wig during the fight, so everyone could see her thin gray hair. She reminded Peter of an evil witch. "What are you doing here, anyway?" she yelled. "Stealing honest people's daily bread."

"Honest people?" Schorsch scoffed. He pointed at Arthur, who was jumping and whining around Peter. "Do honest people steal the prince's dog?"

"I have no idea what you're talking about," van Uffele replied stiffly, but Peter noticed his eyes twitch nervously. Then the shouting and thumping farther up the corridor started again. Van Uffele heard it, too, Peter could tell by his face. He seemed rattled.

"Who is that?" Schorsch asked. "Who else have you locked up down here? Spit it out!"

"I'm not saying another word," van Uffele replied coolly. "Not until you untie me."

"Shut up, you bastard!" Luki punched the bound man and

van Uffele glared at him when a thin rivulet of blood ran from the corner of his mouth.

"If you don't do exactly as we tell you, I'm personally going to feed you to the dogs," Luki continued in a threatening tone. "They're rather hungry, you know."

Peter listened. Between the barking and yelping, he could clearly hear shouts and clanging.

Shouts of a woman. Shouts of a woman he knew very well.

"Mother!" he called out.

And then he ran up the corridor.

Sheltered by the artificial rock, Jakob Kuisl watched as Daniel Pfundner and Master Frießhammer packed the suspicious utensils into crates and chests. Kuisl's eyes were empty, his energy drained, and he felt tired and old.

Too old for this kind of adventure. Too old to protect my daughter.

He had hoped ardently that these two men would lead him to Magdalena, or at least tell him what all those recent murders were about. But now he realized that they had followed the wrong lead. The conversation Magdalena had overheard in Pfundner's house had had nothing to do with the missing girls. What was it the bald man had said to Pfundner?

We must take them away before we're found out.

Magdalena had been convinced the man had spoken about the girls, but he had meant the dies in the grotto. The pair of scoundrels must have expected to use the secret counterfeiting workshop for longer, but the rapid progress on the palace and the masquerade ball had foiled their plans. Now they were getting rid of anything suspicious before anyone discovered the grotto. Kuisl clenched his fists. Those two bastards should climb the scaffold, no doubt—but they weren't the murderers of the girls.

Or were they?

Anni, the dead girl from Au creek, had been forced to work as a prostitute at Pfundner's house, and Elfi and Eva had been whored out to wealthy patricians' houses as well. What about Frießhammer? Kuisl frowned. There must be a connection. Most likely it was right in front of him, obscured by all the wrong leads. Why couldn't he see it?

There was only one way to find out if Pfundner knew anything: Kuisl had to ask him. And the hangman began by doing the easiest thing he could think of.

He stepped forward.

"Damn it, Father," Georg hissed. "What the hell are you doing?"

But it was too late. Pfundner had spotted Kuisl. Even in the dim light of the lanterns, Jakob Kuisl could see the treasurer's face turn white. He tried to imagine what Pfundner was looking at: a huge hangman with a hood who had come to punish him, the counterfeiter caught in the act, by boiling him in seething oil.

"God in heaven!" Daniel Pfundner burst out. He dropped the sack he'd been holding and stared at Kuisl as if he were a ghost. Frießhammer had seen the hangman, too. He squealed like a pig and jumped for cover behind the table. Kuisl raised one hand.

"We need to talk," he said. "I'm not here to—"

In that moment, several things happened simultaneously. Kuisl heard a sound he knew too well from the war: the buzz of a crossbow string. Evidently, the bald Roman wasn't as defenseless as he'd first assumed. He must have kept a loaded crossbow under the table. The hangman instinctively stepped to the side and the bolt flew past him, but in the same instant, one of the bronze dies struck him on the temple. Pfundner appeared to have overcome his fright fast and reached for the next best weapon.

Kuisl saw black for a moment from the heavy blow, but he vaguely perceived Daniel Pfundner reaching for another die. Now Georg came storming out of the shadows and launched himself at the men.

I'm really getting old, Kuisl thought once more as he fell to the ground. *Beaten by a Roman in tin armor and a milksop in a mask . . .*

Meanwhile, Georg had reached Frießhammer and threw him on the table. Harlequin and Roman panted as they fought, sending several crucibles crashing to the ground. Another heavy die hit Kuisl right in the face. He felt warm blood run from his nose.

With the blood came rage.

The hangman struggled to his feet and roared as he threw himself at Daniel Pfundner, who was just reaching for a third die. Before he had the chance to throw it, Kuisl reached him and dealt him such a powerful blow to the chin that Pfundner was hurled against the plaster wall. A chunk of wall came off and shattered into a white cloud. Kuisl raised his fist for another strike, but he was still slightly dizzy. He stumbled and missed. From the corner of his eye, he saw Georg fighting Frießhammer's tin sword with his wooden one.

Daniel Pfundner used the brief respite to grab a fire poker that was leaning against one of the wooden tubs. Kuisl dodged the blow and the poker scraped across his beard like a botched shave. Seething with anger, the hangman grabbed the heavy tub and hurled it into Pfundner, who screamed out in pain and staggered backward. Nonetheless the treasurer managed to run toward the stairs, and Kuisl followed him, gasping for breath. He had almost caught up with Pfundner when he slipped and fell on the icy steps.

"Jesus bloody Christ, stop, you goddamn bastard!"

Cursing, Kuisl scrambled to his feet, but Pfundner had already reached the door to the grotto. He ran outside and slammed the door shut behind him. Kuisl threw himself against the door, but it wouldn't budge. The treasurer must have locked it from the outside.

Kuisl angrily hammered his fists against the rock, which turned into white plaster dust and crumbs bit by bit. The hangman was like a growling giant trapped inside the mountain.

Blood flowed from his nose and forehead, and still he rammed his shoulder against the wall again and again. He might not have been the fastest, but he was still strong. Very strong.

Once, twice, three times he threw himself against the plaster wall.

On the fourth go, he was through.

Kuisl staggered outside. He couldn't see Pfundner anywhere, but the moon shone brightly and the hangman soon spotted tracks leading away from the grotto. Pfundner appeared to be dragging his right leg—Kuisl must have hit him hard. He thought about Magdalena, who had almost become Pfundner's whore, and he was filled with deep hatred. If he caught hold of the dirty bastard, he'd hang him by his own genitals.

But first he needed to talk to him.

Jakob Kuisl followed the tracks like a wolf that had smelled blood. He hoped Georg could handle the Roman by himself. If he let Pfundner get away now, he'd never find out whether the man knew anything about the murders.

The tracks led from the grotto into the forest, along a low wall, then they turned abruptly to the right, where a man-high boxwood hedge and wilted rosebushes were sugarcoated with powdery snow. Kuisl followed the hedge until he reached a sort of entrance. Someone had tried to conceal their tracks in a hurry. Behind the gap in the hedge, another hedgerow led left and right in a wide arch. Kuisl soon realized why Pfundner had chosen to run here.

He stood at the entrance to a labyrinth.

Even though the treasurer tried to conceal his footprints, Kuisl could still make them out in the snow. He followed them to the right, around a bend . . .

And stared at untouched snow.

The hangman cursed softly.

Smart little prick . . .

He had fallen for one of the oldest tricks, one he'd made use of himself several times during the war. Pfundner had taken a few steps in one direction and then walked back in his own prints. Kuisl turned around and was soon back at the spot where the treasurer appeared to have turned. There was a small gap in the hedge and a pile of snow in front of it.

The snow that had fallen off the branches when Pfundner crept through the opening.

Kuisl bent down, pushed through the gap, and found more tracks on the other side. He clenched his teeth and hurried on. How big was this accursed labyrinth? Kuisl knew that the nobility liked to build such mazes out of hedges, some as large as entire villages. This one must have been quite new and probably merged with the forest behind it, which made it even more difficult to navigate.

Kuisl realized he wasn't really wearing enough clothes for a long walk outside and knew that the same went for the treasurer in his silly costume. On top of that, Pfundner was injured, and the hangman saw more and more drops of blood in his tracks. Perhaps they came from the fight, or maybe he'd scratched himself on the thorns in the hedge. Kuisl was bleeding, too, though only a little. At least the cold was helping him think straight again.

Despite his body mass, Kuisl was starting to feel cold. He knew he couldn't run through this maze forever. Most importantly, he would have to find his way back out later. Absentmindedly, he played with the frayed edge of the hangman's cloak.

Loose threads . . .

He remembered a Greek myth he'd once read as a child. It had been written in an old book his father had bought off a peddler. Some hero or other had chased a beast through a labyrinth and, to avoid getting lost, he'd used a thread.

Kuisl hoped this labyrinth wasn't so big that he'd end up naked.

He opened the seam at the bottom of the cloak and tied the

thread to one of the rosebushes. Then he continued to follow the tracks.

The amount of blood in the prints was still increasing and, judging by the tracks, Pfundner's leg was getting worse. He appeared to have fallen several times, too. He wouldn't last much longer. From time to time Kuisl thought he heard panting and scraping behind the hedgerows. The treasurer couldn't be far. Whenever the tracks led to a deadend, Pfundner had pushed his way through the hedge, and parts of his costume hung caught in the thorns.

When Kuisl came to the next fork in the path, clouds suddenly pushed in front of the moon and the night turned pitch-black. A cold wind picked up and blew white clouds of snow through the hedgerows. The footprints became almost invisible. Kuisl uttered a curse. He couldn't lose the treasurer now.

"Pfundner!" he shouted against the howling wind. "If you can hear me, listen! I don't want to hurt you!"

For a while, everything remained silent. Then Kuisl heard someone laugh hoarsely nearby.

"Let's hear it, then!" the treasurer shouted back. "But don't think I'll agree to anything you suggest. I don't even know who you are."

I'm your hangman, Kuisl was about to say, but he thought better of it.

"It doesn't matter who I am. The only thing you need to know is that I don't care what you're doing in that grotto. Whether you forge money or steal the throne from under the elector's arse, it's all the same to me."

"Is that right?" Pfundner's voice sounded a little uncertain. "And why are you following me, then?"

"What do you have to do with the dead girls?"

The treasurer didn't say anything for a while, then he broke out in loud laughter. "Oh, that's why you're after me? Because you think I'm this killer of girls everyone's been talking about?"

In fact, Kuisl had no idea. He was still completely in the dark regarding the identity and motive of the murderer. First he'd suspected Master Hans, then Conrad Näher or one of the other council members, but every lead had turned out false. In the course of his long life, the hangman had solved many cases, but this time he seemed to have reached his wits' end.

And now he was standing in a labyrinth of ice and snow, freezing his arse off. It was maddening.

"I believe you know something," Kuisl continued while the cold crept up his legs like needles. "The dead girl from Au creek, Anni, she was working for you as a whore. And her friends Elfi and Eva were also prostitutes in wealthy homes, sent by van Uffele. They were punished and executed as befits female criminals, but why did they have to die? What was their crime? And what do you know about it? Is van Uffele behind it all?"

"By God, I swear I have no idea," Pfundner shouted against the wind. He sounded much closer now, as if he was standing behind the nearest hedge. "Why do you even want to know? You're not from the city guard, are you? Or did Loibl send you?"

Kuisl replied with a question: "Why did Anni have to die? Speak up, and I swear I'll leave you in peace."

"Who gives a damn about those girls?" Pfundner yelled. "They're nothing but dirty harlots. They come to Munich like birds in the spring, and some don't make it through the winter. Who cares?"

I care, Jakob Kuisl thought. *I care about those girls. Most of all, I care about my Magdalena.*

"Why did Anni have to die?" he repeated.

"I don't know," Pfundner whined. "Jesus, do you have any idea how cold it is? I hadn't seen that . . . Anni for quite a while. She was no longer any good to me, and I told van Uffele, too. He sent me a new girl."

And I know who that was. Kuisl ground his teeth, but he reined in his anger.

"Why was she no longer any good to you?" he asked calmly. He sensed he was close to solving the mystery.

"Because . . . because she was *pregnant,* damn it!" Pfundner burst out. "The stupid wench let herself fall with child. Who needs a pregnant whore? I told her to get rid of it and gave her a pile of thalers to keep quiet. She probably bragged about it, and someone robbed her and cut her throat. I don't know anything else, I swear."

Kuisl forgot to breathe for a moment. Pfundner's words hit him harder than the bronze die had earlier. One sentence in particular.

Who needs a pregnant whore?

He thought of all the individual murders that had looked like executions. Strangling, drowning, impaling, burying alive . . . Punishments for women.

For murderesses.

The hangman picked up his thread and made his way back toward the exit.

I told her to get rid of it . . .

"Hey, what are you doing?" Pfundner screamed behind him. "Why are you leaving? I . . . I need your help! I'm freezing and injured. Get me out of here, I beg you! By God, don't leave me alone in this goddamned labyrinth. Help me!"

But the hangman was no longer listening.

For the first time since he'd set foot in Munich, he knew he was on the right track. He hurried back through the maze while Pfundner's calls for help grew fainter and fainter.

The Anger Wolves and Au Dogs held trial in a storage room deep down below the silk manufactory. The boys sat on bales of cloth, broken looms, dusty chests, and rolls of yarn, glaring at their two prisoners, the director of the manufactory, Lucas van Uffele, and the brothelkeeper, Joseffa. The two Venetians were tied up in the next cell, their wounds dressed as well as the boys had been able to in the basement.

Magdalena sat leaning against a bundle of old rags, exhausted and shaken. She still had a pounding headache and felt sick. Whenever she tried to stand up, everything went black. Van Uffele and Joseffa must have made her drink at least half a bottle of brandy the night before, most likely mixed with some drugs, and she'd been unconscious for almost twenty-four hours. Now she knew how her father felt after he'd gone on a bender.

But she was still alive—unlike Anni, Elfi, and perhaps Eva, too. The boys had searched every room in the basement for the girl but found nothing. At least Paul's life was no longer in danger.

Magdalena cast a loving glance at Peter, who was sitting between her and the sleeping Paul like an attentive guard. When her elder son had opened the door to her prison cell, she had squeezed him tighter than she ever had. Then they had rushed to Paul's side. Peter had done a good job as doctor. The injury wasn't as bad as they'd first feared—the bullet had gone right through. They'd been able to loosen the tight bandage and dress the wound with fresh strips of cloth. And now he was sound asleep, his breathing regular. Magdalena knew that as soon as they were back at the executioner's house, Walburga would give him the medicine he needed. But before they left this cursed building for good, she wanted to make van Uffele and Mother Joseffa talk.

She wanted to solve the mystery of the dead girls once and for all.

"What are you going to do with us?" van Uffele snarled, tugging at his ties. "Kill us? You don't have the guts. And why should you? We haven't done anything. So what's all this nonsense about?"

"You hire out your weavers as prostitutes to patricians," Magdalena said, struggling against nausea. She tried hard to sound calm and confident. "Whoremongering is illegal. You're earning your money through the misery of those girls."

"Boohoo, how sad," Mother Joseffa jeered. "Is that why you came to work here? To find that out?" She grinned wide enough for everyone to see her rotten black teeth. "Then you probably talked to our girls about it. Agnes, Carlotta, and all the others . . . They earn more in one night with a client than in two weeks at the loom. Most would do anything to be one of the chosen ones."

"Last time I spoke with one of your *chosen ones,* all she did was cry and wipe the blood from her thighs," Magdalena replied, full of hate. "Carlotta was still a virgin. So don't talk to me about how kind and generous you are, or I'm going to vomit."

Joseffa shrugged. "We never dragged anyone to those houses, not Carlotta, not you. No one watched you while you walked to Pfundner's. It was your decision, and you did it."

"Oh, and in case you think you can tell your pathetic little story to the guards," van Uffele added, glaring at her, "remember who our clients are. Rich citizens, patricians, even a few courtiers . . . Rest assured, no one will believe you. Who are you, anyway? Did the guards send you? Loibl, perhaps? Are you sniffing around here on his behalf?"

Magdalena ignored van Uffele's questions. "Speaking of the court," she said and pointed at the small spaniel, who was snoozing peacefully at Peter's feet. All the other dogs had disappeared. "You stole the the prince's dog. The electress isn't going to be pleased, and not even your oh-so-wealthy friends will be able to help you. That alone should be enough to see you thrown into a dark hole and left to rot."

"The dog just turned up one day," Joseffa objected. "Just like the other mutts. How were we supposed to know it was the prince's dog?" She smirked and looked at Magdalena with wide eyes. "Bah! It's just another story you made up."

"We didn't make up anything," Peter said. "The prince's

nursemaid stole the dog and gave it to her boyfriend. She told me so herself. And that boyfriend gave the dog to you. You knew very well it was the prince's dog. You were probably going to ask for a horrendous ransom."

"And you are going to tell on us at court?" van Uffele jeered. "Who are you? The emperor of China? They wouldn't even let you in the servants' entrance in your rags. Only through a rat hole." He wrinkled his nose. "You stink. Like all of you. You're nothing but smelly little rats."

"I know the prince," Peter said coldly. "And believe me, I'm going to tell him everything. And you will count yourselves lucky if they hang you before drawing and quartering you."

A certain tone in Peter's voice silenced van Uffele. Apparently, he wasn't quite as certain anymore that Peter wasn't telling the truth.

"You can believe my son," Magdalena assured him. "Peter knows the crown prince. And he's going to make your life hell—unless you do exactly as we tell you."

"Who the hell are you?" van Uffele yelled.

But Magdalena still didn't answer.

We are the Kuisls from Schongau, she thought. *And we eat people like you for breakfast, you slimy Munich fop.*

"You're welcome to disbelieve us," she said after a while. "Or you can cooperate. Then the crown prince might not find out who locked up his darling dog and almost let it starve."

"Hey!" Schorsch called out. "That's not what we agreed on. We want our reward."

The other boys grumbled, and Magdalena raised a placating hand.

"You'll get your reward. But now I finally want to know what the story is with the three girls. Anni, Elfi, and Eva. Two are dead, the third missing. Not to mention all the other girls that have been murdered in and around Munich for decades. What's your connection? Spit it out!" She pointed at the injured Paul, who was twitching in his sleep, and her voice became cutting. "My son needs a doctor. By God, if you don't start talking right now—"

"All right, all right," van Uffele cut her off. "I think I'm beginning to understand why you're here. I'm guessing you're a friend of the three girls? Well, I can tell you that we had nothing to do with the deaths of Anni and Elfi. I swear by everything dear to me. I also swear that we didn't want to kill you. We only wanted to give you a fright and find out who sent you."

"The oath of a swindler and a brothelkeeper?" Luki laughed derisively, and the other boys joined in. "You can stick that up your arse." He took a menacing step toward the director. "Speak up! You heard what Peter's mother asked. Or would you like me to punch out one tooth after the other?"

Van Uffele hesitated. Then he looked at Mother Joseffa and gave her a nod. The old woman cleared her throat.

"It's true," she began. "Anni, Elfi, and Eva all worked as prostitutes. But not for long. The silly geese got pregnant. A poor young girl with a child and no husband . . ." She snorted. "In this city, you're worth about as much as the dirt on the shoes of the rich. So we did what we always do in such cases. We helped those stupid girls. Only Eva didn't want to let us help her at first. Said she wanted to keep the child and got more and more hysterical. In the end, she almost gave us away and we had to lock her up. But finally she saw sense and let us take her there. All in secret, of course—we put a blanket over her on the cart. We don't want to risk our heads for a pregnant wench like her, after all. It's enough that we have to spend a fortune on her."

Magdalena held her breath.

"What . . . what did you do to her?" she asked hoarsely. "Where did you take the three of them?"

"Well, you know, where girls like them can get rid of unwanted children," van Uffele replied. "We've been doing it for years. The girls lose the child, then they leave town and try their luck somewhere else. Girls like those come and go. The only thing that matters is that they shut up and don't talk about us." He shrugged. "To be honest, we never thought much about it. Until the thing with Anni and Elfi. But surely it was just a nasty coincidence."

"Where did you take the girls?" Magdalena asked again, more urgently. A terrible thought had taken root in her mind. *"Where?"*

Mother Joseffa tilted her head, a wide grin spread across her face. "Well, to a place where we know it's going to work. Believe me, there's no better place for an abortion in all of Munich."

15

As the creaking of the carriage wheels moved farther and farther away, Simon slowly walked toward the Deiblers' house.

It hadn't been easy to persuade Doctor Geiger's personal driver to take him to this disreputable part of town. The man simply hadn't been able to comprehend why someone would leave a masquerade hosted by the electress to visit the Munich hangman, and late at night, too. Geiger had joined Simon in the carriage but alighted at his house.

In the pale light of the moon, the building appeared much eerier to Simon than it ever had. The hangman's house grew out of the city wall like a huge black boil. Behind it, Simon could see the outlines of the strange tower the people of Munich called Faustturm—fist tower—because of the shape of its roof. The trees and bushes behind the low wall looked like cowering trolls just waiting to pounce on Simon.

Dull candlelight shone in the windows of the ground floor, so the Deiblers seemed to be home. Peter and Paul had probably come home by now, too, just like Barbara.

And Eva was probably still unconscious in the apothecary's chamber.

Concern for Eva and his family had caused Simon to leave the ball abruptly and rush here as fast as he could—most of all, however, it was fear for his little Sophia. He'd have to take his chances on his own, as he had no idea where Jakob Kuisl and Georg had disappeared to.

Simon opened the gate and walked down the icy path to the front door. His knocking echoed loudly in the stillness of night. Several cats meowed inside, but nothing happened. Simon knocked again.

"Anyone home?" he called out eventually.

Finally he heard footsteps in the hallway, the door was opened, and Walburga stood in front of him. The hangman's tall wife looked exhausted, her usually well-kempt hair hung down in a tousled mess. When she recognized Simon, she smiled. But it took her a few moments, as if she had to orient herself first.

"Oh, it's you," she said eventually. "I hadn't expected you back so soon. Did you find Magdalena at the ball?" She looked around. "And where are Jakob and Georg?"

"They'll be here soon," Simon replied. He rubbed his arms, shivering. "May I come in?"

Walburga looked confused for a moment, then she gave a little laugh. "Of course, how silly of me. You must be freezing."

She accompanied him into the living room. The cradle was still in the corner. Simon hurried over to it and saw to his relief that his daughter was peacefully asleep inside.

"She is such a sweet child." Walburga stood next to Simon, looking adoringly at the little girl. "She's like a ray of sunshine on these cold days. I'm truly glad to have her here." Suddenly, she seemed very sad. "I was never granted the fortune of children of my own."

"Where is your husband, Walburga?" Simon asked abruptly.

The hangman's wife leaned down and brushed Sophia's cheek. "He went back to Loibl. Said there was something else they needed to discuss. I'm sure he'll be back soon."

"And Peter and Paul? Barbara?" Simon grabbed her arm. "What about Eva?"

"Eva is sleeping just as peacefully as Sophia. The others . . ." Walburga pulled her arm free and sat down at the table. "I don't know. It's a . . ." She paused. "A strange night, isn't it?" Then she jumped up again. "You must be starving. I'll get you some soup—"

"I don't need soup, Walburga. I need answers." Simon gently pushed Walburga back onto her chair and sat down beside her. "I have so many questions."

The hangman's wife looked at him blankly. She brushed a strand of hair from her eyes and ran her tongue across her dry lips. "What do you mean?"

"Well, for example, I wonder whether Eva really did talk about a ball a few hours ago," Simon replied. "I was under the impression that she was unconscious and unable to talk."

Walburga smiled wanly. "I told you she only awoke very briefly. Then she went straight back to sleep."

"Well, unfortunately we couldn't find Magdalena at the ball. And I don't believe she was ever there. Most likely she's still at the manufactory. But I met someone else at Nymphenburg Palace, the honorable Doctor Geiger. Do you remember what I told you about my visit to the lunatic asylum with Geiger? About old Traudel, who was saying all those strange things?"

Walburga frowned. "The crazy woman? You said she was crazy, didn't you?"

"Yes, she's crazy. But not crazy enough not to remember anything. She said she knew who'd been murdering all those girls for decades. And she said she promised not to tell. I wonder who she made that promise to."

The hangman's wife laughed. "Perhaps to Satan himself?"

"No, I believe it was someone who was at the asylum with her a long time ago. Someone who, unlike her, was released. Perhaps because they had connections, or perhaps they were considered healed. I think that someone poured their heart out to Traudel back then." Simon looked closely at Walburga. "Do you know what Traudel screamed over and over when we tried to calm her down? She screamed: 'it's your fault, all your fault,' again and again. I think I finally know who she meant."

"Is that so?" Walburga wet her lips again. "And who is that supposed to be?"

"Us men." Simon paused for a long moment before continuing.

"Apart from Traudel, only men were in the room. Doctor Geiger, the guard, and myself . . . We men are to blame for everything. Isn't that right, Walburga? Isn't that what you told Traudel more than twenty years ago?"

Walburga didn't reply, and Simon continued, more urgently. "It was *you* who shared her cell at the lunatic asylum. Doctor Geiger told me about it earlier. They keep a good record of their patients there. The warder told us so himself. That's what gave me the idea to ask Doctor Geiger to take a look. The record also tells us why you were admitted back then. It was the death of your child. When it died so soon after birth, you were consumed by grief. Your husband took you to the asylum because he didn't know how to help you anymore. His name is recorded, too." Simon shook his head thoughtfully. "I wonder why he didn't tell us about that. Was he embarrassed, or was it because he's been suspecting something for a while?"

"Little Monika," Walburga said. Her eyes became glassy. "Moni. We already had a name for her. I hope the Lord doesn't let the unbaptized child suffer in purgatory for too long."

"When I heard you'd been at the asylum with Traudel, several other details suddenly made sense to me," Simon said. "The whole time I was wondering how all those murders were linked. They were all young girls, and the same amulet was found with each of them. We always thought it showed the Virgin Mary." He pulled out the amulet he and Jakob Kuisl had found on Eva. "But then I remembered where I've seen this kind-looking woman before: in the Altenstadt basilica, back home in the Priests' Corner, where the fourteen holy helpers are depicted. The woman on the medallion isn't Mary but Saint Margaret, the patron saint of pregnant women."

Simon held up the amulet. It dangled right in front of Walburga's nose now, but she didn't seem to see it. Her eyes were focused on a point in the distance.

"A warning to the others," the hangman's wife whispered suddenly. "But they didn't listen. No one listened to me."

"You also wear an amulet like this, Walburga, don't you?" Simon said softly. "You always hid it from us. But when we arrived home with Eva, you forgot to take it off. Probably because you were too surprised to see us with Eva — with the same Eva you had just buried alive." Simon was still holding up the amulet, dangling it to and fro. "You quickly took it off, but I caught a glimpse of it. I thought it was just a talisman like so many women wear around their necks, what of it? I wondered why you tried to hide it."

"Saint Margaret," Walburga replied in a monotone, her eyes now following the pendant. "Her own father reported her because she converted to Christianity. When the judge desired her, she rejected him. He threatened her, tortured her — but Margaret didn't waver. She resisted man."

"Unlike the poor girls who sought you out," Simon said. "Am I right? You punished them because they were pregnant. Because they got involved with the devil in the shape of men."

"Oh God, no!" Walburga shook her head vigorously. "Every

child is a gift of God. It isn't a sin to conceive one. But it's a deadly sin to murder it. That's why they deserved to die."

Simon nodded, trying to understand what was going on in Walburga's sick brain. She had deceived them for so long. Walburga, the child-and-animal-loving hangman's wife who'd been present during almost all their discussions. Who had listened to everything. Who had a vast knowledge of herbs, poisons, and medicines.

And to whom the young girls of Munich had been coming for decades when they needed an abortion.

Walburga's own child had died years ago. She had loved it more than anything in the world, and she hadn't been able to conceive another. And then all those women flocked to her, asking her to kill their unborn children. The insanity that had probably always slumbered in Walburga must have broken out. Most likely she had already committed her first murders before she was admitted to the asylum and told old Traudel about them. The men were at fault, but the women who slept with them and now wanted to rid themselves of the unwanted fruit had to die. Because they were murderesses in Walburga's eyes. When they sought out the hangman's wife and asked for a remedy against the unborn child, they signed their own death sentences.

Anni and Elfi must have come to Walburga as well, just like the young patrician woman. *And Eva?*

"Where is Eva?" Simon asked again.

Walburga's gaze suddenly turned clear again, and she looked at him sternly, like a forbidding mother goddess.

"She decided against the child and therewith for death. There is no way out. She is going to receive her just punishment. Just like the other one."

"The . . . other one?" Simon frowned. Was there another woman locked up in the house?

Magdalena? Was that the reason he couldn't find his wife?

Simon's hand went to the small knife he always carried with him. It was a stiletto that always served him well as a doctor. He had hoped he wouldn't have to use it. Perhaps it had been a mistake not to tell anyone else of his plan. He should have told Doctor Geiger. But now it was too late.

"Who else are you keeping here?" Simon asked. His heart started to race all of a sudden. "Speak up. Before my father-in-law comes home and gets hold of you. I don't want to hurt you."

Walburga scrutinized him. "Hmm. I don't think anyone's coming," she said after a while, almost to herself. "Or Jakob would have arrived long ago. No, you're on your own. You had a suspicion, nothing else." Then her face took on a look of surprise, as if she'd only just realized something. "And you don't know that she's pregnant, either, do you? You don't know what she was going to do, that *hussy*." She spat out the last word like a piece of rotten fruit.

"Who?" Simon croaked. "Who are you talking about?"

His heart was beating faster and faster, beads of sweat forming on his forehead. Surely it couldn't still be the coffee. Or could it? He'd already felt a little dizzy at Nymphenburg Palace, slightly delirious. His thoughts had raced. But now his pulse appeared to increase. What was happening to him? He hadn't touched anything in the executioner's house, had nothing to drink or eat. Had Walburga nonetheless managed to poison him? Just as she'd tried to do to his father-in-law? Simon thought of Kaspar Hörmann, the old drunkard, and his terrible death.

Had his heart raced the same way toward the end?

Walburga was still watching him. Then she nodded, as if she'd reached a decision. "She didn't tell any of you," she muttered. "Perhaps not even her sister. Only that fool she's now mixed up with. I must say, she's a big disappointment to me. It's hard to believe Sophia has such a loose woman for an aunt. Shame on her. But he that will not hear must feel. This time, the man is going to share her punishment."

Simon finally understood. His mouth was bone dry, his whole body trembled.

"Ba . . . Barbara," he panted. "You . . . have . . . Barbara . . ."

His strength failed him and he fell off his chair. Lying on the ground, he stared up at Walburga, who stood above him like an angry giant. Somewhere cats meowed, but it sounded strangely far-off. What was happening to him?

"What . . . how . . . ," he managed to say.

"What poisoned you?" Walburga smiled. "Every man has his weakness. At first I thought about poisoning the mouthpiece of Jakob's pipe, but then suspicion would have fallen on me too soon. That's why I decided to break in at the tavern and smear his mug with wolfsbane. Many men love beer, and so did Master Hans. Henbane and hemlock — mixed together, they're easily poured into anyone's mug in the blink of an eye." She watched Simon as if he were an interesting experiment. "With you, it was the coffee. It's so bitter that it isn't hard to add poison. I didn't think you'd even come back from that dirty masquerade, but apparently your digestive system works very slowly. I think next time I'll use more devil's trumpet."

She disappeared from Simon's field of vision with long, booming strides. The ground trembled as in an earthquake. The ceiling seemed ready to crush him at any moment. Somewhere above him loud fanfares grew to an infernal noise.

Then Simon felt like his head burst into a thousand pieces.

"You send your pregnant girls to *Walburga?*"

Magdalena stared at Mother Joseffa. She tried to figure out what that news meant. An awful suspicion crept through her.

"Of course. Where else?" Joseffa gave her an innocent look. She was still tied up on the ground next to van Uffele in a storage room of the manufactory's basement. The boys watched them with hostile expressions and kept checking their fetters, as though they feared their prisoners might yet get away.

"Walburga is the wife of the Munich executioner," the old woman continued. "Everyone knows that she's an expert on poisons and medicines. Girls have been going to her for abortions for decades."

Magdalena winced. *For decades . . .*

She thought of the mummy in the rock cellar. Michael Deibler had most likely already been the Munich hangman at the time. Anni had died of deadly nightshade. Perhaps Elfi, Eva, and the young patrician woman had been poisoned in a similar way?

Could it be?

"You . . . you took Eva to see Walburga, too?" Magdalena asked hesitantly.

"Yes, we already told you," van Uffele snarled, pulling at the ropes. "This morning. In the end, she said herself that she didn't want the child. It would only have brought trouble, for both us and her. So we took her to Walburga, secretly, on a cart. It's always the same deal. Walburga gets rid of the child, with ergot or mugwort or whatever. If the girls come too late, she uses a needle. No one's as good as her. She rarely ever loses a girl."

Joseffa nodded. "Then she puts them on a raft and makes sure they leave Munich. She's always made good money out of it. And we've never heard from the girls again. A pleasant outcome for everyone."

Magdalena winced again. *Never heard from the girls again . . .*

"We can't afford for any of the girls to talk," van Uffele added. "Our clients are too rich and powerful."

"And what happened with Eva this morning?" Magdalena asked again.

"It was a little strange, actually. Walburga seemed somewhat"— Joseffa searched for the right word—"off. Eva was very late to come to her. We thought Walburga would have to use the needle. But she just gave her a potion and hurried off to the raft landing with Eva, even though it was still so early."

Magdalena shivered. Could Walburga really be behind all those murders?

But why should she do such a thing? Magdalena had gotten to know the hangman's wife as a warmhearted person who loved children. It didn't make sense. And yet, Magdalena didn't feel comfortable at the thought of her little Sophia still being home alone with the hangman's wife. And what about Barbara? She needed to go back to the executioner's house as soon as possible. But first she needed to help Paul.

And many other people.

Magdalena leaned down to Paul, who was still sound asleep. The wound had stopped bleeding. She breathed a sigh of relief—he seemed to be over the worst. She turned to Peter and the other boys, who had been listening in silence.

"Listen, you take Paul to that Doctor Geiger on Sendlinger Street right now. The doctor knows his father, so hopefully he'll help Paul."

Peter looked surprised. "But why don't we take him to the executioner's house, to Father and Walburga?"

"Trust me," Magdalena replied. She didn't know who was at the executioner's house at the moment, but considering what she'd just found out, she felt it was safer to take Paul to Doctor Geiger.

"And you?" Peter asked. "What about you?"

"I'll come as soon as I can." Magdalena jutted out her chin with determination. "But first I must go and tell the girls upstairs what's been going on at the manufactory. They ought to decide for themselves what they want to do with those two pigs. It's not my call."

She thought of Carlotta, fifteen years young, lying upstairs crying and bleeding, robbed of her virginity and dignity; of Agnes, beaten to a pulp by the Venetians; of all the other girls who worked hard for a pittance and whose hopes of having a good life in the big city had melted away like snow in the sun.

Magdalena prayed they'd conquer their fear and choose freedom.

But she wasn't sure.

His cloak billowing behind him, the hangman rode through the
forest near Munich, followed closely by his son. As on their way
to the ball, they sat on their borrowed horses, but they'd left the
donkey behind—along with Simon, whom Kuisl hadn't been
able to find in a hurry. But time was of the essence. Jakob Kuisl
had a terrible suspicion.

And if he was right, not only Eva and Magdalena, but his
granddaughter, too, were in the gravest of dangers.

Kuisl had heard Daniel Pfundner's screams for a long time.
They had still echoed faintly from the labyrinth in the palace
gardens when he'd returned to the artificial grotto to find his son.
In the meantime, Georg had subdued his adversary and tied him
with ropes from one of the chests. They left him lying in the
grotto—Kuisl hadn't had time for explanations; he merely asked
Georg to follow him as fast as he could. On their ride back to
town, Kuisl told his son what he'd learned from Pfundner.

"So, Anni had an abortion," Georg panted, struggling to keep
up on his skinny gray. "And the other girls, too, most likely. So
what? That's not a reason to race back into town like this. And
we still don't know where Magdalena is."

"I'm pretty certain we'd never find Magdalena at the masquerade because our dear Walburga lied to us," Kuisl replied
grimly. "Your sister's probably still at the silk manufactory, and
we worried for nothing."

Georg looked confused. "Why should Walburga lie to us?"

"Because all those dead girls came to her for their abortions.
She sent us on a fool's errand." Kuisl urged his horse into a faster
pace and Georg followed him through the dark forest, repeatedly getting struck in the face by low branches. Both men still

wore their costumes, which were rather worse for wear by now. It was bitter cold.

"I'm the biggest idiot in Bavaria," Kuisl swore. "Why didn't I figure it out sooner? All the time I was searching for a connection between the individual cases, and it was right under my nose. It wasn't just the amulets." He counted on his fingers. "Anni was pregnant. When I cut her open, I saw that her uterus was slightly swollen. But I didn't think much of it—we were investigating a poisoning, after all, not a pregnancy. The mummy had a small bag with herbs on her. They still smelled very faintly of mugwort—an herb commonly used for abortions. And Elfi, the impaled girl, also carried a bag of herbs. Deibler told me about it but I didn't read much into it. Stupid me!" He slapped his forehead. "Every one of the dead girls either had an abortion or had bought herbs for one. I bet you anything that the young patrician woman was pregnant, too. And where do you go if you want to get rid of an unborn child? Well?"

"To . . .to the midwife?" Georg guessed.

"Not in Munich, where the midwives live in the city under strict municipal supervision." Kuisl shook his head grimly. "No, you go to the hangman's wife—in secret. Everywhere in the country, the wives of executioners know a lot about poisons and healing medicines, just like my beloved Anna-Maria. But Walburga is a true artist on the subject."

"Are you saying Deibler's wife has been murdering young girls for all these years because they asked her for an abortion?" Georg gave his father an incredulous look.

"I can't tell you with absolute certainty and I don't yet know her motive—although I've got a hunch," Kuisl said thoughtfully. "But all those girls sought out Walburga and ended up dead. And think of the poisoned beer mug. Who apart from us hangmen knew that the mugs were kept at the inn? Only Walburga, the Munich executioner's wife. I'm guessing she poisoned

Master Hans, too, before quartering him. He must have known something."

"That time when Hans was sneaking around the executioner's house . . ." Georg hesitated. "If you're right, then he wasn't after Barbara at all, but . . ."

"After Walburga." The hangman kicked his horse in the sides, whereupon it whinnied and trotted a little faster. "Hans probably wanted to search the house for evidence but couldn't get in. But I was so blinded by my hatred for him that I immediately thought he was after my Barbara. Hans in turn thought *I* might know something. He told Barbara as much in the cemetery. But I didn't know a thing. Because I was too foolish — or too old . . . ," he added sullenly.

"Drowning, impaling, burying alive . . ." Georg listed. "They're all punishments used for women. For murderesses . . ."

"For child murderesses in particular." Kuisl nodded. "That's how it's written in the Constitutio Criminalis Carolina, which sets down the laws for the judgment of capital crimes. We thought a hangman was behind the murders, someone from the Council of Twelve. But a hangman's wife often knows just as much about punishment. Impalement is an ancient form of punishment, usually used before drowning. As executioner, Deibler has the Carolina book of laws at home — I leafed through it yesterday. The pages describing the punishments for women have been highlighted ever so faintly." The forest thinned out, and soon the road led through frozen fields, gleaming silver in the moonlight.

"But . . . but if you're right," Georg thought out loud, "wouldn't Walburga's husband have noticed something? I mean, all those years . . ."

"That's what we must find out."

The city wall loomed as a huge black shadow behind the fortifications. Father and son rode toward the Sendling Gate, which was shut at this time of night.

"Damn it, we should have thought of that," Georg said. "We already paid a fortune to get out, I hardly think they'll let us back in that easily."

Kuisl grinned. "I think they will. I saw who's on duty."

Georg looked at his father with surprise but didn't say anything. Instead, he climbed off his panting horse and knocked on the small door beside the gate. A short while later, the hatch opened and a familiar face appeared. It was Lainmiller, the same old guard from a few nights ago.

"Are you stupid or drunk?" he barked. "No one gets in this late. Come back tomorrow."

"Sure, and then we tell Loibl that you earn good money opening the gate for a black carriage every week," Kuisl replied drily. He raised one eyebrow. "By the way, if you're waiting for it — it's not coming back tonight. Its drivers had an . . . accident. I'm afraid they're indisposed. For a while."

Lainmiller turned pale. "What . . . what . . . ," he stammered.

"Don't ask, just open the damned door," Kuisl ordered. "Then I might reconsider telling Loibl."

In a heartbeat, the bolt was pulled across. Kuisl pushed the door open and the guard aside. In passing, he handed him the reins of his horse.

"The fat one belongs to Alois, the wagon driver." He pointed to the back. "And the skinny one is the knacker's. If you take them back for me, I'll forget all about the business with the carriage. You have my word as a hangman."

"A . . . hangman?" Lainmiller gasped.

But Kuisl had already hurried on.

Followed closely by Georg, he ran alongside the city wall until they saw the executioner's house in front of them.

A figure stood outside. It held a sword in its hand and watched them expectantly. When Kuisl came closer, he realized the sword was a very particular one.

An executioner's sword.

Michael Deibler was waiting for them.

A steady jolting and creaking crept into Barbara's dreams. They hadn't been pleasant dreams—she vaguely remembered slimy black eels that wound themselves around her and smothered her. When she opened her eyes, she saw the night sky.

Where in God's name was she?

The next thing Barbara noticed was the cold. She was shivering all over, her teeth chattered, and she felt her hair stand on end. What happened? Her head was as heavy as lead, but she tried to remember.

She had been atop Old Peter with Valentin. She told him about the pregnancy and Valentin had mentioned Walburga. He persuaded Barbara to seek out the hangman's wife with him and explained to her that Walburga was a true artist when it came to ending unwanted pregnancies, even if a woman had waited as long as Barbara had. No one was as nimble with the needle as she. And she also used poppy juice and other remedies so one barely felt a thing. Good old Walburga! Why hadn't she thought about confiding in her sooner?

Is that why she was feeling like this? Had Walburga given her a sleep potion? Had the hangman's wife already gotten rid of the thing in her belly? But then why was she outside somewhere and not in a bed? Barbara was covered with only a thin blanket, a holey sheet that stank of blood and urine.

She tried to sit up but couldn't.

What the hell?

She was bound. As she grew more and more awake, she also realized a gag was blocking her mouth. She whimpered quietly and her heart started to race. Then she heard a muffled sound from beside her. She turned her head and saw Valentin, who was bound and gagged just like her. He stared at her with wide eyes and tried to tell her something, but he only managed a strangled gasp through the gag.

But someone else spoke.

"Looks like you woke up," a familiar voice said. "Bad girl! Just be glad your father will never find out. He'd fret for the rest of his days."

Barbara looked up. Indeed, it was Walburga. What was going on here? The hangman's wife was pulling her and Valentin on a hand cart. Walburga was looking straight ahead, and her broad back almost looked like that of a man. But her voice was high and severe like that of an angry mother.

A very angry mother.

"You haven't told your father, have you?" she asked with a cutting voice, still with her back to Barbara. "I'm sure he would have led you back onto the right path. But now it's too late. You have sinned and must be punished. Together with the man who brought you. You're both guilty. Guilty of the attempted murder of an unborn child. You have been sentenced and will receive your just punishment."

Barbara couldn't believe her ears. Was she still dreaming? That couldn't possibly be Walburga speaking. Not the kindly hangman's wife who took care of Sophia so lovingly, putting cream on every little scratch. But it definitely was her voice.

"I'm so disappointed in you, Barbara," Walburga continued her tirade. "I welcomed you into my house, gave you shelter, trusted you. And how do you thank me? Not only do you get pregnant by some fellow in Schongau, but you continue just the same way in Munich, getting involved with the first lad that comes your way. And then you ask me to kill your child. As if it was some kind of . . . bug you can simply squash. Don't you understand? Doesn't anyone understand? Life is a gift from God, and it's a deadly sin to extinguish it. You may never kill what you receive. Ever!"

Meanwhile, the cart bounced along a wider lane. Barbara tried to recognize the passing houses. Were there no night watchmen? Walburga probably knew exactly which way she needed to go to avoid the guards. And if anyone happened to look out one of the few illuminated windows, they'd only see a knacker's journeyman carting a dead cow through town.

Barbara's memory slowly returned. The three of them had sat at the table in the executioner's house. Barbara had told Walburga about the pregnancy, and also that she couldn't feel any tenderness toward the creature in her belly. Walburga had listened, remained silent for a long time, and eventually handed her and Valentin a steaming cup each. Hot, sweet mulled wine, the hangman's wife had said with a smile, to warm her up and prepare her for what was to come.

That's where her memories ended.

Barbara still didn't understand what exactly Walburga was planning to do. Apparently, she and Valentin were being punished. But hadn't the hangman's wife helped so many other girls like her before? So why this anger, this nightmare, now? Barbara winced in horror as realization sank in.

Had the other girls been punished, too?

Impaling, drowning, burying alive . . .

Next to her, Valentin desperately tried to sit up, but the fetters were well tied. He panted and groaned and moved his head from side to side wildly, his face turning red.

"Hush," Walburga said. She turned around for the first time, and Barbara looked at her pale face. Her expression was blank, her eyes glowed like coals. Her straggly hair fell down over her forehead.

Like someone possessed, Barbara thought. *Walburga is possessed by the devil.*

"There's no point in struggling," the hangman's wife said to Valentin, who was still gasping and making incomprehensible sounds. "God has passed his judgment. The moment you came to me with the wish to kill, your fate was sealed."

Something whimpered, and it took Barbara a moment to realize that it was neither her nor Valentin, but Sophia. Walburga carried her in a scarf tied around her broad chest. Sophia looked at Barbara with round, curious eyes. Walburga stroked the little girl's head lovingly.

"Take a good look at your niece, Barbara," Walburga said in a gentle voice. "Your sister conceived this child. She has a clubfoot, but Magdalena loves her more than anything. And you don't want your child just because its father is a shifty good-for-nothing and long gone?" She shook her head. "You should have thought about that sooner."

She turned away and continued to pull the cart through the lanes and alleyways. She spoke half to herself.

"Your poor child was always going to die. If it wasn't me, you'd have asked someone else to abort it, or killed it yourself after birth. I've seen it too many times. It's better I do it myself—in the name of God, as always. I'm sure the little one won't have to suffer in purgatory for long, no child does. Unlike you two. Murder is a deadly sin. I'm very sorry, Barbara, I like your family. But this punishment comes from God. God pronounces the sentence, I'm merely his executioner."

Now they could hear the soft murmur of water somewhere ahead. Barbara thought they were nearing a stream. The lane widened, and Barbara could see the tower of Old Peter in the distance, where she and Valentin had spent such happy moments only hours ago. The houses retreated from her field of vision, and she thought they must have reached some kind of square.

Suddenly Barbara knew where they were.

A few more steps, then the cart stopped. The rushing of water was now very loud.

"I think this is a good place for your execution," Walburga

said calmly. "Countless sentences have been carried out here. When bakers bake poor bread, they're held under water here. Back in the old days, child murderesses were drowned here in a sack. I also chose this place for that arrogant little patrician." She nodded, happy with her decision. "This way, I know the whole city is going to talk about it. Perhaps some people will finally start to think — although I doubt it, not after such a long time. I must set an example. And that's why I thought of something special for you."

Walburga leaned over Barbara and Valentin and pulled off the thin blanket. Barbara noticed that their feet were wrapped in something — a large sack, which Walburga now started to pull over both of them.

"You're going to be drowned together," the hangman's wife said. "Man and woman. The women are the murderers, but the men are at fault. It's always the men's fault."

With those words, Walburga pulled the sack over Barbara's and Valentin's heads and tied it up. Then she pulled the cart the last few meters to the Rossschwemme. One of the last thoughts flitting through Barbara's mind as she writhed in the foul-smelling sack was that she'd sat at Katzenweiher Pond in Schongau not two weeks ago, thinking about taking her own life. Now someone was trying to drown her, but she would fight to the last.

She wanted to live.

"Two selfish lovers, united in death," Walburga muttered.

Then the hangman's wife tilted the cart and the sack slid off, dropping into the water with a splash.

And Sophia started to scream.

The devil wore shaggy black fur, he was as large as the whole room, and his eyes gleamed red like hellfire. Caustic acid dripped from the trident in his claws. He roared loudly as he hurled the weapon at Simon.

With a shout of fear, Simon rolled to the side and the trident shot straight through the floor next to him. It vanished in a puff of smoke, just like the devil. Instead, a hunchbacked, snickering witch stared at Simon, first turning into Walburga, then into a huge black bird, and finally into a hissing adder. Simon tossed and turned, closed his eyes, and when he opened them again, the room had suddenly become tiny, as tiny as the smallest crate, and he could not move. His throat tightened and he struggled for breath.

"This . . . isn't . . . real," he gasped. "Not . . . real."

In the farthest corner of his brain, Simon knew all those mythical creatures and visions couldn't be real. He'd been unconscious for a short while, but he remembered very well that Walburga had put poison in his coffee. What was it she said when she left?

Next time I'll use more devil's trumpet . . .

Simon knew devil's trumpet was one of the ingredients in witches' flying ointment, a mythical potion witches applied to their brooms to make them fly. He doubted the ointment could actually make brooms fly, but it definitely had the power to send a person on a trip. He'd read that the plant evoked terrible nightmares that seemed like reality, making a person believe they were flying through the air, accompanied by various demons. He'd also heard of cases where youths drank a decoction of devil's trumpet in the woods on a dare, or because they wanted to experience heaven and hell on earth.

Definitely hell, he thought while the room around him grew into infinity and filled with an inky blackness.

Simon's thoughts raced, ideas flashed through his mind like colorful lightning bolts. His only luck was probably that he hadn't finished the cup of coffee in the rush to get to Nymphenburg Palace. He remembered that Walburga had offered him a second cup, too. If he'd drunk it all, he'd be dead now or insane for good.

Like Walburga . . .

He squeezed his eyes shut tightly and opened them again repeatedly, trying to banish the visions. Through a blurry haze, he saw he was in a chamber whose walls appeared to tremble slightly, like the skin of a large animal. Black cats brushed around his legs. Were they real? He wasn't sure. Simon guessed he was somewhere in the executioner's house. Perhaps Walburga had dragged him into the cellar in case of unexpected visitors. Or to the attic? This house was so damn big, he could be anywhere.

His chest ached as if several of his ribs were broken. He felt sick, but at least he could think halfway straight again.

With a huge effort, Simon scrambled to his feet. The ground beneath him was as soft as marshland, and he fell repeatedly. Cats meowed somewhere. Simon held on to the wall and felt his way along, searching for a way out. Maybe Walburga had left the house. If he made it onto the street, he could call for help.

He stumbled on until he felt a cold metallic bolt under his hand. Was this a way out? A door appeared in front of his eyes, growing smaller and larger by turns. Simon took a deep breath and pulled on the bolt. The door creaked open. Ice-cold air blew in his face. It was pitch-black behind the door, and it smelled musty and a little sweet.

The cold store, he thought immediately. *This must be the cold store.*

Simon had seen Walburga bring up cold beer from the basement several times in the last few days. Many houses had a cellar like this deep in the ground, where perishable goods were kept. Such cellars remained cold even in the middle of summer. At least he knew that he was in the basement. Now he only needed to find the stairs.

He was about to turn away when the drugs played another trick on him. He heard a ghostly moaning from the darkness of the cold store, then the shadows became lighter and he saw a naked young woman lying on the ground between the crates and kegs of beer.

Simon knew some kinds of drugs could also cause sexual hallucinations. Well, at least better than the hairy black devil from earlier. The girl was pretty to look at, with long blonde hair and firm breasts, even though they were pale and blue from the cold.

Blue from the cold . . . ?

Simon blinked. Could this girl be not a vision at all? He looked again. The outlines became blurry, the body throbbed like a huge heart, but the woman looked strangely familiar.

Eva!

Walburga must have locked her up naked down here so she'd slowly freeze to death—another one of her cruel execution methods. Eva still appeared unconscious, or perhaps the crazy woman had drugged her. Either way, one thing was for certain: if Eva stayed down here for much longer, she would die.

Another wave of nausea gripped Simon. He fought it down and staggered into the cold store. If he fell unconscious now, he and Eva would be finished.

"Eva?" he whispered, bending down to the girl. "Eva, can you hear me? We must get out of here, or we'll freeze."

Suddenly Eva's face turned into that of an old woman. Her mouth twisted into a grin full of black stumps. The old woman giggled nastily, and bugs crawled out of her nose.

"Not . . . real," Simon kept telling himself. "Not . . . real . . ."

He grabbed Eva and dragged her out of the cold store. Her skin felt as cold as dead meat.

"We must get you warm," Simon panted. "Up into the living room."

He looked around. The walls came closer and retreated again, but for a brief moment, Simon had seen the stairs in a twitching gap. The path to freedom. He stumbled toward it while the gap appeared to close again. Then he remembered Eva. He couldn't leave her down here. She needed warmth as soon as possible.

He turned back around and grabbed her under the arms. Eva was as heavy as a lead weight, and she appeared to flow continuously through his fingers like a liquid.

When Simon looked back, the stairs were still there, even though they gleamed like a swift black stream.

He pulled Eva up the stairs, step by step. The door upstairs was only leaned shut. For a moment, everything spun around him, then he was in the hallway. Three more steps, two, one . . . The door to the living room. Its edges glowed like a ring of fire.

Simon pushed it open and stumbled into the room with Eva. Pulsing, life-giving warmth enveloped them.

Simon collapsed with Eva in his arms in front of the tiled stove. He didn't know whether he'd survive or whether the drug would take his life. He had no idea whether Walburga would come back at any moment and cut him to pieces as she'd done with Master Hans. But he no longer cared.

He was consoled by the fact that the naked girl in his arms felt just like his Magdalena.

"I . . . love . . . you," he whispered. "Magdalena . . ."

With this last soothing thought, he fell asleep with the naked girl and three purring cats by his side.

Barbara fell into the water and the world became chaos.

Next to her, Valentin pulled at his fetters. They were so close, as if they were one creature with four arms and four legs. The water flowed in through the sack, the cold pricked like needles. Barbara pressed her mouth shut as well as she could with the gag and tugged and floundered like an animal.

This is how they kill cats, she thought. *Cats and child murderesses. Am I a murderess?*

All at once she was filled with a deep sense of calmness, and she stopped struggling. Perhaps it was for the best. This life had battered and bruised her so many times, why should she fight for it now? Still, Barbara felt sad. She had only just found the man she loved and now it was all over. Would they stay together in heaven? At least she'd see her beloved mother again soon.

Valentin, on the other hand, didn't accept his fate so easily. He kept tugging at the ropes. The sack had reached the bottom, where it sank into the mud. The cold numbed Barbara's limbs. She was so tired, so awfully tired. Not much longer now . . .

Suddenly she felt a hand on her arm. Valentin! He'd actually managed to free himself. And now he was trying to undo her ties. But they had become impossibly tight in the water, it was hopeless. Yet Valentin persisted, pulling and fumbling on the strings. The urge to breathe was getting stronger.

Open the sack and swim up, Barbara wanted to tell him. *You can't save me. Save yourself.*

But Valentin wasn't giving up, though his movements became slower and weaker. Barbara couldn't see anything in the dark, but she saw his face in her mind's eye.

Valentin. My dear Valentin.

Barbara's senses gave up, blackness flooded her soul.

Valentin . . .

In that moment, when she almost didn't feel anymore, someone grabbed her by the collar and lifted her as if she were a puppy. The water drained away, she breathed delicious fresh air. Had they gone to heaven? Was dying this easy? But then she heard Sophia scream and realized someone must have pulled the sack out of the water just in time. She landed hard on the ground beside the Rossschwemme. The fabric ripped open and a cold winter breeze brushed her face. The stars sparkled above.

Next to her, Barbara heard Valentin breathe heavily. He'd freed his hands completely by now and was just about to take off her gag.

"Take your hands off my daughter. I'd rather do that myself."

A big hand tore Barbara's gag off and a knife cut through her bonds.

Her father stood above her.

Gasping for breath, Barbara held out her arms to him like she used to do as a small child, when she wanted him to pick her up. His hair and beard were dripping wet, his clothes clung to his body so his rough-hewn muscles stood out. Her father looked very, very angry.

And yet his eyes shone with a love she had never seen in him before.

"Thought you could just leave me like that, girl," Jakob Kuisl growled. His voice sounded strangely broken, creaking like old wood. "But I won't let you go that easy." He pointed at Valentin. "You can explain him later."

Trembling, Barbara came to her feet. In the light of the moon, she saw Georg and Michael Deibler at the edge of the Ross-schwemme stream. The Munich hangman was holding a huge executioner's sword in his hands. For a brief moment, Barbara thought he was raising it against Georg, but Deibler was approaching Walburga, who was standing with her back against the railing of one of the many bridges. She was holding the crying Sophia to her chest.

"It's over, Burgi," Michael Deibler said with a calm, steady voice. "No matter what you've been doing, it's over now."

"It's never over!" Walburga screamed. "Never! The killing of innocent children is going to go on forever. Someone had to do something. I . . . I . . . ," she broke off, her lips trembling.

"I should have known." Michael Deibler spoke softly, almost to himself. "All those years, decades . . . When did it start, Burgi? Before the asylum? I should have taken you sooner. But I thought I could do it by myself." He shook his head and lowered his sword. "My God, I'm so sorry. Sorry for you, but especially for all those poor girls . . ."

"Moni," Walburga whispered. She looked at her husband with big eyes and squeezed the crying child tightly. "Our beloved Moni . . . The Lord took her from us and didn't grant us any more children. But I wanted one more than anything." Her gaze turned cold. "And then . . . then that hussy comes and asks me to get rid of her child. I complied, as always. But only a few weeks later, I see her dancing with the lads at the Jakobi Fair. And she didn't even look at her little sister. She had killed her unborn child just to climb in bed with the next man." Walburga's voice had become shrill. Barbara couldn't believe this was the same Walburga who had baked fragrant cookies and gingerbread for her nephews only the day before.

"Someone needed to punish the whore. So I drugged her with poppy juice and walled her in. A just punishment for a child murderess. And all the others received their just punishments, too."

"Pregnancy outside of wedlock is forbidden," Georg now said, who was standing next to Deibler. "And abortion, too. You only needed to hand those girls over to the guards. Why did you kill them?"

Walburga stared at him as if she'd only just realized there were other people present beside her husband. She laughed out loud.

"Don't you understand? They'll always do it, even if it's forbidden. Someone's always willing, there are countless herbs and remedies. If I don't do it, they do it themselves or they find a midwife. It's been the way since the beginning of time. Someone had to make a stand. Sometimes it takes a bang for everyone to hear."

"Damn it, Burgi!" Michael Deibler shouted. "Shut up! Please, shut up." He walked toward his wife with his sword raised. "I can't listen to your crazy talk any longer. Those girls were no murderesses. They were desperate young women who didn't know what else to do. It's the men's fault. That's what you've been saying a lot lately. And you're right. But they are never held accountable, and the women are left alone in their misery. That's the real problem." He turned to Jakob Kuisl, who had wrapped his warm coat around the shivering Barbara. Valentin had managed to stand up, too, and they watched the unlikely couple, the short, stocky Deibler and his tall wife.

"Believe me, Jakob," Deibler said. "I've had a feeling, for days now. But I didn't know for certain until I saw Loibl earlier. A young man had been to see him, apparently Elfi's secret boy-friend. He hadn't shown up until now because he was afraid of being accused of murdering her."

"I think I've seen him before," Kuisl said thoughtfully. "At the cemetery, someone ran away from me. He must also be the one who decorated Elfi's grave."

"Anyway, the fellow told Loibl that Elfi had gone to see my wife for an abortion. She didn't know whether the child was from one of her clients or her boyfriend. And the two of them hadn't saved enough money to get married yet. After Elfi left to see Walburga, he never saw her again. That's when I knew for sure."

"She sinned gravely!" Walburga screamed. "That's why she had to be punished severely. Her boyfriend wanted to keep the child, even if it wasn't his. But Elfriede was selfish, so I impaled her. The deserved punishment for a murderess."

"Just like you executed Master Hans as a traitor. Am I right?" Kuisl said. "Each one received their own special punishment."

"That swine," Walburga hissed. "Some bastard told him about me on the rack in Weilheim. Probably a boyfriend of one of those hussies. Reckoned he'd save his pathetic little life with that bit of information. Hans strung him up and started to sniff around here in Munich. He wanted to hand me in so he'd become the new Munich executioner. Most of the time, killing was a sad duty for me, but in his case . . ." She smiled. "The knife wasn't very sharp, so it took a long time. And he could watch until the end."

Sophia cried louder and louder. Walburga still stood at the bridge railing with her, the stream rushing beneath her. The hangman's wife stroked the child, her eyes became clear again, and for a moment she was the kindhearted woman Barbara had met about a week ago.

"Don't cry, my darling," Walburga soothed little Sophia. "Everything's going to be fine. Everything's going to be better soon."

"Give me the child, Burgi," Michael Deibler commanded.

Walburga looked up with astonishment. "But . . . but she's staying with me, isn't she? She's such a dear little child, same eyes as our Moni . . ."

"But she's not our child," Deibler said quietly. "Sophia is Magdalena's daughter. And that's why she's going back to her mother, who loves her more than anything."

"The . . . the Lord gave me this child," Walburga said, her voice weak. She held Sophia tight. "He took my Moni and gave me Sophia. You can't take away a gift from God."

Deibler took another step toward his wife, sword raised. "Give me the child, Burgi."

Walburga lifted the crying girl into the air. "Not another step," she threatened. "Or else . . . or else I'll throw her into the stream."

"Then you'll also be a child murderess, just like all your victims," Deibler replied. "Is that what you want? Tell me, Burgi, is that what you want?"

Walburga hesitated, wrestling with herself. Tears ran down her pale cheeks, her fingers gripped Sophia's legs hard, making the girl scream even louder. Finally, the hangman's wife appeared to have reached a decision. Gently she placed Sophia on the ground, as if the child were made of glass. Georg ran over and picked up his niece. Then he carried her away, speaking softly to her.

Walburga now stood alone at the railing. Michael Deibler stood a step or two away from her, sword still in hand. After a while, he dropped it. With a loud clanking, the sword fell onto the icy cobblestones. Deibler slowly stepped toward his wife.

"My dear Burgi," he said softly, as if he were talking to a child. "I've always loved you, and I still do, even after everything you've done."

"I know, Michael." Walburga smiled. "I know. That's why you're my husband. My good husband, and my hangman."

Michael Deibler nodded. He closed the gap between them and

held his wife for a long time. Hangman and hangman's wife stood at the railing like a loving old couple in a moonlit night. Then Deibler gave Walburga a little push, and she toppled over the hip-high railing without a sound. For a brief moment, her hands were still visible above the water's surface, like a final goodbye. Then she disappeared in the ice-cold black waters of the city stream.

"My only love," Michael Deibler whispered.

He left his sword lying where it was and walked away with his head hung low.

A lonesome old man, aimless and without a future. All alone in this world.

Georg ran to the bridge railing and looked down.

"She's gone," he said. "She'll probably turn up at one of the weirs tomorrow, frozen stiff." He clenched his fists angrily. "She deserved a much harder death, damn it! All those poor girls she killed . . ."

"Many who deserve a painful death live," Kuisl replied. "And others who deserve to live, die. That's just the way of the world."

"And you're just letting him go?" Georg asked, pointing at the dark outline of Michael Deibler at the end of an alleyway. "He must have known something. He was her husband."

"Believe me, he has been punished enough. And I don't think he knew anything for certain, even if he suspected. Perhaps, secretly, he wanted all this to end. That's why he always supported us during the investigation."

"I . . . I must thank you," Valentin said and held out his hand to Kuisl. "If it hadn't been for you—"

"I'll deal with you later, lad," Kuisl growled. "Now we must go and see how Eva is doing and, most importantly, we must find Magdalena. We ran here as soon as we heard Sophia cry, we never even went inside the executioner's house." He turned to his daughter with a smile. "Your niece saved your life. If she hadn't . . ."

Barbara no longer listened. Something warm was running down her legs.

In the light of the moon, she saw it was blood.

About an hour later, Magdalena sat next to Peter on a bench upholstered with leather in the house of Doctor Malachias Geiger.

She kept casting worried glances at the door to Geiger's treatment room. The high-ceilinged hallway they were in was hung with portraits of other Geigers, all of them physicians and scientists who enjoyed a formidable reputation throughout Bavaria, as Magdalena had learned. Stairs led down to the ground floor and a large reception room. A massive tiled stove spread a cozy warmth through the whole house. Somewhere a clock ticked quietly—an item becoming increasingly popular in the homes of patricians.

Magdalena thought of her own house in Schongau. It was drafty, some of the windows were merely covered with tanned hides, and the floor of the treatment room was scratched and covered in old bloodstains. Doctor Geiger must have been making a fortune with his wealthy patients.

And yet he had agreed to help the Kuisls—even though he knew they couldn't pay more than a few stained coins.

Jakob and Georg sat opposite her. The hangman kept picking up his pipe and sucking on the cold mouthpiece. Magdalena knew it always calmed her father. He ground his teeth; his beard was gray and shaggy. At least both he and Georg were wearing shirts and vests again instead of their tattered costumes.

They had met here at the doctor's house and fallen into each other's arms. Her father had never believed that his daughter was dead, but he'd thought her still at the manufactory. As usual, he hadn't been able to put his emotions into words. But Magdalena had known by his embrace how much her father loved her and had feared for her. He had almost suffocated her.

So far, Jakob Kuisl had only told her in a few brief words what had happened at Nymphenburg Palace and at the Ross-schwemme afterward. Magdalena's suspicion had been right: Walburga was the serial killer they had been looking for. But now she was dead, drowned in one of Munich's icy streams.

Others were still fighting for their lives.

"Is Barbara going to die?" Peter asked quietly.

Magdalena gave a start. "Oh God, no!" She tried to smile, but didn't succeed entirely. "What makes you think that?"

Peter shrugged. "Georg said there was a lot of blood on Barbara's legs. If a person loses too much blood, they die. That's why Father always says cupping's not good."

"Your father talks a lot of nonsense," Kuisl grumbled. It was the first thing he'd said in a long while. But then he returned to his brooding silence and sucked on his pipe. The fact that he wasn't treating his younger daughter himself but trusting a studied physician instead showed Magdalena how nervous he was. His hands were shaking, his gaze empty.

"You're right, my darling." Magdalena wrapped her arms around her son. "But don't worry, Barbara is going to be fine."

But Magdalena wasn't entirely certain. Barbara appeared to have lost a lot of blood, and Magdalena had an idea why. But she didn't know any details.

At the silk manufactory, she'd made sure the girls learned about the crimes of van Uffele and Joseffa. As promised, the Au and Anger boys had removed the fetters of the two scoundrels and left the building — not before the boys pocketed anything of value and, of course, took with them the prince's dog. They'd agreed that Peter would take Arthur back to the Residenz in exchange for the reward the following day.

Magdalena was disappointed by how few of the young women had chosen to leave the silk manufactory that night. Carlotta had stayed, too, probably in the hope of saving enough money to start a better life soon. At least Agnes had decided to turn her back on the manufactory for good and return home. She had hugged Magdalena tightly in farewell and wished her all the best.

At Geiger's house, Magdalena had expected to find only Peter and Paul, but to her enormous surprise, she learned that Simon, Eva, and Barbara had been taken to the doctor as well.

Since then they had sat here and waited for news from the treatment room.

Paul was asleep in a chamber next door, freshly bandaged. There was nothing else Magdalena could do for him right now, but Doctor Geiger had reassured her that the bullet went clean through and wouldn't leave any lasting damage. Paul would be able to move his arm again soon. And Eva was recovering, too.

Geiger hadn't told them anything about the condition of Simon and Barbara, however, and had rushed straight back into the treatment room. Her father might know something, but he wasn't saying.

After a while, Kuisl cleared his throat. "Peter?" he said to his grandson. "Do me a favor and check on your brother, will you?"

Peter looked surprised. "But Paul's asleep . . ."

"I said, go check on your brother."

Peter stood up tiredly and walked into the small room, the sweet smell of herbs in firepans wafting over to them from the door. When Peter had gone, the hangman turned to his daughter.

"We're lucky this quack Geiger seems to like your Simon," he began. "Apparently, they drove back to Munich together, and your husband must have talked such nonsense that the doctor thought he might have been poisoned. That's why he sent a messenger to the executioner's house. Otherwise, we'd never have made it here this fast."

"Walburga *poisoned* Simon?" Magdalena shot up from her seat. "And you only tell me now?"

"Judging by your husband's stammering when we found him at the house, he was poisoned with devil's trumpet, a rather mild poison, although it causes nasty dreams. But I'm confident he'll survive. And Eva, too, even though she was very cold. But Barbara . . ." Kuisl paused for a long moment, eyeing Magdalena. "You knew, didn't you? You all knew."

"What do you mean?" Magdalena asked reluctantly.

The hangman brought down his fist on the armrest of his chair. "I may be old, but I'm no fool, damn it. I've been healing folks for too long not to know what the blood between Barbara's legs means." He pointed the stem of his pipe at Magdalena. "Barbara was pregnant and is miscarrying. She could die if the child has been in her womb for too long. How far along was she, huh?" He spun around and glared at Georg. "How far?"

Georg raised his hands defensively. "I don't know for sure, I swear. Two, three months?"

"Three months," Magdalena said. "It was one of the traveling jugglers from the Schongau church fair. He pushed her into the hay and took what he wanted."

"Jesus Christ, and you only tell me now?" Kuisl clenched his fists. "I'm doing everything I can to find Barbara a husband here in Munich, and now I find out she's been pregnant all along? Do you have any idea what the shame and disgrace would have meant for our family? We may be dishonorable, but that would have robbed us of our last remaining scrap of dignity."

"We were hoping the fiancé would have thought the child was his," Magdalena said. "That was the plan. But that no longer matters. There isn't going to be a child now. Barbara may be dying. And all you can think of is some drivel about honor and dignity. Shame on you, old man."

Magdalena had never spoken this rudely to her father before. But instead of raising his hand against her, he slumped in his seat as if all strength had suddenly drained from him. The sight hurt Magdalena worse than any beating.

Georg appeared to sense that this was something between father and daughter so he rose quietly.

"I'll go check on Paul, too," he said. "And make sure Peter doesn't do anything stupid."

They sat in silence for a while, listening to the ticking of the large clock downstairs.

"I only ever wanted the best," Kuisl said eventually. "For you, for Georg, for Barbara . . . Since your mother died, I've had to make so many decisions on my own." He shook his head tiredly. "Who knows what you womenfolk want? My Anna-Maria, yes, she understood you. But an old ass like me . . ."

Magdalena took his callused hand in hers. He was still trembling slightly. "You've made many good decisions, Father. For Barbara, too." She sighed. "Can't you understand why we didn't want to tell you? You can be so . . . so . . . angry."

"I know." Kuisl nodded. "You were probably right not to tell me." He hesitated. "That young lad who was in the sack with Barbara . . . I sent him away. But I've got a feeling he'll be back. Do you know who he is?"

Magdalena smiled thinly. "I've got a hunch. If I understood correctly, they went to see Walburga together. So she must have told him about her pregnancy. I think the two of them have become very close in the last couple of days."

"So he's just another bloody good-for-nothing—" Kuisl flared up.

But in that moment, the door to the treatment room opened. Doctor Malachias Geiger came out. He wore a blood-smeared apron and looked at them seriously. Magdalena's throat tightened.

"So?" she croaked. She squeezed her father's hand as hard as she could.

"I think . . ." Geiger paused and wiped the sweat off his forehead. "Well, I think she'll get through."

With slow movements, he untied his apron and hung it on a hook next to the door. "She lost a lot of blood, and unlike too many of my colleagues, I don't believe in the benefits of bloodletting. But with wine and a lot of rest, she should recover. I'd like to have her taken to the Hospice of the Holy Ghost." He gave them a sad look. "But she lost the child. And I can't promise she'll ever bear children again."

Despite this sad news Magdalena felt a huge weight fall off her. She knew Barbara was in the best of hands with Doctor Geiger. There was probably no better doctor in all of Bavaria. Geiger had helped Paul, Simon, and Eva, who had already been taken to recover at the hospice. He'd heal Barbara, too.

"We . . . we owe you our deepest gratitude," she started awkwardly. "Unfortunately, our trip to Munich used up all our—"

Geiger waved dismissively. "I don't work at the hospice for money, either. Anyway, your husband already paid me." He grinned, and Magdalena looked at him with astonishment.

"How?" she asked.

"Well, we had a little time to talk in the carriage back to Munich. Doctor Fronwieser was very agitated after I gave him Walburga's name. And I got the strange feeling that something wasn't right. Nonetheless he remembered to hand me a treatise. It appears he wrote it himself." Geiger turned to the bloody apron and pulled the pages Magdalena knew all too well out of its pocket.

"I've only skimmed through it so far, but it sounds very interesting. I'd like to make it available to a wider readership." He scratched his chin. "Hmm. Though I still don't understand how your husband came to be poisoned by devil's trumpet. And why he was holding a naked, half-frozen girl in his arms." The doctor gave Magdalena a curious look. "Do you have any idea?"

"Um, the thing with the naked girl is news to me, too," Magdalena replied uncertainly. "But I'm sure there's an explanation."

"Anyhow," Geiger shrugged. "Your husband is welcome to spend the next few days in one of my spare rooms until he feels better. I'm sure he'd like to tell me more about his treatise. It appears he also owns a book on microscoping. All very interesting stuff." The doctor looked over at Jakob Kuisl, who sat with his eyes closed. Magdalena noticed he was holding on to a small amulet.

It was the amulet of Saint Margaret.

Magdalena guessed her father had found it at the executioner's house. She might have been mistaken, but it looked as though her sullen, cynical giant of a father uttered a silent prayer of thanks.

Wonders never cease, she thought. *He must be getting old.*

"Oh, and this gentleman must be Doctor Fronwieser's father-in-law?" Malachias Geiger asked. "May I ask what profession—"

"My father also works as a healer," Magdalena cut him off quickly. "It runs in the family."

"Oh? In the family?" Geiger raised an eyebrow. "Just like with my family." He pointed at the numerous paintings in the hallway. "The Geigers are a dynasty of physicians, did you know? Have been for centuries."

Thoughtfully, Magdalena gazed at the portraits, a row of ancestors so long she couldn't see the end of it in the dark of the sparsely lit hall. Then she smiled, and her voice was clear and steady.

"I hope one day they'll say the same about the Kuisls."

EPILOGUE

AT THE HOSPICE OF THE HOLY GHOST IN MUNICH,
a few days later . . .

WHEN BARBARA OPENED HER EYES, the sun shone warm and friendly through one of the windows in the hospice's infirmary. A hint of spring was in the air. The logs in the stove by the door crackled and filled the large, low-ceilinged room with a pleasant warmth.

Barbara closed her eyes again for a moment, shutting out the smells and sounds around her: the groaning and soft whimpering of the other patients, the occasional laughter and conversations of the visitors. About a dozen patients were currently being cared for at the infirmary, and until yesterday, Eva had been one of them. The two young women had gotten along well. Eva had told Barbara that she'd wanted to keep her child, but Mother Joseffa had pushed for an abortion. A pang shot through Barbara, and her hand went to her abdomen.

My child . . .

She felt guilty and didn't know why.

When Barbara opened her eyes again, Valentin sat by her bed. He smiled when he saw her look of surprise.

"I only popped out to fetch a little more hot water from the kitchen," he explained and wiped a damp towel across her forehead. Barbara sighed with pleasure; the warmth felt good. Valentin had hardly left her side in the last few days. Following the treatment at Doctor Geiger's house, the young musician had taken her to the infirmary and cared for her like a baby. The bleeding had stopped and she hadn't become infected, as was often the case with miscarriages. It really looked as if the worst was over—even though Doctor Geiger had told her that she'd probably never have children.

Barbara's face darkened again.

"Is the water too hot?" Valentin asked, misinterpreting her expression. "Or would you rather have some wine, or—"

She shook her head. "It's . . . it's fine, Valentin. Tell me about the world outside, will you? I'm afraid I've been sleeping for so long. How is my family?"

"They're well and back at the Radl Inn at Au." Valentin grinned. "Although your sister complains about the fleas and lice in the bedrooms without pause. Your father hopes you'll be well enough to travel in one or two days." He hesitated. "Though your brother-in-law might stay a little longer. Doctor Geiger is so excited about his treatise that he wants to publish it at his own expense. The two of them are spending a lot of time together at Geiger's house. Apparently, Doctor Geiger has offered your brother-in-law his assistant's job. He's not happy with his current assistant, they say."

Barbara sat up in her bed. "But that would mean . . ." she started excitedly.

Valentin nodded. "That sooner or later, your sister and her family would move to Munich, yes. Geiger is working on gaining citizenship for them, but something like that takes time. They also have to consult the Schongau City Council. After all, the people there would lose their town physician. But Geiger has influential friends, both in the council as well as at court."

"I don't think Lechner, the Schongau court clerk is going to like that." Barbara smiled. "As far as I know, Lechner personally recommended Simon at court. But only to find a dog, not to get a job as a doctor here."

"Peter is going to move here sooner, though," Valentin continued. "He'll start at the Jesuit college soon." He winked at Barbara. "After he returned the prince's lapdog, he and the prince spent much time together. Apparently, the prince nagged and nagged at his mother until she got Peter a place at the school." Valentin shrugged. "When his parents move here, Paul will probably attend a public school—if he ever goes back to school at all. Lately he's been doing nothing but hanging out with the Anger street kids. Today he's sporting a decent black eye, but he seems very proud of it."

"That's fantastic news!" Barbara called out. "The Kuisls are moving to Munich."

She immediately noticed how weak she still was and sank back into her pillow. She was still overcome by waves of fever every few hours. And yet she couldn't help but smile. The thought that a part of her family was moving to the magnificent capital was simply too good. Until recently, they had all lived together at the Schongau executioner's house down in the stinking Tanners' Quarter, and now the world was opening to them. Anything was possible.

For me, too?

Barbara told herself that the miscarriage had been a stroke of luck. At least there was no longer a reason for her to marry—she was free. And yet she frequently caught herself thinking of the unborn child. What would have become of it? A hangman, a midwife, or something else entirely? But God seemed to have other plans for her. Barbara's lips tightened. At least she was alive—unlike all those girls Walburga murdered over the years.

Some fishermen from the hospice had found the hangman's wife in one of the weirs the following day. Officially it was an accident, but Michael Deibler had told Captain Loibl the truth. The Munich hangman had become an old man overnight. People said it was grief for his dearly beloved Burgi, and for the greater part, that was probably the truth. They were saying Deibler wouldn't be holding the position as hangman for much longer. The city would soon need a replacement.

"There is other news, too." Valentin tore Barbara from her thoughts. "I heard they finally caught those coin counterfeiters — and you'll never guess who was part of it. The Munich mint master himself, Frießhammer. Apparently, his trial is going to begin soon. And another high-ranking patrician is supposed to have had his hand in it, too, but the city hall won't let anything out." He frowned. "Oh, and the silk manufactory your sister was locked up in is going to be closed down. Apparently, the production of silk isn't working out in Bavaria after all — it's too cold, to begin with. But allegedly it's got something to do with that scoundrel van Uffele, too. He's deep in debt to numerous patricians, and they've thrown him into debtor's prison, together with Mother Joseffa. Someone reported them for procuring."

"Serves them right." Barbara nodded grimly. Magdalena had visited her the previous day and told her everything about van Uffele and Joseffa. Barbara had been very annoyed at the fact that those two criminals, who brought so much misery to so many young women, should get away unpunished. But it seemed there was justice in the world after all. Barbara hoped they rotted in prison.

The conversation with Valentin helped her forget her own fears for a while. But now it was time to ask the one question she'd been putting off asking. She'd lain awake for half the night because she'd been afraid of Valentin's reply. She couldn't wait any longer.

"Valentin . . ." she began reluctantly. "You and me . . . Do you think . . ." She couldn't go on.

Valentin squeezed her hand. "You don't have to say anything. Of course you'll go back to Schongau with your family and —"

"But I don't want to, damn it!" Barbara burst out. "I want to stay with you. It took so long to find someone like you. I . . . I thought I'd never—"

Tears streamed down her face, she broke off again. Now it was out. What an idiot she was! Throwing herself at him, practically begging for his affection—when a man is supposed to woo a woman. She had ruined everything. Now Valentin would probably mutter a few hollow phrases and go. For good.

But he didn't.

"Barbara," Valentin said gently. "I'd like to ask you something." Without paying any attention to his surroundings, he knelt down beside her bed and looked at her seriously.

"Will you marry me?"

Barbara froze. Silent tears still ran down her face, but she nodded. Some of the other patients stared curiously, but she didn't care. She thought she was in a dream, or perhaps her fever had returned. But slowly she realized that this was reality.

"Yes, I will," she said eventually, sniffling.

Valentin awkwardly pulled a ring out of his pocket. It was made of silver and sparkled in the light of the few candles in the infirmary.

"It's proper silver," he said with a smile and held the ring out to her. "Not the cheap stuff those counterfeiters were making. I played at countless weddings to be able to afford it, but none of those weddings was as beautiful as our own is going to be."

He put the ring on Barbara's finger, but she looked at him anxiously.

"I . . . I'm afraid it's not going to be that easy. There's still my father. If Magdalena is already moving to Munich with her family, he won't let me leave, too. Especially not for a dishonorable musician," she added glumly.

Valentin winked at her. Unlike her, he didn't seem worried at all.

"Just wait and see. I spoke with someone earlier who's got a lot of influence with your father. We had a good talk, even though it cost me many beers. But it was worth it."

Barbara looked at him with surprise. "Who do you mean?"

"Just wait and see." He gave her a kiss on the forehead, and a warm wave washed through her body, from the top of her head right down to her toes.

"You'll see," Valentin said. "Everything's going to be fine."

Two men stood in the watchman's room atop Old Peter and gazed into the distance, where the Alps rose as a white ribbon on the horizon. The mountains looked close enough to touch. An unusually warm breeze for February brushed around the tower. Both men were smoking, the haze from their pipes blowing toward city hall.

"Schongau lies somewhere in that direction," Georg said, pointing southwest. "If you look closely, you can even make out Hoher Peißenberg."

Jakob Kuisl enjoyed the view in silence. He was filled by a pleasant emptiness following the excitement of the last few days. He felt as though the warm wind were blowing straight through his head, clearing it, and leaving him with a slight headache. For this one moment, the hangman felt at peace with himself. He breathed deeply.

"A nice spot," he grumbled. "Though I don't believe just anyone's allowed up here. How did you do it?"

Georg winked at him conspiratorially. "Let's say I know someone who knows the tower watchman. He told me a keg of brandy would go a long way."

Kuisl kept his eyes fixed on the mountains as if they were precious church murals. He couldn't remember the last time he'd simply been together with his son like this. When Georg was still a child, they used to catch trout together in the Lech River, or roam the forest for hours, hardly speaking a word.

Now, too, they stood in silence for a long while before Georg spoke again.

"What happened to that Pfundner? You know, the counterfeiter you followed into the labyrinth?"

Captain Loibl had told them that Frießhammer, the master of the mint, was found the night of the masquerade. A pair of lovers had sought out the grotto for a stealthy rendezvous and had found the tied and half-frozen master of the mint. A carriage had left from the grotto's entrance shortly beforehand, evidently without its load—the dies and other utensils had soon given Frießhammer away. But so far, people had only been talking about one counterfeiter, not several.

"Apparently, they also arrested the carriage driver and two other helpers," Kuisl replied, still studying the mountains. "They're still looking for a fourth man. A bookshop keeper caught the fellow trying to pay with false money. A scrawny little man, dressed like a dandy." Kuisl shrugged. "I don't think they'll find him now. The three helpers are going to be hanged, Frießhammer decapitated."

"Deibler's got his hands full in his old age." Georg scratched his beard and took a drag on his pipe. "Although the master of the mint is getting off pretty lightly. Usually, coin counterfeiters get boiled in oil or are quartered."

"They say there was some sort of deal with the city. In return, the name of his partner remains secret."

"Does that mean Pfundner simply gets away with it?"

"You can ask him on judgment day." Kuisl spat. "Loibl told me today that they found Pfundner in the labyrinth yesterday, stiff like one of the statues in the park. He didn't find his way out that night and froze to death. They only found him yesterday because of all the snow in the last couple of days. Apparently, he lay caught in one of the prickly hawthorn hedges. Seems he tried to find the way out to the last."

"I can't say I feel sorry for him," Georg said. "Judging by what

Magdalena told us, he was a real degenerate. A heart of ice—
and now the rest frozen, too."

Kuisl's gaze darkened like a thunderstorm on a sunny day at
the mention of his elder daughter's name. Magdalena had told
him that she and Simon were moving to Munich before the year
was out. Her tone had told Kuisl that she wouldn't tolerate any
objections. He couldn't order her around any longer. And perhaps it was for the best. For Peter, for Simon, for everyone . . . He
was an old man whose busy life was nearing its end. But he had
nothing to be ashamed of, damn it. He had always done the best
he could for his family.

That only left Barbara.

"I think I'll ask the Schongau knacker again what he thinks of
Barbara," Kuisl said thoughtfully. "He's not a bad fellow, if only
he washed from time to time. Barbara would still be close to
home and could lend a hand at my place, too."

Georg cleared his throat. "That's what I wanted to talk to you
about. I met up with that young fellow this morning, the one
who took Barbara to see Walburga. Valentin is his name . . ."

"A proper good-for-nothing," Kuisl growled, biting the stem
of his pipe. "I heard he's a city musician and plays at weddings
and all sorts of dodgy feasts. It's high time I took Barbara back to
Schongau."

"Well, he's not that bad a fellow, actually. And Barbara likes
him. And he can provide for himself and his family. People are
always going to need music."

The hangman turned to look at Georg, taking his pipe from
his mouth for the first time. "Hang on a minute. Are you trying
to tell me my Barbara ought to marry that . . . that fiddle-playing
gallows bird?" Kuisl snorted derisively. "Forget it. I'll never consent to that."

"Whatever you say." Georg nodded. He gazed at the mountains and took another drag on his pipe. Another long silence followed.

"By the way, I'm not going back to Bamberg," Georg eventually said. "Uncle Bartholomäus left a few days ago, but I'm not going to follow him."

"Not . . . follow him?" For the second time, Kuisl was astounded. "For God's sake, and you only tell me now? Just like that? What happened? Did he throw you out?"

"Uncle Bartholomäus is going to retire soon and the city is looking for a new hangman. I've already been told it's not going to be me. I have no future in Bamberg."

"And in Munich . . . ?" Kuisl asked cautiously.

"Deibler has offered me the position of his journeyman. I'd soon be able to complete my master's certificate and become the new Munich executioner. Deibler would put his word in for me." Georg moved his head from side to side. "We get on well, and he badly needs help after what happened with his wife."

"Hmm. A great offer." Kuisl tightened his grip on the railing, his gaze went blank, but his voice remained calm. "I'm sure you'll accept. Congratulations. It's a great honor to become the executioner of Munich. Widmann from Nuremberg is going to hate having a Kuisl as the hangman in the city of the elector."

Georg shrugged. "Well, I'm not sure I want the job. You know, Munich is such a big city, with too many people, everything's so noisy . . . At the end of the day, I'd rather be somewhere quiet." He paused. "Where I'm at home. Where my ancestors are buried."

Kuisl's heart beat faster. "Which means . . . ?"

"Well, I might just come home to Schongau." Georg smiled. "I hear the hangman is looking for a new journeyman—and one day, a successor. And if I find a nice girl from Peiting or Steingaden, Barbara won't need to help you at home."

"And can stay in Munich with her good-for-nothing fiddler." Jakob Kuisl sucked hard on his pipe, making the embers glow red-hot in the night. He stared grimly at some distant point on the horizon. Suddenly he laughed out loud. It was warm laughter, echoing through the lanes of Munich. Several pedestrians looked up curiously.

"Nicely orchestrated." The hangman grinned. "So, you only come to Schongau if Barbara's allowed to stay here and marry her goddamned musician. Who thought of that plan? You or Magdalena? Or that lousy city fiddler?"

"One comes up with all sorts of plans over a few Munich beers." Georg winked at his father. "That's one of the few reasons I'd truly regret not taking the position in Munich. No one brews a better beer."

"And no one's cheekier than you." Kuisl elbowed his son in the ribs, but then he placed his arm around Georg's shoulder and held him tight. Thus, together, they stood at the tower railing and watched the smoke from their pipes unite as one cloud and slowly drift off.

Father and son, no more, no less.

AFTERWORD

(A warning, as always, to read this part only after finishing the book — spoiler alert! Unless you're one of those people who like to know the villain from the start . . .)

This is the seventh installment of the Hangman's Daughter saga but the first to take place in my hometown of Munich. Why only now? Well, to be honest, because I love beautiful hotels! I enjoy traveling for research, exploring new cities, and making myself at home in cozy hotel rooms — art nouveau, preferably — far away from my noisy, exhausting family. In my own city, however, I would have struggled to justify a hotel room . . . On top of that, I used to believe I knew Munich very well already. I was born here, after all, a proper child of Munich. So what was there for me to discover? How wrong I was!

When the lovely guide from Stattreisen city tours accompanied me through *my* Munich in the name of research for the first time, I felt like a tourist. There was so much I hadn't seen before, so much I didn't know. The capital of Bavaria is like a snake that has molted at least a dozen times since its founding over eight hundred years ago: from its beginnings as an insignificant settle-

ment at a toll bridge to the sophisticated Italian era of Electress
Henriette Adelaide to the classical buildings erected under Ludwig I to the city of the rich and famous, the home of FC Bayern,
and the cultural metropolis of today . . .

If you want to discover the Munich of the seventeenth century,
you must look closely—or engage a good tour guide, like I did.

For this novel, too, an initial spark kindled my imagination—
the beginning for everything you're holding in your hands. This
time it was a note in Reinhard Heydenreuter's *Kriminalgeschichte
Bayerns,* a book on the criminal history of Bavaria, in which I
read to my horror that during the seventeenth and eighteenth
centuries, more women were executed for child murder than for
witchcraft in the electorate of Bavaria. Not the notorious witch
trials, but the uptight ways of dealing with sexuality were the
main affliction of the day—at least for women.

Most women thus executed were young, unmarried mothers
who killed their newborn out of desperation or had an abortion.
They were convicted of so-called *Leichtfertigkeit* (frivolity)—
prohibited extramarital intercourse—which had been punish-
able with drastic sentences following torture since the sixteenth
century. Worse than the sentence itself for many women was the
social ostracism.

Intercourse was only permitted in marriage, but a future husband needed to have enough money and practice a decent job
within a guild to obtain permission to marry. You can imagine
that many young people didn't want to wait until they were married. If the accident happened, it was the woman who bore the
brunt of it. Attempted abortion was punished with deportation
or banishment, successful abortion or child murder with death.
Men convicted of frivolity generally got away with fines. It was
especially bad under Elector Maximilian and his Catholic regime
in Bavaria. The ramifications of this ludicrous law are a pervad-
ing theme of this novel.

If you think we've left those dark times behind, take a look around. In India, scorned lovers douse women in acid, in parts of Africa they remove or mutilate young girls' external genitalia, and in some areas of Nepal women are still forced to retreat into menstruation huts during their time of the month because they are considered impure. Oh, and I'm sure crazy anti-abortion activists like Walburga, the hangman's wife, also exist outside the USA, where doctors have been killed in the name of God because they fought for the right to abort. With that in mind, this historical novel is more relevant than one might first think. History always repeats itself, just dressed in a different outfit.

I tried to describe the locations in *The Council of Twelve* as closely to historical reality as I was able to find out, although many have changed significantly or no longer exist. The names of most characters are historically correct, including the hangmen in the Council of Twelve. I only changed some first names or used a middle name instead to avoid confusion. Unfortunately, Jakob and Johann were very popular names for men back then. As far as I know, the only portrait of any council member in existence is of Nuremberg executioner Johann Michael Widmann, so I made up the physical features of all the other hangmen. I must thank several of my faithful readers for all their help with my research. And also various city archives that helped clear up many mistakes.

I must admit, however, that I invented the meeting of the executioners' guild in Munich. It's not unlikely that such meetings took place, though. Around the year 1500, for example, a guild meeting of hangmen in the Swiss city of Basel has been well documented, enabling me to borrow some of the rituals. (Not all, though, because they were just too bizarre. For example, the guild master's right leg had to be bared and his foot in a tub of water . . .)

A masquerade like the one I describe at Nymphenburg Palace

might very well have taken place. In her interesting biography about the Bavarian electress Henriette Adelaide, Roswitha von Barys writes about costumed amazons, Romans, Muscovites, shepherds, Greeks, Chinese, Arabs, and Romani. Over the years, the electoral couple appeared as a pair of Turks, Persians, Native Americans, and innkeepers. Kerll, the court music director, and treasurer Pfundner also were historical characters — although I'm sure they weren't as unpleasant in real life as I described them. Doctor Malachias Geiger existed, too, and was a famous and respected physician from a dynasty of doctors in Munich and all of Bavaria.

The so-called Kipper- und Wipperzeit (literally the "tipping and seesaw period") takes a special place in this book. This period of financial crisis had its climaxes in the 1620s and 1680s. Precious silver coins were mixed with cheap copper, tin, or lead, leading to immense inflation in the entire German Empire. The name of the period relates to the seesawing and tipping of scales while trying to sort heavier coins from lighter ones. Often, the territorial sovereigns had a hand in it themselves and, as a result, the population suffered poverty and hunger. Contemporary pamphlets make frequent mention of it.

I invented the storyline about the Munich treasurer and the master of the mint participating in such a crime, but I think the plan is genius. All right, the dies were probably guarded much too closely for it to work in reality. Never mind — the truth can afford to turn a blind eye from time to time in crime novels. That's the advantage of being a novelist as opposed to a virtuous author of nonfiction.

I must mention that I don't know of a serial killer in Munich during the seventeenth century, or at least none who executed his victims like a hangman. The most spectacular case from the time is probably the trial of the Pämb family, called the Pappenheimers, which is mentioned in the novel. The family was ac-

cused of murdering 120 people, robbing 28 churches, setting 26
fires, and conjuring 21 hailstorms. During their execution in
1600, the mother's breasts were cut off and rubbed in the faces of
her sons. The men were partially broken on the wheel, partially
impaled, and finally burnt alive. My stomach turns at the thought
of the large Munich crowd cheering and applauding at the execution. But those were the times.

One location in the novel was particularly important to me: the
Au silk manufactory. When I read about it for the first time, I
couldn't imagine that there really was a silk factory in the cold
Munich of the seventeenth century. But it's true, and there were
even two of them, one at Jakobsplatz Square and the other one at
Au. If you dig a little deeper, you find a true industrial-crime
drama.

A certain Dr. med. Johann Joachim Becher convinced Elector
Ferdinand Maria to go ahead with this unlikely plan in 1664.
They hired Italian specialists, engaged in industrial espionage in
Venice, and planted mulberry trees populated with silkworms in
the court gardens and other parks around Munich. From then
on, only Bavarian silk could be sold in Bavaria—true to the
motto by Kurt Tucholsky: Germans, buy German bananas!

Someone named Lucas van Uffele was appointed director of
the manufactory, a rather shady character who began looking for
investors all over Bavaria. And just like today, there were plenty
of fools willing to invest in a dubious business venture. None of
them ever saw their money again. In 1672, after only six years,
the manufactory was shut down. Van Uffele fled to Augsburg in
the dead of night, was caught, taken back to Munich, and locked
up in Falkenturm Tower for several years (an excellent read on
the subject: Hermann Wilhem, *In der Münchner Vorstadt Au*).
That was the end of one of the most bizarre chapters in Munich's
history.

By the way, the electress's lapdog did indeed run away, in 1675 . . .

Have I ever mentioned that history always writes the best stories? It's anecdotes like these that made me become an author of historical fiction!

As always, I have many people to thank for the fact that an initial idea turned into a novel of more than five hundred pages.

My first thanks goes to Barbara Reis from Stattreisen Munich, who guided me through my hometown and knew the answer to nearly all of my curious questions. The same goes for Karin Niederländer, my tour guide at Au. Dr. Manfred Heimers from the Munich city archive helped me with the names, and the State Coin Collection provided me with information about the Kipper- and Wipper period and coin minting in the seventeenth century.

Dieter Brenner from the Haus der Seidenkultur (House of Silk Culture) in Krefeld helped me learn about silk. A good read on the subject is Ursula Niehaus's novel *Die Seidenweberin,* which I found very helpful during my research.

Professor Dr. Matthias Graw, head of the Munich Institute for Forensic Medicine, patiently answered all my questions regarding the yucky subjects of poisoning, decomposition, and mummification. Dr. Thomas Puyol helped me in the broad field of gynecology, and, as always, my father helped with medical questions as well. Thanks, Papa, for letting me call you about every tiny medical issue! (And I don't mean the countless hypochondriacal questions pertaining to my own person. Everyone gets older . . .) My clumsy Latin translations were proofread by Professor Dr. Manfred Heim from the Catholic theological faculty of the LMU Munich.

I can't forget to thank the lovely ladies from the ever-supportive Ullstein Publishing, in particular Nina Wegscheider, Sarah

Ehrhardt, Marion Vazquez, Pia Götz, and Siv Bublitz, and, of course, my favorite editor, Uta Rupprecht, who is as precise as she is kind. Gerd, Sophie, and Martina from the agency were my trial readers, just like my wife, Kathrin, who always lends a friendly ear to all my questions and fears, and always comes up with good ideas. And last but not least, thank you to my friend Oliver Kuhn, who unknowingly gave me the idea for the villain in Tuscany. Thank you to you all, you're the best. Until the next book!

Sincerely, your still hopelessly romantic
Oliver Pötzsch